MIND DIMENSIONS

BOOKS 0, 1, & 2

DIMA ZALES

♠ MOZAIKA PUBLICATIONS ♠

This is a work of fiction. Names, characters, places, and incidents are either the product of the author's imagination or are used fictitiously, and any resemblance to actual persons, living or dead, business establishments, events, or locales is purely coincidental.

Published by Mozaika Publications, an imprint of Mozaika LLC.
www.mozaikallc.com

Cover by Najla Qamber Designs
www.najlaqamberdesigns.com

Print ISBN: 978-1-63142-408-3

THE THOUGHT READERS

MIND DIMENSIONS: BOOK 1

DESCRIPTION

Everyone thinks I'm a genius.

Everyone is wrong.

Sure, I finished Harvard at eighteen and now make crazy money at a hedge fund. But that's not because I'm unusually smart or hardworking.

It's because I cheat.

You see, I have a unique ability. I can go outside time into my own personal version of reality—the place I call "the Quiet"—where I can explore my surroundings while the rest of the world stands still.

I thought I was the only one who could do this—until I met *her*.

My name is Darren, and this is how I learned that I'm a Reader.

1

Sometimes I think I'm crazy. I'm sitting at a casino table in Atlantic City, and everyone around me is motionless. I call this the *Quiet*, as though giving it a name makes it seem more real—as though giving it a name changes the fact that all the players around me are frozen like statues, and I'm walking among them, looking at the cards they've been dealt.

The problem with the theory of my being crazy is that when I 'unfreeze' the world, as I just have, the cards the players turn over are the same ones I just saw in the Quiet. If I were crazy, wouldn't these cards be different? Unless I'm so far gone that I'm imagining the cards on the table, too.

But then I also win. If that's a delusion—if the pile of chips on my side of the table is a delusion—then I might as well question everything. Maybe my name isn't even Darren.

No. I can't think that way. If I'm really that confused, I don't want to snap out of it—because if I do, I'll probably wake up in a mental hospital.

Besides, I love my life, crazy and all.

My shrink thinks the Quiet is an inventive way I describe the 'inner workings of my genius.' Now that sounds crazy to me. She also might want me, but that's beside the point. Suffice it to say, she's as far as it gets from my datable age range, which is currently right around twenty-four. Still young, still hot, but done with school and pretty much beyond the clubbing phase. I hate clubbing, almost as much as I hated studying. In any case, my shrink's explanation doesn't work, as it doesn't account for the way I know things even a genius wouldn't know—like the exact value and suit of the other players' cards.

I watch as the dealer begins a new round. Besides me, there are three players at the table: Grandma, the Cowboy, and the Professional, as I call them. I feel that now-almost-imperceptible fear that accompanies the phasing. That's what I call the process: phasing into the Quiet. Worrying about my sanity has always facilitated phasing; fear seems helpful in this process.

I phase in, and everything gets quiet. Hence the name for this state.

It's eerie to me, even now. Outside the Quiet, this casino is very loud: drunk people talking, slot machines, ringing of wins, music—the only place louder is a club or a concert. And yet, right at this moment, I could probably hear a pin drop. It's like I've gone deaf to the chaos that surrounds me.

Having so many frozen people around adds to the strangeness of it all. Here is a waitress stopped mid-step, carrying a tray with drinks. There is a woman about to pull a slot machine lever. At my own table, the dealer's hand is raised, the last card he dealt hanging unnaturally in midair. I walk up to him from the side of the table and reach for it. It's a king, meant for the Professional. Once I let the card go, it falls on the table rather than continuing to float as before—but I know full well that it will be back in the air, in the exact position it was when I grabbed it, when I phase out.

The Professional looks like someone who makes money playing poker, or at least the way I always imagined someone like that might look. Scruffy, shades on, a little sketchy-looking. He's been doing an excellent job with the poker face—basically not twitching a single muscle throughout the game. His face is so expressionless that I wonder if he might've gotten Botox to help maintain such a stony countenance. His hand is on the table, protectively covering the cards dealt to him.

I move his limp hand away. It feels normal. Well, in a manner of speaking. The hand is sweaty and hairy, so moving it aside is unpleasant and is admittedly an abnormal thing to do. The normal part is that the hand is warm, rather than cold. When I was a kid, I expected people to feel cold in the Quiet, like stone statues.

With the Professional's hand moved away, I pick up his cards. Combined with the king that was hanging in the air, he has a nice high pair. Good to know.

I walk over to Grandma. She's already holding her cards, and she has fanned them nicely for me. I'm able to avoid touching her wrinkled, spotted hands. This is a relief, as I've recently become conflicted about touching people—or, more specifically, women—in the Quiet. If I had to, I would rationalize touching Grandma's hand as harmless, or at least not creepy, but it's better to avoid it if possible.

In any case, she has a low pair. I feel bad for her. She's been losing a lot tonight. Her chips are dwindling. Her losses are due, at least partially, to the fact that she has a terrible poker face.

Even before looking at her cards, I knew they wouldn't be good because I could tell she was disappointed as soon as her hand was dealt. I also caught a gleeful gleam in her eyes a few rounds ago when she had a winning three of a kind.

This whole game of poker is, to a large degree, an exercise in reading people—something I really want to get better at. At my job, I've been told I'm great at reading people. I'm not, though; I'm just good at using the Quiet to make it seem like I am. I do want to learn how to read people for real, though. It would be nice to know what everyone is thinking.

What I don't care that much about in this poker game is money. I do well enough financially to not have to depend on hitting it big gambling. I don't care if I win or lose, though quintupling my money back at the blackjack table was fun. This whole trip has been more about going gambling because I finally *can*, being twenty-one and all. I was never into fake IDs, so this is an actual milestone for me.

Leaving Grandma alone, I move on to the next player—the Cowboy. I can't resist taking off his straw hat and trying it on. I wonder if it's possible for me to get lice this way. Since I've never been able to bring back any inanimate objects from the Quiet, nor otherwise affect the real world in any lasting way, I figure I won't be able to get any living critters to come back with me either.

Dropping the hat, I look at his cards. He has a pair of aces—a better hand than the Professional. Maybe the Cowboy is a professional, too. He has a good poker face, as far as I can tell. It'll be interesting to watch those two in this round.

Next, I walk up to the deck and look at the top cards, memorizing them. I'm not leaving anything to chance.

When my task in the Quiet is complete, I walk back to

myself. Oh, yes, did I mention that I see myself sitting there, frozen like the rest of them? That's the weirdest part. It's like having an out-of-body experience.

Approaching my frozen self, I look at him. I usually avoid doing this, as it's too unsettling. No amount of looking in the mirror—or seeing videos of yourself on YouTube—can prepare you for viewing your own three-dimensional body up close. It's not something anyone is meant to experience. Well, aside from identical twins, I guess.

It's hard to believe that this person is me. He looks more like some random guy. Well, maybe a bit better than that. I do find this guy interesting. He looks cool. He looks smart. I think women would probably consider him good-looking, though I know that's not a modest thing to think.

It's not like I'm an expert at gauging how attractive a guy is, but some things are common sense. I can tell when a dude is ugly, and this frozen me is not. I also know that generally, being good-looking requires a symmetrical face, and the statue of me has that. A strong jaw doesn't hurt either. Check. Having broad shoulders is a positive, and being tall really helps. All covered. I have blue eyes—that seems to be a plus. Girls have told me they like my eyes, though right now, on the frozen me, the eyes look creepy. Glassy. They look like the eyes of a lifeless wax figure.

Realizing that I'm dwelling on this subject way too long, I shake my head. I can just picture my shrink analyzing this moment. Who would imagine admiring themselves like this as part of their mental illness? I can just picture her scribbling down *Narcissist* and underlining it for emphasis.

Enough. I need to leave the Quiet. Raising my hand, I touch my frozen self on the forehead, and I hear noise again as I phase out.

Everything is back to normal.

The card that I looked at a moment ago—the king that I left on the table—is in the air again, and from there it follows the trajectory it was always meant to, landing near the Professional's hands. Grandma is still eyeing her fanned cards in disappointment, and the Cowboy has his hat on again, though I took it off him in the Quiet. Everything is exactly as it was.

On some level, my brain never ceases to be surprised at the discontinuity of the experience in the Quiet and outside it. As humans, we're hardwired to question reality when such things happen. When I was trying to outwit my shrink early on in my therapy, I once read an entire psychology textbook during our session. She, of course, didn't notice it, as I did it in the Quiet. The book talked about how babies as young as two months old are surprised if they see something out of the ordinary, like gravity appearing to work backwards. It's no wonder my brain has trouble adapting. Until I was ten, the world behaved normally, but everything has been weird since then, to put it mildly.

Glancing down, I realize I'm holding three of a kind. Next time, I'll look at my cards before phasing. If I have something this strong, I might take my chances and play fair.

The game unfolds predictably because I know everybody's cards. At the end, Grandma gets up. She's clearly lost enough money.

And that's when I see the girl for the first time.

She's hot. My friend Bert at work claims that I have a 'type,' but I reject that idea. I don't like to think of myself as shallow or predictable. But I might actually be a bit of both, because this girl fits Bert's description of my type to a T. And my reaction is extreme interest, to say the least.

Large blue eyes. Well-defined cheekbones on a slender face, with a hint of something exotic. Long, shapely legs, like those of a dancer. Dark wavy hair in a ponytail—a hairstyle that I like. And without bangs—even better. I hate bangs—not sure why girls do that to themselves. Though lack of bangs is not, strictly speaking, in Bert's description of my type, it probably should be.

I continue staring at her as she joins my table. With her high heels and tight skirt, she's overdressed for this place. Or maybe I'm underdressed in my jeans and t-shirt. Either way, I don't care. I have to try to talk to her.

I debate phasing into the Quiet and approaching her, so I can do something creepy like stare at her up close, or maybe even snoop in her pockets. Anything to help me when I talk to her.

I decide against it, which is probably the first time that's ever happened.

I know that my reasoning for breaking my usual habit is strange. If you can even call it reasoning. I picture the following chain of events: she agrees to date me, we go out for a while, we get serious, and because of the deep connection we have, I come clean about the Quiet. She learns I did something creepy and has a fit, then dumps me. It's ridiculous to think this, of course, considering that we haven't even spoken yet. Talk about jumping the gun. She might have an IQ below seventy, or the personality of a piece of wood. There can be twenty different reasons why I wouldn't want to date her. And besides, it's not all up to me. She might tell me to go fuck myself as soon as I try to talk to her.

Still, working at a hedge fund has taught me to hedge. As crazy as that reasoning is, I stick with my decision not to phase because I know it's the gentlemanly thing to do. In keeping with this unusually chivalrous me, I also decide not to cheat at this round of poker.

As the cards are dealt again, I reflect on how good it feels to have done the honorable thing—even without anyone knowing. Maybe I should try to respect people's privacy more often. *Yeah, right.* I have to be realistic. I wouldn't be where I am today if I'd followed that advice. In fact, if I made a habit of respecting people's privacy, I would lose my job within days—and with it, a lot of the comforts I've become accustomed to.

Copying the Professional's move, I cover my cards with my hand as soon as I receive them. I'm about to sneak a peek at what I was dealt when something unusual happens.

The world goes quiet, just like it does when I phase in . . . but I did nothing this time.

And at that moment, I see *her*—the girl sitting across the table from me, the girl I was just thinking about. She's standing next to me, pulling her hand away from mine. Or, strictly speaking, from my frozen self's hand—as I'm standing a little to the side looking at her.

She's also still sitting in front of me at the table, a frozen statue like all the others.

My mind goes into overdrive as my heartbeat jumps. I don't even consider the possibility of that second girl being a twin sister or something like that. I know it's her. She's doing what I did just a few minutes ago. She's walking in the Quiet. The world around us is frozen, but we are not.

A horrified look crosses her face as she realizes the same

thing. Before I can react, she lunges across the table and touches her own forehead.

The world becomes normal again.

She stares at me from across the table, shocked, her eyes huge and her face pale. She rises to her feet. Without so much as a word, she turns and begins walking away, then breaks into a run a couple of seconds later.

Getting over my own shock, I get up and run after her. It's not exactly smooth. If she notices a guy she doesn't know running after her, dating will be the last thing on her mind. But I'm beyond that now. She's the only person I've met who can do what I do. She's proof that I'm not insane. She might have what I want most in the world.

She might have answers.

2

RUNNING AFTER SOMEONE IN A CASINO IS HARDER THAN I imagined, making me wish I'd downed fewer drinks. I dodge elbows and try not to trip over people's feet. I even debate phasing into the Quiet to get my bearings, but decide against it because the casino will still be just as crowded when I phase back out.

Just as I begin to close in on the girl, she turns the corner into a hall leading to the main lobby. I have to get there as quickly as I can, or she'll get away. My heart hammers in my chest as I fleetingly wonder what I'll say to her when I catch up. Before I get far with that thought, two guys in suits step directly into my path.

"Sir," one of the guys says, almost giving me a heart attack. Though I'd spotted them in my periphery, I was so focused on the girl that I hadn't truly registered their presence. The guy who just spoke to me is huge, a mountain in a suit. This can't be good.

"Whatever you guys are selling, I'm not interested," I say, hoping to bluff my way out of this. When they don't look convinced, I add pointedly, "I'm in a rush," and try to look beyond them to emphasize my haste. I hope I look confident, even though my palms are sweating like crazy and I'm panting from my run.

"I'm sorry, but I must insist that you come with us," says the second guy, moving in closer. Unlike his rotund monster of a partner, this guy is lean and extremely buff. They both look like bouncers. I guess they get suspicious when some idiot starts running through the casino. They're probably trained to assume theft or something else shady. Which, to be fair, does make sense.

"Gentlemen," I try again, keeping my voice even and polite, "with all due respect, I really am in a rush. Any way you can frisk me quickly or something? I'm trying to catch up with someone." I add that last part both to deflect suspicion of nefarious activity and because it's the truth.

"You really ought to come with us," the fatter one says, his jaw set stubbornly. They each keep one of their hands near their inner jacket pockets. Oh, great. Just my luck, they're armed.

Struggling to find a way to deal with this unexpected event, I channel the natural fear from my situation into phasing. Once I enter the Quiet, I find myself standing to the side of our not-so-friendly duo, with the world mute again. I immediately resume running, no longer caring about bumping into the immobile people blocking my way. It's not rude to shove them aside here, since they won't know any of this, nor feel anything when the world returns to normal.

When I get to the hall, the girl is already gone, so I move on to the lobby and methodically search for her. Seeing a girl with a ponytail near the elevator, I run over and grab her. As I turn her to get a look at her face, I wonder if my touch will also bring her into the Quiet. I'm pretty sure that's what happened before—she touched me and brought me in.

But nothing happens this time, and the face that looks at me is completely unfamiliar.

Damn it. I've got the wrong person.

My frustration turns to anger as I realize that I lost her because those idiots delayed me at the most critical moment. Fuming, I punch a nearby person with all my strength, needing to vent. As is always the case in the Quiet, the object of my aggression doesn't react in any way. Unfortunately, I don't really feel better either.

Before I decide on my next course of action, I think about what happened at the table. The girl somehow got me to phase into the Quiet, and she was already there. When she saw me, she freaked out and ran. Maybe, like me, this was the first time she's seen anyone 'alive' in there. Everyone reacts differently to strange events, and meeting another person after years of being solo in the Quiet definitely qualifies as strange.

Standing here thinking about it isn't going to get me any answers, so I decide to be thorough and take one more look at the lobby again.

No luck. The girl is nowhere to be found.

Next, I go outside and walk around the casino driveway, trying to see if I can spot her there. I even look inside a few idling cabs, but she's not there either.

Looking up at the flashy building towering over me, I consider searching every room in the hotel. There are at least a couple thousand of them. It would take me a long time, but it might be worth it. I have to find her and get some answers.

Although thoroughly searching a building that huge seems like a daunting task, it wouldn't be impossible—at least not for me. I don't get hungry, thirsty, or even tired in the Quiet. Never need to use the bathroom either. It's very handy for situations like these, when you need to give yourself extra time. I can theoretically search every room—provided I can figure out how to get in. Those electronic doors won't work in the Quiet, not even if I have the original key from the room's occupants. Technology doesn't usually function here; it's frozen along with everything else. Unless it's something mechanical and simple, like my wind-up watch, it won't work—and even my watch I have to wind every time I'm in the Quiet.

Weighing my options, I try to imagine having to use physical force to break into thousands of hotel doors. Since my iPhone is sadly another technology casualty of the Quiet, I wouldn't even be able to listen to some tunes to kill the time. Even for a cause this important, I'm not sure I want to go to those extremes.

Besides, if I do decide to search the building, now probably isn't the best time to do it. Even if I find her, I won't be able to go after her in the real world thanks to those idiot guards in my way. I need to get rid of them before determining what to do next.

Sighing, I slowly walk back to the hotel. When I enter the lobby, I scan it again, hoping that I somehow missed her the first time. I feel that same compulsion I get when I lose something around the house. When that happens, I always search the place from top to bottom and then start doing it again—looking in the same places I already checked, irrationally hoping that the third time will be the charm. Or maybe the fourth. I really need to stop doing that. As Einstein said, insanity is doing the same thing over and over again and expecting different results.

Finally admitting defeat, I approach the bouncers. I can spend forever in the Quiet, but when I get out, they'll still be here. There's no avoiding that.

Moving in close, I look in the pocket of the fatter guy to find out what I'm up against. According to his ID, his name is Nick Shifer, and he's with security. So I was right—he's a bouncer. His driver's license is also there, as well as a small family photo. I study both, in case I need the information later.

Next, I turn my attention to the pocket near which Nick's hand is hovering. Looks like I was right again: he has a gun. If I took this gun and shot Nick at close range, he would get a bloody wound and likely fall from the impact. He wouldn't scream, though, and he wouldn't clutch his chest. And when I phase out, he would be whole again, with no signs of damage. It would be like nothing happened.

Don't ask me how I know what happens when you shoot someone in the Quiet. Or stab him. Or hit him with a baseball bat. Or whack him with a golf club. Or kick him in the balls. Or drop bricks on his head—or a TV. The only thing I can say is that I can unequivocally confirm that in a wide variety of cruel and unusual experiments, the subjects turn out to be unharmed once I phase out of the Quiet.

Okay, that's enough reminiscing. Right now, I have a problem to solve, and I need to be careful, with the guns being involved and all.

I smack my frozen self on the back of the head to phase out of the Quiet.

The world unfreezes, and I'm back with the bouncers in real time. I try to look calm, as though I haven't been running around like a crazy man looking for whoever this girl is—because for them, none of that has happened.

"Okay, Nick, I'll be happy to accompany you and resolve this misunderstanding," I say in my most compliant tone.

Nick's eyes widen at hearing his name. "How do you know me?"

"You read the file, Nick," his lean partner says, obviously unimpressed. "The kid is very clever."

The file? What the hell is he talking about? I've never been to this casino before. Oh, and I would love to know how being clever would help someone know the name of a complete stranger on a moment's notice. People always say stuff like that about me, even though it makes no sense. I debate phasing into the Quiet to learn the second guy's name as well, just to mess with them more, but I decide against it. It would be overkill. Instead I decide to mentally refer to the lean guy as Buff.

"Just come with me quietly, please," Buff says. He stands aside, so that he's able to walk behind me. Nick leads the way, muttering something about the impossibility of my knowing his name, no matter how smart I am. He's clearly brighter than Buff. I wonder what he would say if I told him where he lives and that he has two kids. Would he start a cult, or shoot me?

As we make the trek through the casino, I reflect on how knowing things I shouldn't has served me well over the years. It's kind of my thing, and it's gotten me far in life. Of course, it's possible that knowing things I shouldn't is also the reason they have a file on me. Maybe casinos keep records on people who seem to have a history of beating the odds, so to speak.

When we get to the office—a modest-sized room filled with

cameras overlooking different parts of the casino—Buff's first question confirms that theory. "Do you know how much money you won today?" he asks, glaring at me.

I decide to play dumb. "I'm not sure."

"You're quite the statistical anomaly," Nick says. He's clearly proud of knowing such big words. "I want to show you something." He takes a remote from the desk, which has a bunch of folders scattered on its surface. With Nick's press of a button, one of the monitors begins showing footage of me playing at the blackjack table. Watching it, I realize that I did win too much.

In fact, I won just about every time.

Shit. Could I have been any more obvious? I didn't think I'd be watched this closely, but that was stupid of me. I should've taken a couple of hits even when I knew I would bust, just to hide my tracks.

"You're obviously counting cards," Nick states, giving me a hard stare. "There's no other explanation."

Actually, there is, but I'm not about to give it to him. "With eight decks?" I say instead, making my voice as incredulous as possible.

Nick picks up a file on the desk and leafs through it.

"Darren Wang Goldberg, graduated from Harvard with an MBA and a law degree at eighteen. Near-perfect SAT, LSAT, GMAT, and GRE scores. CFA, CPA, plus a bunch more acronyms." Nick chuckles as if amused at that last tidbit, but then his expression hardens as he continues. "The list goes on and on. If anyone could do it, it would be you."

I take a deep breath, trying to contain my annoyance. "Since you're so impressed with my bona fides, you should trust me when I tell you that no one can count cards with eight decks." I have no clue if that's actually true, but I do know casinos have been trying to stack the odds in the house's favor for ages now, and eight decks is too many cards to count even for a mathematical prodigy.

As if reading my mind, Buff says, "Yeah, well, even if you can't do it by yourself, you might be able to pull it off with partners."

Partners? Where did they get the idea that I have partners?

In response to my blank look, Nick hits the remote again, and I see a new recording. This time it's of the girl—of her winning at the blackjack table, then working a number of poker tables. Winning an impressive amount of cash, I might add.

"Another statistical anomaly," Nick says, looking at me intently. "A friend of yours?" He must've worked as a detective before this gig, seeing as how he's pretty good at this interrogation thing. I guess my chasing her through the casino set off some red flags. My reaction was definitely not for the reasons he thinks, though.

"No," I say truthfully. "I've never seen her before in my life."

Nick's face tightens with anger. "You just played at the same poker table," he says, his voice growing in volume with every word. "Then you both started running away just as we were coming toward you. I suppose that's just a coincidence, huh? Do the two of you have someone on the inside? Who else is in on it?" He's full-on yelling at this point, spittle flying in every direction.

This fierce grilling is too much for me, and I phase into the Quiet to give myself a few moments to think.

Contrary to Nick's belief, the girl and I are definitely not partners. Yet it's obvious she was here doing the same thing I was, as the recordings clearly show her winning over and over.

That means I didn't have a hallucination, and she really was in the Quiet somehow. She can do what I can. My heart beats faster with excitement as I realize again that I'm not the only one. This girl is like me—which means I really need to find her.

On a hunch, I approach the table and pick up the thickest folder I see.

And that's when I hit the biggest jackpot of the night.

Staring back at me from the file is her picture. Her real name, according to the file, is Mira Tsiolkovsky. She lives in Brooklyn, New York.

Her age shocks me. She's only eighteen. I thought she'd be in her mid-twenties—which would conveniently fit right within my datable age range. As I further investigate the information they've compiled on her, I find the reason I was fooled by her age: she intentionally tries to make herself look older to get into casinos. The folder lists a bunch of her aliases, all of which are banned from casinos. All are aged between twenty-one and twenty-five.

According to the folder, she does this cheating thing professionally. One section details her involvement in cheating both in casinos and underground gambling joints. Scary places by the sound of it, with links to organized crime.

She sounds reckless. I, on the other hand, am most decidedly not reckless. I use my strange ability to make money in the financial industry, which is much safer than what Mira does. Not to mention, the kind of money I bring in through legitimate channels makes the risks of cheating in casinos far outweigh the benefits—especially given what I'm learning today. Apparently casinos don't sit idly by while you take their money. They start files on you if they think you're likely to cheat them, and they blacklist you if you get too lucky. Seems unfair, but I guess it makes business sense.

Returning my attention to the file, I find little personal information beyond her name and address—just other casinos, games, and the amounts she's won under different aliases, plus pictures. She's good at changing her appearance; all the pictures feature women who look very different from one another. Impressive.

Having memorized as much of Mira's file as I can, I walk over to Nick and take my own file from his hands.

I'm relieved to find that there's not much to this folder. They have my name and address, which they must've gotten from the credit card I used to pay for drinks. They know that I work at a hedge fund and that I've never had problems with the law—all stuff easily found on the web. Same goes for Harvard and my other achievements. They probably just did a Google search on me once they knew my name.

Reading the file makes me feel better. They're not on to me or anything like that. They probably just saw me winning too much and decided to nip the situation in the bud. The best thing to do at this point is to placate them, so I can go home and digest all this. No need to search the hotel anymore. I have more than enough information about Mira now, and my friend Bert can help me fill in the rest of the puzzle.

Thus resolved, I walk back to myself. My frozen self's face looks scared, but I don't feel scared anymore because I now have a plan.

Taking a deep breath, I touch my frozen forehead again and phase out.

Nick is still yelling at me, so I tell him politely, "Sir, I'm sorry, but I don't know what or whom you're talking about. I was lucky, yes, but I didn't cheat." My voice quavers on that last bit. I might be overacting now, but I want to be convincing as a scared young man. "I'll be happy to leave the money and never come back to this casino again."

"You *are* going to leave the money, and you won't ever come back to this *city* again," corrects Buff.

"Fine, I won't. I was just here to have fun," I say in a steadier but still deferential voice, like I'm totally in awe of their authority. "I just turned twenty-one and it's Labor Day weekend, so I went gambling for the first time," I add. This should add an air of sincerity, because it's the truth. "I work at a hedge fund. I don't need to cheat for money."

Nick snorts. "Please. Guys like you cheat because you like the rush of being so much smarter than everyone else."

Despite his obvious contempt for me, I don't reply. Every remark I form in my head sounds snide. Instead I just continue groveling, saying that I know nothing, gradually becoming more and more polite. They keep asking me about Mira and about how I cheat, and I keep denying it. The conversation goes in circles for a while. I can tell they're getting as tired of it as I am—maybe more so.

Seeing an opening, I go in for the kill. "I need to know how much longer I'll be detained, sir," I tell Nick, "so that I can notify my family."

The implication is that people will wonder where I am if I don't show up soon. Also, my subtle use of the word 'detained' reminds them of the legality of their position—or more likely, the lack thereof.

Frowning, but apparently unwilling to give in, Nick says stubbornly, "You can leave as soon as you tell us something useful." There isn't much conviction in his voice, though, and I can tell that my question hit the mark. He's just saving face at this point.

Doggedly continuing the interrogation, he asks me the same questions again, to which I respond with the same answers. After a couple of minutes, Buff touches his shoulder. They exchange a look.

"Wait here," Buff says. They leave, presumably to have a quick discussion out of my earshot.

I wish I could listen in, but sadly it's not possible with the Quiet. Well, that's not entirely true. If I learned to read lips and phased in and out very quickly, I could probably piece together some of the conversation by looking at their frozen faces, over and over again. But that would be a long, tedious process. Plus, I don't need to do that. I can use logic to figure out the gist of what they're saying. I'm guessing it goes something like this: "The kid's too smart for us; we should let him go, get doughnuts, and swing by a strip club."

They return after a few minutes, and Buff tells me, "We're going to let you go, but we don't want to see you—or your girlfriend—here ever again." I can tell Nick isn't happy about having to abandon his questioning without getting the answers he wanted, but he doesn't voice any objections.

I suppress a relieved sigh. I half-thought they'd rough me up or something. It would've sucked, but it wouldn't have been unexpected—or perhaps even undeserved, given that I did cheat. But then again, they have no proof that I cheated. And they probably think I'm clever enough to cause legal problems —particularly given my law degree.

Of course, it's also possible that they know more about me than what's in the file. Maybe they've come across some info about my moms. Oh yeah, did I mention that I have two moms?

Well, I do. Trust me, I know how strange that sounds. And before there's any temptation, I never want to hear another joke on the subject. I got enough of that in school. Even in college, people used to say shit sometimes. I usually made sure they regretted it, of course.

In any case, Lucy, who is my adoptive mom—but is nonetheless the most awesome mom ever—is a tough-as-nails detective. If these bozos laid a finger on me, she'd probably track them down and personally kick their asses with a baseball bat. She also has a team that reports to her, and they would likely chime in, too. And Sara, my biological mom—who is usually quite peace-loving—wouldn't stop her. Not in this case.

Nick and Buff are silent as they lead me out of their office and through the casino to the cab waiting area outside.

"If you come here again," Nick says as I get into an empty cab, "I'll break something of yours. Personally."

I nod and quickly close the door. All he had to do was ask me nicely like that. In retrospect, Atlantic City wasn't even that much fun.

I'm convinced I won't ever want to come back.

3

I START MY POST-LABOR DAY TUESDAY MORNING FEELING LIKE A zombie. I couldn't fall asleep after the events at the casino, but I can't skip work today. I have an appointment with Bill.

Bill is my boss, and no one ever calls him that—except me, in my thoughts. His name is William Pierce. As in Pierce Capital Management. Even his wife calls him William—I've heard her do it. Most people call him Mr. Pierce, because they're uncomfortable calling him by his first name. So, yeah, Bill is among the few people I take seriously. Even if, in this case, I'd rather nap than meet with him.

I wish it were possible to sleep in the Quiet. Then I'd be all set. I'd phase in and snooze right under my desk without anyone noticing.

I achieve some semblance of clear thought after my first cup of coffee. I'm in my cubicle at this point. It's eight a.m. If you think that's early, you're wrong. I was actually the last to get into the office in my part of the floor. I don't care what those early risers think of my lateness, though. I can barely function as is.

Despite my achievements at the fund, I don't have an office. Bill has the only office in the company. It would be nice to have some privacy for slacking off, but otherwise, I'm content with my cube. As long as I can work in the field or from home most of the time—and as long as I get paid on par with people who typically have offices—the lack of my own office doesn't bother me.

My computer is on, and I'm looking at the list of coworkers on the company instant messenger. Aha—I see Bert's name come online. This is really early for him. As our best hacker, he gets to stroll in whenever he wants, and he knows it. Like me, he doesn't care what anyone else thinks about it. In fact, he probably cares even less than I do—and thus comes in even later. I initially thought we would talk after my meeting with Bill, but there's no time like the present, since Bert is in already.

"Stop by," I message him. "Need your unique skills."

"BRT," Bert replies. *Be right there.*

I've known Bert for years. Unlike me, he's a real prodigy. We were the only fourteen-year-olds in a Harvard *Introduction to Computer Science* course that year. He aced the course without having to phase into the Quiet and look up the answers in the textbook, the way I did in the middle of the exams. Nor did he pay a guy from Belarus to write his programing projects for him.

Bert is *the* computer guy at Pierce. He's probably the most capable coder in New York City. He always drops hints that he used to work for some intelligence agency as a contractor before I got him to join me here and make some real money.

"Darren," says Bert's slightly nasal voice, and I swivel my chair in response.

Picturing this guy as part of the CIA or FBI always puts a smile on my face. He's around five-four, and probably weighs less than a hundred pounds. Before we became friends, my nickname for Bert was Mini-Me.

"So, Albert, we should discuss that idea you gave me last week," I begin, jerking my chin toward one of our public meeting rooms.

"Yes, I would love to hear your report," Bert responds as we close the door. He always overacts this part.

As soon as we're alone, he drops the formal colleague act. "Dude, you fucking did it? You went to Vegas?"

"Well, not quite. I didn't feel like taking a five-hour flight—"

"So you opted for a two-hour cab ride to Atlantic City instead," Bert interrupts, grinning.

"Yes, exactly." I grin back, taking a sip of my coffee.

"Classic Darren. And then?"

"They banned me," I say triumphantly, like it's some huge accomplishment.

"Already?"

"Yeah. But not before I met this chick." I pause for dramatic effect. I know this is the part he's really waiting for. His own experience with girls thus far has been horrendous.

Sure enough, he's hooked. He wants to know every detail. I tell him a variation of what happened. Nothing about the Quiet, of course. I don't share that with anyone, except my shrink. I just tell Bert I won a lot. He loves that part, as he was the one who suggested I try going to a casino. This was after he and a bunch of our coworkers got slaughtered by me at a friendly card game.

He, like most at the fund, knows that I know things I shouldn't. He just doesn't know *how* I know them. He accepts it as a given, though. In a way, Bert is a little bit like me. He knows things he shouldn't, too. Only in his case, everyone knows the 'how.' The method behind Bert's omniscience is his ability to get into any computer system he wants.

That is precisely what I need from him now, so as soon I finish describing the mystery girl, I tell him, "I need your help."

His eyebrows rise, and I explain, "I need to learn more about her. Whatever you can find out would be helpful."

"What?" His excitement noticeably wanes. "No, Darren, I can't."

"You owe me," I remind him.

"Yeah, but this is cyber-crime." He looks stubborn, and I mentally sigh. If I had a dollar for every time Bert used that line . . . We both know he commits cyber-crime on a daily basis.

I decide to offer him a bribe. "I'll watch a card trick," I say, making a Herculean effort to inject some enthusiasm into my voice. Bert's attempts at card tricks are abysmal, but that doesn't deter him one bit.

"Oh," Bert responds casually. His poker face is shit, though. I know he's about to try to get more out of me, but it's not going to happen, and I tell him so.

"Fine, fine, text me those aliases you mentioned, the ones that 'fell into your lap,' and the address you 'got by chance,'" he says, giving in. "I'll see what I can do."

"Great, thanks." I grin at him again. "Now I have to go—I've got a meeting with Bill."

I can see him cringing when I call William that. I guess that's why I do it—to get a rise out of Bert.

"Hold on," he says, frowning.

I know what's coming, and I try not to look too impatient.

Bert is into magic. Only he isn't very good. He carries a deck of cards with him wherever he goes, and at any opportunity—real or imaginary—he whips the cards out and tries to do a card trick.

In my case, it's even worse. Because I showed off to him once, he thinks I'm into magic too, and that I only pretend I'm not. My tendency to win when playing cards only solidifies his conviction that I'm a closet magician.

As I promised him, I watch as he does his trick. I won't describe it. Suffice it to say, there are piles of cards on the conference room table, and I have to make choices and count and spell something while turning cards over.

"Great, good one, Bert," I lie as soon as my card is found. "Now I really have to go."

"Oh, come on," he cajoles. "Let me see your trick one more time."

I know it'll be faster for me to go along with him than to argue my way out of it. "Okay," I say, "you know the drill."

As Bert cuts the deck, I look away and phase into the Quiet.

As soon as the world freezes, I realize how much ambient noise the meeting room actually has. The lack of sound is refreshing. I feel it more keenly after being sleep-deprived. Partly because most of the 'feeling like crap' sensation dissipates when I'm in the Quiet, and partly because outside the Quiet, the sounds must've been exacerbating a minor headache that I only now realize is there.

Walking over to motionless Bert, I take the pile of cards in his hand and look at the card he cut to. Then I phase back out of the Quiet.

"Seven of hearts," I say without turning around. The sounds are back, and with them, the headache.

"Fuck," Bert says predictably. "We should go together. Get ourselves banned from Vegas next time."

"For that, I'll need a bigger favor." I wink at him and go back to my cubicle.

When I get to my desk, I see that it's time for my meeting. I quickly text Bert the information he needs to search for Mira and then head off to see Bill.

BILL'S OFFICE LOOKS AS AWESOME AS USUAL. IT'S THE SIZE OF MY Tribeca apartment. I've heard it said that he only has this huge office because that's what our clients expect to see when they visit. That he allegedly is egalitarian and would gladly sit in a cube with low walls, like the rest of us.

I'm not sure I buy that. The decorations are a little too meticulous to support that theory. Plus, he strikes me as a guy who likes his privacy.

One day I'll have an office too, unless I decide to retire first.

Bill looks like a natural-born leader. I can't put my finger on what attributes give this impression. Maybe it's his strong jaw, the wise warmth in his gaze, or the way he carries himself. Or maybe it's something else entirely. All I know is he looks like someone people would follow—and they do.

Bill earned major respect from me when he played a part in legalizing gay marriage in New York. My moms have dreamed of getting married for as long as I can remember, and anyone who helps make my moms happier is a good person in my book.

"Darren, please sit," he says, pulling his gaze from his monitor as I walk in.

"Hi William, how was your weekend?" I say. He's probably the only person in the office I bother doing the small-talk thing with. Even here, I ask mainly because I know Bill's answer will be blissfully brief. I don't care what my coworkers do in general, let alone on their weekends.

"Eventful," he says. "How about you?"

I try to beat his laconic response. "Interesting."

"Great." Like me, Bill doesn't seem interested in probing beyond that. "I have something for you. We're thinking about building a position in FBTI."

That's the ticker for Future Biotechnology and Innovation Corp; I've heard of them before. "Sure. We need a position in biotech," I say without blinking. In truth, I haven't bothered to look at our portfolio in a while. I just can't recall having biotech-related assignments recently—so I figure there can't be that many biotech stocks in there.

"Right," he says. "But this isn't just to diversify."

I nod, while trying to look my most serious and thoughtful. That's easier to do with Bill than with most other people. Sometimes I genuinely find what he says interesting.

"FBTI is going to unveil something three weeks from now," he explains. "The stock is up just based on speculation on the Street. It could be a nice short if FBTI disappoints—" he pauses for emphasis, "—but I personally have a hunch that things will go in the other direction."

"Well, to my knowledge, your hunches have never been wrong," I say. I know it sounds like I'm ass-kissing, but it's the truth.

"You know I never act on hunch alone," he says, doing this

weird quirking thing he often does with his eyebrow. "In this case, maybe a hunch is understating things. I had some of FBTI's patents analyzed. Plenty of them are for very promising developments."

I'm convinced that I know where this is leading.

"Why don't you poke around?" he suggests, proving my conviction right. "Speak with them and see if the news is indeed bigger than what people are expecting. If that's the case, we need to start building the position."

"I'll do what I can," I say.

This generates a smile from Bill. "Was that humility? That would be a first," he says, seemingly amused. "I need you to do your usual magic. You're up for the challenge, right?"

"Of course. Whatever the news is, you'll know by the end of the week. I guarantee it." I don't add 'or your money back.' That would be too much. What if I get nothing? Bill is the type of person who would hold me to the claim.

"The sooner the better, but we definitely need it before the official news in three weeks," Bill says. "Now, if you'll excuse me."

Knowing that I'm dismissed, I leave him with his computer and go to my cube to make a few phone calls.

As soon as they hear the name Pierce, FBTI is happy to talk to me. I make an appointment with their CTO and am mentally planning the subway trip to their Manhattan office in SoHo when Bert pings me on Instant Messenger.

"Got it," the message says.

"Walk out with me?" I IM back.

He agrees, and we meet by the elevator.

"This chick is crazy," Bert says as I press the button for the lobby. "She leads a very strange life."

Outside his card tricks, Bert knows how to build suspense. I have to give him that. I don't rush him, or else this will take longer. So I just say, "Oh?"

"For starters, you're lucky you have me," he says, his voice brimming with excitement. "She's long gone from that address you found 'by chance.' From what I can puzzle out, that name—Mira—is her real one. Only that name disappeared from the face of the planet a little over a year ago. No electronic trail at all. Same thing with some of those aliases."

"Hmm," I say, giving him the encouragement I know he needs to keep going.

"Well, to get around that, I hacked into some Vegas casino databases, going on the assumption that she would play there as well as in Atlantic City, and sure enough, they had files on some of the other aliases that you mentioned. They also had additional names for her."

"Wow," is all I can say.

"Yeah," Bert agrees. "At first, only one led to any recently occupied address. She's clearly hiding. Anyway, that one alias, Alina something, had a membership at a gym on Kings Highway and Nostrand Avenue, in Brooklyn. Hacking into their system, I found out that the membership is still used sometimes. Once I had that, I set a radius around that gym. People don't usually go far to get workouts."

"Impressive," I say, and mean it. At times like this, I wonder if the business about him being a contractor for some intelligence agency is true after all.

"Anyway, at first there was nothing," he continues. "None of the aliases rent or own any apartments or condos nearby. But then I tried combining first names of some of these aliases with the last names of others." He pauses and looks at me—to get a pat on the back, I think.

"That's diabolical," I say, wishing he would get to the point already.

"Yes," he says, looking pleased. "I am, indeed . . . She, on the other hand, isn't very imaginative. One of the combinations worked. She's partial to the first name of Ilona. Combining Ilona with a last name of Derkovitch, from the Yulia Derkovitch alias, yielded the result I was looking for."

I nod, urging him on.

"Here's that address," he says, grinning as he hands me a piece of paper. Then he asks more seriously, "Are you really going there?"

That's an excellent question. If I do, she'll think I'm a crazy stalker. Well, I guess if you think about it, I am kind of stalking her, but my motives are noble. Sort of.

"I don't know," I tell Bert. "I might swing by that gym and see if I can 'bump into her.'"

"I don't think that will work," he says. "According to their database, her visits are pretty sporadic."

"Great." I sigh. "In that case, yes, I guess I'll show up at her door."

"Okay. Now the usual fine print," Bert says, giving me an intense stare. "You didn't get this from me. Also, the name I found could be a complete coincidence, so it's within the realm of possibility that you might find someone else there."

"I take full responsibility for whatever may occur," I tell Bert solemnly. "We're even now."

"Okay. Good. There's just one other thing . . ."

"What?"

"Well, you might think this is crazy or paranoid, but—" he looks embarrassed, "—I think she might be a spy."

"What?" This catches me completely off-guard.

"Well, something else I should've said is that she's an immigrant. A Russian immigrant, in case you didn't get it from the unusual-sounding names. Came here with her family about a decade ago. When combined with these aliases . . . You see how I would think along these lines, don't you?"

"Right, of course," I say, trying to keep a straight face. A spy? Bert sure loves his conspiracy theories. "Leave it with me," I say reassuringly. "If she's a spy, I'll deal with it. Now let me buy you a second breakfast and a cup of tea. After that, I'm off to SoHo to meet with FBTI."

4

I MAKE THE TRIP TO SOHO. THE SECURITY GUARD AT THE FBTI building lets me in once he knows I have an appointment with Richard Stone, the CTO.

"Hi Richard, I'm Darren. We spoke on the phone." I introduce myself to a tall bald man when I'm seated comfortably in a guest chair in his office. The office is big, with a massive desk with lots of drawers, and a small bookshelf. There's even a plasma TV mounted on the wall. I take it all in, feeling a hint of office envy again.

"Please call me Dick," he says. I have to use every ounce of my willpower not to laugh. If I had a bald head, I'd definitely prefer Richard. In fact, I think I'd prefer to be called Richard over Dick regardless of how I looked.

"Okay, Dick. I'm interested in learning about what you guys are working on these days," I say, hoping I don't sound like I relish saying his nickname too much.

"I'm happy to discuss anything outside of our upcoming

announcement," he says, his tone dickish enough to earn that moniker.

I show interest in the standard stuff he's prepared to say, and he goes on, telling me all the boring details he's allowed to share. He continues to talk, but I don't listen. Tuning people out was one of the first things I mastered in the corporate world. Without that, I wouldn't have survived a single meeting. Even now, I have to go into the Quiet from time to time to take a break, or I'd die from boredom. I'm not a patient guy.

Anyway, as Dick goes on, I surreptitiously look around. It's ironic that I'm doing exactly the opposite of what everyone thinks I do. People assume I ask pointed questions of these executives, and figure things out based on their reactions, body language, and who knows what else.

Being able to pick up on body cues and other nonverbal signals is something I want to learn at some point. I even gave it a try in Atlantic City. But in this case, as usual, I rely on something that depends far less on interpretive skills.

When I've endured enough bullshit from Dick, I try to invoke a frightened state of being so I can phase into the Quiet.

Simply thinking myself crazy is not that effective anymore. Picturing myself showing up like a dumbass at that Brooklyn address Bert gave me for Mira, on the other hand—that works like a charm.

I phase in, and Dick is finally, blissfully, quiet. He's frozen mid-sentence, and I realize, not for the first time, that I would have a huge edge if I were indeed able to read body cues. I recognize now that he's looking down, which I believe is a sign that someone's lying.

But no, instead of body language, I read literal language.

I begin with the papers on his desk. There's nothing special there.

Next, I roll his chair, with his frozen body in it, away from the desk. I love it when people in the Quiet are sitting in chairs with wheels. Makes this part of my job easier. In college, I realized I could get the contents of the final exams early by reaching into the professor's desk or bag in the Quiet. Moving the professors aside, though, had been a pain. Their chairs didn't have wheels like corporate office chairs do.

Thinking of those days in school makes me smile, because the things I learned in college are genuinely helpful to me now. This snooping in the Quiet—which is how I finished school so fast and with such good grades—is how I make a living now, and quite a good living at that. So, in some ways, my education really did prepare me for the workforce. Few people can say that.

With Dick and his chair out of the way, I turn my attention to his desk. In the bottom drawer, I hit the mother lode.

FBTI's big announcement will be about a device that will do something called 'transcranial magnetic stimulation.' I vaguely remember hearing about it. Before I delve deeper into the folder I found, I look at the bookshelf. Sure enough, on the shelf is something called *The Handbook of Transcranial Magnetic Stimulation*. It's funny. Now that I know what I'm looking for, I realize that aside from reading body language and cues like that, someone doing this 'for real' likely would've noticed this book on the shelf as a clue to what the announcement would be. In fact, the shelf contains a couple more books on this subject. Now that I think about it, I notice they have less dust on them than the other books on the shelf. Sherlock Holmes would've been proud of my investigative method—only my method works backwards. He used the skill of deductive reasoning, putting the clues he observed together to develop a conclusion. I, however, find evidence to support my conclusion once I know what the answer is.

Returning to my quest for information about the upcoming announcement, I read the first textbook I noticed on the subject. Yes, when I have to—or want to—I can learn the more traditional way. Just because I cheated when it came to tests doesn't mean I didn't legitimately educate myself from time to time. In fact, I did so quite often. However, my education was about whatever I was interested in at the moment, not some cookie-cutter program. I cheated simply because I was being pragmatic. The main reason I was at Harvard was to get a piece of paper that would impress my would-be employers. I used the Quiet to attain the mundane requirements of my degree while genuinely learning about things important to me.

When I do decide to read, the Quiet gives me a huge edge. I never get drowsy, even if the material is a little dry. I don't need sleep in the Quiet, just like I'm not a slave to other bodily functions in there. To me, it feels like it took maybe an hour to finish the part of the book about the magnetic version of stimulation—and it was actually interesting in certain parts. I even skimmed a few other stimulation types, which seem invasive compared to TMS, as the book calls it. I didn't absorb it all, of course—that would require re-reading—but I feel sufficiently ready to tackle the rest of the folder I found in Dick's desk.

I catch myself writing the report to Bill in my head. In layman's terms, TMS is a way to directly stimulate the brain without drilling into the skull—which the other methods require. It uses a powerful magnetic field to do so—hence the

'Magnetic' in the name. It's been around for a while, but was only recently approved by the FDA for treating depression. In terms of harm—and this is not from the book but my own conjecture—it doesn't seem worse than getting an MRI.

It takes me only a brief run through the papers in the folder to realize that the FBTI announcement will exceed everyone's expectations. They have a way of constructing a TMS machine that is more precise than any before, while being affordable and easily customizable. Just for the treatment of depression alone, this device will make a significant impact. To top it off, the work can also lead to better MRI machines, which may open up a new market for FBTI.

Realizing I have enough information, I phase out.

Dick's voice is back. I listen to his closing spiel; then I thank him and go home.

I log in to work remotely, and write up my report in an email. I list all the reasons I think we should go long FBTI and my miscellaneous thoughts on why it would be a good investment.

I set the delivery of my email for late Friday evening. It's a trick I use sometimes to make it appear to my boss and coworkers that I work tirelessly, even on a Friday night, when most people go out or spend time with their families. I copy as many people as is reasonable and address it to Bill. Then I click send and verify that the email is waiting in my outbox. It'll sit there ready and waiting until it goes out Friday night.

Given how much money I'm about to make for Pierce Capital Management, I decide to take the rest of this week off.

5

SHOWING UP UNINVITED IS NOT THE ONLY THING THAT MAKES ME nervous about my plan to visit Mira. Another thing that worries me is the fact that the address in question happens to be in Brooklyn.

Why do people do that? Why live in the NYC boroughs? My moms are guilty of this as well—their choice, Staten Island, is even crazier. At least the subway goes to Brooklyn. Nothing goes to Staten Island, except the ferry and some express buses. It's even worse than New Jersey.

Still, I don't have a choice. Brooklyn is the location of the address, so off to Brooklyn I go. With deep reservations, I catch the Q train at City Hall and prepare for the epic journey.

As I sit on the subway, I read a book on my phone and occasionally look out the window. Whenever I do, I see graffiti on the walls of buildings facing the tracks. Why couldn't this girl live someplace more civilized, like the Upper East Side?

To my surprise, I get to my stop, Kings Highway, in less than an hour. From here, it's a short walk to my destination, according to my phone's GPS.

The neighborhood is . . . well, unlike the city. No tall buildings, and the signs on businesses are worn and tacky. Streets are a little dirtier than Manhattan, too.

The building is on East 14th Street, between Avenues R and S. This is the only aspect of Brooklyn I appreciate. Navigating streets named using sequential numbers and letters in alphabetical order is easy.

It's late in the afternoon, so the sun is out, but I still feel unsafe—as though I'm walking at night under an ominous-looking, ill-lit bridge in Central Park. My destination is across a narrow street from a park. I try to convince myself that if people let their children play in that park, it can't be *that* dangerous.

The building is old and gloomy, but at least it's not covered in graffiti. In fact, I realize I haven't seen any since I got off the train. Maybe my judgment of the neighborhood was too hasty.

Nah, probably not. It *is* Brooklyn.

The building has an intercom system. I gather my courage and ring the apartment door from downstairs.

Nothing.

I start pressing buttons randomly, trying to find someone who might let me in. After a minute, the intercom comes alive with a loud hiss and a barely recognizable, "Who's there?"

"UPS," I mumble. I'm not sure if it's the plausibility of my lie or someone just working on autopilot, but I get buzzed in.

Spotting an elevator, I press the up arrow, but nothing happens. No light comes on. No hint that anything is working.

I wait for a couple of minutes.

No luck.

I grudgingly decide to schlep to the fifth floor on foot. Looks like my assessment of the neighborhood was spot on after all.

The staircase has an unpleasant odor to it. I hope it's not urine, but my nose suggests it is. The noxious aroma on the second floor is diluted by the smells of boiled cabbage and fried garlic. There isn't a lot of light, and the marble steps seem slippery. Watching my step, I eventually make it to the fifth floor.

It's not until I'm actually staring at the door of 5E that I realize I don't have a good plan. Or any plan at all, really. I came this far, though, so I'm not about to turn around and go home now. I go ahead and ring the doorbell. Then I wait. And wait. And wait.

After a while, I hear some movement inside the apartment. Focusing, I watch the eyehole, the way I've seen people do in the movies.

Maybe it's my imagination, but I think a shadow comes across it. Someone might be looking at me.

Still no response.

I try knocking.

"Who is this?" says a male voice.

Shit. Who the hell is that? A husband? A boyfriend? Her father? Her pimp? Every scenario carries its own implications, and few promise anything good. None I can think of, actually.

"My name is Darren," I say, figuring that honesty is the best policy.

No answer.

"I'm a friend of Mira's," I add. And it's only when the words leave my mouth that I recall that she lives here under a different name. Ilona or something.

Before I can kick myself for the slip, the door swings open. A guy who appears to be a few years older than me stands there looking at me with tired, glassy eyes.

It takes a moment for me to notice one problem. No, make that one huge problem.

The guy is holding a gun.

A gun that looks bigger than his head.

The fear that slams my system is debilitating. I've never been threatened with a gun before. At least, not directly like this. Sure, the bouncers in Atlantic City had guns, but they weren't aiming them in my direction at point-blank range. I never imagined it would be this frightening.

I phase into the Quiet, almost involuntarily.

Now that I'm looking at my frozen self with a gun to his/my face, the panic is diluted. I'm still worried, though, since I am facing the gun in the real world.

I take a deep breath. I need to figure out my plan of action.

I look at the shooter.

He's tall, skinny. He's wearing glasses and a white coat with a red stain on it.

The white coat looks odd—and is that red spot blood, or something else? Questions race through my mind. Who is he? What is he doing in there that requires a gun? Is he cooking meth? It *is* Brooklyn after all.

At the same time, I can't shake the feeling that the guy does not look like an average street criminal. There is keen intelligence in his eyes. His uncombed hair and the pens and ruler in the pocket of his white coat paint a strange picture. He almost looks like a scientist—albeit on the mad side.

Of course, that does not rule out the drug angle. He could be like the character on that show about a teacher who cooks meth. Although, come to think of it, that same show made it clear that you don't do that in an apartment building. The smell is too strong to keep the operation hidden, or something like that.

Now that I've had some time to calm down in the Quiet, I get bolder. I begin to wonder if the gun is real. Or maybe I'm just hoping it's fake. Gathering my courage, I reach out to take it from the guy's hand.

When my fingers touch his, something strange happens. Or stranger, rather.

There are now two of him.

I look at the picture, and my jaw proverbially drops.

There is a second guy in the white coat, right there, and this one is moving. I'm so unaccustomed to the idea of people moving while I'm in the Quiet that I lose my ability to think, so I just stand there and gape at him.

The guy looks at me with an expression that's hard to read, a mixture of excitement and fear. As if I were a bear standing in the middle of a Brooklyn apartment building hall.

"Who are you?" he breathes, staring at me.

"I'm Darren," I repeat my earlier introduction, trying to conceal my shock.

"Are you a Reader, Darren?" the guy asks, recovering some of his composure. "Because if you're a Pusher, I will unload that gun in your face as soon as we Universe Split, or Astral Project, or Dimension Shift, or whatever it is you people call it. As soon as we're back to our bodies, you're dead, Pusher."

He has an unusual accent—Russian, I think. That reminds me of Bert's theory that Mira is a spy. Maybe he was right. Maybe she travels with a whole gang of Russian spies.

I only understand one thing about what the Russian guy is saying: he knows that I'm at his mercy when we get back. That means that he, like me, understands how the Quiet works.

The terms he's using sort of make sense to me. All except 'Reader' and 'Pusher.' I know that even if I were this 'Pusher,' I wouldn't want to admit it and get shot. He probably realizes that as well.

"I am sorry, I don't know what you're talking about," I admit. "I don't know what a Reader or a Pusher is."

"Right," the guy sneers. "And you're not aware of our bodies standing over there?"

"Well, yeah, of that I'm painfully aware—"

"Then you can't expect me to believe that you can Split, but not be one of us—or one of them." He says that last word with disgust.

Okay, so one thing is crystal clear: Reader is good, Pusher is bad. Now if only I could find out why.

"If I were a Pusher, would I just show up here like this?" I ask, hoping I can reason with him.

"You fuckers are clever and extremely manipulative," he says, looking me up and down. "You might be trying to use some kind of reverse psychology on me."

"To what end?"

"You want me dead, that's why, and you want my sister dead too," he says, his agitation growing with every word.

I make a mental note at the mention of 'sister,' but I don't have time to dwell on it. "Would showing up like this be the best way to kill you?" I try to reason again.

"Well, no. In fact, I've never heard of Pushers doing their dirty work themselves," he says, beginning to look uncertain. "They like to use regular people for that, like puppets."

I have no idea what he's referring to, so I continue my attempts at rational discourse. "So isn't it possible that I'm simply a guy searching for answers?" I suggest. "Someone who doesn't know what you're talking about?"

"No," he says after considering it for a moment. "I've never heard of untrained, unaffiliated people with the ability to Split. So why don't you tell me what you're doing here, outside my door."

"I can explain that part," I say hurriedly. "You see, I met a girl in Atlantic City. A girl who made me realize that I'm not crazy."

At the mention of Atlantic City, I have his full attention. "Describe her," he says, frowning.

I describe Mira, toning down her sex appeal.

"And she told you her name and where she lives?" he asks, clearly suspicious.

"Well, no," I admit. "I was detained by the casino when they thought we were working together to cheat the house. I learned a few of her aliases from them. After that, I got help from a friend who's a very good hacker."

There I go again, using honesty. I'm on a roll. I don't think I've ever said this many truthful statements in such a short time.

"A good hacker?" he asks, looking unexpectedly interested.

"Yes, the best," I reply, surprised. That's the completely wrong thing to focus on in this story, but as long as he's not angry and trigger-happy, I'll stick with the subject.

He looks me straight in the eyes for the first time. He seems uncomfortable with this. I can tell he doesn't do it often.

I hold his gaze.

"Here's the deal, Darren," he says, his eyes shifting away again after a second. "We're going to get back. I won't shoot you. Instead I will snap your picture. Then I'll text it to my sister."

"Okay," I say. I'll take a picture over a bullet any day.

"If you do anything to me before she gets here, she'll have proof that you were here," he elaborates.

"That makes sense," I lie. So far, there's very little of this that makes any sense at all. "Do whatever you think will help us resolve this misunderstanding."

"The only way to resolve it is to get proof that you're not a Pusher."

"Then let's get that proof," I say, hoping I'll get bonus points for my willingness to cooperate.

"Okay," he says, and I can tell that his mood is improving. "You must agree to submit to a test, then. Or a couple of tests, actually."

"Of course," I agree readily. Then, remembering the red stain on his coat, I ask warily, "Are they painful, these tests?"

"The tests are harmless. However, if it turns out that you're a Pusher, you better pray my sister isn't here at that point."

I swallow nervously as he continues, "I would just shoot you, you see. But Mira, she might make your death slow and very painful."

I rethink some of my fantasies about Mira. She's sounding less and less appealing. "Let's just do this," I say with resignation.

"Okay. Walk slowly to your body and touch it in such a way that I can clearly see it. Don't Split, or I will shoot you."

If 'Split' is what I think it is—as in phasing into the Quiet—

then how would he be able to tell if I did do it? Though it seems unlikely, I decide not to push my luck. Not until I know the results of his tests.

"I'm ready," I say, and demonstratively touch my frozen self on the forehead.

6

THE SOUNDS ARE BACK. THERE ARE NOW ONLY TWO OF US.

He's less intent on shooting me—so I know I didn't just hallucinate our conversation.

As I watch, he reaches into a pocket under his white coat and takes out a phone. Then he snaps a picture of me and writes a text.

"You go first," he says.

I walk into the apartment, the gun pressed to my back, and gape at my surroundings, struck by what I'm seeing.

The place is a mess.

I'm not the kind of guy who thinks it's a girl's job to keep a place neat. But after a certain point, I am the kind of guy who thinks, 'what kind of slob is she?' I'm not sexist, though. I think the guy with the gun to my back is just as responsible for this mess as she is. An episode of that show about hoarders could be filmed here.

Pulling me from my thoughts, the guy makes me go into a room on the left.

It appears to be some kind of makeshift lab—if the lab had a small explosion of wires, empty frozen meal boxes, and scattered papers, that is.

"Sit," he says.

I comply.

He grabs a few cables off the floor, some kind of gizmo, and a laptop, all the while trying to keep the gun pointed at me. Whatever he's setting up is ready in a few minutes.

I realize that the cable things are electrodes. Still holding the gun, he applies them to my temples and a bunch of other places all over my head. I must look like a medusa.

"Okay," he tells me when it's ready. "Split, and then come back."

I'm still so much on edge that phasing into the Quiet is easy. Within an instant, I'm standing next to my frozen body, watching myself. I look ridiculous with all the electrodes.

I momentarily debate snooping through the apartment, but decide against it. Instead I phase back out, anxious to see what's coming next.

The first thing I hear is his laptop beeping.

"Okay," he says after a pause. "Right before you Split, you were at the very least showing an EEG consistent with a Reader."

"I know this is a good thing, but you don't sound too confident," I say. As soon as I say it, I regret it. Reader is good. Why would I say anything that might instill doubt? But I can't help it, because I also want to know more about myself. Getting answers was the whole crazy reason I came here in the first place—well, that, and to confirm I'm not alone.

He looks around the room, then finds a nook to put the gun in. I think this officially means he's warmed up to me.

"I've only tested myself extensively, and have run preliminary tests on my sister," he says, glancing at me again. "I have my father's notes, but I'm not confident this is conclusive. Aside from that, I have no idea if Pushers would have the same EEG results." He furrows his brows. "In fact, it's quite likely they might."

His trust is like a yo-yo. "Isn't there a better test you can do?" I say before he reaches for the gun again.

"There is," he says. "You can actually try to Read."

I keep any witty responses related to reading books to myself. "Will you at least tell me what Readers and Pushers are?" I ask instead.

"I can't believe you don't know." He squints at me suspiciously. "Haven't your parents told you anything?"

"No," I admit, frustrated. "I have no idea what you mean or what parents have to do with anything." I hate not knowing things, did I mention that?

He stares at me for a few moments, then sighs and walks up to me. "My name is Eugene," he says, extending his hand to me.

"Nice to meet you, Eugene." I shake his hand, relieved by this rather-civilized turn of events.

"Listen to me, Darren." His face softens a bit, his expression becoming almost kind. "If what you say is true, then I'll help you." He raises his hand to stop me from thanking him, which I was about to do. "But only if you turn out to be a Reader."

I have never wished to be part of a clique so badly in my life.

"How?" I ask.

"I'll teach you," he says. "But if it fails, if you can't Read, you have to promise to leave and never come back."

Wow, so now the rules have changed in my favor. I won't be killed, even if I'm this Pusher thing. Nice.

"We need to hurry," he adds. "My sister's on the way. If you're a Pusher, she won't care about your situation."

"Why?" I ask. In the list of pros and cons as to whether or not I should date Mira, the cons are definitely in the lead.

"Because Pushers had our parents killed," he says. The kind expression vanishes. "In front of her."

"Oh, I'm so sorry," I say, horrified. I had no idea Mira had gone through something so awful. Whoever these Pushers are, I can't blame her for hating them—not if they killed her family.

Eugene's face tightens at my platitude. "If you're a Pusher and she catches you here, you'll be sorry."

"Right, okay." I get that point now. "Let's find out quickly then."

"Put this on your fingers," Eugene says, and grabs another cable from the shelf.

I put the device on. It reminds me of a heart-rate monitor, the kind a nurse would use on you at a hospital.

Eugene starts something on his laptop and turns the computer toward me.

There's a program on the screen that seems to be tracking my heart rate, so my theory was probably right.

"That's a photoplethysmograph," he says. When he sees my blank stare, he adds, "How much do you know about biofeedback?"

"Not much," I admit. "But I do know it's when scientists use electrodes, similar to the ones you used on me before, to measure your brain patterns." I recall reading about it in the context of a new way to control video games in the future, with your mind—as nature clearly intended. Also to beat lie detectors, but that's a long story.

"Good. That's neurofeedback, which is a type of biofeedback," he explains. His voice takes on a professorial quality as he speaks. I can easily picture him teaching at some community college. Glasses, white coat, and all. "This is a simpler feedback." He points at my fingers. "It measures your heart-rate variability."

Another blank stare from me prompts him to explain further.

"Your heart rate can be a window into your internal emotional state. There is a specific state I need you to master. This device should expedite the training." He looks uncertain when he says 'should'—I'm guessing he hasn't done much of this expedited training before.

I don't care, though. From what I know of biofeedback, it's harmless. If it keeps Mira from shooting me, sign me up.

"Anyway, you can read up on the details later. For now, I need you to learn to keep this program in the green." He points to a part of the screen.

It's like a game, then. There's a big red-alert-looking button activated in the right-hand lower corner of the screen. Next to it are blue and green buttons.

"Sync your breath to this," he says, pointing at a little bar that goes up and down. "This is five-in and five-out breathing."

I breathe in sync to the bar for a few minutes. Whatever leftover fear I had evaporates; the technique is rather soothing.

"That's good," he says, pointing at the important lower corner. The red button is gone, and I'm now in the blue. I keep breathing. The green light eludes me.

I see the graph the software keeps of my heart-rate

variability. It begins to look more and more even, almost like sine curves. I find it cool—even if I have no idea what that change means in terms of being able to Read.

The feeling this experience evokes is familiar, mainly because of the synchronous breathing. Lucy, my mom, taught me to do this as a meditation technique when I was a kid. She said it would help me focus. I think she secretly hoped it would reduce my hyperactivity. I loved the technique and still do it from time to time. It's something she told me she learned from one of her old friends on the force—a friend who passed away. You're supposed to think happy thoughts while doing the breathing, according to her teachings. Since I'm thinking of Lucy already, I remember fondly how she told me that she didn't know how to meditate just because she was Asian, which was what I used to think. It was the first lecture I received on cultural stereotypes, but definitely not the last. It's a pet peeve of both of my moms. They have a lot of pet peeves like that, actually.

Thus thinking happy thoughts, I try to ignore the bar, closing my eyes to do the meditation Lucy taught me. Every few seconds, I peek at the screen to see how I'm doing.

"That's it," Eugene says suddenly, startling me. When I open my eyes this time, I see the curves are even straighter, and the button is green.

"You did that much too easily," he says, giving me a suspicious look. "But no matter. Do it again, without looking at the screen at all."

He takes the laptop away, and I do my 'Lucy meditation.' In less than a minute, he looks at me with a more awed expression.

"That is amazing. I haven't heard of anyone reaching

Coherence so quickly before on the first try," he says. "You're ready for the real test."

He gets up, gets the gun, and puts it in his lab coat pocket. Then, much to my surprise, he leads me out of the apartment.

I'm especially puzzled when he walks across the hall and rings the doorbell of the neighboring apartment.

The door opens, and a greasy-haired, redheaded young guy looks us over. His eyes are bloodshot and glassy.

Without warning, everything silences.

Eugene is pulling his hand away from my frozen self. He must've done that trick his sister pulled on me at the casino. He must've phased in and touched me, bringing me into the Quiet. It's creepy to think about—someone touching my frozen self the way I've touched so many others—but I guess I need to get used to the idea, since I'm no longer the only one who can do this.

Eugene approaches the guy and touches him on the forehead. I half-expect the guy to appear in the Quiet, too.

But no. There are only five of us: a frozen Eugene and me, the moving versions of us, and this guy, who's still a motionless statue.

I watch, confused, as Eugene just stands there, holding the guy's forehead. He looks so still that he begins to remind me of his frozen self.

Then he starts moving again. His hand is not on the guy's head anymore.

"Okay," he says, pointing at the guy. "Now you do the same thing. Place your hand on his skin."

I walk up to the guy and comply. His forehead is clammy, which is kind of disgusting.

"Okay, now close your eyes and get into that same Coherence state," Eugene instructs.

I close my eyes and start doing the meditation. And then it happens.

I'M SO FUCKING STONED. THAT WAS SOME GOOD SHIT PETER SOLD me. I've gotta get some more.

I feel great, but at the same time a part of myself wonders—why the hell did I smoke pot? My hedge fund does random urine tests on occasion. What if I get tested?

And then it hits me: *I* am not stoned. *We* are stoned. I, *Darren,* am not. But I, *Nick,* am.

We are Nick right now.

We are listening to "Comfortably Numb" by Pink Floyd, which is also how we feel.

I, Darren, tried pot before. I didn't like it nearly as much as I, Nick, like it right now.

We get a craving, but we're too lazy to get anything to eat.

The doorbell rings.

Wow.

Can that be a delivery? We don't recall ordering, but ordering something—pizza or Chinese—sounds like a great idea right about now. We reach for the phone when the doorbell rings again.

Oh yeah, the door.

Who's at the door? we wonder again, with a pang of paranoia this time.

I, Darren, finally get it: it's Eugene and me ringing the doorbell.

We get up, walk to the door, and open it after fumbling with the locks.

We're looking at Eugene, Mira's older brother, and some other dude, who I, Darren, recognize as myself. We wonder what the deal is.

SUDDENLY, I'M STANDING IN THE CORRIDOR, MY HAND NO longer on Nick's forehead. I stare at Eugene, my mouth gaping and heart racing at the realization of what I just did.

"Eugene, did you want me to get inside this pothead's mind?" I manage to ask. "Is Reading 'Mind Reading'?"

Eugene smiles at me, then walks to his frozen self and touches his own temple, bringing us out of the Quiet. Then he makes some bullshit excuse to confused Nick for ringing the doorbell, and we walk back to Eugene's apartment.

"Tell me everything you just experienced," he says as soon as the door closes behind us.

I tell him. As I go on, his smile widens. He must've seen the same thing when he touched the guy. From his reaction, I guess this means I can Read, and since this apparently removes any suspicions he had about me, I also assume that Pushers can't Read. I think I'm starting to figure out at least a few pieces of the mystery.

This was the test—and incredibly, I passed.

7

WHAT I DID WAS NOT EXACTLY HOW I IMAGINED MIND READING—not that mind reading is something I imagined much. The experience was like some kind of virtual reality, only more intense. It was like I was the pothead guy. I felt what he felt. Saw what he saw. I even had his memories, and they came and went as though they were mine.

But at the same time, I was also myself. An observer of sorts. I experienced two conflicted world views. On the one hand, I was Nick, feeling high, feeling numb, feeling dumb, but at the same time, I was myself, able to not lose my own consciousness. It was a strange merger.

I want to do it again—as soon as possible.

"Do you want tea?" Eugene asks, dragging me out of my thoughts, and I realize we somehow ended up at the kitchen table.

I look around the room. There are a bunch of beakers all over the place. Is he running some kind of chemistry experiment in here? A red stain on the counter, near an ampule with remains of that same red substance, matches the stain on Eugene's white coat. At least it's not blood, as I had originally thought.

"I will take your silence as a yes to tea." Eugene chuckles. "I'm sorry," he adds, joining me after setting the kettle on the stove. "The first time we Read is usually not as confusing as that. Nick's intoxicated state must've been an odd addition to an already strange experience."

"That's an understatement," I say, getting my bearings. "So how does this work?"

"Let's begin at the beginning," Eugene says. "Do you now know what a Reader is?"

"I guess. Someone who can do that?"

"Exactly." Eugene smiles.

"And what is a Pusher?"

His smile vanishes. "What Pushers do is horrible. An abomination. A crime against human nature. They commit the ultimate rape." His voice deepens, filling with disgust. "They mind-rape. They take away a person's will."

"You mean they can hypnotize someone?" I ask, trying to make sense of it.

"No, Darren." He shakes his head. "Hypnosis is voluntary—if the whole thing exists at all. You can't make people do something they don't want to do under hypnosis." He stops at the sound of the kettle. "Pushers can make a person do anything they want," he clarifies as he gets up.

I don't know how to respond, so I just sit there, watching him pour us tea.

"I know it's a lot to process," Eugene says, placing the cup in front of me.

"You do have a gift for stating the obvious."

"You said you came here to get answers. I promised I would provide them. What do you want to know?" he says, and my heart begins to pound with excitement as I realize I'm about to finally learn more about myself.

"How does it work?" I ask before he changes his mind and decides to test me some more. "Why can we phase into the Quiet?"

"Phase into the Quiet? Is that what you call Splitting?" He chuckles when I nod. "Well, prepare to be disappointed. No one knows for sure why we can do it. I have some theories about it, though. I'll tell you my favorite one. How much do you know about quantum mechanics?"

"I'm no physicist, but I guess I know what a well-read layman should know."

"That might be enough. I'm no physicist myself. Physics was my dad's field, and really this is his theory. Have you ever heard of Hugh Everett III?"

"No." I've never heard of the first two either, but I don't say that to Eugene.

"It's not important, as long as you've heard of the multiple universes interpretation of quantum mechanics." He offers me sugar for my tea.

"I think I've heard of it," I say, shaking my head to decline the sugar. Eugene sits across from me at the table, his gaze intent on mine. "It's the alternative to the famous Copenhagen interpretation of quantum mechanics, right?"

"Yes. We're on the right track. Now, do you actually understand the Copenhagen interpretation?"

"Not really. It deals with particles deciding where to be upon observation with only a probability of being in a specific place—introducing randomness into the whole thing. Or something along those lines. Isn't it famous for no one understanding it?"

"Indeed. I doubt anyone really does. Even my dad didn't, which is why he said it was all BS. He would point out how the whole Schrödinger's cat paradox is the best example of the confusion." As he talks, Eugene gets more and more into the conversation. He doesn't touch his tea, completely immersed in the subject. "Schrödinger meant for the cat theory to illustrate the wrongness, or at least the weirdness of that interpretation, which is funny, given how famous the cat example became. Anyway, what's important is that Everett said there is no randomness. Every place a particle can be, it is, but in different universes. His theory is that there is nothing special about observing particles, or cats—that the reality is Schrödinger's cat is both alive and dead, a live cat in one universe and a dead one in another. No magic observation skills required. Do you follow?"

"Yes, I follow," I say. Amazingly enough, I actually do. "I had to read up on this when we wanted to invest in a firm that was announcing advances in quantum computing."

"Oh, good." Eugene looks relieved. "That might expedite my explanation considerably. I was afraid I would have to explain the double-slit experiment and all that to you. You've also heard of the idea that brains might use quantum computing in some way?"

"I have," I say, "but I've also read that it's unlikely."

"Because the temperatures are too high? And the effects are too short-lived?"

"Yeah. I think it was something along those lines."

"Well, my dad believed in it regardless, and so do I. No one really knows for sure, wouldn't you admit?" Eugene says.

I never really thought about it. It's not something that was ever important to me. "I guess so," I say slowly. "I read that there are definitely *some* quantum effects in the brain."

"Exactly." He takes a quick sip of tea and sets it aside again. I do the same. The tea is bitter and too hot, and I'm dying for Eugene to continue. "The unlikelihood that you mention is about whether consciousness is related to quantum effects. No one doubts that some kinds of quantum processes are going on in the brain. Since everything is made of subatomic particles, quantum effects happen everywhere. This theory just postulates that brains are leveraging these effects to their benefit. Kind of like plants do. Have you heard of that?"

"Yes, I have." He's talking about the quantum effects found in the process of photosynthesis. Mom—Sara—emailed me a bunch of articles about that. She's very helpful that way—sending me articles on anything she thinks I might be interested in. Or anything she's interested in, for that matter.

"Photosynthesis evolved over time because some creature achieved an advantage when using a quantum effect. In an analogous way, wouldn't a creature able to do any kind of cool quantum calculations get a huge survival advantage?" he asks.

"It would," I admit, fascinated.

"Good. So the theory is that what we can do is directly related to all this—that we find ourselves in another universe when we Split, and that a quantum event in our brains somehow makes us Split." He looks more and more like a mad scientist when he's excited, as he clearly is now.

"That's a big leap," I say doubtfully.

"Okay, then, let me go at it from another angle. Could brains have evolved an ability to do quick quantum computations? Say in cases of dire emergencies?"

"Yeah, I think that's possible." Evolution is something I know well, since Sara's PhD thesis dealt with it. I've known how the whole process works since second grade.

"Well, then let's assume, for the sake of this theory, that the brain has learned to leverage quantum effects for some specific purpose. And that as soon as the brain does that anywhere in nature, evolution will favor it. Even if the effect is tiny. As long as there's some advantage, the evolutionary change will spread."

"But that would mean many creatures, and all people, have the same ability we do," I say. I wonder if I have someone else who doesn't understand evolution on my hands.

"Right, exactly. You must've heard that some people in deeply stressful life-or-death situations experience time as though it's slowing down. That some even report leaving their bodies in near-death experiences."

"Yes, of course."

"Well, what if that's what it feels like for regular people to do this quantum computation, which is meant to save their lives or at least give their brains a chance to save them? You see, the theory asserts that this *does* happen and that all people have this 'near-death' quantum computation boost. All the anecdotal reports that mention strange things happening to people in dire circumstances confirm it. So far, the theory can be tied back to natural evolution."

"Okay," I say. "I think I follow thus far."

"Good." Eugene looks even more excited. "Now let's suppose that a long time ago, someone noticed this peculiarity—noticed how soldiers talk about seeing their lives pass before their eyes, or how Valkyries decide on the battlefield who lives and who dies . . . That person could've decided to do something really crazy, like start a cult—a cult that led to a strange eugenics program, breeding people who had longer and stronger experiences of a similar nature." He stands, tea forgotten, and begins to pace around the room as he talks. "Maybe they put them under stress to hear their stories. Then they might've had the ones with the most powerful experiences reproduce. Over a number of generations, that selective breeding could've produced people for whom this quantum computing under stress was much more pronounced—people who began to experience new things when that overly stressed state happened. Think about it, Darren." He stops and looks at me. "What if we're simply a branch of that line of humanity?"

This theory is unlike anything I expected to hear. It seems farfetched, but I have to admit it makes a weird sort of sense. There are parts that really fit my own experiences. Things that Eugene doesn't even know—like the fact that the first time I phased into the Quiet was when I fell off my bike while somersaulting in the air. It was exactly like the out-of-body experience he described. An experience I quickly discovered I could repeat whenever I was stressed.

"Does this theory explain Reading?" I ask.

"Sort of," he says. "The theory is that everyone's minds Split into different universes under some conditions. As Readers, we can just stay in those universes for a longer period of time, and we're able to take our whole consciousness with us." He draws in a deep breath. "The next part is somewhat fuzzy, I have to admit. If you touch a normal person who's unable to control the Split like we can, they're unaware of anything happening. However, if you touch a Reader or a Pusher—another person like us—while in that other universe, they get pulled in with you. Their whole being joins you, just like I joined you when you touched my hand earlier today. When you touch someone 'normal,' they just get pulled in a little bit—on more of a subconscious level. Just enough for us to do the Reading. Afterwards, they have no recollection of it other than a vague sense of déjà vu or a feeling that they missed something, but even those cases are extremely rare."

"Okay, now the theory sounds more wishy-washy," I tell him.

"It's the best I've got. My dad tried to study this question scientifically and paid the ultimate price."

I stare at Eugene blankly, and he clarifies, "Pushers killed him for his research."

"What? He was killed for trying to find these answers?" I can't hide my shock.

"Pushers don't like this process being studied," Eugene says bitterly. "Being the cowards that they are, they're afraid."

"Afraid of what?"

"Of 'normal' people learning to do what we do," Eugene says, and it's clear that he's not scared of that possibility.

8

I SIP MY TEA QUIETLY FOR A WHILE. EUGENE COMES BACK TO THE table and sits down again, sipping from his own mug. My brain is on information overload. There are so many directions this conversation could go. I have so many questions. I've never met anyone who even knew the Quiet existed, let alone knew this much about it—other than Mira, of course, but chasing someone through a crowded casino doesn't technically qualify as 'meeting.'

"Are there other theories?" I ask after a few moments.

"Many," he says. "Another one I like is the computer simulation one. If you've seen *The Matrix*, it's relatively easy to explain. Only it doesn't answer as many things as the Quantum Universes explanation does. Like the fact that our abilities are hereditary."

I was initially curious about the computer simulation theory, but the heredity angle stops me dead in my tracks.

"Wait, does every Reader have to have Reader parents?" I ask. In hindsight, it's obvious from what he's said thus far, but I want it spelled out.

"Yes." He puts his now-empty teacup down. "Which reminds me. Who are your parents? How could you not have known that you're a Reader?"

"Hold on." I raise my hand. "Both parents must be Readers?"

"No." He looks upset for some reason. "Not both. Just one." It's obvious that this is a sensitive subject for Eugene.

Before I can question him about that, he continues, "I don't understand why your parents didn't tell you about this. I always thought this was an oral tradition, a story that every family who has the ability passes from generation to generation. Why didn't yours?"

"I'm not sure," I say slowly. Sara never told me anything. In fact, it was just the opposite. When I told my moms about falling off that bike and seeing the world from outside my body, they told me I must've hit my head. When I repeated the feat by jumping off a roof and told them of another out-of-body excursion, they got me my first therapist. That therapist eventually ended up referring me to my current shrink—who's the only person I've spoken to about this since then. Well, until I met Eugene, that is.

Eugene gives me a dubious look in response. "Really? Neither your mother nor your father ever mentioned it?"

"Well, I didn't know my father, so he's the more likely candidate, given that my mom never said anything," I say, thinking out loud. Based on the confusion on his face, Eugene isn't getting it. Why would he, though? My history isn't exactly common for your typical American family. "I was conceived through artificial insemination," I explain to him. "My father was a guy who contributed to a sperm bank in Israel. Could he have been one of us—a Reader?"

My genius father. What a joke. I rarely tell people this story. Having two moms can be awkward enough. The fact that Sara went shopping for good sperm to have a smart kid—that's just icing on the cake. But that's exactly what she did. She and Lucy went to Israel, found a high-IQ donor bank, and got one of them knocked up. I think they went overseas to make sure I would never, ever meet the father. Now you can see why I consider my shrink's job too easy. Whatever happens, blame the mother.

"What? No, that can't be," Eugene says, interrupting my ruminations. "It has to be your mother. Giving sperm like that is not something our people would do. It's forbidden."

"What do you mean?"

"We have rules," he says, and it's clear something about this upsets him again. "In the old days, all Readers were subject to arranged marriages—hence the whole selective breeding theory, you see. Today things are more liberal, but there are still a number of restrictions. For example, a Reader's choice of spouse, regardless of how powerful he or she is, is considered personal business now, but the expectation is that he or she be a Reader."

I file away the mention of 'powerful.' I'm curious how one can be more or less powerful when it comes to Reading, but I have other questions first. "Because of the selective breeding thing?" I ask, and Eugene nods.

"Right. It's about the blood. Having children with non-Readers gets you banned from the Reader community." He pauses before saying quietly, "That's what happened to my father."

Now I understand why this is a sensitive topic. "I see. So your mother wasn't a Reader? And that's forbidden?"

"Well, technically, marrying non-Readers and having children like me and Mira is no longer forbidden. You don't get executed for it, like in the old days. It *is* highly frowned upon, though, and the punishment for it is banishment. But that's not an issue in your case. What you're talking about—a Reader giving sperm—is forbidden to this day, as it can lead to mixing of the blood and is untraceable."

"Mixing? Untraceable?" I'm completely confused now.

"A Pusher mother might somehow get impregnated by Reader sperm," Eugene explains. "Readers consider that an abomination, and, according to what my dad told me, so do Pushers. They wouldn't give sperm either. The risk is admittedly infinitesimally small, since Pushers themselves wouldn't dare risk getting pregnant that way. Also, mixing aside, Readers like to keep tabs on everyone, even half-bloods like me, and sperm bank pregnancy would prevent them from keeping an account of the whole Reader family tree. Or at least it would require oversight of the whole process, which would be complicated."

That makes sense. But this leads to only one logical conclusion. Sara, my biological mother, must be a Reader. How could she keep this from me—her son? How could she pretend I was crazy?

"I'm sorry, Darren," Eugene says when I remain silent. "You must have even more questions than before."

"Yes. Your gift for understatement doesn't fail you," I tell him. “I have hundreds of questions. But you know what? You know what I really want to do?”

“You want to Read again?” he surmises.

He’s spot on. “Can we?”

“Sure.” He smiles. “Let’s ring some doorbells.”

9

I HAVE TO ADMIT, I LIKE EUGENE. I'M GLAD I MET HIM. IT'S refreshing to have another smart person to talk to, besides Bert.

It takes us a few minutes to choose our next 'volunteer,' a tall guy in his mid-twenties who lives a few doors down from Eugene and Mira.

"Hi Brad," Eugene says. "I ran out of salt as I was cooking. Mind if I borrow some?"

The guy looks confused. "Salt? Um, okay, sure. Let me see if I can get some." As he turns away, Eugene winks at me. As we agreed, I phase in and touch Eugene's forehead to bring him into the Quiet.

It works, as expected. We are in the Quiet, which I guess, given Eugene's favorite theory, might be another universe of some kind. I don't dwell on the many questions about this alternate reality, if that's what it is. I have something much more interesting to do. I walk up to Brad, touch his temple with my index finger, and close my eyes.

Then I do the breathing meditation.

WHAT THE FUCK? WHO RUNS OUT OF SALT? THE THOUGHTS running through our mind are less than flattering toward Eugene. And who's this other guy? His boyfriend? Wouldn't surprise us. We always suspected that Mira's geeky brother was gay.

I, Darren, realize that Brad knows both Eugene and Mira. And I know I only have seconds before I play his memory to the current moment, which Eugene told me would force me out of the guy's head. So I try to do something different. As Eugene instructed me earlier, I try to 'fall' deeper into Brad's mind.

I picture myself lighter than air. I visualize myself as a feather, slowly floating down into a calm lake on a windless day. I become a sense of lightness.

And then it happens.

We are in a movie theater. We are on a date. We look at the girl sitting next to us, and I, Darren, can't believe my eyes. We're sitting next to Mira. When we start making out with her, I, Darren, think that maybe I really have gone crazy. But no, there is a simpler explanation. I get it when I try falling deeper again.

We're standing in front of Mira's apartment door holding flowers. "These are for you," we say when she opens the door.

We feel pretty slick. The flowers are a means to an end. We want to get our hot neighbor into bed.

"Oh, how sweet," she says drily when she sees us. "Am I supposed to swoon now?" She then proceeds to tell us exactly what she thinks we're planning. I, Darren, realize that she must've done what I'm doing. She must've Read Brad's mind—or maybe she just used common sense. Why else does a guy give a girl flowers?

We're surprised at our neighbor's bluntness. Impressed, even. We admit that, yes, we want to sleep with her, but that she should still take the flowers. She does. Then she sets the ground rules. Nothing serious. She has no time for relationships, she says. A movie, dinner, and, if she thinks we're worth it afterwards, maybe she'll go to our place. That's it. Just a one-time thing, unless the whole thing goes exceptionally well. In that unexpected eventuality, she might, maybe, initiate another encounter.

We agree. What sane guy wouldn't?

I, Darren, experience the dinner and the movie. It's awesome. All of it.

We get back to our—Brad's—apartment.

We're in the bedroom. We're kissing Mira. I, Darren, am jealous that an asshole like Brad gets to do this with Mira. That feeling doesn't last, though. We're immersed in the experience. Mira's perfect naked body. Her lips on ours. It's everything we ever hoped it would be.

Unfortunately, it's too much of everything we ever hoped it would be. I, Darren, can feel us—Brad—losing control. No amount of baseball stats will pull this guy back from the edge. Just like that, we have a problem. Apparently Mira is a little too good-looking, because before I, Darren, even realize what's going on, things happen somewhat . . . prematurely.

Mira's reaction to the situation is admirable. She's not mad, she insists. She says not to worry about it. Says she had a good time. She isn't fooling us, though. She leaves quickly and never speaks to us about this night, or anything else for that matter, again.

I'm back in my body in the Quiet, and the first thing I do is punch Brad in the face.

"What are you doing?" Eugene exclaims, looking at me like I'm crazy.

"Trust me," I say, resisting the urge to also kick the guy. What a loser. Not only did he sleep with Mira, he didn't even have the decency to be good at it. "He doesn't feel it. Right?"

"Well, yeah," Eugene admits. "At least I highly doubt he feels it. But it looks disrespectful."

It's almost too bad that Brad can't feel the punch. I debate punching him once we phase out, but decide against it. I mean, what possessed me? Mira isn't my girlfriend to be overprotective about. She might not even like me when we meet. One thing is clear, though. Without having said a word to her in real life, I like her.

It's shallow, I know. I'd like to say it's based on the fact that I liked talking to her as Brad at that dinner—which I did. But truthfully, I just want to see her body again. I have to kiss her again. It's weird. I wish I had been in someone else's mind for this, my second Reading. I wish it hadn't been Brad. I really need to find a boring person whose mind I can do this Reading thing with.

"Let's phase out," I tell Eugene, and without waiting for his answer, I touch my forehead.

The world comes back to life, and Brad brings us the stupid

salt. Eugene thanks him, and we walk back toward Eugene's apartment.

"How was that?" Eugene asks on the way.

He has no idea this thing happened between his sister and his neighbor. I decide to respect whatever shred of privacy these two have, and at least not mention anything to Eugene.

"That was a good start," I say. "I think we should go outside and do some more."

"Eugene," a pleasant female voice says. A voice I just heard in Brad's memory. "Who the fuck is this?"

I look up and find myself staring down the barrel of a gun. Again.

10

OKAY, I AM OFFICIALLY SICK OF GUNS BEING POINTED AT ME. Even guns pointed by a beautiful girl I just saw naked in someone's mind.

"Mira, put the gun down," Eugene says. "This is Darren. I just texted you his picture. You didn't get it?"

She frowns, still holding the gun trained on me. "No, I haven't checked my phone. Does your text explain how this creep stalked me all the way here from Atlantic City?"

"No, not exactly," Eugene admits. "But you have to cut the guy some slack. He tracked you down, but he has a good reason to be persistent. You're the first other Reader he's ever met."

I can tell that this knowledge surprises her. "How can I be the first Reader he's met?" she asks skeptically. "What about his parents? What about the other Readers from wherever his home is?"

"Manhattan," I supply helpfully. "And in regards to parents, I'll be having a very serious conversation with my mom about this very subject. For some reason, she didn't tell me anything about this. And I've never met my father, but Eugene convinced me that he couldn't have been a Reader because my mother got his sperm from a bank."

As I'm talking, Mira looks at me with more and more curiosity. "A sperm bank?" she repeats.

"Yes. My mom, she wanted a child, but couldn't bring herself to be with a guy, I guess." Thinking of my mom in this context is weird, at best.

"Why? Does she hate men?"

Did Mira just say that approvingly?

"She likes women," I say. "I have two mothers." I'm not sure why I added this last part. Usually you have to ask probing questions for a lot longer before I reveal such personal information.

To her credit, Mira hardly blinks at that. Instead she says with a frown, "If she got sperm from a bank, that would mean she voluntarily mated with a non-Reader. Why would she have done that? Surely she knew she'd get exiled, like our dad."

"That's a good point," Eugene says. "I can't believe I didn't see that when Darren first mentioned it to me."

"You say that like you're surprised I could make a good point," Mira says to her brother, but her tone is more teasing than sharp. "Don't forget, you wouldn't survive a day without me—the dumb, uneducated one."

Eugene ignores her statement. "Can we get out of this hallway?" he says. "I want to get something to eat."

Mira finally lowers the gun and puts it back in her purse. "Fine, I'll be right back." She goes into the apartment. I look at Eugene questioningly, but he just shrugs.

She's back momentarily. She changed from her heels and

dress into jeans and sneakers. I wonder where she's been, so dressed up. She looks great in the simpler outfit, though, and I can't help thinking back to my experience in Brad's head.

As I'm sifting through the hot pictures in my mind, she tells Eugene, "Are you seriously going out like that?" She gestures toward his stained lab coat.

He mumbles something and disappears into the apartment as well. When he comes out, the lab coat is gone, and he's wearing a long-sleeved T-shirt that looks two sizes too big. Mira shoots him an exasperated look, but doesn't say anything else. Instead she walks over to the elevator and presses the button.

"I don't think that works," I say, remembering having to go up all those stairs.

"Trust me," she says. "It's just the first floor that doesn't work."

And she's right. The elevator comes, and we're able to exit on the second floor. From there, it's only a single flight of stairs to get out of the building.

"What exactly does it mean to be exiled?" I ask as we walk in the direction of the bigger street, Kings Highway, in search of a place to eat.

"It's complicated," Eugene says, looking at me. "Our dad was exiled from the community of Readers in St. Petersburg, Russia, and that was pretty bad. He couldn't visit his childhood friends and family. Readers in Russia, in general, are much more traditional, but it was especially bad almost thirty years ago, when I was born. It was terrible for him, he told us."

"But he did it for Mom," Mira adds.

"And for us. He left it all so he could have children with her." Eugene sounds proud of his father. "Thankfully, it's different here. In present-day America, especially the New York City area, the Readers' community is more open-minded. They recognize us as Readers—unofficially, at least."

"Yeah, just so they can make sure we don't openly use our skills," Mira says with a touch of bitterness.

"I think they have other ways to enforce that," Eugene says, glancing at his sister. "Besides, we all know how stupid it would be to reveal our existence to the rest of the world, half-bloods or not. No, they're genuinely less traditional here. At least now they are. But when you were born, Darren, things could've been worse." He gives me a sympathetic look.

"None of this explains why my mom didn't tell me about Readers, though," I say, still bothered by the thought of Sara hiding such important information from me.

"Maybe she was ashamed of being shunned," Mira suggests, shooting me a look that suggests she's not entirely over my stalking her. "Or she didn't want you to learn how to Split and Read. Maybe as you were growing up, she decided you wouldn't be able to keep the Readers' secret. No offense, but you don't look like the kind of guy who can keep your mouth shut."

"But she must've realized I'd discovered it. I as much as told her that as a kid," I say, refusing to rise to the bait. I have more important things to worry about than Mira's sharp tongue. I'm tempted to go to Staten Island right now, but I know it makes more sense to learn more from these two first, so I can ask my mom the right questions. Maybe then I'll be able to get answers and understand what happened.

"I'm sorry," Eugene says with a hint of pity.

"Oh, poor Darren, Mommy didn't tell him," Mira counters, her voice dripping with venom. "At least she's alive. Maybe that's why she is alive—because she knows how to keep a secret. She doesn't run around asking troublesome questions like our idiot father." As she says this, her hands ball into fists, and I see her blinking rapidly, as though to hide tears. She doesn't cry, though. Instead, she glares at her brother and says caustically, "The father whose steps you seem determined to follow, I might add."

"I thought you supported my research," Eugene says, clearly hurt.

She sighs and falls silent as we pass through a small crowd gathered in front of some yogurt place. "I'm sorry," she says in a more conciliatory tone when we're through. "I do support what you're doing. I support it to spite the fuckers who killed Dad—and because it could give us a way to make them pay for what they did. I just can't help thinking that all of this could've been avoided if he'd just researched something else. Alzheimer's, for example."

"I understand," Eugene says.

We walk in an uncomfortable silence for a few minutes. I feel like an intruder.

"No offense, Darren," Mira says as we stop at a traffic light. "It's a difficult subject."

"No problem," I say. "I can't even imagine how you feel."

We walk in a more companionable silence for another block or so.

"Are you leading us to that diner again?" Mira eventually asks, wrinkling her nose.

"Yes," Eugene says, a faint smile appearing on his lips.

Mira rolls her eyes. "That place is a real dump. How many cases of food poisoning does it take for you to realize it? Let's go to the sushi place on Coney Island. It's closer."

"Right, raw fish is the solution to health concerns," Eugene says, unsuccessfully trying to mimic Mira's very distinctive brand of sarcasm.

They fight about the place for the rest of the way. I'm not surprised at all when Mira gets her way. She seems like the kind of person who always does. I don't mind in this case, though. If choosing the place had been up for a vote, Mira would've had mine as soon as she mentioned food poisoning.

Listening to their bickering, I wonder how interesting it must be to have a sibling. Or frustrating. I mean, what would it be like to have a younger sister? Especially one who's as reckless as Mira? I shudder at the thought.

"Table for three," Eugene tells the waiter when we enter the place.

"Ilona?" A deep voice says, and Mira winces. "Ya tebya ne uznal." Or at least that's what it sounds like. It's coming from a tall, well-built guy with a tattoo in the shape of an anchor on his muscular forearm.

Mira walks over to him, hugs him, and kisses him on the cheek. They start talking out of earshot from us. Eugene crosses his arms and eyes the guy suspiciously.

"Can we get a table as far away as possible from that man?" he asks the waiter.

"I can put you in the privacy of one of our tatami rooms," the waiter offers.

"Thank you," I say, and slip a twenty into his hand. "Please make it the furthest one."

Mira heads back to us. She puts a finger to her lips when her back is to the guy.

We are quiet until we get to the tatami room.

"I will not discuss it," Mira says when we sit down.

Eugene glares at her. She doesn't even blink, opening her menu and pointedly ignoring her brother.

"I thought I told you not to do that anymore," Eugene says in a hushed tone. "I thought I told you not to deal with thugs. You won't find him—but you will get yourself killed. Or worse."

"Ot-yebis' Eugene," Mira says, her face getting flushed. Whatever she just said, Eugene takes a breath and stops talking.

The waiter comes, asking what we want to drink. Mira orders hot sake, showing the waiter what must be a fake ID. I stick with green tea, as does Eugene.

I'm dying of curiosity. Did I mention it's one of my few weaknesses?

It feels risky, but I can't help myself. I phase into the Quiet and watch the frozen faces of Mira and Eugene carefully.

They don't seem to be in the Quiet with me. If what Eugene said is true, pulling them in requires explicitly touching them. That's good. I don't plan to do that.

I walk out of the little alcove room the waiter gave us and go through the restaurant, searching for the guy Mira spoke to when we first arrived. His table is empty, with only dirty plates and a check lying there. Apparently he was on his way out when we entered.

I walk through the frozen patrons to the door. Outside, I spot my target. He hasn't gone far.

First, I look in his pockets. Anton Gorshkov, his New York driver's license tells me. Along with his age, height, and address on Brighton Beach. That doesn't tell me much. But I now have a new trick I've been itching to try again—the whole Reading thing.

I touch his forehead. I do the meditation. I realize as it starts that the process is a little quicker now.

We watch Ilona—whom I, Darren, know as Mira—walking toward us. We don't know the men she's with. We barely recognize her without the tight dress and heels she's usually wearing.

"Anton, kakimi sud'bami?" she says to us. It should've sounded like gibberish to me, Darren, but I gleefully realize that I understand exactly what she said. The approximate meaning is: "I'm surprised to see you here, Anton." And I'm aware of the full, subtle meaning of her words, which doesn't translate to English. In general, I understand every thought that goes through Anton's head. Apparently language doesn't seem to matter when it comes to Reading, which makes a weird kind of sense.

We shrug and say, "What are you doing here?"

"Decided to grab a bite to eat," Ilona/Mira responds in Russian.

"Who are the wimps with you?" we say. Again, the translation is approximate. The word for 'wimps' has a more insulting connotation in the original Russian.

"Math geeks," she answers. "I consult with them on how to improve my game."

We have a flashback to playing cards with Ilona. She's good. One of the best. We try to look at her companions, but she blocks our way.

"They work exclusively with me," she says. Then, seeing our stubborn look, she adds, "Viktor introduced us."

We now lose any inclination to look at the math geeks. Not when Viktor is involved. People who cross that guy lose their heads. Literally. There was a rumor that Viktor tapped Ilona, and perhaps it's true. We really don't want anything to do with him.

"It was good seeing you. Maybe I'll see you at this weekend's big game?" she says.

"I doubt it," we say. "I first need to collect some money."

I, Darren, try to go deeper.

Suddenly, it's late evening, and we're beating a guy in an alley. He's refused to get protection. Who does he think he is? Every Russian-owned business in this neighborhood pays protection money to Anton. Our fist aches, but we keep on pounding. No pain, no gain, we joke to ourselves. I, Darren, am horrified, but go deeper still.

Now we're sitting at a card game. We have a gambling 'hard on,' as we call it. I, Darren, can't believe my eyes.

In this dark room, filled with cigarette smoke and sketchy-looking characters whom we—Anton and me—find scary, there is Ilona. Or Mira, as I, Darren, remind myself.

She's wearing a tight dress, showing off her impressive cleavage.

We look at our cards. We have two pairs. We are golden. We bet to the limit.

She drops out. *Can she read our 'tells'?* we wonder, impressed.

The game moves forward.

Ilona wins the next round, calling one guy's bluff. We had no clue the fucker was bluffing. She deserves her reputation as a card prodigy.

As far as we know, she's never been accused of cheating. But we wonder how such a young, pretty thing can be this good without something up her sleeve. Then we chuckle at the realization that, in fact, she has no sleeves. With that strappy little dress, there's no fucking way she can be hiding cards.

Maybe someone at the table is cheating, and she's the partner? If that's the case, we'll keep our mouth shut. These men are not the kind of people you can accuse of cheating and live.

After seeing the game through, I, Darren, have had enough.

I AM OUT OF ANTON'S HEAD. THE EXPERIENCE OF BEING SOMEONE else, even a lowlife like him, is beyond words. I'm going to do this over and over, until I get sick of it—which is probably never going to happen. It's so cool.

Right now, though, instead of enjoying the novelty of this experience, I'm wondering about Mira's sanity. I recall reading something about underground gambling and links to organized crime in her file in Atlantic City, but seeing it through this degenerate's eyes really put things in perspective for me.

Mira is nuts to be doing this. Why is she doing it? A Reader like her has to have a safer way to make money. Does she need something else in the criminal society? Eugene dropped a few hints about her looking for something or someone, but I still don't get it. A green monster in me wonders if she finds these men appealing. Anton did think of some scary guy who maybe had her protected or something like that.

Whatever the answers, I will not find them anytime soon. I have no intention of letting Mira know I learned any of this.

If she knew I snooped like this, it would kill whatever little trust she has in me—if she has any, that is.

11

I RE-ENTER THE RESTAURANT AND FIND MY WAY BACK TO OUR little room. Then I touch myself on the forehead.

I'm back in my body. The sounds return.

"I must admit I love these places," I say, making small talk to cover any weirdness in my demeanor. "It's like a little piece of Japan in the middle of Brooklyn. This one isn't as hardcore as some I've seen. At least we're allowed to keep our shoes on."

Mira and Eugene comment on how some places in Brooklyn are more like that. Some do make you take your shoes off, and their servers wear kimonos.

I breathe easier. I officially got away with the little bit of snooping.

We all examine the menus.

"So, Darren, how long can you stay in the Mind Dimension?" Mira says nonchalantly, resuming the conversation.

"Mira," Eugene says, reddening as he looks up at his sister. "That's not very polite."

"Why is that not polite?" I ask, surprised. "Isn't Mind Dimension what she calls the place you guys 'Split' into? The place I call the Quiet?"

"The Quiet? How cute," Mira says, making me wonder if sarcasm is just the way she normally talks.

"Yes, Darren, that's what she's talking about," Eugene says, still looking embarrassed. "But what you don't know—and what Mira wants to take advantage of—is that this question is very personal in Reader society."

"Well, we're not in Reader society," Mira counters. "We're outcasts, so anything goes."

"Why is it such a big deal?" I ask, looking from brother to sister.

"In the Reader society proper, it's like asking someone how much money he's worth, or the size of his penis," Eugene explains as Mira chuckles derisively. "The time she asked you about is the measure of our power. It determines Reading Depth, for example, which is how far you can see into your target's memories. It also determines how long you can keep someone else in there. I'm surprised you even ask this, Darren. It seems self-evident how important this time is, since even without knowing about Reading Depth, there's the simple matter of longer subjective life experience."

"Of what?" I almost choke on my green tea. "What do you mean 'longer subjective life experience'?"

"You have got to be kidding me," Mira says, downing a shot of her hot sake. "Don't you know anything? I feel educated all of a sudden, and this is coming from a high school dropout."

I don't even question the dropout comment. I'm still on the life experience thing.

"You don't age while in the Mind Dimension," Eugene says. "So the longer you can stay there, the more you can experience."

"You don't age?" I can't believe I didn't think of it myself. If you don't eat or sleep, why am I surprised that you don't age?

"No, there's no aging that anyone's ever noticed," Eugene says. "And some of the Enlightened, the most powerful among us, can and do spend a long time in there."

I just sit there trying to readjust my whole world, which is becoming a common occurrence today.

When the waiter comes back, I order my usual Japanese favorite on autopilot. Eugene and Mira order as well.

"It's not that strange, if you think about it," Mira says when the waiter is out of earshot. "Time stands still there, or seems to."

"We don't know that," Eugene says. "It could also be that we're not there in a real, physical sense. Only our minds, or more specifically, our consciousness."

Mira rolls her eyes at him, but my mind is blown. "I was always bored when I spent too much time in there. I only used it when I was under some time crunch," I tell them, realizing all the opportunities I missed so far. "If I had only known . . . Are you saying that with every book I read in the physical world, I was literally wasting my life away—since I could've done it in the Quiet and not aged by those hours?"

"Yes," Mira says unkindly. "You were wasting your life away, as you are wasting ours right now."

She uses sarcasm so much that I've already become accustomed to it. It barely registers now. I'm more caught up in thinking about all the times I wasted hours of my life and the many millions of things I could've done in the Quiet. If only I had known that it would add more time to my life—or rather, not take time away from it. All this time, I thought I was just taking shortcuts.

"Well, I'm so glad I met you guys," I say finally. "Just knowing this one thing alone will literally change my life."

"Oh, and Reading wouldn't have?" Eugene winks.

I grin at him. "For that too, I'm forever in your debt and all that."

"Why don't you repay that debt a little by answering my question," Mira says, looking at me.

"Will you tell me yours if I tell you mine?" I joke.

"See how quickly his gratitude dissipates and turns into the usual tit for tat?" Mira says snarkily to Eugene.

I'm so flabbergasted by all the revelations that it barely registers that Mira just made a joke about tits.

"It's a deal," Eugene says, answering for his sister.

We pause our conversation when our food arrives. Eugene is served a three-roll special, Mira has a sushi bento box, and I have my sashimi deluxe. I'm a big fan of sushi—to me, it's like an edible work of art.

Returning to our discussion of how long I can stay in the Quiet, I say, "I can't give you an exact amount of time." Grabbing a piece of fatty salmon with my chopsticks, I explain, "As I said, I eventually get bored and phase out."

"But what's the longest you've ever been inside?" Eugene asks, adding a huge wad of wasabi into his tiny soy sauce bowl.

"A couple of days," I say. "I never really kept track of time."

Mira and Eugene exchange strange looks.

"You don't fall out of the Mind Dimension for a couple of days?" Mira says.

"What do you mean 'fall out'? I get bored and touch my skin to phase out. Is that what you mean?"

They exchange those looks again.

"No, Darren, she means fall out," Eugene says, looking at me like I'm some exotic animal. "When we reach our limit to being in that mode, what you call the Quiet, we involuntarily re-enter our bodies. For me, that happens after about fifteen minutes, which is considered pretty standard."

"I'm slightly above average for Readers, and practically a prodigy for a half-blood," Mira says, echoing his stare. "And my max time is a half hour. So you must see how this sounds to us. You're saying you can stay there for two entire days—or even longer, since you've never been pushed out."

"Right," I say, looking at them. "I never realized that was anything abnormal—well, more abnormal than going into the Quiet in the first place."

Eugene looks fascinated. "That would mean your mother had to have been extremely powerful. Almost at the Enlightened level, if you've never been forced out thus far."

"But if you get forced out, can't you just go right back in?" I say, confused.

"Are you messing with us?" Mira's eyes narrow.

"I think he really doesn't know," Eugene says. "Darren, once we get pushed out, we can't go right back in. The recuperation time is proportional to how long we can stay there, though it's not directly related. There's a strong inverse correlation between short recovery times and longer times in the Mind Dimension. So the elites get the best of both worlds: a short recovery time and a long time inside. How it all works in the brain is actually my area of research."

"Eugene, please, not the neuroscience again," Mira says with exasperation before turning her attention to me. "Darren, if you truly don't know about recuperation time, then your power must be off the charts. Only I didn't think a half-blood could have that much power." The look she gives me now is unsettling. I think I prefer disdain. This look is calculating, as though she's sizing me up.

"You have to let me study you," Eugene tells me. "So we can figure out some answers."

"Sure, I guess. It's the least I can do," I say uncertainly.

"Great. How about tomorrow?" Eugene looks excited.

"Hmm. Maybe the day after?"

He smiles. "Let me guess, you're going to spend a whole day going around Reading people's minds, aren't you?"

"Good guess," I say, smiling back.

"Okay. Thursday then," he says. He looks ecstatic at the prospect of putting more electrodes to my head.

"So, I can't Read another Reader's mind?" I ask as I eat a piece of pickled ginger. This is a question that's been bothering me for a bit.

"No. But I bet you wish you could," Mira answers, downing the last of her sushi.

"It's only possible to do that to someone before they learn to Split for the first time, when they're children," Eugene explains. "Once people have experienced the Split, they simply get pulled into your Mind Dimension with you if you try to Read them."

"And if you and I manage to Split at the same time?" I ask. "Would we see each other in there?"

"Now you're getting into very specific and rare stuff," Eugene says. "It's almost impossible to time it that perfectly. Dad and I managed it only once. Even if you did, you'll find that, no, you see the world still, as usual, but you don't encounter each other. The only way to have a joint experience is to pull someone in. If either of you touches the other, the other will get pulled in. Once that happens, you'll be using up the time of the person whose Mind Dimension you're in."

"Using up the time?" I ask, finishing the last bit of my sashimi. This was amazing fish, I realize belatedly.

"As you bring people with you, your time is shared with them. If I pull you in, together we would stay in my Mind Dimension for about seven or eight minutes—about half of my fifteen-minute total. Similarly, how deep you go into someone's memories is half your total time."

The Reading Depth thing gives me an idea. If what Eugene says is right, then I think I have a better gauge of my 'power' based on my Reading of Eugene and Mira's neighbor, Brad. That sci-fi flick that he and Mira watched at the theater left the big screen at least six months ago—which means that I can spend at least a year in the Quiet.

As blown away as I am by this realization, something prevents me from sharing this information with my new friends. They looked awestruck at the mention of two days. What would they say to a year? And how do I reconcile this and being a half-blood? How powerful is Sara, to give birth to someone like me?

"What's the maximum power a Reader can have?" I ask instead.

"That's something even people who are part of the regular Reader society probably don't know," Mira says. "And even if they did, they wouldn't share that information with us."

"There are legends, though," Eugene says. "Legends of the Enlightened, who were wise well beyond their years. It was as though they'd led whole extra lifetimes. Of course, some of these stories seem more like mythology than history."

Myth or not, the stories sound fascinating. Before I get a chance to think about them, however, I'm interrupted by the waiter who brings our check. I insist on paying despite a few feeble complaints from Eugene. It's part of my thank you to them, I say.

When we exit the restaurant, I tell them, "I wish we could talk for hours on end, but there's something I have to do now."

"You could pull us into the Mind Dimension and chat away; this way you wouldn't be late for your appointment," Mira says, giving me a sly look.

"Mira." Eugene sounds chiding again.

She must be breaking another Reader social rule I'm not aware of. Using someone for time, perhaps? It doesn't matter. I wouldn't mind doing what she's asking if I wasn't dying of curiosity. "It's not about being late," I explain apologetically. "It's about asking my mom some serious questions."

"Oh, in that case, good luck," Mira says, her voice sympathetic for the first time.

"Thanks. Do you guys know where I can rent a car around here?"

Going to Staten Island from Brooklyn, or from anywhere for that matter, is best to do by car. There's a ferry from downtown, but no thanks. That requires taking a bus afterwards. And the ferry is unpleasant enough by itself.

Though Eugene and Mira don't know about rentals, my trusty phone does. According to it, there's a rental place a couple of blocks away. Since it's on the way to their apartment, I get an armed escort to the place—Mira with her gun. I'm grateful for that, as I'm still not a fan of their neighborhood. On our short walk, we talk some more about Readers. Despite Mira's complaints, Eugene starts telling me about his research.

It sounds like he's trying to find neural correlates that accompany what Readers do. That discovery might lead to knowing how the process works. He thinks he knows approximately what goes on, all the way up to the Split. After that moment, things get complicated because technology is finicky in the Quiet, and the instruments remaining in the real world don't register anything—proving that no time passes in the real world after we phase in.

I only half-listen. It all sounds fascinating, but in my mind, I'm already having a conversation with Sara.

When we reach the rental place, I enter both Eugene's and Mira's phone numbers into my phone, and they get mine. We say our goodbyes. Eugene shakes my hand enthusiastically. "It was great to meet you, Darren."

"Likewise," I say. "It was great meeting you both."

Mira walks up to me, and gives me a hug and a kiss on the cheek. I stand there wondering if that means she likes me, or if it's just a Russian thing. Whatever the reason for her actions, it was nice. I can still smell a hint of her perfume.

When they begin to head back, I turn to enter the car rental place. Before I do, I'm pulled into the Quiet again.

It's Mira.

"Darren," she says, "I want to thank you. I haven't seen Eugene this happy, this animated, for a long time."

"Don't mention it. I like your brother," I say, smiling. "I'm glad I had that effect on him."

"I also wanted to say that, as he *is* my brother, I, above all, don't want to see him hurt."

"That makes sense." I nod agreeably.

"Then we have an understanding," she says evenly. "If this whole thing is a lie, I'll be extremely upset." Her eyes gleam darkly. "To put it in other words, if you hurt my brother in any way, I will kill you."

She turns around and walks to her frozen body, which is standing a few feet away.

I don't get a hug this time around.

12

I'M DRIVING THE PIECE-OF-SHIT CAR I PICKED UP AT THE RENTAL place. They didn't have anything nice, but at least this thing has Bluetooth, so I'm listening to Enigma's "T.N.T. for the Brain" from my phone on the car speakers. I raise the volume to the max.

In a confused stupor, trying to digest everything I've learned today, I follow my phone's GPS directions. I know I need the Belt Parkway and the Verrazano Bridge after that, but once I get on Staten Island, I typically get lost—usually only a few blocks from where my moms live.

I called ahead to make sure they were home, but mentioned nothing of what I want to discuss. I plan to ambush them with my questions. They deserve it. I love them dearly, but I've never been angrier with them than I am now—not even during my rebellious mid-teen years. I'm especially mad at Sara.

Alternative lifestyle aside, Sara and Lucy are living,

breathing stereotypes of two similar, yet different, kinds of moms.

Take Sara, for instance. She's a Jewish mom to the core. Never mind that she's the most secular person you'll ever meet. Never mind that she married a non-Jew, which isn't kosher. She still regularly hints—and sometimes outright says—that since I've finished my degree from a good school (of course), I should meet a nice girl (meaning a Jewish girl) and settle down. At twenty-one. Right. And she has all the usual guilt-trip skills down to a T. For example, if I don't call for a couple of days, I get the whole 'you don't need to trouble yourself to call your own mother; it's not like I'm in any way important,' et cetera, et cetera. And then there's the weird stuff, like if I'm out late and make the mistake of mentioning it to her, she'll want me to text her when I get home. *Yeah.* Never mind that on other nights—when I don't talk to her—I might not come home at all, and she's fine with my lack of texting.

Lucy is no better. Well, in truth, Lucy is better now. She only expects a call from me once a week, not daily. But when I was growing up, she was worse than Sara. She must've read that book about being a Tiger Mom and tried to apply it literally, with probably the worst possible subject—me. In hindsight, I think I had ADHD when I was a kid. When it came to the violin lessons she tried to force me to take, I 'accidentally' broke a dozen of the stupid instruments to test her resolve. When I broke the last one (over another student's head), I was expelled, and that did it for musical initiatives. Then there were the ballet lessons. I was kicked out for beating up a girl, which was not true. I knew from a very early age that you don't hit girls. Another girl pushed the victim, but I, because of my reputation in the class, took the rap. Lucy also wanted me to learn her native Mandarin. I don't care if I mastered a little bit from her when I was a baby, or that I can string together a few sentences even to this day; that was just not going to happen. If I'd studied Mandarin for her, I would've had to take Yiddish lessons for Sara, too. Oy vey.

So, finishing school early and going to Harvard was partially an attempt to make my mothers happy, but even more so a means to get away from their overzealous parenting techniques and experience some freedom in Boston. Not to mention that finishing college allowed me to get a job and my own place as soon as possible. Ever since I gained some distance, my love for my family has deepened greatly.

As I pull into their driveway, I see three cars outside. I recognize the extra car as Uncle Kyle's old Crown Victoria.

Great, he's here. That's the last thing I need.

"Hi Mom," I say when Sara opens the door. I've never really seen much of myself in her, which makes me wonder that much more now about who my father might have been. We both have blue eyes, and I could've inherited her height, I guess. At five foot seven, she's tall for a woman. She seems particularly tall when, like now, she's standing next to my other mom. Lucy is barely above five feet tall, but don't let her size deceive you. She's tough. Plus, she has a gun—and knows how to use it.

"Hi sweetie," Sara says, beaming at me.

"Hi Mom," I say again, this time looking at Lucy.

"Hi Kitten," Lucy says.

Hmm. Are they trying to embarrass me in front of Uncle Kyle?

"Hey Kyle," I say with a lot less enthusiasm as I walk in.

He smiles at me, a rarity from him, and we shake hands.

I have mixed feelings when it comes to Kyle. Even though I

mentally call him uncle, he's not my blood relative. Sara was an only child. He's a detective who works with Lucy. As former partners, I guess he and Lucy are close—a camaraderie I don't pretend to understand, having never put my life in danger the way they have.

I imagine my moms decided to ask Kyle to come around when I was growing up so I'd have a male role model in my life. However, their choice for the task couldn't have been worse. As far back as I can remember, I've butted heads with Kyle. Pick an issue, and we're likely to be on opposite sides of it. Doctor-assisted suicide, the death penalty, cloning humans, you name it, and you can be sure we've had a shouting match over it. I like to think of myself as a free thinker, while Kyle clings to what was digested and fed to him by some form of authority, never stopping to question anything.

The biggest mystery to me is actually why someone so traditional even accepts my moms' relationship. My theory is that he has a mental disconnect. I imagine he tells himself that despite their marriage, they're just best friends who live together.

I also think he has a rather tragic crush on Lucy. He would call it brotherly love, but I've always been skeptical. Especially given his very professional, cold attitude toward Sara, a woman he's known for over twenty years. An attitude that was chilly all along, but grew downright frigid after the huge fight they had when he decided to discipline me with a belt when I was nine. I was clever enough to scream and cry like a banshee, and predictably, Sara had a major fit. She actually threw a vase in his face. I think he had to get stitches. After that, he only used words to discipline me, and his interactions with Sara became even more aloof.

Having said all that, after I stopped needing to deal with Kyle regularly, I began to feel more fondness for the bastard. I know he usually means well. He's the closest thing to a father figure I have, and he did come around a lot, generally with good intentions. He told me cool stories about back in the day when he and Lucy kicked ass and took names—stories Lucy never chose to share, for some reason. And I wouldn't be half as good a debater now if not for all that arguing with him. For better or for worse, he played a role in the person I've become, and that's an honor usually reserved for people you consider close.

"How's work?" Kyle asks. "Are we due for another financial meltdown anytime soon?"

Kyle isn't a fan of anyone in the financial industry. I can forgive that; few people are fans of them. Or should I say of us? Also, only a tiny portion of the population understands the difference between bankers and hedge fund analysts, or can tell any financial professional from another.

"Work is great," I respond. "I'm researching a biotech company that's going to use magnetic waves to manipulate human brains for therapy."

Lucy narrows her eyes at me. She knows I'm trying to start an argument again. But I have to hand it to Kyle: this time, he doesn't take the bait. Usually he would go into some Luddite bullshit about how frightening and unnatural what I just said sounds, how dangerous it is to mess with people's brains like that. But no, he doesn't say anything of the sort.

"I'm glad you're making a name for yourself at that company," he says instead. Is that an olive branch? "I was just on my way out, but I'll see you at Lucy's birthday party in a few weeks."

"Sure, Kyle," I say. "See you then."

He walks out, and Lucy walks out with him. He probably came to get her advice on a case. He does that to this day, despite not having been her partner for decades.

"When will you grow up?" Sara chides, smiling. "Why must you always push people's buttons?"

"Oh, that's rich, you defending Kyle." I roll my eyes.

"He's a good man," she says, shrugging.

"Whatever," I say, dismissing the subject with a single word. The last thing I'm interested in right now is an argument about Kyle. "We need to talk. You should actually sit down for this."

Alarm is written all over Sara's face. I'm not sure what she imagines I'm going to say, but she has a tendency to expect the worst.

"Should we wait for your mother?" she says. They both say that in reference to the other, and it's always funny to me. *Your mother.*

"Probably. It's nothing bad. I just have some important questions," I say. Despite everything, I feel guilty that I've worried her.

I notice that she pales at the mention of important questions.

"Are you hungry?" she asks, looking me up and down with concern. *Please, not the too-thin talk again.* If it weren't for Lucy intervening, my own lack of appetite, and my stubbornness, I would be the chubbiest son Sara could possibly raise. And the fatter I'd get, the happier Sara would be as a mom. She would be able to show me around and say 'see how fat he is, that's how much I love him.' I know she got that 'feeding is caring' attitude from Grandma, who wouldn't rest until you were as big as a house.

The fact that Sara doesn't pursue the food topic now shows

me how concerned she is. Is it some kind of guilt thing? Does she suspect what I'm about to ask?

"No, thanks, Mom. I just had some sushi," I say. "But I would love some coffee."

"Did you go out partying all night?" She appears even more worried now. "You look exhausted."

"I didn't sleep well last night, but I'm okay, Mom."

She shakes her head and goes into the kitchen. I follow. Their house is still unfamiliar. I preferred the cramped Manhattan apartment where I grew up, but my moms decided a few years back that it was time for the suburbs and home ownership. At least they have some of the same familiar furniture I remember from childhood, like the chair I'm now sitting in. And the heavy round kitchen table. And the cup, red with polka dots, that she hands to me. My cup.

"I smell coffee," Lucy says, coming back.

"I made you a cup, too," Sara says.

"You read my mind," Lucy responds, smiling.

I decide I'm not going to get a better segue than that. Is it literally true? Can Sara Read Lucy's mind?

"Mom," I say to Sara. "Is there something important you want to tell me about my heritage?"

I look at them both. They look shell-shocked.

"How did you figure it out?" Lucy asks, staring at me.

"I'm so sorry," Sara says guiltily.

The vehemence of their reaction confuses me, considering my relatively innocuous question. I haven't even gotten to the heavy stuff yet. But it seems like I'm onto something, so I just say nothing and try to look as blank as I can, since I'm not sure what we're talking about. I sense we're not exactly on the same page.

"We always meant to tell you," Sara continues, tears forming in her eyes. "But it never seemed like a good time."

"For the longest time, until you were in your mid-teens, we couldn't discuss it at all. Even among ourselves," Lucy adds. She isn't tearing up, but I can tell she's distraught. "We even tried reading books about it. But the books recommend saying it as early as possible, which we didn't do . . ."

"Saying what?" I ask, my voice rising. I'm reasonably certain I'm about to find out something other than what I came here to verify, since I'm not aware of any books about Reading.

Sara blinks at me through her tears. "I thought you knew . . . Isn't that what you want to talk about? I thought you used some modern DNA test to figure it out."

A wave of panic washes over me. I try not to phase. I want to hear this.

"I want to know what you're talking about," I say. "Right now."

I look at them in turn. Daring them to try to wiggle out of it. They know they have to spill the beans now.

"You were adopted, Darren," Lucy says quietly, looking at me.

"Yes," Sara whispers. "I'm not your biological mother." She starts to cry, something I've hated since I was a little kid. There's something wrong, weirdly scary, about seeing your mom cry. Except—and the full enormity of it dawns on me—she's not my birth mom.

She never has been.

13

HOW WOULD ANYONE REACT IN MY SHOES?

I don't know if it's seeing my moms so upset or the news itself, but I can't take the flood of emotion for long. I phase into the Quiet. Once the world around me is still, I pick up the coffee cup and throw it across the room. It shatters against the TV, coffee spilling everywhere. I get up, grab the empty chair next to the one where my frozen self is sitting, and hurl it across the room after the cup, yelling as loudly as I can. I stop myself from breaking more stuff, though; even though I know it will go back to normal after I phase out, it still feels like vandalism.

Then I take a couple of deep breaths, trying to pull myself together.

This explains things—things that Eugene and Mira told me about. Sara didn't lie to me. She never had my ability. She reacted to my descriptions of the Quiet as a normal person would. I should probably feel relieved. I feel anything but.

Why would they not tell me? After all, it's not like we haven't had conversations about being adopted. We had them all the time. Sort of. We talked about how Lucy didn't give birth to me, but loves me just as much as Sara who, allegedly, did. This would've been just more of the same.

I take more deep breaths. I sit on the floor and perform the meditation I have used four times already today.

I begin to feel better—well enough to continue talking, at least. I look at the shocked expression on my frozen face. I reach out and touch myself on the elbow. The gesture is intended to comfort the frozen me, which, once I do it, seems silly. The touch brings me out of the Quiet.

I take a deep breath more demonstratively in the real world. "If you're not my biological mother," I manage to say, "then who is?"

"Your parents' names were Mark and Margret," Lucy says. To my shock, she's crying too—something I've almost never seen her do. A knot ties itself in the pit of my stomach as she continues, "Your uncle might've told you stories about Mark."

I'm almost ready to phase into the Quiet again. She said 'were.' I know what that means. And I have heard of Mark. He was the daredevil partner who worked with Lucy and Kyle.

"Tell me everything," I say through clenched teeth. I'm trying my best not to say something I'll regret later.

"Before you were born, we really did go to Israel, as we always told you," Sara begins, her voice shaking. "It's just that what happened there was different from what you know. Our friends Mark and Margret approached us with a crazy story, and an even crazier request."

She stops, looking at Lucy pleadingly.

"They said someone was out to kill them," says Lucy in a more even voice. "They said Margret was pregnant, and they wanted us to raise the child. To pretend it was our own." She gets calmer as she tells this, her tears stopping. "We always wanted a child. It seemed like a dream come true. They were the ones who came up with the whole sperm bank story. They said the danger they were in could spill into your life if anyone ever found out about the arrangement. I know it sounds like I'm making excuses for not telling you, but when they got killed, just as they moved back to New York to be near you . . ."

"Lucy and Mark were close," Sara jumps in, wiping away the moisture on her face. "Back then, they worked in the organized crime division together. Lucy and I just assumed the unit where they all worked had something to do with why Mark was killed, which is why I begged your mother to switch to another division." She looks at Lucy again, silently urging her to continue with the story.

"I investigated their deaths," Lucy says. "But I still, to this day, have no idea who killed them and why. The killer left no clues. The crime scene was the most thoroughly investigated one in my career—and nothing. All I know is that Margret was shot in the back in her own kitchen, and it looked like Mark was killed a few seconds later when he tried to attack the person who shot her. There were no signs of a break-in."

My mind's gone numb. How am I supposed to feel about something like this happening to the biological parents I never knew existed? Or about them giving me to their friends to raise, even though they knew they'd be putting Sara and Lucy in danger?

I can't take it anymore, so I phase into the Quiet again.

Once everything is still, I walk up to Sara, whose face is frozen in concern. I still love her, just as much as I did on my way here. This changes nothing. I've always loved Lucy the same as Sara, despite knowing we're not related by blood. As far as I can tell, this is no different.

I put my hand on Sara's forearm and try to get into the state of Coherence, as Eugene called it. I'm so worked up that it's much more difficult this time. I don't know how long it takes before I'm in Sara's memories.

WE'RE EXCITED DARREN IS GOING TO VISIT.

I, Darren, feel ashamed somehow at the intensity of Sara's enthusiasm. If it makes her so happy, I should probably visit more often.

We're devastated at having the dreaded adoption conversation with Darren, after all these years. Our own little family secret. Before I, Darren, am naturally pushed out by getting to the present moment in Sara's memories, I decide to go deeper. Picturing being lighter, trying to focus, I fall further in.

We're watching Darren pack for Harvard. We're beyond anxious. I, Darren, realize that I am not far enough and focus on going deeper.

We're on a date with Lucy. She's the coolest girl we have ever met. I, Darren, realize how creepy this thing I am doing can get, but I also know that I can't stop. I overshot my target memory mark and need to go back out of this depth, or in other words, fast-forward the memories. I, Darren, do what I tried before when I wanted to get deeper into someone's mind, only in reverse: I picture myself heavier. It works.

We've been obsessing about Israel for months. Our heritage must call us, as our mom Rose said. I, Darren, realize that Rose is Grandma and that I am close—and I jump a bit further this time by picturing myself heavier again.

We're in Israel. It's awesome. Even Lucy's initial grumpy 'there are almost no other Asians here' attitude gets turned around after spending a day at the beach.

We look around the beach. The view is breathtaking. I, Darren, make a note to visit this place someday.

"Hi guys," says a familiar male voice.

We're shocked to see the M&Ms, Mark and Margret, approach our chairs. So is Lucy, we bet. What could they possibly be doing here, in Israel? The last thing anyone expects when going overseas is to meet friends from New York.

I, Darren, see them, and Sara's surprise pales next to mine. It's not like they look exactly like me, Darren. But it's almost like some Photoshop genius took their facial features, mixed them up, added a few random ones, and got the familiar face that, I, Darren, see every day in the mirror.

"What are you doing here?" Lucy asks, looking concerned.

"We need to talk," Mark says. "But not here."

I, Darren, picture feeling heavy again, so I can jump forward a little more.

We're listening to the M&Ms' crazy tale.

"Who's after you? If you don't tell me, how am I supposed to help?" Lucy says in frustration after they're done. We feel the same way. We can't believe our friends are springing this on us and telling us next to nothing.

"Don't ask me that, Lucy. If I told you, I'd put you and, by extension, the unborn child in danger," Mark says. I, Darren, realize that his voice is deep, a lot like the voice I hear on my voicemail. My voice.

"But what about you?" we say, looking at Margret. "How will you be able to go through with this?"

Margret, who has been very quiet through this conversation, begins crying, and we feel like a jerk.

"Margie and I are both willing to do whatever it takes to make sure our child lives," Mark says for her. "Regardless of how much it hurts us to distance ourselves this way."

"So you won't come back to New York?" Lucy asks. That's our girl, always the detective, trying to put every piece together.

He shakes his head. "My resignation is already prepared. We'll stay in Israel until the baby is born, then come back to New York for the first year of the baby's life to help you guys, and then we'll move to California. We hope you can come visit us in California once the baby is older. Tell her—or him—that we're old friends." Mark's voice breaks.

"But this makes no sense," Lucy says, echoing our thoughts. "If you're going to quit and move anyway, the child should be safe enough—"

"No," Mark says. "Moving barely mitigates the risk. The people who want us dead can reach us anywhere. Please don't interrogate me, Lucy. Just think how wonderful it would be to have a child. Weren't you guys always planning to adopt?"

"We couldn't think of better people to trust with this," Margret says. "Please, help us."

We think she's trying to convince herself of her decision. We can't even imagine how she must be feeling.

"We'll pay for everything," Mark says, changing the subject.

We're in complete agreement with Lucy's objections to the

money, but in the end, the M&Ms convince us to accept their extremely generous offer—money we didn't even know they had. We know what Mark's approximate salary range is, since he works with Lucy, and he can't be making that much more than she is. To someone with that salary, this kind of money is unheard of. Nor is it likely that Margret makes that much. We wonder if having so much money has something to do with the paranoid story of people coming after them.

I, Darren, however, don't think it's the money. Could it be the Pushers? After all, Pushers killed Mira and Eugene's family. Could they be behind killing mine? Learning more about Pushers becomes much more personal for me all of a sudden.

I, Darren, can't take any more of this unfolding tragedy. I might come back here someday, but I can't handle it right now. Still, like a masochist, I progress into the memories.

We're driving back from Margret and Mark's funeral. We haven't spoken most of the way. We have never seen Lucy this upset.

"Please talk to me, hon," we say, trying to break the heavy silence.

"I was the one who found the bodies," Lucy says, her voice unrecognizable. "And I did the most thorough sweep of the crime scene. And with all that, I have nothing. It's like a perfect, unsolvable crime from one of your detective stories. I can't take it. I owe it to Mark to find the fucker who did this . . ."

"Don't be so hard on yourself," we say. "You'll figure it out. If you can't, no one could."

"We should have moved," Lucy says.

She hits a weak spot—our own guilt. We wish we had told Mark and Margret not to come to New York for that first year, not if they were in that much danger. But we didn't tell them that. We could've offered to come to California for a year. Something. The biggest source of our guilt, though, is that we thought the M&Ms were crazy. We didn't delve deeper into their story because it led to the most miraculous result—Darren. But now that Mark and Margret are dead, they are vindicated. We don't think they were crazy anymore. We just feel horrible for doubting them and not preventing this disaster somehow.

I, Darren, officially can't take any more. I jump out of Sara's head.

I'M BACK IN THE QUIET, LOOKING AT SARA. MUCH OF MY ANGER has dissipated. How can I be angry after I just experienced how this woman feels about me? I feel a pang of guilt for having invaded my mother's privacy to get the truth, but it's over and done with now.

I walk toward myself and touch my elbow.

Though I'm out of the Quiet, Sara is still pretty much motionless, waiting for my reaction.

"I don't know what to say," I say truthfully.

"It's okay. It's a lot to process," Lucy says.

"You think?" I say unkindly, and immediately regret it when she winces.

"I'm sorry it took us so long to tell you," Sara says, looking guilty.

"Even today, you told me under duress," I say, unable to resist. I guess I still feel bitter about that—about being kept in the dark for so long.

"I guess that's true," Sara admits. "Like Lucy said, we had a hard time talking about this for years. Once you don't talk about something, it becomes this strange taboo. But if you didn't already know, what were you asking about before?" She gives me a puzzled look.

"Never mind that now," I say. No way am I ready to spout some crazy talk about being part of a secret group of people who can freeze time and get into the minds of others. I was only going to bring that up when I thought Sara was a Reader herself. "The most important thing is that what you told me doesn't change anything for me."

I know from just Reading her mind that this is what she most wants to hear. I mean it, too. Yes, I'm mad and confused now, but I know with time what I just said will be one hundred percent true. It will be as though this adoption conversation never happened.

For those words, I'm rewarded by the expressions of relief on their faces.

"If you don't mind, I want to go home right now. I need to digest all this," I tell them. This is riskier. I know they would rather I stay and hang out. But I really am beyond exhaustion at this point.

"Sure," Sara says, but I can tell she's disappointed.

"We're here to answer any questions you might have," Lucy says. Her expression is harder to read.

Lucy is right. I might have questions later. But for now, I kiss and hug them before getting out of there as quickly as I can.

The drive to Tribeca happens as if in a dream. I only become cognizant of the actual mechanics of it when I start wondering where to park. Parking in the city is a huge pain, and is the reason I don't own a car. I opt for one of the paid parking lots, despite having to pay something outrageous for it tomorrow. Right now, I don't care. Anything to get home.

Once I get to my apartment, all I have the energy to do is eat and shower. After that, I fall asleep as soon as my head hits the pillow.

14

It's amazing what a good night's sleep can do for the psyche. As I'm eating my morning oatmeal, I see the events and revelations of the prior day in a brand-new light. Even the adoption thing seems like something I can deal with.

I try to put myself in my moms' shoes. Let's say my friend Bert told me a strange secret. Let's further suppose he asked me not to tell it to anyone, and then died. Surely that would count as sort of like someone's dying wish. And as such, it would undoubtedly be hard to reveal the secret in those circumstances. Could that be part of the reason for my moms' lack of communication?

Now that I'm more rested, I also realize another aspect of my new situation: I might have some family I've never met. Grandmothers and grandfathers I didn't know existed. Maybe uncles and cousins. All of these new family members are probably out there in the mysterious Reader community. It's too bad Eugene and Mira are not part of said community. If they were, I would have a way of getting introduced to other Readers. Maybe I'd even meet my extended family and learn more about my heritage.

Also, now that I'm not so stressed, knowledge of my newfound skills begins to excite me. I mean, think of the possibilities. It reminds me of middle school, when I first mastered the Quiet. I'd had a ton of fun sneaking into the girl's locker room unnoticed, reading my first girlfriend's diary, spying on hot older women . . . Now that I think about it, there was definitely a pattern to my early use of the Quiet.

All those things, however, pale in comparison to what Reading will let me do. It's almost best that I only learned about it now, when I'm more mature and better able to use this power responsibly.

The choice for my first destination is easy.

Finishing breakfast, I get dressed. I grab a Blu-ray disk that I should've returned ages ago and go to the third floor of my building.

I only went out with Jenny a few times. She's not in any way special among my ex-girlfriends, except for one thing—proximity. She lives in my building, which naturally makes her my first stop. Now what was I saying about being mature enough to handle this responsibly?

Stopping in front of her apartment door, I ring the doorbell.

Jenny opens the door. "Darren?" she says, looking at me. I'm tempted to deny it, to say that I'm not Darren, but figure she's not in the mood for jokes.

"I found this movie I borrowed from you," I say instead. "I wanted to give it back."

"Oh. Okay, I guess. I'm just surprised to see you." She doesn't look just surprised, though—she looks angry. Or at least a little unnerved. Figuring there's no time like the present, I phase into the Quiet.

There had been a slight buzzing in the hallways of my apartment building, something I only realize now because it's gone. It's interesting how we ignore constant noises like that. I started becoming more cognizant of just how much we don't register about our surroundings when I first began phasing into the Quiet. So much happens around us that our conscious mind misses.

I touch Jenny's forehead. Though I had been conflicted about touching women in the Quiet, I decide that this is different. Or that Reading is worth it. It's easy to convince myself to let go of certain principles when they get in the way of something I really want.

I try to get into Coherence. It's even easier this time. As soon as I'm in, I do the lightness bit in order to jump deeper into her thoughts—otherwise all I'll see is her opening the door for me, which is boring.

WE'RE AT A CLUB, MAKING OUT WITH A GIRLFRIEND IN ORDER TO get attention from the guys. Though this is not where I, Darren, intended to end up, I'm content to stay for a little while. I try to absorb every moment. We dance and grind with Judy, but it's all just for fun, a way to get attention. Eventually I, Darren, lose interest and try to go deeper.

We're getting ready to meet with Darren again. We're a little sad about our relationship with him. He used to be so hot—until he paid attention to us. At that point, his appeal dropped drastically. Why does that always happen to us?

No, we have to stop being our own worst critic. It could be Darren who's the problem, not us. When we saw him at that party in the penthouse, he seemed so confident and cocky, exactly what turns us on. But then he didn't ask us to go to his place that night, coming up with some lame coffee date instead. That's on him. Unless of course we start worrying about being a slut. We wish one day the inner critic would just shut the fuck up.

We pick the outfit for this evening very carefully. The new bra and panties should go a long way. I, Darren, think I recognize what day this is, so I jump further, to the part of her life I actually came here to witness.

Darren is standing without his shirt in our bedroom. He's in great shape. We hope we turn him on. As things progress, we worry a lot less about anything, instead focusing on what we're feeling as we give in to the purely physical part of ourselves.

When the experience is over, I, Darren, jump out.

I'M BACK IN THE QUIET. OKAY, YEAH. I WANTED TO EXPERIENCE what sex is like for a girl. And what better way to do so than to find out what it would be like to have sex with *me*? Not to mention, I'm not entirely sure how I'd feel about experiencing sex as a girl with a guy who's not me. There's no way I'm sharing this with my therapist. She'd have a field day with it.

Both Coherence and moving about in people's memories are getting easier for me already. This reminds me of when I first discovered being able to go into the Quiet.

Skills improve with experience. With the first few trips into the Quiet, it took being near death to activate the strange experience. A fall from a bike was only the first. There was also a fall off a roof into a sandbox, and a bunch of other stunts culminating in the time I fell into that manhole. Crazy, right? Who falls into a manhole? According to my moms, their childhood nickname for me was Taz, after the Tasmanian Devil from the cartoons. That's how much trouble I used to get into. But at least it gave me practice when it came to near-death experiences.

Then it started happening under less dire circumstances, like the time I got into a fight with our school bully, John. I still hate that guy. I momentarily contemplate finding him, Reading his mind, and messing with him. I decide against it for now. I would need to locate the prick, and that's too much of a bother at the moment.

Eventually, getting into the Quiet would happen when I did something as insignificant as watch a good horror movie. Progressively I got to where I am today, where any slight worry or nervousness can be harnessed for phasing in. I wonder what the path was like for Eugene and Mira. I'll have to remember to ask them.

Thinking of those two makes me wonder if I should stop messing around and go see them. No, I decide. Not yet. Not until I have some more Reading fun.

I look at Jenny. She's clutching the door, like she wants to close it as soon as possible. I feel a pang of guilt, and I phase out.

"Sorry if I intruded," I say. "I guess I should've left this by the door. I just figured, since we agreed to stay friends, it would be a good idea to bring this to you."

"Yeah, sure," she says. It doesn't take Reading to know she didn't actually want us to be friends when she said that. "It was nice of you to bring this back, and I'm glad you didn't just leave it by the door like some stranger."

"Okay, thanks. Sorry I bugged you. I'll see you around," I say. It's awkward, but I don't regret this. Jenny looks like she knows she's missing something, but since I'm sure there's no way she'll ever guess what just happened, I don't worry about it.

The door closes, and I'm ready for a drive around the city.

On a whim, I decide to go to the gym. There are plenty of people I can Read there. Plus, it would be nice to get a workout. I exercise mostly out of vanity, but at the same time, I do like to hear how good exercise is for your mind as well as your body. More bang for the buck.

Instead of my usual Tribeca location, I go to the Wall Street branch—I have a car, after all, so I figure I may as well use it. The Wall Street gym is classier.

By the time I get there, which isn't far, I curse the car idea. I would have gotten here much faster on foot, considering the traffic and the time it takes to find a parking spot. That's Manhattan for you. It's got some minuses.

I walk through the big revolving glass doors. This gym in general, and this location specifically, is very high end. Its membership price is ridiculous, but hey, I can afford it. It's nice and clean, which is a huge bonus for me. I might be a little OCD when it comes to cleanliness.

I wonder if it would make sense to exercise in the Quiet anymore. I used to do it on occasion when I was in a rush, but that was before I knew you don't age in there. Now that I know about the aging thing, it seems logical that muscles wouldn't grow bigger from any exercise performed in the Quiet. And growing muscles is really the only reason I do this.

Still, I'm not one hundred percent sure that it would be

useless to exercise in the Quiet in general. Certainly some skills stay with you. Just the other week, when I was convinced to play my first game of golf, I practiced in the Quiet so my game would be more impressive to my coworkers. The practice definitely helped, meaning some kind of muscle memory was retained. Another question for Eugene, I guess.

For now, I opt for a real-world workout.

I'm doing chest presses when I see a familiar face. We have a lot of celebrities at this gym, so I try to recall who this is. Then it hits me. Can that really be who I think it is? It's possible—his bank's headquarters are near here. If he did go to a gym open to the public, this would be the one he'd go to.

To make sure I'm right, I approach him.

"Excuse me, can you please spot me?" I ask, pointing at the bench I'm using.

"Sure," he says. "Do you need a lift?"

"I got it," I say, and I do. That's him. Jason Spades, the CEO. The man is a hero to us at the fund. His is the only bank that weathered the shit storm that befell most others—and he got a lot of the credit for it. From what I heard, his fame is well deserved.

"Thanks," I tell him when I'm done with my set.

He walks away, and on a whim, I phase into the Quiet. It's particularly easy in the gym—the heart is already racing, which to the brain must not be far from being frightened or otherwise excited.

It's very odd to see people holding heavy weights suspended in midair, though. It seems like their hands should fail any second.

I walk up to Jason Spades and touch his temple. It's time to flex my Reading muscles some more. I have to work on the meditation to get into the Coherence state for a moment. Next, I picture myself light as a feather. I'm hoping to enter his mind further than what seems to happen by default.

"GO TO THE GYM TODAY, TAKE A DAY OFF, AND DO SOME gardening. You can't beat yourself up like this," our wife tells us at the breakfast table. "This kind of stress will give you a heart attack."

"You don't understand, babe. It's going to be the worst quarter results in the company history. Back in the day, CEOs jumped out of windows over this sort of thing," we say. We are grateful for her support, but we can't help feeling that she just doesn't get it. The enormity of it. Everything we've worked for is going to be ruined. No weekends, no vacations, endless sleepless nights—all for nothing.

We also think about the other thing, the thing we haven't even mentioned to her. How a trader was taking unauthorized risks and lost a big chunk of the bank's money. We're going to be held responsible by the investors for that, too. Combined with the quarter results, we'll look like an idiot—just like the rest of the bank CEOs. This is not the legacy we'd been hoping for.

I, Darren, decide I've had enough and jump out.

I'M SPEECHLESS, TORN BETWEEN EMPATHY AND GLEE.

I do feel bad for Jason. It's painful to see legendary people like that fall. His disappointment is intense. His wife is getting him through it, though, and that's encouraging. Maybe there is something to the whole marriage thing after all. And he's probably wrong about his wife—I bet she understands what's about to come down. She probably just knows the right things to say to her husband. On a slightly more positive side, I'm glad he wasn't contemplating something insane, like blowing his brains out. I don't know what I'd do in that case. Would I try to stop him? Probably I would, though how to start that conversation without seeming like a lunatic is beyond me.

Anyway, I can't dwell on these depressing thoughts. Not when Jason's tragedy can be my get-rich-ridiculously-quick scheme.

I phase out, and on an impulse, I take out my phone. Did I mention I love smartphones? Anyway, I bring up my trading app. The bank's stock is the highest it's been in the past four years. Clearly nobody has any idea what's about to happen.

I have to act. I check on the price of put options. Those are basically contracts with someone assuring you they'll buy from you at an agreed-upon price within a given time period. It turns out that an option to sell at a lower price than where the stock is right now is dirt-cheap. That's because put options are like insurance, and in this case, people are betting the price will be steady or higher. I have thirty-two thousand dollars in cash in my trading account, and I use it all to buy the put options.

With some very conservative assumptions, if the stock drops even ten percent, I'll still be able to make a lot, either by selling the options or exercising them. If the stock completely tanks, like that of the 'too big to fail' banks during the crisis, I might end up making a cool million from the money I just invested. And, of course, I'll invest more of my money when I'm near a computer. There's only so much you can do on the phone. I think I might even put all of my savings into this, though I have to be careful. The SEC might wonder about me if I go overboard. Also, what if I Read someone else and get an even better tip? My money would be locked up for a few weeks. Though, I have to admit, it's hard to picture a better scenario.

And regarding the SEC, I wish I knew at what point someone shows up on their radar. Not that they'd have anything on me, even if they noticed my activity. They work on proof, unlike the casinos—proof like phone conversations or email records. Things they would not have in my case. Still, I don't want the bother of an investigation.

I can't believe Mira makes her money playing cards with criminals. This way is so much easier. I really hope she doesn't do it for money. If I find out that's the case, and offer Eugene and her some money, I wonder if they would accept. Somehow I think she might be too proud, but I ought to try. I'm feeling very generous right now. I've never had any trouble with money, even without the job at the fund, but now, with Reading, I see that I will quickly reach a new level of financial independence.

I'm so wired now, I have to go harder on myself during the rest of the workout. Lifting heavy weights seems to clear my mind. I'm not sure if that's a common experience or just me being weird. There's only one way to find out, so I Read a few minds to investigate. According to my informal gym-based study, other people also feel good after lifting weights. Good to know.

When I'm done with the gym and get in my car, I text Amy. She's an acquaintance from Harvard. That's another reason to go there, by the way—to make important connections that help you get jobs.

Networking is not why I want to meet with Amy today, however. I do it because she's crazy, in exactly the way I need.

She wants to do sushi, and after some back-and-forth, I give in. I guess I'll have sushi for the second day in a row. It's a good thing I like the stuff so much.

We meet at her favorite midtown place and catch up. She works at another fund, so it's easy to convince her this is just an impromptu networking session. Except I'm here for a different reason.

Amy is into extreme experiences of all sorts. In some ways, she's the opposite of me. For example, she's just bitten into Fugu sashimi. Fugu is that poisonous blowfish that the Japanese never allowed their emperor to eat. The fish contains tetrodotoxin, a neurotoxin fatal to humans and other creatures. If the chef messed up Amy's order, it could be deadly. Each fish has enough poison to kill around thirty people. And Amy's eating it like it's nothing. That's the sort of person she is. It's perfect for me, so I phase into the Quiet.

Amy is still, chopsticks carrying their potentially deadly load into her mouth. She isn't cringing or anything. I have to respect her for that.

I approach her and get into her mind, not bothering to rewind events.

We're chewing the Fugu. I, Amy, can't get enough of the stuff, while I, Darren, am severely disappointed. The flavor is much too subtle for me. It doesn't really taste like much of anything. Given the health risks, I would've expected this to taste like lobster multiplied by a hundred.

I go deeper.

We're flying in a plane. This is our first non-tandem jump, and we feel the adrenaline rush just getting on the plane. When it takes us to fifteen thousand feet, we get our first 'feargasm,' as we like to call it.

When we eventually make the jump, the feeling of free fall overwhelms us with its intensity. It's everything we thought it would be, and more. Through it all, we don't forget the most important thing—and after sixty seconds of bliss that seem like a millisecond, we pull the cord to open the parachute.

We're already wondering what to do next. Maybe jump naked? Maybe under the influence of some substance?

The flight after the parachute opens gets boring, so I, Darren, seek something else.

We're snowboarding this time . . .

I GET OUT OF AMY'S HEAD EVENTUALLY. THANKS TO HER, I'M able to cross off ninety percent of my bucket list. Through her eyes, I have surfed, bungee jumped, rock climbed, snowboarded, and even done BASE jumping with a wing suit.

I would never have done any of these things for real, particularly since yesterday I found out something that I'm still trying to wrap my head around: I can extend my subjective lifespan by just chilling in the Quiet. That means I have a lot more to lose than regular people.

I insist on paying for Amy's lunch. It's the least I can do to pay her back for the experiences I just gleaned through her eyes. I definitely got closer to understanding what drives her and other people like her to do these seemingly crazy things. Most of it was awesome—especially jumping out of that plane.

Of course, it wasn't awesome enough for me to risk my life. But now, thanks to Reading, I won't have to. I can just hang out with Amy again. I think I might be getting lunch with her more often now.

After I'm in the car again by myself, I, unbelievably, feel like I might've had enough Reading for today. I want to get together with my new Brooklyn friends a day early.

I text Eugene, and he excitedly invites me over.

Now the stupid car will finally come in handy.

15

I park in front of Eugene and Mira's building after an uneventful drive over. The spot is near a fire hydrant, but far enough away from it not to get a ticket. The nice thing about hydrant spots like this is that there's no one in front of the car. This makes parallel parking, a skill I haven't fully mastered, easier. No parking meters either, just a regular spot that's only a problem during Monday morning street cleanings. Impressive. I guess one nice perk of Brooklyn is being able to park like this on the street.

I make my way over to the building entrance. A friendly old lady holds the door for me. Apparently I don't look like a burglar to her, the way she just lets me walk right in. I'm glad, because this way I don't have to play with the intercom again.

Before the door closes behind me, I get that feeling again.

Someone's pulled me into the Quiet.

The door is frozen halfway between open and shut, the world is silent, and I'm standing next to frozen me and unfrozen Mira. I briefly wonder what part of my body she touched to get me to join her before I notice the wild look in her eyes and forget everything else.

"Mira, what's going on?"

"There isn't time," she says, running to the stairs. "Follow me."

I run after her, trying to make sense of it.

"They found me," she says over her shoulder. "They found us."

"Who found you?" I ask, finally catching up.

She doesn't answer; instead she stops dead in her tracks. There are men standing like statues on the staircase heading up to the first floor.

Finally coming out of whatever shock she's in, she goes through the pockets of a tall burly man wearing a leather jacket. Not finding whatever information she was looking for in his wallet, she touches his temple and appears to be concentrating in order to Read.

When she's done, she takes a gun from the man's inner pocket and shoots him. The sound of the shot, even with a silencer on the gun, nearly deafens me, and I put my hands up to my ears. She just keeps shooting, over and over. Then, when the gun begins to make clicking sounds, she uses the empty gun to beat the man's face into a bloody pulp. I've never seen anyone as angry, as out of control, as she is. Tears of frustration well up in her eyes, but none fall.

"Mira," I say gently. "You're not going to kill him that way. He'll still be alive when we phase out of the Quiet."

She goes on with her grisly attack until the gun slips from her fingers. She turns to me, the tears falling now. She brushes them away impatiently, clearly embarrassed that I've seen her lose control like this. "I know that—trust me, I know. It doesn't make a fucking bit of difference, anything I do to them. But I needed that." She takes a breath, pulling herself together. "And now we have to run."

"Wait," I say. "Can you please explain to me what's going on?"

"These fuckers' friends just kidnapped me," she says, pushing her way through the rest of the 'dead' man's three companions.

"What? How?"

"They're after Eugene," she says, running even faster up the stairs. "They're taking me hostage in case they don't find him at home. They want to use me to smoke him out. Only, he *is* home."

"What do they want with him?" I ask, confused. Eugene is one of the nicest people I've ever met. I just assumed this whole kidnaping business with Mira had something to do with her gambling adventures. The four men sure look like the same kind of guys as the one we ran into at the sushi restaurant yesterday. Why would they be after Eugene?

"I don't have time to explain, Darren," she says, and stops on the second floor. She turns to me and sizes me up, as though looking at me for the first time.

"Listen," she says, "I won't make it to the next floor, let alone the apartment. I'm about to fall out of the Mind Dimension—I can already feel myself slipping. Me running here was a desperate attempt. Even if I didn't pull you in, I wouldn't have made it. So, I need your help."

"Of course—what do you need?" I'm scared. I haven't seen Mira like this before. Sarcastic—yes; angry—a couple of times, sure. Even amused. But not vulnerable like this.

"You have to promise to save my brother."

"I will," I say, and it comes out very solemn. "But can you tell me what's going on?"

"Okay, pay attention. I might not have the time to repeat it. I need you to go into the Mind Dimension, the Quiet as you call it, as soon as my time's up. Once you're there, once you've stopped time for everyone around you, you have to come back up these stairs and go all the way to the apartment. Take one of their guns on the way—" she points at the men downstairs, "—and shoot the door lock to get into the apartment. Pull Eugene in to join you in your Mind Dimension. Tell him these guys are on their way up." She says it all in one breath, wiping her eyes and nose with her sleeve. It might be disgusting from anyone else, but somehow Mira makes even this display endearing. "If you pull this off, if you get him out of this fucking mess, I'll be forever in your debt."

"I'll do it, Mira," I say, beginning to think coherently. "I promise, I'll get him out of the building. I'm parked right outside. It shouldn't be a problem."

"Thank you," she says. The next moment, she's next to me. She hugs me, and I clumsily hug her back. I don't know how to act around a woman in such distress. I pat her back gently, hoping it makes her feel better.

Then she stands on her tiptoes and kisses me. The kiss is deep and desperate, her lips soft against mine. It's completely unexpected, but I return the kiss without a second thought, my mind in complete turmoil. So much for coherent thinking.

"Tell Eugene I'm sorry," she says, pulling away after a few moments. "Tell him this is my fault. I led them here. They picked me up at the gym, and I had some mail on me."

"The gym?" I say, a sick feeling in my stomach.

"Yes. I'm so fucking stupid. I took the mail out of the mailbox in the morning. They found it on me. Our address was on it," she says bitterly.

"Your gym is how my friend found you," I admit. "You used one of your older aliases there. I'm so sorry. I should've told you that."

"No, you didn't know the danger we're in. This is definitely on me. I should've asked you how you found me. And I should've changed gyms. We should've fucking moved a long time ago—"

"Where are you now, and more importantly, who are these people? You have to tell me before your time is up," I interrupt urgently.

"The men in this building are working with the ones who picked me up. I don't know for sure, but I think they're all involved with the people who killed our parents. The same Russian crew. The same Pusher is probably pulling their strings. Eugene can tell you more. I'm in the car where the friends of the assholes downstairs put me. At first they knocked me out somehow, maybe with chloroform or a shot. I don't remember. I don't have any bruises, so I doubt they hit me on the head. When I came to, about twenty or so minutes after, I Split and Read the driver. They gave our address to someone, which led to the group that came here. They work quickly; I didn't expect them to already be here. The ones holding me are going to this address in Sunset Park." She hands me a little piece of paper. I commit the address on the paper to memory. "After that, I Split again and ran here on foot. But it was too far. If I hadn't run into you—"

I phase out before she's able to finish her last sentence.

Suddenly I'm standing downstairs again, next to the still-closing door.

Mira is gone.

As she instructed me, I instantly phase into the Quiet.

I run, even though rationally I know I have plenty of time. Unlike Mira, I can spend an insanely long time in the Quiet.

As I'm running, I digest the fact that after she pulled me in and her time ran out, I got pushed out. This is something I wondered about—what happens if you pull someone in, but then get out of the Quiet yourself. Looks like your guest in the Quiet is tied to you. If you get out, they get out.

My contemplation of the rules of this bizarre new world is interrupted by the people on the stairs. The guy in the leather jacket is back, standing there like nothing happened—which makes sense, since nothing actually has happened, at least not outside Mira's Quiet session. I take his gun as she suggested. I'm very tempted to Read them, but I decide to do the important part first.

I run up to the fifth floor. As I turn into their hallway, I see Eugene. He's wearing a ratty hoodie with dorky pajama pants underneath. I fleetingly wonder what happened to the white coat.

He's throwing out the garbage. I don't need to shoot the lock off their door after all.

I touch him, and in a moment he's staring at me, confused.

"Eugene, Mira is in trouble," I tell him instead of hello.

"What? What do you mean?" He looks alarmed.

"Please let me explain. She was just here, in the Quiet. She said she was kidnapped. She said they're after you."

"Who's after me?" He looks panicked now. "What are you talking about?"

"Come with me," I say, figuring a picture is worth a thousand words. "I'll tell you what she told me on the way down. You need to see them."

"See whom?" he asks, but follows me anyway. "Can you just explain?"

"There are some kind of mobsters who came here for you. I'm taking you to them," I say and pick up speed. "Mira said they're the same people who killed your parents. That some Pusher controls them. She said you would be able to explain this to me."

"And now they have her?" he asks from behind me, his voice low.

"Yes. She's in a car, being taken to a place in Sunset Park. I have the address," I say as we make our way to the four men on the stairs. "This is the problem," I say, pointing at them.

Eugene approaches the men. There is an unrecognizable, almost frightening expression on his face.

Without asking any more questions, he approaches the man wearing a blue tracksuit and touches the guy's temple. I decide to also indulge in Reading, since I'm waiting for Eugene anyway. I walk up to the guy in the leather jacket whose gun I didn't need.

WE'RE DRIVING TO THE ADDRESS WE WERE TEXTED. WE'RE HAPPY we called shotgun, as Boris, Alex, and Dmitri are still bitching about having to share the backseat. Alex, who sits in the middle, apparently spreads his knees too wide for the others' comfort.

Haste was of the essence when we got the call, so we had to

leave the restaurant, bill unpaid and food unfinished, and get into Sergey's car. Top priority and all that.

"Wait here," we tell Sergey—the driver—in Russian. I, Darren, understand this again, though the words sound foreign in my mind.

Next, we hand Sergey our phone with a picture of the target. If the target happens to waltz into the building behind us, Sergey is supposed to text us immediately.

I, Darren, am able to feel a more pronounced mental distance between myself and my host, whose name is Big Boris. I'm less lost in the experience, and I'm glad about that. I guess I'm getting better at this Reading business. His mind seems less of a mystery to me with this little bit of extra distance.

Encouraged, I try to focus on how he—or I, or we—got the idea to come to this building. Specifically, I'm looking for more details on this phone call he/I/we were recalling. All of a sudden, I'm there.

We're at the restaurant eating lamb shish kebab when we get a phone call. We look at the phone and see the number we memorized long ago, and the name 'Arkady' on the screen. A piece of meat gets stuck in our throat. It's the boss, and he always makes us nervous.

"Go to the location I'm going to text you immediately," he says, and we promptly agree.

We're not done with the meal, but we don't voice our annoyance to the boss. Not into the phone, and not even to the crew as we tell them what's what. We wouldn't dream of crossing Arkady; he's the craziest, toughest, most ruthless son of a bitch we've ever met.

I, Darren, repeat Arkady's phone number to myself over and over, so I can remember it in case it comes in handy later.

Luckily, I'm very good when it comes to remembering numbers. Still, I need to write this down, along with the address where Mira is being kept, as soon as I can.

I realize that I managed to jump around Big Boris's mind without the usual feeling of lightness. Though with hindsight, I think I did feel light; it was simply on a subconscious level, like I was on a strange mental autopilot. I'll need to play around with this some more, this jumping about in people's minds, but now is not the time. I need to jump out of this mind and get Eugene out of this mess.

When I'm out of Big Boris's head, Eugene is staring at me.

"I couldn't find any confirmation that these men are the same people who killed Mom and Dad," he says.

"That's not the thing to focus on right now," I respond. "We have to get you out of this first. Then we have to rescue Mira."

"Sorry, you're right." He shakes his head like he's disgusted with himself. "There's no time to think about revenge—not that I'm in a position to do anything to them right now anyway. I'm not good at thinking under pressure."

"It's fine. But we have to be careful," I tell him, remembering what I just saw. "Their driver knows what you look like."

"I got that much out of Boris," he says, pointing at the short stocky guy in the tracksuit whose mind Eugene just Read. I internally chuckle, realizing the reason Big Boris needs the 'Big' distinction. He's the second Boris in the group.

"Walk with me," I say. "I want to show you where I'm parked."

As I lead Eugene to my car, I ask, "Is there a back exit from your building somewhere?"

"Not that I know of," he says, scratching his head as we stop in front of my parked car.

"How about a way to the roof?"

"That's through the sixth floor," he says, pushing his glasses further up his nose. "I think I can get there if I need to."

"Okay. Hopefully you won't have to. First, we need to try for the main door. They're walking up the stairs. It will take them time to get to your floor. I have an idea—follow me," I tell Eugene and head back to the building.

I run up the stairs, pushing the mobsters out of my way. Eugene follows. I pull the elevator door on the second floor. It's locked. I run to the third floor and do the same thing, getting the same result. The door on the fourth floor opens. So far, so good. I keep running, checking near the elevator doors on every floor until we get to the top, on the sixth.

"Okay, Eugene. Here's my plan: they think your elevator is broken. That gives you a good chance. As soon as I phase out and you're in the real world, press the elevator button. Since the elevator's on the fourth floor, it should get to you in plenty of time. No one is by the elevator on any of the other floors, so there's little risk of any slowdowns."

"Got it, Darren." He smiles for the first time since I've seen him today. "You know, I could've come up with this plan on my own. You're basically telling me to take the elevator down and walk out."

"Yeah, I guess I am. Also, pull up your hoodie and try to hunch as you walk out. Go straight to the car. That's where I'll be waiting, keeping it running," I say. This sounds doable, but I wouldn't want to be in Eugene's shoes right now. "If something goes wrong, run for the roof and text me. I'll phase into the Quiet and come talk to you. Can you phase in every few seconds and walk down to check on the bad guys' progress?"

"Yes," he says. "Since I'll only be spending a small fraction of my available time in each instance, I should be able to re-enter the Mind Dimension without waiting a long time in-between. Thank you."

"Thank me when this is over," I say and begin to walk down the stairs again. He continues to follow me.

"Darren," he says when we reach my frozen body in the lobby. "If something happens to me, promise you'll help Mira."

"I promise," I say. I have no idea how I'll do that, but it occurs to me that the last thing Mira made me promise was that I would save him if she didn't make it. Maybe it wouldn't be so bad having a sibling after all, the way these two look out for each other.

"Don't look guilty as you get out of the building," he says, looking in the direction where Sergey, the driver, is waiting for his comrades.

"Same to you," I say. "See you in a few minutes."

We shake hands.

I take a breath and touch my frozen self on the forehead. The sounds of the world come back.

16

I DO MY BEST TO AVOID LOOKING SUSPICIOUS, IN CASE SERGEY IS watching me from the car. I pat my pockets, take out the car keys, and confidently walk back. The image I'm trying to project is: silly me, I forgot something in the car. I might not win an Oscar for my acting, but hopefully the performance will be enough to keep us off the Russians' radar.

As soon as I'm in the car, the first thing I do is fish out the pen I used to sign the receipt for this car rental and the receipt itself. On the back, I write the address and phone number I kept in my head.

Then I start the car.

I've never been this antsy. I stare at the car's digital clock, but it seems to have stopped. It feels like half an hour has passed when a single digit on the clock advances one minute.

The plan initially seemed simple enough—just wait for Eugene. I didn't expect the suspense to be this torturous. I take a deep breath and mentally count to thirty. It doesn't work.

There *is* something I can do, though, so I phase into the Quiet.

I'm in the backseat of the car. My frozen self is in the front. I've always wondered how the body I get in the Quiet decides where to show up. Of course, there is Eugene's mention of this possibly not being a real body. That still doesn't answer it completely. Whatever I inhabit now, who decided it should appear in the backseat? How did it get there? Why not show up, say, outside the car?

I open the door and get out. Now that he can't see me staring, I can get a better look at Sergey. He seems to be bored, so I assume I didn't raise his suspicions. Good. I also note the car he's driving is actually pretty nice—a Mercedes, no less. Apparently crime does pay.

I walk into the building. The goons are now approaching the second floor. It's scary how close they're getting to Eugene.

I run all the way up to the fifth floor.

Thankfully, I see Eugene opening the elevator door. This is it. The plan is working.

I go back to the car and phase out.

The noises are back, and the digital clock in the car is supposed to work normally; only it's still crawling. I wonder if using the Quiet messes with your time perception. I mean, how long can a few minutes last?

After what seems like another half hour of worry, but really is only three minutes according to the clock, I phase into the Quiet again. Eugene is still not out of the stupid elevator on the second floor.

I go back, phase out, wait ten seconds, and go back in. I repeat this a couple of times until I see the elevator door open. Yes! Finally.

Since I'm here anyway, I walk up to check on the mobsters. They're between the fourth and fifth floors. Satisfied, I go back to the car to phase out again.

Another few seconds, and I can't take it anymore. I phase into the Quiet yet again. Eugene is walking to the door in the lobby. His hoodie is pulled up all the way. His hunching is terribly fake, but as long as he doesn't look like himself, we should be out of this mess in a few seconds. I go back to the car and get out of the Quiet again, only to return a few seconds later.

Eugene is walking toward me. Sergey, the driver, is looking at him with too much concentration. Oh, no. I walk up to the car and touch Sergey's temple.

We're looking at a strange guy who just left the building in a very suspicious manner. He's trying to hide his face, so we can't see it, but we think he could be the target. Since we know we're here on Arkady's orders, we have to cover our ass. We take out our phone and text Big Boris about seeing something suspicious. Now it can't be said that we fucked up.

Done Reading the driver, I run back to the car and phase out. I swivel the steering wheel. My foot is on the gas. I shift the gear in the drive position. Then I phase into the Quiet again.

Eugene is a few steps away from the car. I walk up to him and touch his wrist. A moment later, another Eugene stands next to me, this one fully animated.

"I made it," he says on a big exhale, like he's been holding his breath this whole time.

"No. We're far from out of this. Sergey, the driver, just recognized you."

"Fuck. What do we do?"

"You'll jump into the car, and as soon as you close the door, I'll step on the gas. Buckle up as soon as you can—it might be a bumpy ride."

"Thank you again, Darren," he starts saying, and I wave dismissively.

"As I said before, thank me once we're out of this." Hurrying back to the car, I take a deep breath and phase out of the Quiet.

The next few actions happen in a blur. Eugene runs to the door and jumps into the car. As he closes the door, I stomp on the gas pedal, and we're at the first intersection in seconds.

As we pass the next intersection, I realize that I have no idea where I'm going, but it doesn't matter as long as it's away from that building. On a whim, I decide to keep going straight, and pump the gas again.

I'm going fifty miles per hour when I see the next light turning red a few feet away.

I'm forced to phase into the Quiet. This time, it's particularly eerie. I've never done this in a moving car before. The sounds of the engine, which was working overtime to get us moving faster, are gone. That's strange enough, but what's weirder is that the car itself is standing still. Everything in my brain tells me it should at least move a few extra feet according to the law of inertia, but it doesn't. It's as still as a rock.

I realize I should've done this phasing business at the last intersection. Or even the one before that. It's too late now, though, so I might as well get on with it.

This gives me a chance to check for any pursuers. I walk out of the car and look inside. Through the front window, I see expressions of sheer horror on both my own and Eugene's faces. I walk to Eugene's side and reach into the window. Touching his neck makes Eugene's Quiet incarnation show up in the back seat.

"Darren, what the fuck are you doing? You can't Split like this, in the middle of a car chase."

"Why not?"

"Well, for starters, when you get back, you increase the chance that you'll lose control of the car."

"We'll have to chance it—I'll be careful," I promise. "I had to do it because there was a red light at that intersection."

"Shit," Eugene says, following my gaze. Though here in the Quiet the light is actually dead, he doesn't doubt my powers of observation. And I'm sure he finally understands: the red light means we'll need to stop, and stopping is not a good idea when you've got a car full of very bad Russian dudes on your tail.

"Let's split up," I say. "I'll check out this intersection, and you go back and check on our new Russian friends."

"Okay," he says, turning around and running back toward his building.

I walk more leisurely to the intersection. Eugene has more distance to cover, and I want to give him a head start.

When I'm standing under the traffic light, I turn left and observe the road.

The closest car is about half a block away. I walk toward it. It's a small car, but that doesn't fill me with confidence. Small or not, if it T-bones us, it will hurt.

I open the car door. The speedometer is unreadable—another example of defunct electronics in the Quiet.

I Read the driver. Through his eyes, I learn that he's going thirty miles per hour. I also learn that he's late and is about to speed up. It's unclear what the final speed will be, but I believe he's about to give a noticeable push on the gas.

I make some quick estimates and decide that this guy will prevent me from turning right or going forward. I'll have to at least slow down at the intersection and make sure his car passes.

On the plus side, the car behind this one is a block away. Since I still have a little time while Eugene does his recon, I run to that car and learn its speed as well. It's also going thirty, but its driver isn't in a rush. He's the type of safe driver who slows down a little before getting to an intersection—which is rare, but admirable.

I walk back to my rental and spot Eugene running back. I have to say, I'm impressed with his speed.

"It's not good, Darren," he says when I'm within hearing distance. "They're in the lobby already, and Sergey's ready to pursue us."

"Damn it," I say, resisting the temptation to kick the car in frustration. "I have bad news, too. We have to actually stop on that light. At least to let this one reckless asshole through."

"Okay, but after that, if the path is clear, we need to go," he says urgently. "I Read them some more. They indeed have orders to kill me—and for running and causing them a headache, Big Boris has decided to make it slow if he gets the chance."

"Then it sounds like we don't really have a choice," I say, trying not to wonder what Big Boris would do with *me*. I'm not on the hit list, but I bet to him it would be guilt by association with equally dire consequences. "There's another car after the one that's the problem, but I think I can make it. Just tell me, should I turn right here or go straight? Do you have any idea where we're going?"

As I ask the last question, I realize that I should've brought it up much sooner.

"There's one place we can go," Eugene says. "Mira and I aren't welcome there. It's the community where Readers in Brooklyn live. It's a long shot, but I can't think of anyone else who could help. They're located on Sheepshead."

"And Sheepshead is where, exactly?" I'm forced to ask. My Brooklyn geography isn't very strong. All I know is the Brooklyn Bridge and, as of recently, Mira and Eugene's apartment.

"Go straight for a bit, then turn left on Avenue Y. It will be a wider street that we'll approach after a few more blocks. Once on it, we go straight, then right on Ocean Avenue. Straight from there until you hit the canal, after that you have to turn left . . ."

"All I got is that I'm going straight for now. Give me a heads up a block before we get where I need to turn."

"Okay," he says. "We should Split again shortly and see where they are at that point."

"Good plan," I say and approach the car.

"Careful," he reminds me.

I take a few breaths and prepare for getting back into driving. I even get into the car in the back, hoping it reduces the disorientation I might get somehow. I touch the back of my head, and the next moment I'm in the driver's seat of the car, my foot instinctively moving from the gas to the brake.

The braking is sudden, and my sushi lunch threatens to come back up. As soon as the car with the guy in a rush passes, I slam the gas again and go on red. The car behind the one that we let through is approaching, but we clear the intersection safely.

We get lucky on the next couple of streets—the lights are green. It's a miracle that we haven't killed a pedestrian. In Manhattan, we would've definitely killed someone by now. People there jaywalk left and right.

"Avenue Y is next," Eugene reminds me, though I actually saw this one coming—courtesy of alphabetically ordered street names. We just flew by W, and this one is X.

"It's yellow," I say, looking ahead. "It'll be red by the time we get there."

"Let's repeat what we did last time," he suggests, and I immediately agree.

I phase into the Quiet and pull Eugene in with me. We split up the same way we did the last time.

As I reach Avenue Y, I see that we're about to have a big problem.

There are too many cars here to safely repeat our earlier maneuver.

I Read the minds of the drivers who'll be closest to the intersection by the time we arrive. It seems like no one is in a rush, or plans to speed. But it doesn't matter—we still won't make it.

"They're already approaching Avenue T," Eugene says when he gets back.

That means they're five blocks away.

"How fast are they going?"

"They're insane—pushing a hundred miles an hour. You saw the Mercedes they're driving."

Our luck is just getting worse. My piece-of-shit rental

would be pushing its limits if I tried going that fast, even if I was willing to risk it—which I'm not.

"Can we afford to wait for the light to change?" I ask.

"Not according to my calculations. We have to run the red light, and we have to turn right on the next street. We need to get off this main street so they can't easily catch up with us. It's my mistake. I should've had you turn and zigzag the streets earlier."

"I guess we'll need to phase out regularly and time the turn just right," I say doubtfully. It sounds like we don't have a choice.

The next minute is probably the most nerve-wracking of my life.

I phase in every second, check the intersection, and come back to the car. Over and over. It's hard to drive when you come back, and it's impossible to calculate this whole thing exactly. Still, I think—and Eugene verifies—that I can make the turn if I slow down just a tiny bit to let the Honda closest to us pass by.

The phasing out makes this process play out slowly, like a frame-by-frame sequence in a one-second-long movie stunt.

The Honda gently kisses our back bumper. Brakes screech all around us. I phase into the Quiet to learn what the other drivers will do in reaction to the chaos about to take place. Meanwhile, I also learn what they think of my maneuver, me, and all my ancestors. Out of the Quiet, they express their frustration with a deafening orchestra of honking. That cacophony of car horns and swearing is followed by a loud bang.

The Beemer we just cut off ended up getting rear-ended by an old station wagon. I feel a mixture of guilt and glee. Though no one is visibly hurt, the accident is my fault. On the flip side, however, this might actually slow down our pursuers.

I push the gas and turn the wheel to the right, getting off Avenue Y as Eugene recommended.

"I can't believe we made it," he says. "Now we need to go a roundabout way, and Split to check on our tail."

On Avenue Z, I turn again, and we reach Ocean Avenue uneventfully. The only issue is that we're unable to find our pursuers in the Quiet. At least, not by looking a few blocks behind. We take it as a good sign. We must have lost them.

"Now drive to Emmons Avenue and turn left," Eugene says. "You can't miss it."

He's right. I'm soon faced with the choice of either driving into some kind of canal or turning.

"It's not that far now," he says as we drive a few blocks down Emmons, following the water. I'm glad we're not being pursued at this point; this area is full of traffic.

"Make a left at that light," Eugene tells me. "We're almost there."

Before I get a chance to actually turn, however, the passenger-side mirror explodes.

17

I PHASE IN, AND THE NOISE OF THE BUSY STREET STOPS. I PULL Eugene in with me. As we exit the car, we start looking around.

"Darren, look at this," Eugene says. He sounds more scared than I've heard him since we started this whole mess.

He stands a few feet to the right of the car and points at something in the air. When I take a closer look, my heartbeat spikes. It's a bullet. A bullet frozen in its path. A bullet that just missed the car. The sibling of the one that must have shattered that mirror.

"Someone's shooting at us," I say stupidly.

Eugene mumbles something incomprehensible in response.

Coming out of our shock, we frantically search the cars behind us. It doesn't take long to find the source of the bullets. Not surprisingly, it's our new friends.

How did they manage to get this close? How could I be so stupid—why hadn't I checked on them for so long? Why was I so convinced we'd lost them?

“Eugene, we need to get to wherever it is we’re going. And we need to do it fast,” I say.

“It’s very close. If we turn now, we’ll almost be there. Just a few more blocks.”

“It might as well be miles if they shoot us.”

I’ve never been shot at before, and I hate the feeling. I’m not ready to get shot. I haven’t seen enough, done enough. I have my whole life ahead of me—plus all that extra time in the Quiet.

“Darren, snap out of it.” I hear Eugene’s voice. “Let’s see if we can make this left turn.”

Assessing the situation, we quickly realize that our chances of making this turn unscathed are very small. A Jaguar is coming toward us on the opposite side, driving at thirty-five miles per hour—and we’ll likely crash into it if we take a sharp left turn. Still, we don’t overthink it. A car crash with a seatbelt and an airbag beats getting shot. I think.

I walk to the car, take a calming breath, and phase out. As I’m pulling the wheel all the way to the left, I try my best not to phase into the Quiet out of fear.

With a loud screeching noise, my side of the car touches the Jaguar’s bumper. The impact knocks the wind out of me, but the seatbelt holds me, and the airbag doesn’t activate. Happy to have made it this far, I slam the gas pedal harder. The car makes all sorts of unhappy sounds, but at least we made it through that deadly looking turn relatively unscathed.

When we’re midway through the block, I phase in and get Eugene to join me.

We look at our handiwork back at the beginning of the street. As a result of our crazy turn, the Jaguar hit the Camry in front of it. Its bumper is gone, and the once-beautiful car is pretty much totaled. I think the guy inside will have to be hospitalized—which I feel terrible about. Furthermore, the entire intersection is jammed with cars. Unless they plan to go through them, our trigger-happy friends can't pass.

Still, Eugene walks over to Read Sergey's mind, just in case.

"Darren, I'm such a fucking idiot," he says, slapping his hand to his forehead.

"What is it?"

"They know where we're going. Their boss texted them the address. That's how they caught up with us. I should've realized that if they're working with a Pusher, he or she would know the location of the Readers' community. That they would know we're likely to head that way."

"It's too late to blame yourself now," I tell him. "Let's just get there."

"I'm not sure we'll make it. Sergey plans to ram this car." He points at the tiny Smart Car that happens to be the smallest of those involved in the jam, and I realize that we have a problem. Our pursuers can go through the blocked intersection after all.

"We already have a little bit of a head start," I say, trying to summon optimism I don't feel. "We'll just have to make it."

"Okay," Eugene says. "From here, we can actually walk to our destination on foot before we get back into the real world. This way, you'll know the exact way there."

We take the walk. I realize we'll make it when we see the wall of the gated community that is our destination. Whether Sergey rams that car successfully or not, we can do this.

We're a mere three blocks from where we need to be.

When we get back to the car, I phase back out.

I push the little rental to its limits. I'm going eighty, the tires screeching as I make the next turn. I hear the loud bang behind us and know that Sergey followed through with his plan; the Smart Car is probably toast by now.

It's too late for our pursuers, though. We've reached the gate that separates us from our destination. I stop the car in the middle of the street and am about to phase into the Quiet when I'm pulled in instead by someone else.

"Eugene, you beat me to it," I say when everything goes still. Only when I look to my right, I don't see Eugene.

I see someone else—someone I've never met before.

18

THE GUY IS HOLDING A HUGE MILITARY KNIFE. THREATENINGLY. I don't know what to make of it, since we're in the Quiet. I'm not sure what will happen to me if he uses the knife on me. Not that I care to find out. He doesn't look like someone who makes idle threats. I make a mental note to find out the risk of death in the Quiet. I know injuries don't stick. And yes, I cut myself to find out. Wouldn't anyone? My shrink thought it was 'interesting' that I cut myself in my delusional world—I recall her talking some nonsense about the physical pain helping me deal with some fictitious emotional one.

"I've seen that one before," the guy says, pointing the knife at frozen Eugene. "But who the fuck are you?"

I gape at him. I don't know what to make of his muscular build, short haircut, and military clothing. Is he some kind of Reader security guard?

"I'm only going to ask one more time," he says, and I realize I didn't respond to his question.

"My name is Darren," I say quickly. "I guess I'm a Reader."

"You guess?"

"Well, it's new information to me, so I'm not used to announcing it. Eugene and Mira are the first Readers I've ever met."

The guy's eyebrows lift, and he unexpectedly chuckles. "I've got news for you. If what you say is true, then today—right now—is the first time you've met a real Reader. Few of the people inside consider the Tsiolkovsky orphans that."

"You sound like you consider them Readers, though," I say on a hunch.

"No one gives a rat's ass what I think; I'm just a soldier. But I say if you can spend more than a second in the Mind Dimension and can Read a single thought, you're a Reader. I'm a simple person with simple definitions, I guess. Who cares how you got to be that way?"

"That makes sense," I say. "I'm sorry, I didn't catch your name."

"You didn't catch it because I didn't give it," the guy says, all traces of amusement gone. "It's Caleb. And knowing my name isn't going to help you, unless you have an explanation for what you and Eugene are doing here. This is private property."

"His sister Mira was just kidnapped. Eugene barely escaped getting killed. There are men coming after us as we speak," I try to explain. "Or at least they'll be here once we leave the Mind Dimension."

"How many?" he asks, coming to attention. The bit about Mira seems to have made an impression.

"There are five of them. They're driving a Mercedes; they could be here any second."

"What else should I know about them?" Caleb asks, his hand tightening on the knife.

"They're some kind of a Russian gang or something. Sergey, two Borises—"

"I don't give a shit what their names are," Caleb interrupts me. "If they're armed and heading this way, we won't be bonding on that level."

"Okay," I say. I have a bad feeling in the pit of my stomach.

"Stay here and don't move. Sam and I have sniper rifles pointed at your heads. If you so much as sneeze, we'll blow your brains out."

I don't have a clue who Sam is, but it doesn't look like Caleb's interested in answering questions right now. As I'm trying to come to grips with his threat, he leaves the car, and in a minute I'm forcefully phased out of the Quiet.

"Eugene, don't move," I say hurriedly. There's a red laser dot on his chest, as though someone has a gun pointed at him—which is apparently the case.

"Why?" he asks, confused.

I phase back into the Quiet instead of answering. I'm afraid of even talking while someone is pointing a sniper rifle at me. What if Caleb thinks my lips moving qualifies as movement and shoots? When I find myself in the backseat again with the world silent, I pull Eugene in.

"I just spoke to some scary-looking dude who's guarding this place. He pulled me in," I explain.

"Did whoever it was say they'll help?"

"Not exactly. He said not to move and that they have guns pointed at us." I swallow. "I saw a laser pointer on you."

"I see," Eugene says, surprisingly calmly. "We'll probably be okay. They'll most likely go Read our pursuers to verify you told them the truth."

"And on the off chance they don't?" I ask, though I can guess the answer.

"In that case, they'll let us resolve our differences with the people following us."

"Great. And we're supposed to just sit and wait?"

"I know I will. The Readers don't usually issue empty threats. If you were told not to move, don't move."

Annoyed with Eugene's ironclad logic, I phase out.

I sit without moving for about five seconds, until I realize that waiting next to Eugene's building earlier was child's play compared to this. I count twenty Mississippis before I phase in. The Mercedes is halfway between the corner where Sergey rammed that car and our current location. The fancy car is barely dented, but Reading Sergey's mind, it seems he doesn't agree with my assessment. He's furious about the damage to his car and determined to make us regret this chase, if he gets the chance. Reading the mind of his friend Big Boris, I get the feeling they'll have to get in line when it comes to doing evil things to us.

I walk back and phase out. I'm now back in the car, waiting for whatever it is that's about to happen.

After what seems like a couple of hours, I think I hear a car motor. As soon as I do, I also hear a gunshot.

I automatically phase in this time. My brain must've thought that shot was directed at me, and this is a near-death experience.

I get out of the car and look at my frozen self. No gunshot wounds. That's good. The only abnormalities about my frozen self are the humongous size of my pupils and the overly white shade of my face. The whole thing makes my frozen self look ghoulish. Eugene is even paler and is holding his head defensively. Like his hands can somehow protect him from a bullet.

I look around. The front end of the Mercedes is visible at the head of the street. I walk closer and realize its tires are in the process of blowing out. They must have been shot.

In a daze, I walk back and phase out.

The sound from the tires exploding reaches my ears now, followed by the screech of steel on pavement as the car continues to careen forward on the exposed rims. Another burst of shots are fired, and I phase into the Quiet again.

This time, just like the last, I didn't intend to phase in. It just happened under stress.

I get out of the car. My frozen self doesn't seem to have any blue in his eyes anymore, his irises swallowed up by the black of his pupils.

I walk to the Mercedes. When I look inside, I wish I hadn't.

I've never seen anything like this before. I mean, I've seen dead bodies in the Quiet, but not of people who were actually dead—or about to be dead—outside the Quiet. This is very different. Very real. These five people have bloody wounds in their chests, and their brains are blown out all over the car.

I feel my gag reflex kick in like I'm about to throw up, but nothing comes out. I'm not sure if it's even possible to puke in the Quiet; it's never happened to me before.

I feel bad about these men getting killed, which is a paradox, given that they were just shooting at me a few minutes ago. I think it has something to do with having Read their minds, like it bound us in some way. There's nothing I can do about it, though; they're gone now.

"Rest in peace," I mutter, walking back to my car. I morbidly wonder what I would experience if I Read one of them right now. Or more specifically, I wonder what I would feel if I catch someone at the right—or wrong—moment, and end up experiencing death firsthand?

I shake my head. I'm not doing that. Besides, I might experience that for myself when I get out of the Quiet; Eugene and I might be the next two targets Caleb shoots.

On the plus side, the Mercedes has no more tires at all. The added resistance should counteract inertia to prevent them from ramming into us—in theory. I'm no expert on blown-out tires.

I walk back to the car and phase out.

A few more shots fire in a blur, and the Mercedes moves a few more feet before it screeches to a stop on its rims. It didn't reach us by at least a hundred feet, but I still feel the need to swallow my heart back into my chest.

Things get suspiciously quiet for a few nerve-wracking seconds, and then the gate shutting us out of the community starts to open.

The guy I met before, Caleb, steps out, with a couple of other dudes who look pretty badass. One of them is toting a sniper rifle. I'm guessing that means he's Sam. He and this Caleb guy look like twins, with their stony, square-jawed faces and hard eyes. Sam is a bit taller, which makes him just short of enormous.

"Darren, Eugene, come with me," Caleb says curtly, and I see Sam shoot Eugene an unfriendly look.

"What about that?" Eugene says, gesturing at the car riddled with bullet holes. He's pointedly avoiding looking at Sam, which I find interesting.

"Both it and your ride will be taken care of. No one will ever find them, or those bodies, again," Caleb assures us.

I manage to feel grateful for having the foresight to say yes to the optional rental car insurance, which seems a bit shallow under the circumstances, even for me.

"Wait," I say, remembering the rental receipt. "I need to get the address where Mira's being kept. It's in the glove compartment."

Caleb walks to the rental and gets the paper I need.

"Here," he says, handing it over to me. "Now, no more delays. We need to have a chat."

And with that, under gunpoint, we enter the private Reader community of Sheepshead Bay.

19

We're taken to some kind of ritzy clubhouse. It's in the middle of an impressive-looking housing community. A house here must cost millions. I didn't even know a place like this existed in Brooklyn—it's more like something you'd expect to see in Miami. Such a lavish compound sort of makes sense, though; Readers should be able to find a bunch of creative ways to make money given their abilities. Or, more accurately, our abilities. I need to get used to the idea that I'm a Reader, I remind myself, remembering the snafu with Caleb earlier.

Inside the clubhouse are an indoor pool, a large fancy restaurant, and a bar. Caleb takes us further in, into what looks like some kind of meeting room.

A dozen people of different ages are here, looking at us intently.

"That really is Eugene," says a hot blond woman who looks to be a few years older than Mira. "I can vouch for that."

"I knew that much," Caleb says, but finally lowers his weapon. "And this guy?"

"Never seen him before," she says, looking at me. I do my best to keep my eyes trained on her face, rather than her prominent cleavage. Being polite can be a chore sometimes.

"He learned about being a Reader yesterday," Eugene explains. Then he gives the blond woman a warm smile. "Hi Julia."

The woman smiles back at him, but her expression changes back to one of concern quickly. "Are you sure he's a Reader?" she says, sizing me up.

"Positive," Eugene says. "You know my family history with Pushers. It was the first thing I checked."

"You have to forgive me, but I must verify for myself," Julia says. "You can be too trusting, Eugene."

So these two somehow know each other. This must be what Eugene was talking about when he said things are less strict in modern New York than they were in Russia during his father's time. Despite being 'exiled,' Eugene and Mira are not completely cut off from other Readers.

"Bring in our bartender," Julia says to a short young guy to her left. He leaves and comes back with a young, extremely pretty woman a few moments later.

"Stacy, I just wanted to tell you about my new guest," Julia says, gesturing toward Eugene. "Put his drinks on my tab."

"Sure thing, Jules," the woman says. She probably expected something more meaningful, being summoned as she was. Stacy begins to walk away when I'm suddenly in the Quiet again, and the woman who knows Eugene—Julia—is standing next to me.

"Now, Darren, I want you to Read Stacy," she says. "Tell me

something about her that no one else can know, and I'll know you're not a Pusher."

This reaffirms what I surmised earlier: Pushers can't Read at all. Otherwise, this test—and the test Eugene did when we first met—wouldn't make sense.

Without much ado, I walk up to Stacy and touch her temple.

WE'RE WALKING INTO THE ROOM WITH JULIA. *OH SHIT, HE'S HERE*, we realize, looking at Caleb. Of all the times we've made a fool out of ourselves, the time we got drunk with Caleb is hardest to forget for some reason. Probably because he's a real man, unlike the rest of the guys here. It's mostly a bunch of rich mama's boys in this community. Well, except for Sam and the other guards.

I, Darren, try distancing myself from Stacy, the way I did in the now-dead Sergey's mind earlier. I latch on to her memory of something involving Caleb, and try to remember what happened. I also notice that the feeling of lightness coming over me is overwhelming this time. If I feel any lighter, I might actually start floating.

"Caleb, you can't drink that as shots. It's sacrilege," we say, watching our favorite customer down a shot of uber-expensive Louis the XIII Cognac like it's cheap vodka.

"How am I supposed to drink it?" he says, giving us a cocky smile. "Show me."

"Are you buying?" we say. "I can't afford a three-hundred-dollar shot."

"Sure," he says. "How much for the whole bottle?"

We grin at him. "You don't want to know. My suggestion would be to switch to good vodka."

"What's good?"

"Try this," we say, pouring a couple of shot glasses of Belvedere, the better of the two pricey vodkas they stock in this place.

We take a shot glass ourselves and cross arms with Caleb, planning to have our shot poured into his mouth, and hoping he does the reverse. "How about a toast?"

When we see the expression on his face, our heart sinks.

"I'm sorry, Stacy. I wasn't trying to hit on you," he says, gently pulling away.

Goddamn it. Not this again. What's wrong with the men in this fucking community? We know most others are probably just rich snobs, but Caleb is their security. What is his deal? And Sam's? It's like a girl can never get laid around here.

I, Darren, distance myself again. I feel a little gross. After all, I'm in the head of a girl who's clearly lusting after this guy. What's worse, from Reading her, I completely understood what it's like to want to take a guy home. I need to get out of Stacy's head, fast.

"OKAY," I TELL JULIA WHEN I'M OUT. "I THINK I HAVE SOMETHING to convince you. She wanted to sleep with him." I point at Caleb. I stress the word 'she' too much, and Julia smiles at my discomfort.

"You men and your homophobia," she says, walking over to Caleb.

In a moment, Caleb's double appears, the animated version of him looking at Julia curiously.

"He says that Stacy was interested in you," Julia tells him.

"That's his proof?" Caleb says, grinning from ear to ear. "That sounds more like an educated guess to me."

"Right, because every woman wants you?" Julia says sarcastically.

"You tell me."

"Not if you were the last man on the planet," Julia retorts sharply.

"Louis the XIII Cognac," I say, tired of their back-and-forth. "Three hundred dollars for a shot; vodka shots; turning the girl down. Any of that ring a bell?"

Caleb's face turns serious. "I do remember that now," he says, frowning at me. "But it doesn't make sense. It was months ago."

He stares at me intently, like he's seeing me for the first time. Julia is also staring. Then they exchange meaningful looks.

"Okay, Darren," Julia says, looking back at me. "You have to be one of us."

She walks toward herself and touches the frozen Julia's cheek.

The world comes to life again.

Julia looks from me to Eugene, then back to me, waiting for Stacy to leave the room. When the bartender is finally outside, the short guy who went to get her closes the door.

"Darren's one of us," Julia says. "I can vouch for that. He's not Pusher scum."

Everyone seems to relax. There had been tension up to this point, but that tension is gone now. They *really* dislike Pushers over here. Given what Pushers did to Eugene's family, and what I suspect they did to my own parents, I can't really blame them.

"That still doesn't explain what that half-blood degenerate is doing here," Sam—Caleb's annoying doppelganger—says. A few people nod their heads and murmur their agreement.

"Watch it, Sam. Eugene is my personal friend," Julia says, staring the guy down. Sam sneers, but keeps quiet. When Julia turns away, however, the look he gives Eugene is even more hostile than before.

"My sister has been taken," Eugene explains, ignoring Sam. "And I think Pushers are behind it."

This last statement gets everyone's attention, even the asshole Sam's.

"Why would Pushers be after Mira?" Caleb says, his eyes narrowing. It sounds like he knows her.

"They're not after her—they're after me," Eugene explains.

"Is this a continuation of that story you told me about your parents?" Julia asks.

Sam scoffs. "You mean that crazy conspiracy theory—"

"Shut it, Sam," Caleb cuts him off. "Let's get the facts without needless commentary."

I can tell Sam is dying to talk back, but decides not to. I guess that means Caleb outranks him or something.

"Please start from the beginning," Julia says to Eugene. "Tell everyone what you told me."

Looks like I was right earlier. There's definitely some kind of history between her and Eugene.

"I believe," Eugene says, giving Sam a hard look, "that my parents were killed because Pushers were trying to kill my father and me."

"Why would they want to do that?" Caleb asks.

"Because of my father's research. He was working on some things they would've found unnatural," Eugene says, and there's anger in his voice. "He was trying to figure out how Reading and Splitting into the Mind Dimension work in the brain."

The room grows tense again.

"That kind of research is forbidden," Sam says harshly, frowning.

"It's not forbidden," Julia corrects him. Like Caleb, she seems to have some authority around here. "As long as the research is never published and is only discussed with peers who are Readers themselves."

"My father was very discreet. Very few people knew what he was working on," Eugene confirms. "I believe something about his research made Pushers think that Readers would gain a big advantage if he succeeded."

"And would we?" an older woman asks. She's been quiet up until now, but from the way everyone looks at her, I can tell she's important.

"I'm not really sure," Eugene says. "I don't know the practical applications of what he was doing—but I imagine so. Any good science has real-world benefits."

"Eugene is more interested in theory, Mom," Julia tells the older woman. "He's above politics."

"So they're trying to kill you because you inherited the same research your dad was doing?" I decide to butt in.

Everyone looks at me with surprise. They probably assume I already know what's going on since I came with Eugene.

"Exactly," Eugene says. "When I used that first test on you to see if you were a Reader, I did it using the method Dad developed back in Russia. The fact that they tried to kill me today is extra evidence he was killed over his work. They missed killing me that day. I was shopping for groceries." He stops and takes a deep breath. "For those of you who don't know, my parents were murdered when their car exploded right in front of our house. My sister was coming back from school—she saw the whole thing."

Julia walks over to him and puts her hand on his shoulder. Her mother frowns, and Sam looks furious. I wonder if he has the hots for Julia, or just hates Eugene because he's a 'half-blood.'

"Was there any proof of his words in the minds of those men you killed outside?" Julia's mother asks.

"Kind of," says Caleb. "Sam and I checked them thoroughly. There were signs of Pusher activity in the mind of the driver. He drove their boss someplace, and the Pusher made him forget what he heard when the boss spoke to the Pusher on the phone. We couldn't get a visual on the Pusher, of course."

"The fact that there's a Pusher involved is good enough reason to help them as far as I'm concerned," Julia says.

"Right. The fact that his sister slutted around the Russian mob has nothing to do with her capture," Sam says, sneering again. I really don't like this guy. If he wasn't so big and scary-looking, I'd strongly consider punching him in the face.

"Mira was trying to find the people who killed our mother and father," Eugene says defensively. "I told her not to, but she wouldn't listen to me."

"Mira isn't someone who'd be easy to control," Caleb says, chuckling. Is that admiration I see on his face?

"Well, if you ask me, the simpler explanation for the kidnapping would be his sister's gambling debt," Sam says. "As to the original explosion, it's more likely that his father's 'friends' from Mother Russia had something to do with it.

Isn't that more plausible than some crazy theory about Pushers?"

"I think the Pusher used the Russian mob for that very reason—so that the police would think the explosion had something to do with what my dad did in Russia," Eugene says, his face turning red with anger. "Only that's bullshit; Dad was the most honest and peaceful man I've ever met."

"Okay," Julia says. "We can debate this until the cows come home, and it won't solve anything. The only way to figure out what's really going on is to rescue Mira—which is what I think we should do."

"Julia, you need to consult your father on this," Julia's mom says, and Julia frowns at her.

"She's right," Sam says. "Jacob would never want to get involved in these exiles' business."

"Well, let's find out, why don't we?" Julia suggests, and walks over to a desk to get a laptop.

20

"What are you going to do?" Julia's mother asks.

"Skype with Dad, if that's what it takes," Julia responds, turning on the laptop.

As her video call is connecting, Julia motions for Eugene and me to come closer. We gather around the computer, and I see a middle-aged man with tired, beady eyes appear on the screen.

An expression of distaste crosses his stern face as he sees Eugene.

"Hello, Jacob, sir," Eugene says respectfully.

"Hi Dad," Julia says.

"Hello," I say politely.

"Who are you?" Jacob asks, staring at me.

"This is Darren, Dad," Julia says, "a new Reader we discovered."

"A new Reader?" he says, watching me intently. "You look familiar to me, kid. Who are your parents?"

"He doesn't know who they are," Eugene jumps in, and Jacob's face reddens at the sound of his voice. I'm glad Eugene volunteered this information because, as embarrassing as it is, I don't know the last names of my parents. Just their first names: Mark and Margret. I need to find out their last names when we're out of this mess. For all I know, I could have extended family in this very room.

"Everyone knows who their parents are," Jacob retorts, but he's not looking at Eugene. He's still boring into me with his beady eyes. "But we'll continue this conversation another time. For now, I'd like to know what this call is about," he says, turning his attention to Julia, "as well as what he—" he gestures at Eugene, "—is doing in our compound."

"Eugene needs our help, Dad," Julia explains. She then proceeds to tell her father a much smoother, more plausible version of the theory about Eugene's parents. She's good. She downplays the research Eugene and his dad worked on, which appears to be controversial in this community. She highlights the Pusher involvement every chance she gets. "So I want to help them and learn more about this matter," she says in conclusion.

"Hell, no," her father says, catching me completely by surprise. "I thought I forbade you from ever consorting with that half-blood."

"This has nothing to do with my personal life; it's about standing up to the Pushers," Julia says, glaring at her father. Her face takes on a rebellious look, making me remember my own interactions with Uncle Kyle.

"My decision is final," Jacob says. "I want him out of the community. He should be grateful our security saved his life. If I had been at the compound, that would not—"

Before Jacob gets a chance to finish his last sentence, Julia closes the laptop with an angry bang.

This seems like as good a time as any for me to phase into the Quiet, and I do.

When everything is still again, I look around. Julia is clearly pissed. Her mother's expression is neutral. Though Sam is standing a bit to the side, he clearly heard the conversation because he looks grimly satisfied.

It's interesting to contemplate the fact that in this room, everyone could be doing what I'm doing right now, at any time. Are people watching me frozen as they do so? It's hard to imagine myself standing there, not moving, not thinking, as someone else goes about his or her business while I'm none the wiser.

Shelving these thoughts for later, I touch Eugene's forearm.

"What do we do now?" I ask him when he joins me in the Quiet. "That was a huge flop."

"I don't know what to say," Eugene says. "I didn't really have a clear plan."

"This Julia, how do you know her? She seems to be sympathetic."

"We had a class together in college. Then, for some reason, she agreed to date me." He smiles ruefully. "But when her father found out my status, he freaked out. He's very traditional."

"And this is supposed to be more open-minded than Russia?"

"That I'm alive is testament to that," Eugene says. "I thought we might have a chance at getting help here because Jacob hates Pushers more than anyone. Under normal circumstances, anyone even remotely in trouble with Pushers automatically becomes an 'enemy of his enemy' kind of friend."

"Except you," I say, looking at him.

"Right. I think my history with Julia hurt our chances. The problem is, this is Mira's life on the line, not mine."

"If you don't mind, I want to talk to Julia some more," I say, unwilling to give up.

"Go ahead," he says. He looks over at her, his face drawn. There's something in his eyes, in the way he watches her, that tells me he's far from over her. Then he shakes his head, looking away. "I'm not sure if it's going to help, though."

Instead of arguing, I walk over to her and pull her in.

"Darren." She smiles at me. "I was about to Split to talk to the two of you. It looks like you beat me to it."

"It's funny how that works," Eugene says. "I have this time-slicing algorithm I developed that simulates—"

"Eugene, I'm so sorry about my dad," Julia interrupts him gently. My guess is that she wanted to stop a science diatribe. I suspect it's not the first time she's done this. "Let's talk about what we can do for Mira, if you don't mind."

"After the conversation with your dad, I thought you wouldn't be able to do anything to help," Eugene responds, science forgotten as worry shadows his face again.

"I'm going with you," she says. "Together, we'll get her out of whatever trouble she's in."

"No," Eugene protests. "That would be too dangerous—"

"I'm doing this." She gives him a steely look. "I've had enough of people telling me what to do."

"No, Julia, I don't mean to tell you what to do." Eugene immediately backtracks. "I just worry about you, that's all . . ."

Her icy glare warms considerably, and she takes a step toward him.

"With all due respect," I interject, "how can you help us,

Julia? This sounds like a job for someone like that." I point at motionless Caleb.

"I'm good at getting into places I shouldn't—picking locks, that kind of thing," Julia says, turning to look at me. "It's a skill that could come in handy in exactly the type of mission I imagine this will become. But you're right, we need Caleb or one of his people. We have to convince him to help without my dad's orders."

"How do we do that?" Eugene asks.

"Can we pay him?" I suggest. With the stock options I got at the gym, money will soon be easy to come by. Even easier than it usually has been for me.

"If you're talking about money, it won't work," Julia says. "But there are other forms of payment."

"What are you suggesting?" Eugene looks puzzled.

"Nothing sinister." Julia grins. "You see, your friend Darren seems to have impressed Caleb. Actually, he impressed both of us with his Reading Depth."

"Oh?" Eugene says, and I recall that this is a sensitive subject for these people. Something like asking about the size of someone's paycheck or his package were the analogies used, I think.

"What does my Reading Depth have to do with Caleb?" I ask.

"Caleb is obsessed with improving his fighting skills," Julia says. "He's already rumored to be the best fighter among the Readers. Still, he's always looking to get better."

"I'm not going to fight him, if that's what you're about to offer," I say, shuddering. I'm not a fan of violence, plus I'm not suicidal. The guy will probably kill me before I get a single punch in.

Julia laughs. If she weren't laughing at my expense, I would say her laugh was nice. In general, she's a very pretty girl. I can see why Eugene likes her, and I can tell that he truly does. I'm less clear why the reverse is true, but it must be, as I catch her giving him decidedly warm glances. It's weird—I always thought geeky types like Eugene didn't do well with women. Of course, this is based solely on my friend Bert, which isn't exactly a valid statistical sample.

"No, Darren, thank you for offering, but I'm not asking you to fight Caleb," she says, still having a hard time keeping a straight face. I'm insulted. How does she know I'm not secretly some Kung Fu master?

"You have an amazing Reading Depth," she continues. "You can offer to take him into the mind of some famous fighters. I suspect he would find the idea intriguing."

Eugene looks from me to her uncomfortably. "But—"

"Eugene, please, I'm trying to help save your sister," Julia interrupts, and Eugene falls silent, his expression smoothing out.

"Can someone actually do that? Bring another person into someone else's mind?" I ask, wondering what Eugene had been about to say. He'd seemed worried about something for a moment.

"Yes," she says, "absolutely. It depletes your power even faster than pulling someone in, but from what I saw, you won't have a problem with that."

"Why can't Caleb do this himself?" I ask. "Why can't he Read some fighter's mind on his own?"

"For all his fighting prowess, Caleb isn't very powerful when it comes to matters of the Mind Dimension," Julia explains. "He can't go back very far at all with his Reading, and he can't do it very often, which is exactly why such an opportunity might appeal to him."

I consider questioning her further to figure out what made Eugene uncomfortable, but then I decide against it. "Fine, I'll do it," I say instead. I can't see any other way to help Mira at the moment, and I find the idea of doing this fighter Reading thing rather intriguing. If Caleb is doing it to get better at fighting, does it mean that by joining him, I could get better, too? Or, more accurately, will I actually learn how to fight as a result of this?

"Great, Eugene, let's go so they can have some privacy," Julia says, grabbing his arm and pulling him back toward their frozen bodies.

"I don't know how to thank you for this, Darren," Eugene says on his way to his frozen body, and I shrug in response, still unsure what the big deal is.

As soon as they phase out, I walk up to Caleb and pull him in.

"Darren," he says with a smirk. "To what do I owe the honor of being pulled into your own personal Mind Dimension?"

"Julia said you might be able to help us, for a price," I begin, and Caleb laughs.

"Did she now? And what did Julia think would be my price?" His grin reminds me of a hungry shark.

"She said you like fighting, in all its forms," I say, hoping I don't sound crazy. "She said I can take you into the mind of a couple of fighters as payment."

"Interesting," he says, crossing his arms. "And did she say anything else?"

"No, just that."

"You really did just learn how to Read yesterday, didn't you,

Darren?" he says, still grinning. "What Julia 'forgot' to mention to you is that very few Readers would agree to offer me this kind of deal."

"Why?" I ask, wondering if I'm about to learn the reason for Eugene's concern.

"Because it's considered a private, almost intimate experience to pull someone else into a Reading," Caleb says, his grin fading. "You get glimpses of the other Reader's mind, and vice versa."

"Oh." I try to keep my jaw from dropping. "What does that feel like?"

"I only did it once," he says, completely serious now. "But that time, it was incredible."

I stare at him for a moment, then shrug. "I don't care," I say. "To save Mira, I'll do it. I'll let you get inside the heads of a couple of people of your choice."

Caleb looks like a happy shark again. "We have a deal then," he says, smiling widely. "I'll let you know whose minds I choose."

Why do I feel like I did something reckless just now?

"Oh, don't make the long face," he says, apparently sensing my sudden unease. "I promise not to deplete your Depth. We both know you can go back very far, so getting to see a few fights shouldn't be a problem at all. We won't see how these men began their careers, only something fairly recent."

"Okay, sure." I decide to worry about it later.

"Good. Now pull Eugene and Julia back in."

I do as he says.

"Here's the plan, people," Caleb barks, taking control of the situation. "Eugene and Darren will leave, looking exceedingly disappointed. Julia, I'll meet you in the parking lot after I get the supplies I'm going to need. We'll pick you gentlemen up on Emmons Avenue."

"Who else is coming with us?" Julia asks. "Not Sam, I presume?"

"You presume correctly," Caleb says. "It will be just me."

"Just you?" Julia frowns.

"Oh, ye of little faith." Caleb smirks at her. "One of me is probably overkill for this mission."

"Yeah, yeah," she says. "I don't doubt your machismo, Caleb; I just want the girl to survive the rescue."

"She will," Caleb assures her. "You have my word on that."

"Okay, then let's get back to our real lives," Julia says.

"Hold up. Darren, there's something you should know," Caleb says, turning toward me. "I've known Mira for a while. She's a good kid. I was going to offer to help Eugene anyway—especially since I knew Julia would do something reckless, and Jacob would hold me liable for her actions regardless of my involvement. Not to mention, I like a good skirmish."

"So I didn't need to agree to this deal?" I say dryly, and he shakes his head.

"Nope. You didn't. But a deal is a deal." He winks at me. "I'm really looking forward to all this."

Leaving the community with apparent dejection, Eugene and I make our way to Emmons Avenue, to the exact place where we caused the last car crash. There are still bits of plastic and glass on the asphalt, but the broken cars have apparently been towed.

I'm deep in thought, trying to understand how I got involved in all this craziness.

"Darren, about taking Caleb into someone's mind," Eugene breaks the silence.

"He already told me; you see into each other's minds," I tell him.

"Oh, good. I'm surprised Caleb was so honest," Eugene says with relief. "Julia should've warned you. She can be kind of ruthless when it comes to getting what she wants."

Before I can reply, we're interrupted by a loud car honk. It's a Hummer—occupied by Caleb and Julia.

Of course Caleb drives a Hummer, I think as I get in.

"Give me that address, Darren. We have a damsel in distress," Caleb says.

I give him the address, and he sets his GPS to the location. With a roar, the Hummer is off, moving through the streets of Brooklyn like a tank.

21

We park in a Costco lot in Sunset Park.

According to Google Maps, the place where they're keeping Mira is an industrial warehouse. What these guys are doing so far from Brighton Beach, none of us have a clue. Brighton Beach is where the Russian Mafia is supposed to be headquartered, according to Eugene. I hope that this actually plays to our advantage. If they do call for reinforcements, it's a twenty-minute drive without traffic, according to Julia's phone. Of course, that assumes the reinforcements are on Brighton Beach, and—this is a big one—that they're going to need reinforcements against the four of us.

Caleb jumps out of his seat and starts rummaging through the trunk of the Hummer.

"Are we shopping for supplies?" I ask, looking in the direction of the huge store. I'm only half-joking.

"I have everything I need," Julia says, hanging a messenger bag over her shoulder.

"They don't sell the type of stuff I need in Costco," Caleb responds, putting what has to be a rifle in a special carry case over his shoulder. "At least not in New York."

He puts on a vest with special pockets and straps the huge knife I saw previously to it, along with a couple of handguns.

"This is for you," Caleb says, handing me a gun.

The seriousness of the situation hits me again. We're going against armed criminals. Just the four of us. A scientist, a girl whose toughness I haven't fully determined yet, and, let's face it, a financial analyst. Caleb is the only person even remotely qualified for this rescue. Despite his unshakable confidence, the odds don't seem right to me.

Not to mention, the people holding Mira have an ace up their sleeve: a hostage.

All we have is our unusual skill set.

Caleb clearly has a plan, though. He leads us to an abandoned warehouse located a short distance from where we parked.

We walk up to the top floor, and Caleb methodically unzips his gun case and starts setting up. The gun is huge and looks very professional—complete with scope and silencer. I wonder if this is what he used to gun down our pursuers earlier. Eugene and Julia, who have been silent for some time, exchange impressed looks. Eugene seems grimly determined, while Julia looks thoughtful.

I gaze around the room we've found ourselves in. It's dusty and dark, despite large, floor-to-ceiling windows—probably because said windows are yellow and covered with grime. Caleb opens one of those windows, lies down on the floor, and aims the huge gun at the industrial warehouse across the street. Then he says curtly, "All right, Darren, pull us in."

I leverage my natural anxiety over what's about to happen and quickly phase into the Quiet. Then I touch everyone in turn, pulling them in.

Once we're all in, we walk down the stairs and cross the road. This part of Brooklyn is so abandoned that being in the Quiet doesn't seem like much of a change. At least not until we cross the road, and Caleb breaks the door with a series of kicks. Even in a scarcely populated area like this, such bold breaking and entering might've gotten us noticed and reported, if it took place in the real world.

"You know, I could've picked that lock," Julia says, looking at what's left of the door on the ground.

"You'll get your chance," Caleb tells her as he walks into the building.

We walk through the door and find ourselves in a large open space. There are a bunch of guys frozen in the process of walking around. They all have guns. Caleb walks between the guys and the windows, looking intently at the building we came from.

His plan is beginning to dawn on me.

He's figuring out how to shoot them from our location across the street. He's triangulating his shots; as soon as we phase back out, he'll shoot.

I'll have to remember to never piss off Caleb.

"Where's Mira?" Eugene asks after examining the hangar.

"Try Reading them," Caleb says without turning. "We need to figure that out, because once we get back to the real world, the information will be lost."

Right. Because you can't Read dead men. A chill skitters across my spine. Caleb is too calm about it. Too poised. His coldness makes me uneasy. I wonder if I, personally, am capable of killing. Even if it's an enemy. Even in self-defense. I don't know, and I hope I don't find out today.

For my Reading target, I choose a big guy near one of the columns. He must be on steroids or growth hormones—or both. Though he's my height, he must be at least two hundred pounds heavier than I am. Being that he's Russian, I wonder if he's trying to look like a bear. He's closer to a gorilla. I catch myself hoping that Caleb doesn't miss this specific dude with his rifle. We wouldn't want to face him in anything but a gunfight.

Putting my hand on his gigantic forehead, I jump in a few hours ago.

We see Mira playing cards with Vasiliy. There is one other guy in the room with her.

"Na huy ti s ney igrayesh?" we say. As usual I, Darren, marvel at understanding this. He, Lenya, was asking a question about why his idiot bro is playing cards with the hostage. Playing cards with a girl who is a renowned card cheat.

He, Lenya, is picturing what he would do with the hostage. We see images of Mira tied up and abused. I, Darren, distance myself almost instantly and nearly puke—though this is not easy to do in my current position. Can you vomit mentally? This almost makes me want to jump out of this asshole's head, it's so sick. I also feel an instinctive need to protect Mira from ever coming near this guy. I feel dirty. The best way to describe the experience is it's as if I'm dreaming of being this scumbag. I am rethinking my earlier squeamishness toward killing.

I shouldn't jump out, however, as he's about to give me key information. I try to focus on what the guy's body is experiencing—an ache from yesterday's workout, soreness in the knuckles from punching someone, anything except those sick rape fantasies. This approach is flawed, though, because focusing on his body makes me realize he's getting turned on from these disgusting thoughts. Thankfully, before I'm forced out of his head from sheer horror, he refocuses on what he should be doing. And that is locking the door in front of him from the outside.

We lock the door, mentally praising Tolik, who is also in the room. At least he has his gun next to him, and isn't letting the bitch distract him. He also forbade untying her legs from the chair. Tolik will keep Vasiliy in check.

We walk out into the corridor and through a maze of concrete hallways until we reach the stairs. Then we go down to the main hall, where the rest of the guards are.

I, Darren, now know where Mira is being held.

I almost jump out, but I decide to try to go even deeper. I want to know who told this guy to lock the door from the outside. That's very specific. Whoever came up with that could've been trying to limit Mira's range of motion in the Quiet—and thus might be the Pusher fuck behind all this.

I jump further.

We're sitting in a banya. I, Darren, learn that a banya is a Russian spa—a bit like a sauna, but much hotter. Given how we, I mean he, feels when in there, it sounds like something I should check out.

I go further still, jumping around scenes from this goon's life.

Aha.

"Keep those doors closed," Piotr says. We look at Piotr and wonder who the fuck he is to be giving orders around here.

I, Darren, realize with disappointment that Piotr is another Russian I saw in the very room we're in now.

I jump out of Lenya's head.

"Darren, let's go," Caleb says as soon as I'm conscious of being myself again.

"Give me a minute," I respond. "I need to check that guy." I point at Piotr, sitting at a desk.

"Hurry," Caleb says.

I walk up to the guy. He looks a tiny bit more intelligent than the one whose mind I was in a moment ago. I place my hand on his forehead.

I'm in, but I don't know where to start. Intuitively I jump around scenes from this guy's life until I find it.

We're watching boxing on TV when another mind enters. Time stops; now there are more of us in his head.

I understand that the guy himself wouldn't have felt the Pusher enter his mind. Apparently people don't consciously notice either us or them when we do our thing. But I am very much aware of it. It's like a ghostly presence. And as I keep Reading, the Pusher begins to give instructions.

'Instructions' is a poor word for it, but I can't think of a better one. In reality, they're almost like experiences the Pusher inserts into the guy's mind. Like the reverse of Reading. The

Pusher inserts experiences and reactions to them. How this will ensure the guy does what he's supposed to, I don't know, but it must work. To me, it feels a little bit like a very detailed story of what Piotr should experience when the time is right.

The experience in this case is pretty simple. 'Pick up the phone' is the first step. The Pusher seems to almost play out a fake memory for his target. Every detail of how it would be to pick up the phone is considered: which hand, the weight of the phone in his hand, and so on.

Next comes the instruction: 'Text all the trusted people with a request to meet at Tatyana Restaurant in an hour.'

Finally, Piotr is instructed to get up and go there himself.

After that, the Pusher's presence disappears. Based purely on the person's presence in this mind, I can't tell whether it was male or female. To my disappointment, whoever it was never came into physical contact with Piotr.

I Read Piotr's mind a little longer. I'm curious what he'll recall of the Pusher influence. As I expected, he remembers nothing. He arrives at the restaurant, slightly amused. *Isn't it strange how sometimes you drive someplace, but don't even remember the driving process?* he thinks.

It seems like the Pusher's influence has caused a mild memory lapse in the target's mind, but overall Piotr acts as though of his own volition. It's interesting to watch how he rationalizes his actions as happening of his own choosing and his memory lapse as one of those times when the conscious mind goes on autopilot and the subconscious takes over. The illusion of free will at its finest. It comes to me all over again how dangerous these Pushers are. Whatever they need done, all they need to do is plant the seed in someone's mind.

Mind-rape, Eugene called it. Now I understand why.

Knowing I won't get any more than this, I decide to jump out of Piotr's mind. People are waiting for me.

WHEN I'M CONSCIOUS AGAIN, CALEB IS STANDING NEXT TO ME looking like he's about to say something snide. I just head for the exit, explaining where Mira is as I move. The group follows.

"That's perfect," Caleb says when I finish my explanation. "If they're that far inside the building, they definitely won't hear my shots."

"Did any one of you Read a guy whose name was Arkady in there?" I ask. No one responds, so I assume they haven't.

We return to the room across the street, on the top floor near the window. Our frozen bodies are hunched near Caleb, who's lying on the floor with his eye to the scope of his rifle. I touch my forehead.

As soon as the phase-out process is complete, Caleb fires the first shot.

Then another.

Then another.

I lose count of the shots, as I'm more focused on plugging my ears. In the movies, silencers work much better than in real life. Despite the elongated device on the end of the barrel of Caleb's rifle, the noise is deafening in this room. I hope the area is abandoned enough that no one hears the shots—or if they do and call the cops, we're out of here before they arrive.

His shooting done, Caleb pushes off the floor to a standing position.

"Now things should go more smoothly in there," he says,

picking up his gun. Wiping down his prints, he leaves the rifle behind and heads for the stairs.

We follow him all the way down to the ground level of the building we've just fired the shots from.

"Darren, take us into the Mind Dimension again," Caleb orders before we exit to the street. "We need to assess the situation."

"Okay, Sergeant," Julia says sarcastically. "Before we go running around again, can you please tell us the plan?"

"The plan will become clearer after we reconnoiter," Caleb says curtly. "The only thing I can tell you now is that with two armed guards in the room with Mira, stealth is of utmost importance. If I were them, I'd shoot the hostage as soon as I caught wind that some shit was going down."

Eugene looks pale, and a shudder runs through me. Without further ado, I phase into the Quiet once again and get everyone to join me.

We cross the street. I'm getting a sense of déjà vu. The door is locked again, which of course makes sense, but is no less annoying.

"Now you can practice picking the lock," Caleb says to Julia. "We want to be in as quickly as we can."

She goes inside her messenger bag and takes out what I assume are the instruments of a professional burglar. I wonder where she learned to do this. Her people seem too ritzy for thieving.

She struggles with the door for only a minute before we're in.

"Will you be able to do this faster when we actually get here?" Caleb asks.

"Yes. I can get it down to twenty seconds," she says.

We enter the hangar we inspected before. Though I'm not surprised by what I see, my gag reflex kicks in, and I barely hold back vomit.

They're all dead. Shot in the head, every single one of them. There's blood, lots of blood everywhere. Though it's my second time seeing a scene like this today, it's not in any way less disturbing.

Julia looks green too, making me feel a bit better about my own sorry state.

Caleb steps over the bodies in his way and just waltzes to the stairs. We gingerly follow, trying to keep our eyes off the dead people.

After a few flights of stairs, we reach a floor that appears to be the one we're searching for. We follow Caleb into the maze of corridors, which, according to Lenya's—the disgusting gorilla's—memories, leads to the room where Mira is held.

There's a guy standing with his back to us at a bend in the corridor, looking toward the door. Another is standing by the door, looking at the hallway. This means there's no way for Mira to come out of the room, nor for us to turn the corner without one of these men raising an alarm. Not good.

"Okay," Caleb says. "We'll need to take these two guards out. Darren, Eugene, this one is yours," he says, pointing at the guy with his back toward us.

"Ours?" Eugene appears confused.

"You need to overpower him," Caleb explains with a sharp smile. "Silently, so the two guards with Mira don't hear us coming."

Caleb is enjoying this, I realize. Eugene must've acted arrogantly toward him in the past, or maybe Caleb is just a sadistic prick. Whatever the case, Caleb is clearly trying to shock the guy. Or is it my buttons he's trying to push?

"I can turn the corner and quickly grab the guy. When he can't move, you stab him," I propose, looking at Eugene.

"Good plan," Caleb says, glancing at me with approval. "I have some extra knives for you gentlemen."

Eugene doesn't seem as hesitant as I would expect at the prospect of stabbing someone. Have I misjudged him? After all, just because someone is a little geeky doesn't mean he can't be tough. Or score a hottie like Julia, I remind myself.

"What are *you* going to do?" Julia challenges Caleb.

"I'll take care of that one," Caleb responds, nodding toward the guy facing us.

"Wait—won't he shoot you as soon as you turn this corner?" Eugene asks. I know he's walking into some sort of smart-ass remark from Caleb.

Instead of answering, Caleb walks back into the hall leading to this turn. Then he pointedly turns the corner. In a blur of motion, the knife is in his hand; the next moment, after a lightning-fast throw, it's in the second guy's chest.

Show-off.

"Any more questions?" Caleb asks. No one responds. "In that case, Julia, see how fast and how quietly you can pick that lock."

Julia takes out her tools and does her thing. It takes her about a minute.

"That won't work," Caleb says when she's done. "But we'll get back to that in a moment."

Without waiting for an invitation, we all barge into the room.

The room still looks like I remember it. Or more accurately, how the now-dead Lenya—the gorilla—remembered it.

It was originally meant to be some kind of storage room. There are no windows, and the walls are painted a dull white color. In some places, the paint is chipping away.

Just like in the memory I obtained, there's a guy with a gun near him, though now he seems to be playing with his phone. It's a little odd, since his phone has a pink case. Just like before, there is Mira, tied to the chair, playing cards with another guard. Only unlike before, they're all frozen in the midst of their activities.

I walk up to Mira and touch her forehead.

As soon as she phases in, her eyes look like they're about to jump out of their sockets. She has an expression on her face I don't recognize. Then I get it—I've never seen her this genuinely happy to see me before. Her eyes scan the room, and she sees Eugene. Her face lights up.

"You did it," she says, turning toward me, and I hear the joy and disbelief in her voice. "You saved him. I don't know how I can thank you."

"I said I would," I say, trying not to think of all the ways I'd want Mira to express her gratitude. For the first time in my life, I understand the motivations of those hero types. For a fleeting moment, I feel like I really did something important. Something impressive. It's a great feeling.

"But what are you doing here?" she says, her expression changing as she fully registers the situation.

"What does it look like?" Caleb says. "We're rescuing you."

"In that case, why did you bring Eugene?" She looks at me like I'm an idiot, and all my heroic feelings deflate. Like I could've stopped a brother from trying to save his little sister?

"It's too dangerous," she says, turning toward Eugene. "You shouldn't have come." She looks from Caleb to Julia to me.

Then at the corridor through the open door. "This is all of you?" she asks, her shoulders slumping.

"It's going to be enough," Caleb says.

She shakes her head. "This is going to be impossible." She doesn't wait for anyone to respond before she walks out of the room. She must not realize that we—well, Caleb—already took out the lion's share of her captors.

"As friendly as ever," Caleb says, giving me a wink. "Julia, go out and then lock and unlock this door again. Try to do it quicker and quieter this time."

We stay in the room to judge Julia's work. After the initial click of the lock, the rest of the stuff she does is pretty subtle, but still audible if you know what to listen for. She seems to finish faster this time.

Caleb waves at us to follow him and walks out of the room —to follow Mira, I presume.

"Do it ten more times," he says to Julia on the way out.

The three of us try to find Mira. We walk a couple of floors up. Everything seems abandoned. We find Mira on the seventh floor, punching the wall in frustration.

"What is it?" Eugene asks her.

"That fuck isn't here," she says, punching the wall again.

"Who?" Eugene says.

"The Pusher. The one behind all this. That chicken shit's not here. That was my main hope, the only silver lining to this. I thought he'd be overseeing the whole thing."

"I Read a mind earlier," I say. "The Pusher who influenced that mind was very careful to avoid revealing himself to his target."

"Then this is pointless. You guys should go back and wait. Maybe he'll show up eventually," she says.

"That's not happening," Caleb says, standing between her and the wall she's been punching. "Here is what *is* happening. You'll try to be as loud as possible as soon as you hear any funny sounds coming from outside your door. Talk loudly, ask questions—or even better, fall from your chair. That would distract them *and* get you out of harm's way."

"Yeah, yeah, don't try to teach a fish how to swim," she mutters. Then she takes a deep breath and glances at Eugene before turning her attention back to Caleb. "Look, even with those dead bodies I just saw downstairs, busting in here is going to be dangerous," she says in a more even tone. "Promise me that Eugene won't take part in this. They took me to smoke him out in the first place, so if you bring him, you'll be playing right into their hands."

"Yes, so he told us. We have a deal," Caleb says before Eugene starts protesting. "I won't force Eugene to come with us."

Mira gives him a disbelieving look, but seems a bit calmer as we make our way back to the room. I get the feeling that there's definite history between Mira and Caleb. I don't like it, not one bit. Though it can't be romantic, can it? He's a little too old for her, and he called her 'kid.' Maybe it's a bond between two kindred, sarcastic, pain-in-the-ass spirits?

When we rejoin her, Julia is still diligently practicing unlocking that lock.

Upon Caleb's request, she does a final run, which is extremely quick. She's way faster and much quieter than she was before. For the first time, I'm beginning to think we can pull this off.

"So what's the exact plan?" I ask.

"While Julia works on the door, Mira falls on the floor with her chair. Then I shoot these two," Caleb says, pointing his index finger in a gun motion at the two frozen guards.

"I'm not sure I can fall like that," Mira says, looking at her frozen self. Her hands are free, but her legs are duct-taped to her chair.

"We'll just have to practice that part as well," Caleb says, his eyes crinkling in the corners. I get the feeling he's going to enjoy this part, too.

"You want to tie me to a chair so I practice falling?" Mira says. She doesn't look happy.

"Exactly." Caleb grins. "See, Eugene, you're not the smartest one in the family."

Eugene and I free the frozen Mira from the chair and place her limp body gently in the corner of the room. I accidentally touch her exposed skin, but nothing happens. I guess once we pulled one Mira into the Quiet, touching her frozen self doesn't produce more Miras. It would have been kind of cool if it did.

Mira sits down in the chair and, muttering something in Russian under her breath, grudgingly allows us to tape up her legs with the duct tape her guards left lying around. She's now set up exactly as her frozen self was a few minutes ago.

She leans her body to the right, but the chair doesn't fall. She shakes it back and forth, and slowly, almost grudgingly, the chair falls over.

"Are you okay, sis?" Eugene asks her.

"Yes. Pick me up," she says, trying to push herself off the floor. Her position looks extremely uncomfortable.

"That was too slow," Caleb says. "Try again."

I get up and walk over to a dingy couch standing in the furthest corner of the room. I take the cushions from it, and lay them on either side of Mira. No point for this to hurt more than it already must.

"Thanks, Darren," she says before she begins shaking the chair again.

The cushions help, but it's clearly an unpleasant practice. She does it again and again over the course of about twenty minutes. We try to give tips—which are usually met with disdain.

Eventually Caleb decides she won't be able to improve further.

About five seconds to fall over is the best she can do.

"We need a different strategy to distract them," I say. "Besides falling, I think you should also start yelling. Scream 'mouse' or 'spider' at the critical moment and start waving your arms, acting like you're freaking out right before you fall."

Julia chuckles. Mira gives me a deadly glare. Caleb is about to say something, but Eugene shakes his head at him behind Mira's back. He must actually think it's a good idea.

"Just do it, sis," Eugene tells Mira. "It won't be the first time. Remember when you jumped on the table—"

"Don't say another fucking word," Mira interrupts him. "I'll do it."

And before her brother has a chance to say anything more, she quickly walks up to her own frozen body—which is now lying on the floor—and touches that version of herself on the cheek. That makes her phase out, and she's no longer in our company.

Only the Mira on the floor remains.

"But I was about to ask her to practice the new strategy," Caleb says with visible disappointment.

I can't help myself. I burst out laughing.

"This is a pretty serious situation, guys," Eugene says, but I can tell he's trying his best to suppress a smile. Despite the danger we're in—or maybe because of it—everyone finds the idea of Mira freaking out like that hilarious. Then again, Eugene implied that she's acted like this before. Maybe when she was little? It's hard to picture it now. I wish I could Read Eugene's or Mira's mind.

We exit the room. Caleb holds the door for everyone, making me wonder why he's being such a gentlemen all of a sudden. As soon as we're all out of the room, I find out.

He's decided to do a little practice on his own.

All I hear is a quiet rustling of clothing, and the next moment Caleb is holding two guns, one in each hand. Two shots fire at the same time. Two men in the room each have a bullet in their head.

I begin to feel even more confident about the success of this mission.

We walk back to our bodies and phase out.

"Any last words?" Caleb says to us all.

"I'm coming with you," Eugene says, his voice filled with determination.

"Of course," Caleb says. "I said I wouldn't force you. But if you volunteer, well, that's a different matter." He hands Eugene a knife. "You're in charge of stabbing the guy in the corridor, remember?"

I get a knife as well. *Great.* As though the gun I was given earlier wasn't bad enough.

We cross the street, for real now. The area is pretty dead, yet it seems infinitely more alive now than when we crossed this road in the Quiet—mainly because all the ambient noises of

Brooklyn are back. With the increase in noise, my adrenaline levels go up as well.

Julia picks the lock on the front door in twenty seconds—just as she said she would. So far, so good. We walk through the hangar. My heart rate becomes a tiny bit calmer. This part isn't all that different from the version in the Quiet. The heavy walls block most of the sounds of the city. The dead men are just as frozen in death here as they were in the Quiet.

"Situation check," Caleb whispers when we're near the stairs.

I phase in, and pull everyone else in with me. We walk up the stairs until we get to the corridor and turn the corner again. In the few minutes it took us to walk across the street and through the hangar, the men have not moved; they stand in pretty much the same positions.

"Good," Caleb says. "We'll do another check, right before turning the corner. This will be my signal." He gives us a thumbs-up sign. Not the most imaginative signal, but it gets the point across.

We walk back and phase out. Now we finally get to make the trip up the stairs in the real world.

We all try to make our walk stealthy, but only Caleb succeeds. We get to the corner, and he does his thumbs-up sign. I phase in and pull them all in again. The men are still standing as they were.

"Are you ready?" Caleb says, looking from me to Eugene.

"Ready," I say.

"Let's get this over with," Eugene says.

I notice Caleb never asked to rehearse this part. I bet I know why: he realizes that if given enough information, Eugene might lose his nerve. Or maybe he thinks I'll lose mine.

We phase out. Everyone looks at me expectantly. I take a deep breath and turn the corner.

My heart is racing a hundred miles per hour, but I ignore it and grab the now-very-familiar Russian as soon as I turn the corner, placing my hand over his mouth to muffle his scream. I hold him as tightly as I can, but he struggles and I know there's very little time.

Out of the corner of my eye, I see Caleb make his move. I can't afford to pay attention to him, though.

I rotate my body, and Eugene is there with the knife. It's unclear if he jabs the guy with it, or if I push the guy onto the knife myself. However, it's quickly clear that it's done—the knife is there, in the man's stomach.

He makes a horrible grunting sound. My own stomach heaves, but I hang tight.

The grunt is echoed by the sounds of another wounded guard—the one Caleb must've thrown the knife at.

The guy I'm holding stops struggling, and I feel him going limp. I don't want to think about what that implies as I let him slide to the floor. Eugene looks pale as he steps back, dropping his knife on the ground.

Caleb is next to the guy by the door already and is holding the man's throat in a tight grip, blocking off air and preventing further sounds.

Julia begins to pick the lock on the door. I walk toward her and Caleb, trying to avoid looking at all the blood.

I hear faint screams inside the room. Mira must have started her performance.

Caleb eases the now-limp body to the floor.

I focus on the good things. The plan is going smoothly.

I try not to think of the gruesome parts.

Not surprisingly, there's a difference between stabbing people in the Quiet and seeing it done in real life. Blood flows. People actually die. The difference is huge. I can also actually throw up in the real world, an urge I fight with all my strength.

Julia is done with the door and looks at Eugene in triumph.

In a split second, her face changes—dread contorting her features. Her fright is contagious. Instantly I turn, so I can see what she sees.

Eugene is still standing next to the man he stabbed, but what he's not seeing, because he's looking away, is that the guy isn't dead, like we thought. He's lying on the floor and holding a gun aimed at us.

Before I can even digest the image in front of me, there is a shot.

It's the loudest thing I've ever heard. It's like my ears explode. Like the most intense thunder you could ever imagine.

Everything seems to slow, and then goes quiet. A very familiar kind of quiet. I realize that I phased in without consciously trying. Near-death experiences are becoming a habit today.

In the safety of the frozen world, I look around. There is a bloody circle on Julia's left shoulder. Her face is frozen in shock. Despite myself, I'm relieved. Though she's clearly been shot, even without being a doctor I know that shoulder wounds are rarely fatal. The real reason for my relief, however, is that my own frozen body is unscathed.

The biggest surprise is Caleb, who I thought was still in the process of laying the dead guard on the ground. In the time it took me to phase into the Quiet, he's already holding a gun. And the gun has smoke around its muzzle. He must've managed to take it out and shoot, almost as soon as the other shot was fired. Or maybe he saw it coming? Maybe he was phasing in every second, assessing the situation around us—something I now realize I should've been doing. Still, Caleb's speed is astounding.

The most incredible part is that I can actually see the bullet. It's a few inches away from the shooter's head.

With dread, I open the door into the room with Mira.

It's bad.

The guy who was playing cards with her is now standing. He's trying to get out of the way of his partner—the more suspicious guard, who's now pointing his gun down at Mira. She, with her chair, is lying on her side on the floor. She completed the difficult maneuver, as we'd planned. Only now it might be for nothing. The noise of the gunshots ruined everything.

I get closer to the suspicious guard and inspect the situation. The muscles in his wrist are taut. He looks like he's about to pull the trigger.

I refuse to accept this.

I touch his forehead.

We're still contemplating what to say in the text to the hostage's brother, whose number we located in the girl's pink phone, when we hear the shots outside the room.

Someone must be trying to free the hostage. Unbelievable. What idiot would even try something so stupid?

We know we need to follow orders, which were very explicit on this. Arkady made us repeat them. If any shit goes down, first order of business is to shoot the girl. After that, we must deal with whoever might've come after her. If we kill her brother, we get a big bonus.

We take the gun and aim. We're pressing the trigger.

I GET OUT OF HIS HEAD. I HAVE NO DOUBT ABOUT IT NOW. HE'S shooting. In his head, I felt my—or I should say *his*—finger squeeze the trigger. His brain already sent the instructions to his arm. In a second after I phase out, a shot will fire. A shot aimed directly at Mira.

If only he was just reaching for his gun. If only his partner would trip and fall to cover her somehow. If only the door was wide open already—I'm right behind it, ready to shoot.

I want to scream. I'm ready to kill. Only it's too late.

I can't just watch Mira die. I have to do something.

Not sure why, I approach the guard who was looming over Mira. The one who was playing cards with her before. Vasiliy, I remind myself.

I touch his forehead.

WE'RE LOOKING AT THE GIRL ON THE FLOOR. WE KNOW WHAT Tolik is about to do. We feel faint regret. We think it's a shame she'll be killed. We think it's a waste of a very nice female specimen.

I, Darren, realize that this one likes Mira in his own crude way. A way that's not altogether different from the way I like her. It makes this experience odd. It also seems to push me further with what I'm trying to do.

Without fully realizing what I'm doing, I focus on his regret. On the fact that he likes her. Even on his lust for her.

I picture it growing. I picture what regretting losing someone very close to me would be like and channel it into Vasiliy. I recall wanting to fuck Mira and channel those memories into him. I recall what losing my grandmother felt like, which has nothing to do with Mira, but seems useful, so I channel that into him, too. It feels like I'm pouring my essence into him. As if for a moment, we merge into the same person.

It feels like I'm achieving something, so I continue further, almost becoming my host.

I think of Tolik. He's my best friend. If I just get in the way of the gun, he'll never shoot. He'll stop, and then I can talk to him, explain why the girl must be spared. I picture us coming up with a scheme. We tell Arkady she's dead. Tolik gets full credit and a huge bonus. She and I disappear from NYC, maybe even from the US. I picture how grateful the girl will be when she realizes she owes her life to me.

I finally picture the simple action that can make it all come together. I need to fall on top of her. From where I'm standing, it will take less than a second to just fall down.

I will feel her body under my own. I'll be her strong protector. A real man. All I need to do now is show a little courage. And then, of course, Tolik will stop. He'll never shoot me. All he needs to see is that she's important, and it will all be over . . .

As if in a trance, I feel almost pushed outside his head. I'm not sure what just happened.

I realize that in reality, there is only one thing I can do. I can open that door, and I can shoot Tolik. And hope I make it—hope I shoot him in time.

My brain screams at the impossibility of making the shot in time, so I try to hope that whatever I did inside Vasiliy's head will help.

I open the door. I push my frozen self out of the way and take his exact position. I close the door behind me.

Now, I try it in the Quiet. A test.

I open the door. My hand is steady. I shoot. His temple is red. It all takes no more than two seconds.

I'm ready. I take a breath and phase out.

I open the door for real this time. My hand is even steadier here than it was in the Quiet.

I hear the Russian's shot as I squeeze the trigger.

22

My own gun fires—but I don't hear it. I phase into the Quiet once more.

Tolik's head is frozen mid-explosion. Bits of his skull and brain are caught mid-flight toward the wall behind him. I killed him, but I don't even register that fact. Instead I focus on something else entirely—and what I see makes me feel like I'm about to burst with joy.

Vasiliy, the guy whose head I was in just a moment ago, is on top of Mira.

He took the bullet that was meant for her.

I roll him off her and see no signs of the bullet having traveled all the way through. It hit him in the right shoulder blade.

Mira is unharmed, other than some minor bruises due to falling with the chair. She hasn't been killed.

I know there is a possibility, however remote, that the bullet is still about to go through Vasiliy. I might've phased in at just the right fraction of a second to make the bullet freeze on its way out.

I run to my body and slam into myself, roughly grabbing whatever exposed skin comes my way.

I am in the real world again, hearing the sharp crack of the shot I just fired.

I rush into the room.

I ignore the sound of Tolik's body falling to the floor where I shot him. My entire focus is on Vasiliy, now crumpled on top of Mira.

He moans in pain.

She's quiet.

My heart sinks.

Tolik's shot must've reached her through Vasiliy's body.

Filled with panic, I roll him off her as fast as I can. His moans become screams at my rough treatment, but I barely notice his pain as I see Mira lying there, alive and unharmed.

Just as she was in the Quiet.

She's strangely silent, however, and I decide that she must be in shock. Feeling a tiny fraction calmer, I start cutting away the duct tape from her legs.

"You're a hero, Darren," Caleb says from the door. For the first time, I hear no sarcasm in his voice. "You should know I don't throw around compliments lightly."

"Help me untie her," I say, not knowing how to respond to that.

"Can't," he says curtly. "I need to bind Julia's shoulder."

I remember Julia's wound and I nod, continuing to work on the tape by myself. Mira still doesn't say a word. Her silence begins to worry me.

Finally, I succeed in cutting through the tape, and Mira

slowly gets to her feet, still without speaking. Then, not looking at me, she walks to the gun that fell from Tolik's hand and picks it up.

She's going to finish Vasiliy off, I realize.

But instead of pointing the gun at the injured mobster, she points it at me.

I barely have a chance to register the tears gleaming in her eyes and the shaking of her hand before I instinctively phase into the Quiet.

Battling my shock and disbelief, I approach her and brush my fingers against her frozen cheek, determined to understand her strange behavior.

Instantly a moving Mira joins me in the Quiet. She wipes the tears from her eyes, looking around the room, and as her gaze lands on me, the expression on her face turns to fury. Stepping toward me, she slaps my face, the way wives do to cheating husbands in movies. Then she punches me in the stomach.

I'm stunned. What the hell is she doing?

"You fucking Pusher!" she says through clenched teeth. "Don't you ever come near me again!"

Before I can react, she turns around and touches her frozen self.

Numb, I look at my own self standing in front of her gun. His face looks more confused than it did on the day I first discovered being able to 'stop time.'

I now know what upset her so much.

I now understand what I did to Vasiliy.

Mira must've phased in after the shots went down. She must've Read Vasiliy. She must've seen the telltale signs of what happened in his mind.

Signs similar to what I saw earlier in Piotr's mind.

Signs of what I refused to really think about, until now.

I *made* Vasiliy protect her with his body.

I made him fall.

I overrode his free will.

I *pushed* him.

I'm what she hates most in the world.

A Pusher.

I touch my confused self on the forehead.

I am back in the real world, with Mira's gun in my face. It's shaking more than it did before.

Is this really how it's going to end? Is she going to kill me? I'm so numb that I just stand there, waiting for it.

But no. She slowly lowers the gun. Then, hurrying over to Tolik's dead body, she picks up her pink phone from the table next to him and runs out of the room.

Finally shaking off my strange numbness, I run after her.

"What the fuck was that?" Caleb yells after me, but I don't have time to explain.

I keep running after her, gaining speed, but she's fast. After chasing her down a couple of flights of stairs, I slow down and then stop. Even if I catch her, I have no idea what I'll say.

Feeling exhausted all of a sudden, I go back and rejoin Eugene and Caleb, who seem very confused. Julia is bleeding, her face deathly pale, and Eugene is hovering next to her. His face is almost as pale as hers.

"What's going on?" Caleb asks, frowning at me.

"Don't ask," I say. "Please."

"Is Mira okay?" he persists.

"I think she is, yes," I answer wearily. "I mean, she's not hurt —physically, at least."

"Fine. Then help me," Caleb says. He gives Eugene the keys and tells us to get the car. Meanwhile, he picks Julia up like she weighs nothing, and starts down the stairs. Everything seems to happen in a haze.

Eugene and I get the car in silence. He looks back toward Caleb and Julia once, then looks around, probably hoping to spot Mira. She's nowhere to be seen, but we find the car in the Costco parking lot, where we left it. I drive to the curb, pull up, and Caleb carefully puts Julia in the back. Caleb reclaims the driver's seat, while I ride shotgun. Eugene gets in the back with Julia. I hear them talking quietly, but make out only her repeated insistence that she's fine.

In five minutes, we're parked at the Lutheran Medical Center. Caleb gets out as soon as the car's stopped. He leans in Julia's window. "You holding up okay?"

"Fine," she says. "Really. I'm okay." She doesn't look okay—she looks like she's about to pass out. Eugene doesn't look much better.

"I'll be right back," Caleb says. "Give me a minute."

As soon as he's gone, I hear the sound of Eugene's text alert go off. I don't know why, but the sound alone fills me with dread.

"Darren," Eugene says after a few seconds. "Mira just texted me. She's on her way here on foot. She says she wants you gone when she arrives."

I don't know what to say. "Okay. I'll go then."

"What happened?" Eugene asks, his face the very definition of confused.

"Talk to Mira," I say tiredly. "Please don't make me explain."

We share an uncomfortable silence. Through the haze surrounding me, I'm aware of Caleb returning a few minutes later with a wheelchair for Julia. How did he get one so quickly? Did he show his gun to someone in the hospital? Surely not, or security would be right behind him, I reason dazedly.

Caleb says something to Eugene and sends him on his way with Julia. Something about making sure she's okay and about being back once he drops 'the kid' at his house. He also suggests some bullshit cover story to explain the gunshot wound. I listen, but I'm mentally somewhere else.

When Eugene and Julia enter the hospital, Caleb starts the car.

"Are you okay, Darren?" Caleb asks me as he pulls out of the hospital parking lot.

"Yeah, sure," I say on autopilot. I'm far from okay, but he doesn't need to know that.

"All right then, I'll take you home. What's your address?"

I give it to him, and he puts it into his GPS.

"Okay, good. Now give me your number, too, and I'll get in touch with you soon. I've almost made up my mind about the first person whose fighting we'll experience."

"Great."

"You're in shock," Caleb says. "It happens sometimes after a battle. Even with the best of us."

I just nod. I don't care about his theories or approval. I don't care about anything. I don't want to think.

My phone rings. It's my mom Sara.

"Do you mind?" I ask Caleb. I think it's very rude to talk on a cell in front of someone.

"No worries," he replies, and I answer the call.

"Hello?" I say.

"Darren, I was beginning to worry," Sara says. This makes my stupor fade a little. Beginning to worry is Sara's default state. I don't believe the woman has ever called me when she was chill. Of course, if she thought I was in even a fraction of the trouble I've been in today, she would go to her second-favorite state—panic about me.

"I'm okay, Mom. I was just busy today." Understatement of the century.

"You aren't mad at us?" she asks, and I immediately realize I've been an ass. I should've called to reassure them about the adoption business from the day before.

"No. We're good, Mom," I say, forcing certainty into my voice. Better late than never, I always say.

She seems to believe me, and we move on to the usual 'how are you' chat that we have every day. The whole thing is surreal.

When I get off the phone, Caleb is just a few blocks from my place. We ride in a companionable silence the rest of the way.

"This is you," Caleb says when we get to my building.

"Thanks for the ride," I say, extending my hand to Caleb. "And for helping us out. That was some good shooting you did."

He shakes my hand firmly. "You're welcome. You weren't bad yourself, and I know these things. Get some sleep," he says, and I nod in agreement.

It's the best idea I've heard in a long time.

I get to my apartment, eat something, shower, and get into bed. Once there, I just sit for a moment, looking outside. It's still light out there, the sun only beginning to set. I don't care, though. I'm exhausted, so I lie down.

When I'm this tired, time seems to slow. It's like my head approaches the pillow in slow motion.

I think about everything that's happened to me today. I think about the things that are about to happen. In those couple of seconds it takes for my head to hit the pillow, I think of anything but the fact that Mira will hate me now. Anything but the biggest question of all.

What am I?

And then my head finally touches the pillow, and I'm out, falling asleep faster than I have in my entire life.

THE TIME STOPPER

A MIND DIMENSIONS STORY

DESCRIPTION

I can stop time, but I can't change anything.

I can access memories, but not far enough.

My name is Mira, and my life is about finding the Russian mobster who killed my family.

Note: This is a short prequel from Mira's point of view. It takes place before Mira meets Darren. For optimal reading experience, we recommend that you read it before proceeding to *The Thought Pushers*, the continuation of Darren's story.

1

"IT'S SO SMOKY IN HERE; IT'S LIKE SOMEONE SET OFF A BOMB."

As soon as I say the stupid line, I Split into the Mind Dimension, and time seems to stop.

Victor is squatting over his chair, about to sit down. If this was still the real world, his legs would hurt in a minute or so. As it is, he's as aware of his muscles as a wax statue would be. Shkillet, a guy at the poker table, is frozen in mid-stare at my body—a position I often find men in. The other players are similarly stuck at what they were doing when I Split. The strangest thing in the room is probably the thick cigar smoke that's no longer moving. It looks eerie, like frozen clouds on an alien world. I don't smell the smoke now, which is a relief. I also don't hear anything other than the sound of my high heels clicking on the floor as I walk around the room.

I look at these men, these dangerous men, and an inner voice tells me, "Mira, no sane woman would voluntarily be here. Not even to merely observe this poker game, let alone play with these savages." It's funny how this inner voice usually sounds like my mom.

"You're dead, Mom," I mentally reply to the inner voice. "And I'm here to find the fucker who killed you. Can't we have an imaginary conversation without all this nagging?"

The inner voice sneers—but that's me. Mom was too nice to sneer.

The Mind Dimension makes it safe for me to walk around the room and peek at my opponents' cards without them being the wiser. When I'm in the Mind Dimension, everything stops in a single moment. No matter what I do here in this alternate world, when I get back to my real body—the body that's still sitting at the table—I'll still be in the same situation as I was before I Split: still being stared at by Shkillet, and still having just said that line about the bomb.

When I first learned I could Split, I was a little girl, and I thought my soul was leaving my body. But that was back when I believed in such things as souls, and God, and goodness—words that are meaningless to me now. Back in those days, I also believed in silly things, like the fact that there is a purpose to life.

I don't any longer. Not since that day.

Since that day, I haven't believed in anything but myself. And sometimes—a lot of times—not even that. That little girl who believed in souls would certainly think I'm a stranger if she met me today.

And maybe, she would think I'm a monster.

Of course, that day did not just dispel my childish illusions. It also taught me more practical things, such as how impotent I am while in the Mind Dimension. How truly powerless. No matter how much I want to, I can't change anything in the real world. Like a ghost, I don't affect the world of the living. Maybe that's what I became that day—a ghost of my former self.

That day. Why does thinking about it always hurt the same way, no matter how much time passes? Why is it so vivid in my mind at a moment's notice?

For that matter, why does trying not to think about something bring that very thing into focus?

My mind flashes to that day as though I'm Reading other people, but it's as if I'm replaying my memories instead of someone else's.

I see myself walking home from school, my backpack heavy on my shoulders. I relive the excitement of seeing my dad's car in the driveway when I get home. He hasn't driven away yet, I think joyously, so I'll get a chance to say goodbye. That last line will be singed into my mind forever, but I don't know it yet.

And then I see the car explode.

I see it go up in flames.

I hear the most horrible sound.

Then... silence.

I open my eyes.

The fire is standing still.

The explosion had scared me so much that I automatically Split into the Mind Dimension, as sometimes happens under extreme stress.

Now in the Mind Dimension, I'm standing next to my other, frozen-in-time, self. She looks as terrified as I feel. I know that if I touch the exposed flesh on her/my body, I will leave the Mind Dimension—and the explosion will continue its destruction.

Leaving would've been a cowardly choice, a choice I didn't

even think to make at the time. I would later regret that bravery —or rather, lack of imagination.

Instead of leaving the Mind Dimension, I run toward the car.

The flames are frozen. Unreal. As if they're made of red and yellow silk.

The full horror of the situation hits me only when I see the expression on Mom's face.

She looks white, or at least the parts of her face that aren't burned do. Her blue eyes are wide open, her irises almost black from her dilated pupils.

I open the car door and try to pull her out. In her body's rigid state, she's like a human-sized doll. As I'm straining under her weight, I know that this is futile. I've never been able to change anything in the real world by what I've done in the Mind Dimension. Still, I'm hoping that today will be different. That Mom will be out of the car in the real world simply because it matters so much to me.

Except the universe doesn't give a fuck what matters to me.

I quiet my mind and touch her face. I begin the Reading process, another brave action that will later haunt me. Like always, Reading her shows me the world through her eyes. I lose myself in her head. For that minute, *I* become *we*. The horror of my mom's last moments becomes mine—so it's me, too, who's beginning to realize we are about to burn alive.

Later, I will think about who caused the explosion and wonder if I can ever un-live it, but right now, I just leave her head and look into the car again.

Dad's face is free of burns. I will later hypothesize that the explosive was on the passenger side. His mouth is half-open in an expression of terror that contorts his whole face. I take all this in and am overcome with another idea that I will later regret.

I run to the side door and touch Dad's face through his open window, not really thinking about what I'm doing. Except I do know what I'm doing. I'm bringing him into the Mind Dimension. That's what touching another Reader does—and that's what Dad is, a Reader, like me and my brother.

Unlike Mom, who doesn't have our abilities.

As soon as I touch his skin, another Dad, a screaming Dad, shows up in the back of the car.

"Nyyyeeet!" He switches to Russian as he always does when he's stressed. Then he registers me and screams, "Mira, honey, no!" His accent is heavier than usual.

"It's okay, Dad," I soothe. "We're in the Mind Dimension."

"It's true. We are." He looks around, terror replaced with a different emotion on his face. A darker emotion that I can't exactly place. "Where is she?" he says after looking at the passenger's seat.

"I took her outside. I was hoping she'd stay outside."

Not saying anything, he gets out of the car and looks at Mom. "She's already burned."

"I know," I say thoughtlessly. "I Read her. She's in a lot of pain."

My dad looks like I flogged him with those words, but he quickly hides his reaction.

"In the real world, where are you standing, sweetie?" he says. "Tell me. Quickly."

"Over there..." I point. "Too far to help you."

"That's good." His shaking voice is filled with relief. "The blast shouldn't reach you there. But you still have to fall on the ground when you get back to your body and cover your ears for me. Promise me you'll do this. It's important."

"I promise, Dad." I'm beginning to understand what I have done to him. By pulling him out, I made sure that he could see himself dying in that car. That he could reflect on it. Dwell on it.

"I'm sorry." My voice also begins to shake. "I shouldn't have pulled you in."

"Don't say that." He smiles at me. It's one of the last smiles I'll have from him. "I'm glad I'll have a chance to... a chance to say good-bye."

I remember my thought right before I Split into the Mind Dimension and realize I had created something like an evil omen. A part of me knows that the idea is irrational, but I feel like I brought all of this on with that prophetic thought. *A chance to say goodbye.*

I squint as though I'm going to cry, but no tears come out.

"Don't." Dad reaches for me. "Let's spend the time we have left remembering the good times. Your Depth is only about a half hour—not enough time to spend on anything but happy memories."

He hugs me and tells me stories, determined to be with me for as long as I can stay, until I run out of Depth and become Inert—unable to go back into the Mind Dimension for a while. As I catch myself enjoying his stories and being with him, I hate myself more and more.

I'll later wonder what kind of bitch I was to extend such a moment for my father, but for now, I'm just happy to have him with me a little longer. For as long as I'm allowed.

"We're running out of time." Dad is trying his best to sound cheerful, but I know he's pretending. "You did the right thing," he says. "I'm really glad you pulled me out."

He's lying. Like my brother, Dad repeats lies to make them sound more convincing.

"To live even a few more minutes, to see you, is a treasure." His eyes look earnest, but I can see the truth. He isn't glad. He's terrified because he knows that as soon as my time runs out, he'll be taken out of the Mind Dimension and pulled back into his frozen body.

Into the explosion.

"There's nothing you can do for us now, Mira," he says. "Please take care of your brother; he's all you've got—"

I don't hear him finish that sentence because my time runs out. I will later grow to resent this limitation, my Depth. This finite amount of what-if time.

If only I could've stayed in the Mind Dimension forever. Then Dad and I could've talked forever. Or we could've explored that frozen-in-time world. Instead, I'm back in my body and the explosion is in my ears again, ears that feel like they might bleed. I fall on the ground, like I promised Dad I would. I welcome the pain of the fall because it numbs the pain from knowing that I don't have parents anymore.

With herculean effort, I pull my mind back to the present. To the poker table and the Russian thugs surrounding me. I really have to get it together. My Depth's being wasted as the seconds turn into minutes. If I run out of time, I'll be Inert for a while—which means no more Reading and having to play fair in this poker game, to boot.

I shake my head and try to focus, determined to forget Mom and Dad for the moment. I try to focus on something else.

Anything else.

To distract myself, I think of how strangely I experience emotions in the Mind Dimension. For example, if I cry there, because my face is dry once I get out, I don't feel as sad anymore. Sometimes things work the other way. I can be terrified when I get into the Mind Dimension, but once there, I'm much calmer. Probably because there I'm safe. So if I get any tears now, they would be gone when I'm back at that table. And tears should be falling down my face right now, but none come. Just like on that day. The worst one of my life—

I have to stop thinking about that day.

So I try to picture talking to my brother about emotions in and out of the Mind Dimension. He would want to study this phenomenon, as he—ever the scientist—would call it. It makes me feel somewhat better. Thinking of Eugene always helps take me out of the darkness, if only for a moment.

"I do take care of him. The poor bastard would've starved long ago without me, Dad." I'd say that to my father if I believed he was listening to me from Heaven. Of course, my father is not in Heaven or Hell—those are just constructs people make up to dull the pain of losing their loved ones. I know that, in reality, he's just gone, and nothing I say can reach him.

And that means I need to stop dwelling on what might've been and focus on the task at hand.

The fucker who put the explosive under my family's car might be in this very room right now.

I take a deep breath, finding comfort in anger and the violent fantasies of what I plan to do to him.

"It's time," I say out loud—though, of course, the frozen people can't hear it. "Let's see if any of you fuckers are thinking of explosions."

2

I'm hoping the guy I'm looking for, the guy who deals with bombs, will be primed by my words and think of setting up one specific explosion. I'll be the first to admit that this tactic is a long shot, but it's the only option I have since my Depth allows me to go back only a few minutes into their memories.

Not for the first time, I envy more powerful Readers. Those like the legendary Enlightened, the most powerful Readers of all, who have enough Depth to relive whole months, if not years, of someone's life. Someone like that would get the answer directly without any gimmicks, but I can't. There are no shortcuts for Readers like me. Given that Depth is spent at twice the speed when you Read, I have to be careful about running out of my measly half hour.

Whatever Depth I spend on Reading is going to be worth it in this case, though. Trying to learn the truth is why I come to these games. Well, that and the money from the wins—but there are better ways to make money gambling than coming here. Safer ways.

My strategy for today is to spend only seconds of my Depth on people I think as unlikely candidates, leaving extra time—even if it's just a few minutes—for the others.

One such unlikely candidate is Shkillet, the guy who's staring at me in the real world.

Shkillet is not his real name, but a street alias. Probably has something to do with his too-thin pasty-looking face. He resembles one of those skeletons we had in science class before I dropped out of school. The Russian word for skeleton sounds a lot like the word *skillet*, only with a *yet* sound at the end. Shkillet's lisp could be the reason for the *sh* sound at the beginning.

Or I could be completely wrong. I was pretty young when we left the Motherland, and I do get some of these little ethnic things confused now and then—which drives my brother nuts.

I look at Shkillet's cards. He's not holding anything I need to worry about. But he is staring at me—the real-world me. In fact, if I drew a line from his pupils to that me, it would land directly on her/my boobs. Boobs that are nicely displayed in my red strapless dress, thanks to the Victoria's Secret pushup bra.

I intended that effect, but I'm still annoyed. Fucking men.

Stepping around him, I take off his shirt.

I know it seems weird that I'd undress someone, especially someone this unattractive, but I do have a purpose. I'm looking for tattoos. Over the course of my investigation, I've learned that a man's tattoos in the Russian criminal underworld reveal a lot about him. Well, only for the ones who've been in Russian prisons, but those are the ones I'm looking for. The most dangerous. The ones without souls.

Those who'd plant bombs on innocent families.

Shkillet is what I call skinny-fat. His body is gaunt with his ribcage sticking out, but at the same time, his stomach is flabby. I don't care about his looks, though. All that matters is that he has no tattoos. He does have a large birthmark, however, that reminds me of a Rorschach inkblot test. A counselor showed it to me during the one and only time I tried therapy. Most of her inkblots reminded me of people's brains blowing up—understandable, given the reason I went to see her in the first place—but this guy's birthmark looks like an exploding heart.

Okay, so Shkillet either hadn't been to prison back home or nobody bothered to put any ink on him while he was there. Either way, he's not likely to be a high-status criminal and thus probably isn't the person I'm looking for. Therefore, he's good for a measly five-second jump into his head.

I put my hand on his neck as though trying to measure his pulse. Where I touch people in the Mind Dimension never seems to matter, so I go for the least disgusting place. I clear my mind for Reading. The faster this part is, the more Depth I save. Eugene had figured out some techno-widgety new practice for me to improve how quickly I can do this, and I'm grateful for it with situations like this.

The feeling I get just before I'm about to Read someone comes over me, and I make sure I'm sent only a few moments back into his memories.

"It's so smoky in here; it's like someone set off a bomb," the girl says.

The sex bomb is talking about a real bomb, we think of

replying, but decide against it. Not until we see how Victor responds. The guy's insane, and displeasing him is as easy as it is deadly.

This is why we realize that if we go through with our plan for the girl, we'll have to cut her throat afterwards. Had we just wanted to fuck her, then we could probably get away with leaving her alive afterwards—there are no rules against rape in this place. But we want her money, too, and that's why she'll have to die. Victor's underground casinos have only this one rule: retaliations due to game losses are forbidden. We shudder when we remember what had been done to the last guy who tried to pull some shit on a poker game winner. We'll have to ensure we're not caught.

We think about all the things we want to do to her before we kill her off, and get a painful hard-on. We imagine how we'd fill up that oh-so-fuckable pouty mouth of hers. We visualize grabbing those perfect titties, leaving marks, prying open those long legs... Our balls tighten in anticipation.

This is going to be even better than the last time. That whore from two days ago can't even begin to compare to this girl. Looks aside, that bitch hadn't even fought us, just meekly took it. The fight has become half the fun for us over the years. When they fight, and we finally bend them to our will, we feel the rush of power that's almost as fun as the sex itself. With this girl, it'll be even better because she's rumored to be feisty. The sarcastic remarks she's made throughout the game confirm it. So she'll likely fight, and fight well. We fantasize about her scratching our back with her perfectly manicured fingernails before we lock her wrists in a tight grip...

I, Mira, separate my own thinking from Shkillet's in horrified disgust. I need a shower. I need a dozen showers. I'm still in his head, but I can reflect on what I just learned without fully getting out. Separating my thinking this way allows me to spare my brain from getting more of the vile details of what he plans to do to me. Witnessing the memories of what he did to the poor girl he raped two days ago was terrible enough. And while I'm not clear if he killed her afterwards, I'm positive he's planning to kill me.

Given the circumstances, I dive a little deeper into his memories. I need to learn if he's armed and if there's anything else I need to know about.

We look at our cards. One fucking pair. Two more rounds like this, and we'll be completely broke. But not for long, we remind ourselves, feeling the weight of the ceramic knife in the holster in our boot.

It'll be best to do the deed swiftly. It has to happen here on the club premises before the bitch leaves and has the chance to get into her car.

Victor will be furious when they find the body. But he'd never suspect Shkillet. Getting no respect has some advantages —people underestimate us, and therefore, we can get away with anything.

I, Mira, separate again and think quickly. He managed to sneak a ceramic knife into this place. I guess the material didn't trigger the metal detector wands the bouncers pass over everyone's body upon entrance.

Damn it. This changes my strategy completely. I need to make sure to leave plenty of Depth to deal with this development. If one of these other men is the one I came here to find, it's his lucky day, because I'm skipping their vile heads.

Except Victor's. I've been waiting to meet him face-to-face for months because he's always seemed the most likely candidate, given what I've heard about him. There's no way I'm missing that chance now.

As I form a plan, I exit Shkillet's mind.

STILL IN THE MIND DIMENSION, I APPROACH VICTOR AND unceremoniously rip the shirt from his body. As I do so, I note the pair of aces in front of him on the table.

And his tattoos.

Yeah, Victor's been in the Russian jail system—he's a *zek*, as these people call it. Russian tattoos fascinate me. Probably because Dad had one. He served time with a bunch of scientists for objecting to the nuclear arms race during the Cold War. His Reading skills saved his life, enabling him to get out of the prison camp after only a couple of months, but the hellish experience made him desperate to leave the Soviet Union. He waited years until he could, and by then, the Soviet Union was simply Russia. Still, as Dad liked to say about the new regime, "Nothing's changed—KGB still rules."

So now I try to memorize Victor's tattoos. I only recognize the meaning of the stars on his shoulders. *Vor v zakone.* Translated literally, it means 'a thief in law,' but the vernacular is a criminal authority of high caliber.

I examine him more. I've never seen this double-headed eagle tattoo before, though I think this is what the government symbol looked like back in the Czarist Russia. The Statue of Liberty super-imposed on the eagle also doesn't ring any bells. Perhaps Victor hates the Soviet Union and is reliving the pre-revolution glory days with this ink? Coupled with a symbol of America, maybe he's not so fond of communism, too? It's a theory that gains more credence when I realize that a lot of his prison images are anti-authority.

I also notice that Victor is ripped. How can I not? I am, after all, human. He's built like a swimmer, and his abs form a perfect six-pack.

Stop being a danger slut, Mira, I chide myself. *How can you even think about what he looks like after what was in Shkillet's head?*

Or, more importantly, given what I've heard about Victor. This tendency to drool over monsters is something I truly despise about myself.

So, to that end, I decide enough's enough. I need to give Victor a Reading and get the hell out. I'll be only half-empty of Depth, and that will have to be enough.

I put my arm on his chiseled chest, right on the serene face of Lady Liberty. Physical contact made, I concentrate.

I'm going back far enough to see what he did before he came into this room. With any luck, he might've been thinking of blowing up someone's car. If so, Shkillet won't be the only person I'll need to deal with...

We're inside Vera. She moans softly. With her bent over just the way we like, we have a nice view of her naked back. It's sinewy with muscle. In a perfect world, we like our woman to be a bit curvier, but there's something about her that we find attractive enough to overlook that fact. Our previous squeeze had nice love handles, but she, unfortunately, didn't appreciate our interest, instead opting to overdose while we were taking care of business. Women.

Besides the lack of curves on Vera, we also don't approve of the tattoo on her lower back. It's of Madonna holding the baby Jesus. When we fuck someone doggy-style, the last thing we need is a religious symbol staring us in the face, particularly since the tattoo artist made Madonna beautiful. Probably wanted to mess with the heads of everyone who'd ever fuck Vera in the future—which is a large number of people. Or, just as likely, the bitch arranged for the tattoo to have this effect herself.

As our thrusts deepen, she moans louder, and that brings us closer to the edge. In an effort to prolong the sensation, we direct our mind off the fucking and onto irrelevant things, like the dimples above her ass.

Unfortunately, they're actually a turn-on.

So then we try focusing on the little mole on her right shoulder blade. That works for a bit until we notice the way the sweat slicks her skin. Smooth, gleaming skin. Fuck. We lift our head to stare at the blank walls of the VIP room.

I, Mira, disassociate, albeit hesitantly. This is the first time I've ever caught a man fucking a woman, and it's... hot. It's nothing like Reading them while they fuck me. Of course, I'm not here on a hedonistic vacation. Each moment I spend watching this, a double moment is subtracted from my Depth—because that's how Reading works. Eugene explained that we share the time with the target. I guess that means that on some level, everyone can get into the Mind Dimension when touched, but non-Readers are pulled in only enough for us to Read them.

I fast-forward Victor's memories a few minutes into the future.

We're approaching the table and noticing the girl. She's the prodigy we've heard so much about, the only female *katala* we've ever met—though, to be fair, we met most of those card-shark shysters when doing our time in the all-male Gulag.

We look at her, this girl who's squeezed so many people dry at our establishment. She has the cheekbones and nose of Russian nobility. Someone in this girl's lineage must've survived the October Revolution back in 1917. Her features have a slight sharpness to them, along with an air of dignity. It's a contrast to the matreshka-like round face of someone like Vera, who looks like a common Russian farmer's daughter—and probably is.

With those big blue eyes, long eyelashes, and dark waves of hair, this girl reminds us of our daughter's latest pictures. Only Nadia looks much more innocent than this one, we think with a mixture of longing and pride. Keeping Nadia innocent is why we made the sacrifice of not being in her life all those years ago. She probably doesn't even know who we are, so there's no point dwelling on it. And even if she knows, she's in Russia, and we can't go back there.

"It's so smoky in here; it's like someone set off a bomb," the girl who reminds us of our daughter says.

That word—bomb—brings back flashbacks of that day in Chechnya when we lost two of our best comrades. Our heart rate increases, but then we calm down. The girl is just being a spoiled American princess. It happens to all the kids who arrive here. Her Majesty probably expected this illegal gambling club to enforce New York's non-smoking laws.

I, Mira, separate my mind from Victor's and feel a hint of disappointment. The fact that my words bring up his experience in Chechnya, which must've happened a long time ago, makes him unlikely to be the guy I'm looking for. Especially since he seems to have an aversion to explosions—

almost a PTSD-type of reaction. It's not a certainty that he wasn't involved, of course, but it's enough for me to clear him. I'd crossed people off my list based on less credible evidence.

Thus decided, I exit his head.

I'm back in the silent room. I'm not going to Read the other players' minds. I'm going to conserve my Depth instead. I have two more things I have to do.

First, I take a look at the cards everyone else is holding. With the outcome of the next round in my head, I proceed to the second thing and run out of the room. Swiftly, I go through the dark corridor to the nearby bathroom. I check what I came here to check and confirm that it's still there—the thing that'll give me a chance when dealing with Shkillet. I'm a little calmer now and glad I took the time to explore this establishment in another Mind Dimension excursion; otherwise, I wouldn't have known about things hidden in nooks and crannies.

I run back to the room and approach my body. It's always strange seeing myself like that. Being able to examine myself from all angles used to magnify my teenage insecurities. Normal girls can drive themselves crazy with a mirror, but Readers have it much worse. I remember being depressed about the shape of the back of my ankles not long after my fifteenth birthday. Of course, since my parents' death, I haven't thought about shit like that ever again.

I prepare myself for exiting the Mind Dimension and reach out, placing my hand on my frozen self's face.

And just like that, I'm back in my body.

The sounds are back, and so is the smell of smoke. Victor

completes the motion of sitting down in his chair. The dealer finishes dealing. Shkillet stops staring at me, and looks furtively at Victor to see if he would reply to my weird statement.

"What the fuck are you talking about?" says a bald guy who's smoking a cigar. "If someone brought a bomb in here, Victor would put that bomb into that yebanat's ass."

3

THE NEXT FEW ROUNDS OF POKER PROCEED PREDICTABLY, GIVEN that I know which cards everyone is holding, as well as the top cards of the deck. So obviously, I win every round I can. And as I win, I watch Victor's amusement grow. I'm not sure if it's my winning that he finds amusing or the men's reactions. They dare not give me any attitude, but when I sneak a look at Shkillet, I can tell he's barely hiding his anger. Today, out of spite, I've been winning more than I usually do, and two rounds ago, I called Shkillet's bluff—a bluff that would've probably worked if not for my Reading powers.

Since I don't have a lot of Depth left, I decide that now is the time for me to get out of here. Before I wear out my welcome, so to speak.

"Gentlemen." I stand up. "It's been a pleasure."

"Pleasure taking our money, you mean?" Victor, surprisingly, doesn't sound angry. More like he's teasing.

"Sure, that, and it's nice to finally put a face to the name...

Victor." That might've come out too flirtatious, but hell, I'm too wired for finesse at the moment. As I start gathering my stuff, I see Shkillet begin to fidget. I can tell he's about to leave, too. He's determined to put that plan of his into motion.

I put my winnings into my purse and slowly walk out, trying not to look suspicious.

I know I should make a run for it once I'm in the hall instead of implementing my more dangerous idea of confronting him. But I don't. That would be like playing the last rounds of poker so Shkillet would win—something else I could've done, but didn't. He needs a lesson, and I'll enjoy giving it to him. Maybe with him, I'll finally get the chance to figure out if I'm capable of doing what must be done when the time comes. My brother doesn't think I'd take someone's life. He means it as a compliment, but that's not how I take it, and tonight, I'm betting my life that my brother is wrong.

I arrive at the bathroom door. Shkillet hasn't come out of the game room yet. I take out a pack of Marlboro Reds and a lighter from my purse. I don't really smoke, but pretending to smoke has come in handy at times. Being a girl with a cigarette in her hand is a good icebreaker when the room is full of men with lighters. So I'm a sort of social smoker, I guess. But unlike others, I hate every inhalation. Sometimes when I smoke, I can almost feel the stuff making my lungs and teeth yellow and gross.

As I put the disgusting thing in my mouth, the game room door opens. I light up, inhale, and try not to cough while glancing at the door. Shkillet's there, and we make fleeting eye contact before I exhale the smoke.

Bait set, I walk into the bathroom.

I close the flimsy door lock behind me, hang my purse on a

little hook in an effort to free my hands, and run to the toilet as quickly as possible given the slippery floor and my high heels.

The toilet lid is opened, and I catch a glimpse of the disgusting stuff in the bowl when I throw my now-useless cigarette into it. God, would it have been that difficult to flush the shit? The sight and stench of it reminds me of a nightmare I had a few times about a dirty bathroom. And this reality might be worse than that nightmare if I don't hurry up.

I reach for the water tank just as I hear the lock on the door being picked.

Shit. He's faster than I thought he'd be. He must've run down that hall like a maniac.

I frantically lift the heavy tank cover... just as the door lock fails.

"What the hell?" Shkillet says in Russian as he steps inside and sees me standing there with the lid in my hands.

Good. Not what he was expecting. And I capitalize on that by throwing the lid at his head with all my strength.

He's not fast enough to duck.

As he staggers backward with a grunt, I turn and grab the gun in the plastic zipped bag from the tank. I'd found this weapon in one of my earlier excursions in the Mind Dimension. I'm ripping the bag open when someone's hands grab my left arm.

It's Shkillet.

His fingers are like pincers digging into my flesh.

I Split into the Mind Dimension to assess the situation.

The sounds of his panting are gone, and I observe us from my new vantage point.

One of his hands is on my arm, and the other is reaching into his boot for the ceramic knife he's hiding there. His eyebrow is split open—must be where the lid hit him. The blood running from that wound makes his face look ghoulish.

I examine the bag in my hands. I've almost opened it, but I'm not sure if I'll make it before he gets the knife out and uses it. But I can do something else if I aim right.

I look at my statue-like face that's paralyzed in fear. I'll try my best to be calmer when I get back into my head. Calmer and lethal.

Grabbing my hand, I jump out of the Mind Dimension and desperately will my muscles to act. As though in slow motion, my leg kicks backwards, aiming for his shin. My foot connects with something.

"Bitch!" He falls to his knees. I must've hurt his leg.

In the time I bought myself with the kick, I get the gun out. Whirling around, I see the knife already in his hand.

He swings, the knife swishing through the air an inch away from my leg.

Instinctively, I jump to the side, then slam the butt of the gun into his face. It connects with his nose with a disgusting crunch.

He looks stunned for a moment, and I do it again, swinging the heavy handle at his jaw this time.

He tries to grab me, so I hit the back of his head.

He crumples—his head landing right in that disgusting toilet.

Serves the fucker right. Now he'll drown.

I should gloat, but for some inexplicable reason, I get the urge to kick him away, to get his face out of that toilet. Do I actually want to save his life?

I take a closer look at him. His mouth and nose are above the water, so he won't drown in that muck.

Funny, but for someone who was just thinking of saving him, I feel a pang of disappointment. The practical side of me knows I can't let him live. So I take the gun safety off and aim the muzzle at the back of my would-be-rapist-and-murderer's head.

This is it.

Now I just have to pull the trigger.

Is my hand really shaking? What is wrong with me?

This man deserves to die. Maybe not as much as my parents' killer, but he does deserve it. And if I don't kill him, he'll likely come after me. So shooting him is self-defense. Or a pre-emptive strike, if I have to justify my actions.

And apparently I do—because I can't squeeze that trigger no matter how many reasons I come up with for doing so. Like: *he might be too chicken-shit to come after me*. Or: *this might be his first attempt at murder*. And even: *he might change his whole life around after this*. Yeah, right. I'm now grasping at straws to come up with excuses for myself, when the truth is that Eugene was right.

It's not easy to kill a person—even a bad person.

"Is someone in there?" someone says from the other side of the door.

Shit.

I rush to the door and open it a sliver.

"Hey there," I say to the guy at the door, who looks to be one of the bouncers. "I'm just powdering my nose, and I need to change after that. Can you please use the bathroom upstairs?"

The bouncer mumbles something derogatory about women but starts walking away. Taking no chances, I Split again and Read a second of the bouncer's mind. He's going upstairs—that's the good news. The bad news is that he's mentally cursing a specific woman, me, and not, say, women in general, or one of the few other possible women who visit this place, like Vera—Victor's fucktoy from the nearby VIP room.

I guess this makes my decision for me. I can't shoot Shkillet now. The bouncer will know that I was the one who killed him, even if I run as soon as I fire the shot. I'm not keen to find out how Victor would react to my murdering someone in his place.

I could, though, hold Shkillet's head under the water until he drowns. That way, no one would come running right away, and I could get away. Plus, the bouncer wouldn't necessarily think I'd done it—I'm sure he's seen more than one drunk in Shkillet's position.

The big question is whether I can actually do it... since I wasn't able to pull the trigger.

Damn it. I hate that Eugene is right, and today isn't going to be the day I finally prove my worth to myself.

I stuff the gun into my purse and walk through the place, paranoid all the way to the exit that someone's going to notice the size of my purse. Luckily, no one stops me. It makes sense, since the time to distrust someone is when he or she is on the way in, not out. Plus, what male bouncer is going to be staring at my purse instead of my cleavage?

Still, I'm only able to breathe normally when I get into my car and put the gun into the glove compartment. Even though I don't need it, I didn't want to leave it for Shkillet in case he regains consciousness and decides to come after me. I might not be a cold-blooded killer, but that doesn't make me stupid.

The drive back home happens in a post-adrenaline-rush haze, for which I'm thankful. I don't want to think about what just happened. I just want to get home and unwind.

When I arrive at the apartment I share with Eugene, I take

my high heels off and tiptoe into my room, stepping over all the junk in the living room. Not for the first time, I promise myself to tidy up, but obviously, not tonight. Closing my bedroom door, I'm super-grateful that I didn't wake my brother. My earlier plan for a dozen showers forgotten, I get into bed and pass out.

My sleep is interrupted by a recurring nightmare—a skeleton trying to strangle me.

4

"MIRA, IS THAT YOU?"

My brother has this annoying habit of talking to me when my mouth is full or when, like now, I'm under a cascade of blissfully warm water, trying to relax.

"No, Eugene, it's some fucking stranger using our shower!" I slam the sliding door for emphasis.

"Thanks for saying the F word—now I know it's you!" He bangs on the bathroom door. "Come to the kitchen when you're done."

I wish I'd slept instead of tossing and turning all night. Still, the little sleep that I had should keep me going, and this shower is doing wonders.

I put on jeans and a T-shirt and head to the kitchen. My curiosity is piqued because I smell food—an oddity because I don't think anyone is here besides Eugene. Which would mean that, whatever dish the smell is coming from, he would've had to cook it.

"Happy birthday to you," my brother sings when I enter. "Happy birthday to you—"

"Eugene, please stop. My ears are going to wilt." I use humor to cover up the fact that I completely forgot about my birthday. With everything that's happened, it was the last thing on my mind.

"I made pancakes." He puts a plate in front of me when I sit down at the table. "Eighteen. One for each year."

"Is that what those brownish ovals are?" I give him a questioning look. "And isn't it supposed to be a candle for each year, not pancakes?"

"Aha!" He winks and brings his hands out from behind his back. He's holding a cupcake with a lit candle. The strawberry vanilla cupcake from the local Italian bakery that I like. It's a miracle he didn't burn his clothes standing like that.

"Thank you." I take the pastry and place it on the table. "And thanks for wearing a clean lab coat on this special occasion."

"You're welcome." He's acting like he didn't hear my ribbing about the lab coat. "Make a wish."

A wish. All of a sudden, I feel an ache in my chest. None of my wishes are happy. None are normal. A normal girl would wish to meet a nice guy, someone who's fun and good-looking. But not me. I wish I could find my parents' killers and the person who sent them, and then find the will and fortitude to kill them.

"Is something the matter?" Eugene asks.

"No," I lie, smoothing out my frown. "It's silly."

"You wish they were here to say happy birthday?" he says softly, switching to Russian.

I nod. It seems pointless to put it into words. As pointless as wishing.

We share a silence during which I stab the first of my eighteen pancakes with my fork and take a bite.

A bite that I have to stop myself from spitting out.

"Eugene..." I try to swallow the soggy, half-cooked lump in my mouth. "These are awful."

Oh crap. As soon as I see the hurt look on his face, I realize I could've been more tactful. But seriously, these are the worst-tasting pancakes I've ever had.

"Sorry." He demonstratively puts a pancake into his own mouth and chews it. "I did what the algorithm said." His expression doesn't change; if he can taste the problem, he's not showing it.

"They're called recipes, not algorithms." I move the plate toward him. "And I'm sure it called for butter and salt, things that make food yummy—stuff that's clearly missing from these pancake-esque thingies."

"Potato, potahto... Recipes are algorithms." He spears another pancake onto his fork. "And salt and butter are bad for you anyway."

"A lot of good stuff is bad for you." I reach for the cupcake he bought for me and place it on my plate. "And it's funny you brought up potatoes. Did you put that in these pancakes? Because there's this aftertaste—"

"I'm not an idiot, Mira," he says. "If I made potato pancakes, I would call them *draniki*. Do you remember how—"

He doesn't have to finish that question. Of course I remember Mom's draniki. A cross between pancakes and hash browns, they were the most delicious things ever—and a part of my childhood I'll never have again.

I interrupt him by demonstratively blowing out the candle

and taking a bite of my cupcake, making that yumminess-signifying, "Mmmmmmm," as I do so.

Eugene smiles at first, but then his face goes dark, an expression so intense and unnatural for him that it frightens me. And considering he's looking over my shoulder, I'm really hoping it's not a huge-ass spider.

"What's that?" He points in that same direction.

"What's what?" Oh shit. Maybe it's one of those giant cockroaches that thrive in this building's garbage disposal system. Or their competitors, the rats.

"That." He stands up and peers at me. "The black-and-blue claw mark on your arm."

I look at my left bicep. Fuck. It seems that Shkillet left a bruise when he grabbed me yesterday.

"It's nothing." I tug my sleeve down—not that it does much good. "Don't worry about it."

"It's not nothing." An even darker look crosses his face. "How stupid do you think I am?"

"Do you really want me to answer that?" I take a bite of my cupcake and regret it immediately. I know where this is going, and the delicious cupcake begins to taste like cardboard.

"I heard you come in late last night." He sits back down slowly. "You were doing that again. You were consorting with those monsters."

"Calm down." I brush the cupcake crumbs from my fingers.

"How the hell am I supposed to calm down?" He plants his palms on the table, about to shove himself upright again—until I grab his arm. I can feel the tension in him as he yells, "You're coming home with fucking bruises, and you're telling me not to worry about it? It's my job to protect you, and you're on your way to getting yourself killed!"

"Lower your voice, please," I say through clenched teeth. "It's not your fucking job to protect me."

"How can you be so dumb—"

I've had enough. Grabbing the plate from the table, I hurl it toward the stove.

Eugene watches it shatter with utter shock, even though this isn't the first tantrum he's seen me throw in his lifetime. More like the hundredth in the past two years alone.

"Mira, I—" he begins.

"Shut up." I rise to my feet.

"Wait, Mirochka. Seriously, I'm sorry—"

I don't hear the rest because I storm into my bedroom and slam the door shut behind me. Then I crank up some music and begin throwing clothes into a bag: something casual, a gym outfit, and, on a whim, a nice dress I bought months ago after a spree of poker wins. I also throw in some shoes. I want to make sure I have what I need so I won't have to come back here today —because if I do, I'll have to deal with Eugene's sulking.

"I'm not mad," I say when I open the door again. "I just need to get out of the apartment."

"Don't go, Mirochka—"

"Thank you for the birthday wishes." I sling the bag over my shoulder. "I mean it. It was nice."

"You're welcome." He pinches the bridge of his nose. Eugene knows me well enough to know there's no salvaging this situation right now.

Still, I feel like the biggest asshole as I leave the house.

Yoga class helps a little. A pretty boy checking out my

yoga-pants-clad butt helps a little more. After the gym, I head to my favorite sushi place. That and hot sake make me feel almost like a normal person.

Almost like my birthday is worth celebrating.

Determined to enjoy feeling normal for as long as possible, I take a lengthy walk on the Brighton Beach boardwalk. I try to stay focused on the nice weather, but my thoughts eventually turn to my investigation, as they always do these days.

They said my parents' death was a mob-on-mob hit. Eugene Read the detectives investigating the case, and learned that the police had cut short the investigation as soon as they learned of the Russian mob's involvement. But my dad was never in the Russian mob. He was a scientist, like Eugene. It didn't make any sense until Eugene told me something else that he saw in the mind of the detectives: signs of Pushing.

Pushers are the other side of the coin among people who can enter the Mind Dimension. They're like us—except they control people's minds, instead of reading them. And they hate us just as much as we hate them. It's not a huge surprise those evil fuckers are involved in this somehow, especially given Dad's research into our abilities.

As soon as I learned all this, I knew I had to take the investigation into my own hands. My brother honors our parents' memory by focusing on Dad's research, but I do it differently. I do it by trying to hunt down their murderers, and if it drives my brother crazy, so be it. I'm not a little girl anymore. In fact, as of today, I'm officially an adult—though I haven't felt like a child for a long time.

Determined to get back into my earlier birthday-enjoyment groove, I go to the movies. The one I choose is a romantic comedy, and I enjoy it immensely for the fiction that it is.

Those writers make these things so light and fluffy, it's like a fairy tale. In real life—at least in my real life—people are self-destructive, violent liars who will cheat and steal if they can get away with it. Outside of the mob, they put on a façade of civility, but as a Reader, I know what hides behind their polite smiles. In the mob, they don't even try to hide it. The criminals are more honest, in a way. Then again, the depravity of some of the things I Read in Victor's club and other similar places is mind-boggling. I sometimes can't sleep for weeks after getting one of those 'snuff Reads'—

I shake my head. Man, I need to get back some positivity.

To do that, I grab some ice cream before leaving the movie theater. Nothing is more positive than ice cream.

Afterwards, I decide against getting dinner. Instead, I go into the theater bathroom to change into my killer dress, and while I'm at it, I put on some makeup and a pair of high heels. It's time to have some fun and go clubbing. Why the hell not? It's my fucking birthday.

"Are you Russian?" is what I think the guy tries to say to me over the pounding music of the dance club.

"Da," I yell, nodding to the beat.

"Can I buy you a drink?" he says in Russian. Or I assume that's what he says because I catch the Russian word for drink over the noise, and he also puts his hand to his mouth in that universal drinking gesture. Not to mention, he points at the bar.

I look the guy over. Tall, broad-shouldered, he looks like the kind of guy I would've liked if I'd remained normal. Since I'm trying to be normal tonight, I let him buy me a Grey Goose with Red Bull, my party-all-night drink.

I love these Russian-owned clubs, even if sometimes the owners are in the mob. The vodka selection is always topnotch, the DJs are great at mixing the tracks, the music they mix is more to my taste, and the bartenders never ask for ID. I have a fake one, of course, but I prefer not to be asked. What's more, here they never give you that I-know-that-ID-is-fake-but-hey-now-I'm-off-the-hook-little-girl look.

As I sip my drink, the guy introduces himself and gives me some compliments, but I only hear bits and pieces. Finally, I have to lean in and yell into his ear, "I can barely hear you!"

"Would you like to dance?" He leans down, yelling into my ear, and I can finally hear him.

"Absolutely." I'm about to add his name, but realize that I can't remember it. Talk about embarrassing. I can't ask him now. Of course, I can always Split and check his wallet for an ID, so maybe later I'll do that.

He's a great dancer, with a sense of rhythm that I haven't been lucky enough to run into before. And speaking of lucky, I've lucked out in that he's also just the right amount of grabby. Although, after a song or two, with the buzz from the drink starting to hit my brain, I decide that he's not grabby enough. I take his hands and stick them on my butt. He, smart guy that he is, gets the point, and from here on out, there's a lot more touching. He even goes for some ear-nibbling, which I approve of.

We dance like that for at least ten songs. My legs begin to ache, and my head is spinning. I feel great. I feel as if... well, as if it's my fucking birthday.

Another few songs, and I'm grinding against him. He clearly

likes it—that or there's a flashlight in his pocket that I hadn't noticed before.

"Do you want to get out of here?" he asks me eventually.

"Sure." I give him one last grind—in case there's any misunderstanding as to where this night is headed. "Let's go to your place."

He's holding my hand as we start making our way through the crowd, and then, suddenly, he stops.

He's staring at the chest of a gargantuan bouncer.

"Leave," the bouncer growls. He must have sixty pounds' worth of lungs alone; I can hear him clearly over all the noise. "She stays."

"What's the problem?" the guy asks.

"You didn't hear me?" The bouncer starts rolling up his sleeves—never a good sign. In a Russian nightclub, could be a deadly sign.

"It's all right," I yell at my guy. "I know this man."

"You're with him?" His lips become a thin line. "Why didn't you tell me you were with someone?"

I shrug, taking his anger as a compliment. I'd love to tell him the truth, but whatever this shit with the bouncer is about, there's no reason to bring a civilian into it. Especially a guy who showed me a good time.

The guy walks away, shaking his head.

"Upstairs," the bouncer barks. "This way." He leads me up the stairs and points to a closed door with a tinted glass window in it. There's no way I can see what's waiting for me inside.

Damn. I shouldn't have left the gun in my car. Oh well, I think, and open the door.

"Hello," Victor says when the bouncer opens the door for me. "We need to talk."

Of all the clubs owned by shady people, I clearly chose the worst one.

And then I realize there's someone else in the room.

A man I didn't expect to see, let alone this soon.

Shkillet, his face black and blue with the injuries I inflicted, gives me a look that says, "You're dead now, bitch."

5

"YOU HAVE QUESTIONABLE TASTE IN COMRADES, VICTOR." I'M NOT going to let either of them think they've thrown me. Never let them see you sweat—it's a motto I live by.

Shkillet's face reddens, and he reaches for his boot, but stops. "She's trying to disrespect you," he whispers to Victor, loudly enough that I can hear.

"When I want your opinion, Shkillet, I will provide it." Victor rises from his chair as Shkillet's red face turns white. "As for you, my lovely friend—" Victor inclines his head toward me, "—there's a very good reason why he's here."

"And that would be what? You need your toilets licked clean?" I stare at Shkillet, not backing down from the threat I see in his eyes.

"You whore." Shkillet's fingers twitch, likely itching to get to that knife. I know; I've felt that same hatred myself. Thankfully, he elects to spit on the ground instead of trying to skewer me.

"Spit on my floor again, and you'll be licking it off, Shkillet, understand? Also don't speak again until I say you can." If looks actually could kill, Victor's would've already murdered Shkillet ten times over. "Do I make myself clear?"

Shkillet nods, and I can tell it's killing him to do so.

Victor glares at him. "Say it."

Shkillet exhales. "I'll wait for you to ask me to speak, Victor." It sounds as if the words are being pulled from him.

"Now." Victor tugs his sleeves down. "As I was saying, there is a reason he's here, and it's because an accusation has been made."

"An accusation?" I try not to sound challenging—a task I, admittedly, have trouble with on occasion.

"Our comrade here told me some disturbing things about you." Victor leans against a table, arms crossed. "He claims that you work with the cops as a snitch, or worse, that you're a cop yourself."

"What?" I didn't expect that, and I don't have any clever, or even dumb, comebacks for him. "What are you talking about?"

"He said you'd deny it." Victor picks up a shot glass that's been standing on his desk and downs the contents in one gulp. "But his story is rather persuasive, so I figured we should talk."

This is bad. If Victor really believes this, I'm as good as dead. He wouldn't threaten a cop and let her live. Then again, if he truly believed I was a cop, given what I know of Victor, I would already be dead. I debate Splitting and Reading him to figure out what's what, but decide against it. After yesterday, my Depth is fairly low, even if some was recovered in the twenty-four hours that have passed. Still, if I overuse it, I'll go Inert and be unable to Split for many days.

"I'm not a cop." I start to fold my arms in front of my chest, realize it's a defensive gesture, and run my hands through my hair instead. "That's a ridiculous notion that only that syphilitic excuse for a brain could've come up with—"

"Suka." The Russian insult comes out of Shkillet with a snarl.

"I thought I told you to shut it." Victor points one threatening finger at Shkillet. "It's not that ridiculous, my dear. He says cops—your colleagues—did that to his face."

"Cops didn't do it. I did."

"I wasn't done." Now I'm the recipient of Victor's threatening finger. "What he said is just a piece of the puzzle, you see. After that last game yesterday, I asked around."

"And?" I ask, not liking where this is going.

"And you do have a tendency to... How should I put this delicately? To ask some odd questions during pillow talk."

Shkillet sneers, and I try not to blush. It's true that I've slept with a few gangsters. No one too monstrous, mind you, but definitely bad boys. I didn't do it just to get information, though. I was attracted to them—though I'm not sure if that makes it better or worse. Yeah, I did end up asking about explosion experts when a good moment presented itself, and if it just happened to be post-coitus... Well, that's when most men seem to let their guard down.

"I'm just interested in certain things." I shrug. "Maybe I'm looking for someone to do a job for me. To settle a score. That doesn't make me a cop."

Victor stares at me. I meet his gaze. I'm determined not to show any weakness. And right now, my knees are feeling pretty weak. I don't know what Victor has up his proverbial sleeve, and I don't know where he's going with this. I do much better when I have all the information.

"There's also the matter of your name. You claim it's Ilona, but we both know that you also go by Mira and Yulia and a bunch of others."

Crap. Where did he get that from? I thought I'd covered my tracks well. Changing my name was actually for my brother's sake, the going theory being that whoever killed Dad, if controlled by a Pusher, would want Eugene dead as well. But I can't exactly tell Victor that.

"I win large sums of money." I think really hard and really quickly, something I've learned to be good at. "Not just from you, but other legal venues as well. You can check with your people in Vegas. Given that, I think it's only natural for me to want to retain some anonymity."

"I can see that. To a point." Victor takes a big bottle of vodka and refills his shot glass. "But you must see how, bundled together, this doesn't look good."

"No, I don't agree." I shift my weight from one foot to another. "I'd make the worst, most conspicuous undercover cop in the history of undercover work. I mean, I'm usually the only woman at those games. I stick out like a sore thumb."

"She has a point there." Victor waves his shot glass in Shkillet's direction. "Even if I'd use a prettier metaphor to describe her."

"Why are you even listening to her?" Shkillet says in frustration. "She'll say anything to get out of here with her head still attached."

"Because something more is going on here." Victor downs the shot he's been holding. "And I find this one rather interesting."

"Then let me make her talk." Shkillet takes his knife out, his hands practically shaking with eagerness. "Two minutes, and she'll admit that she's a cop, just like I say she is."

"We'll talk about you sneaking a weapon into this establishment in a moment." Victor gives him a furious look. "First, I want to point something out to you. *I* ask the questions. I don't need your help. I'm a good judge of people, and I know she's hiding something. But I also think you're not telling everything."

"Oh, he's hiding things from you," I say, deciding to escalate matters.

"Is that so?" Victor raises his eyebrows, as if I can't possibly know what I'm talking about. "What would he dare hide?"

"The fact that it was me who fucked up his face, as I was trying to explain earlier," I say. "And that's just for starters."

"That's a lie." Shkillet's knuckles whiten around the hilt of his knife. "It was the cops."

"Also, he's hiding the fact that he's disrespected you." I ignore Shkillet's denial. "He's said things behind your back."

"Before you go further, my dear *Ilona*—" Victor holds up his hand, "—you should know that I won't treat a baseless accusation like that lightly."

"Baseless accusation, like calling me a cop?" I narrow my eyes at Victor. "How's this? He said he fucked your mistress. Though I think he actually raped her, because what woman in her right—"

"What the fuck are you talking about?" Shkillet growls, but shuts up when he looks at Victor.

I see why. Victor's face darkens, and it's scary to see, especially since it's most likely me, not Shkillet that he's angry at.

Without a word, Victor reaches into his desk, pulls out a gun, and places it on the desk with a loud clink of metal on glass. "I think you didn't understand me when I said I wouldn't take to this sort of shit lightly."

I nod. "I understood. But did he?" I point to Shkillet.

"You're a cop," Shkillet shouts. "And I sure as hell didn't go near Victor's lady."

"Oh really?" I say. "Then how would I know her name is Vera, if not from you?"

"You're a cop." Shkillet moves the knife from one hand to another, nervously.

"And how about the fact that she has a tattoo on her back of the Madonna holding the baby Jesus? The tattoo with a face you wanted to come all over?" I say. "Do I know that also because I'm a cop? Because you told my 'colleagues' that when they beat you up? How about the claim you made that she has a muscular back with dimples and a mole on her right shoulder? You're trying to say that it was some other fucking rapist who told people that?"

Victor's face is the most frightening thing I've seen in a long time. Shkillet sees it, he sees Victor reach for the gun, and he completely flips out, lunging at me with the knife.

Now I Split—no point in having leftover Depth if I'm dead.

In the Mind Dimension, I walk over to Shkillet so I can Read him to verify his intent. As I suspected, he knows he's a dead man and wants to make sure he takes me down with him.

Fuck. I overdid it with him. I didn't think he'd go for the kamikaze thing. At least he made me look honest, which means Victor will probably not only kill him, but do it slowly. Still, if Shkillet kills me first, his destiny will be only a small consolation for me.

I look at Victor. He's still angry, but confused, too. He didn't expect Shkillet to do what he did either. Like me, he probably didn't think the man had the balls for it.

I look at the path of Shkillet's body and the knife. I try my best to project it another foot, to where my frozen self is. I now know what I have to do.

Somewhat encouraged, I get out of the Mind Dimension.

As soon as my consciousness is back in my body, I begin to twist myself just the right way and step aside, hoping I didn't miscalculate.

Shkillet's knife swooshes through the air an inch from my neck.

I didn't miscalculate, thank God.

Shkillet comes to a dead stop, his beady eyes wide with shock. He can't believe I escaped his attack.

I see a blur of movement so I Split again.

Shit. He recovered too quickly. He's frozen in the process of making a wide swing at me. Unless I do something, he's going to disembowel me with that knife.

I look at Victor. In the few moments that have passed, he's grabbed the gun from his desk. But even if it's my opponent rather than me that Victor intends to shoot, it'll take too long for him to complete that movement, let alone aim the gun and fire it at Shkillet.

Besides, if he did that, there's no telling whether he'd shoot the wrong person—namely, me—given how close I'm standing to Shkillet. I decide against Reading Victor to see who he's going to aim that gun at. I have no Depth to waste on questions where the answer won't help the situation at hand. Instead, I Split back.

Even before my mind is back in my body, I begin mentally playing out a maneuver that I can best describe as a hula-hoop move. I try to do it over and over, to make sure it's the first and only thing that my body does when it gets the mind back. My body moves in the desired motion, but not fast enough, and I feel a burning pain in my side.

A pain that makes me involuntarily Split again.

Please, God, don't let me see myself dying. I turn to look at my frozen body in the Mind Dimension.

I'm in luck. Even though the hula-hoop move wasn't entirely successful, it did get me far enough out of the knife's path. Shkillet only grazed my side. And now he's off-balance.

I Split and get back to real time with a whirling kick to Shkillet's balls, a move I've done many times since starting my investigation. Nothing stops a man as quickly as a hit in that vulnerable place, and no man has ever deserved it more than Shkillet.

As my foot connects, Shkillet squeals loudly and grabs his damaged family jewels. Remembering Victor's unfinished vodka bottle, I grab it, determined to bring it down on Shkillet's head. But before I can, a shot rings out.

My heart feels like it's going to jump out of my ribcage as the room goes silent.

I automatically Split again and look around. My real body doesn't look like it's been shot. There's some more blood flowing from where Shkillet's knife grazed me, but that's it. When I glance at Victor's gun, I can't tell where he's pointing it because the air around the barrel is filled with smoke.

When I turn toward Shkillet, however, I see that the right side of his skull is flying away, with bits of blood and brain matter frozen in the air. So that's where Victor was aiming. And what's more, there's another bullet frozen midway on its trajectory toward Shkillet's chest.

Exhaling in relief, I decide to spend a few more precious moments of my Depth to Read Victor's intentions. If he's planning to shoot me, I want to know about it, even if there's not much I can do to stop him. Then again, maybe I'll throw that vodka bottle at him—get one last shot in before I go.

Inside Victor's head, I experience rage mixed with awe mixed with confusion. It's impossible to tell what he'll do for sure, so I leave the Mind Dimension and get ready to face whatever is in store for me.

Victor looks at Shkillet's bleeding body, then looks at me, the gun pointing at me for a brief, heart-pounding moment, but then he slowly lowers the weapon.

A bouncer rushes into the room. "What the fuck, boss? Your glass door is not that soundproof. If I heard it outside, anyone on the dance floor could've, too."

"We'll need some private cleaning in here." Victor puts his gun down on the table. "And as for the noise, tell the DJ to make up an excuse about a problem with his equipment. Also tell him to announce a half hour of open bar, starting now."

"Got it." The bouncer exhales and rolls his shoulders as he heads out the door. "That'll work, especially the second part."

"I'm not sure what just happened," Victor says when the bouncer leaves. "What you said about Vera was accurate, and only someone who's seen her naked would know those things. But something doesn't ring true because I have a hard time believing he'd dare." Victor waves toward what's left of Shkillet, and shakes his head. "Still, I did underestimate the little creep tonight. I ought to put on his tombstone: 'Shkillet, the underestimated.'"

"I'd make that 'Shkillet, the underestimated rapist.'" I give the dead body a shove with my foot.

"I don't know about that part." Victor extends his hand for the bottle I'm still holding.

"Believe what you want." I hand him the bottle. "Ask around. He was a rapist."

"But did he do that to Vera?" Victor frowns, pouring himself another shot. "That's what I have trouble with. Wouldn't she have told me?"

"She was probably ashamed. It happens a lot with rape victims. All I can say is, if he didn't, he sure lied about it. Just like he lied about me being a cop."

"And you're not?" Victor gulps down the shot. "You moved like some Spetsnaz soldier when he attacked you. It was—"

"I have good reflexes." I have to get his mind off what he thinks he saw. "That's all. It doesn't make me a cop."

"But it does make you an accessory to this." He points to Shkillet. "But here's what bothers me. If he lied and didn't fuck her, how'd he know what she had on her back?"

"Well, we can't ask him now." I shrug. "Maybe he was a peeping tom? That's not strange for a rapist."

"Perhaps." He gives me a suspicious stare. "Or maybe you are. Did you see me fuck her yesterday? Did you watch us and use the info to make it look like he disrespected me?"

"You wish. That's one of *your* voyeuristic fantasies. Besides, wouldn't you close the door and have some bouncer guard it if you were fucking?"

Victor sighs and rakes his fingers through his hair. "Talking to you is as frustrating as talking to Nadia. You're too good of a liar—probably helps you during poker."

I shrug and pretend not to know he's talking about his daughter.

"So." Victor exhales. "The fact that he attacked you could

mean you're right. Maybe he knew that if he didn't attack you, his death would've been... slow."

"You give him too much credit. He's not that smart—only crazy." I twirl my finger next to my temple in a gesture for insanity.

Victor chuckles, but then he stops abruptly and stares at me.

Feeling like I'm under a magnifying glass, I can't help but notice the throbbing in my wound. The adrenaline rush has worn off, and it hurts like a son of a bitch.

"You're bleeding." He frowns.

"It's nothing." I don't want to give him the satisfaction of admitting to weakness. "But thanks for your concern."

"Listen, whatever-your-name-is, I want to continue this conversation someday."

Great. Just what I don't need. I think it, but don't verbalize it.

"In the meantime," he continues, "I'll spread the word that you're under my protection so you won't need to worry about the likes of Shkillet in the future."

I'm at a loss for words. I didn't expect him to say that. That's the third time I'm surprised today. I really should Read people more if I don't want these surprises, but it's tricky because of my limited Depth.

"Here's my card." He hands it to me as if this is a normal business deal. "Call me if you need anything."

I take the card. Then he walks to the door and lets his bouncers in.

"Take her to the hospital," Victor tells the big guy who brought me here earlier. "Put the bill on my tab." He looks at me after the bouncer nods. "I'll be seeing you later, Ilona."

Numb with shock, I let myself be herded through the club.

There's no sign of the guy I'd danced with. Oh well. It's not like that would've been anything more than a one-night stand. I'm nothing if not realistic. There's no room in my life for a relationship.

PATCHED UP AND TIRED AS A DOG, I TAKE A CAB FROM THE hospital to my car.

As I watch the streets whiz by, I have a million thoughts running through my head. They fight with one another, but the one that keeps getting my attention is that I have to get away. Away from Brooklyn, away from gangsters, away from all this shit. I need to let things settle here.

It's a smart idea, but what can I do? Where should I go?

Ideas pop up, then fizzle out. Should I visit Vegas again? No, I'd need a new set of IDs for that, since they're onto me big-time in that town. Monte Carlo is still out of reach; my fake papers aren't good enough for Europe.

As I get home and sneak into my room again, I realize that there is another place I could go. It's closer, and there's less heat for me there, even if it's not that far distance-wise.

By the time I get into bed, I'm on board with my new plan. I'll get a couple of nights of good sleep, get my stitches taken out, patch things up with Eugene, and then grab a bus to Atlantic City.

Has anyone been this excited about a trip to New Jersey before? I don't know, and I don't care. My world becomes all about the softness of my pillow as I fall into a blissful and much-deserved sleep.

THE THOUGHT PUSHERS

MIND DIMENSIONS: BOOK 2

DESCRIPTION

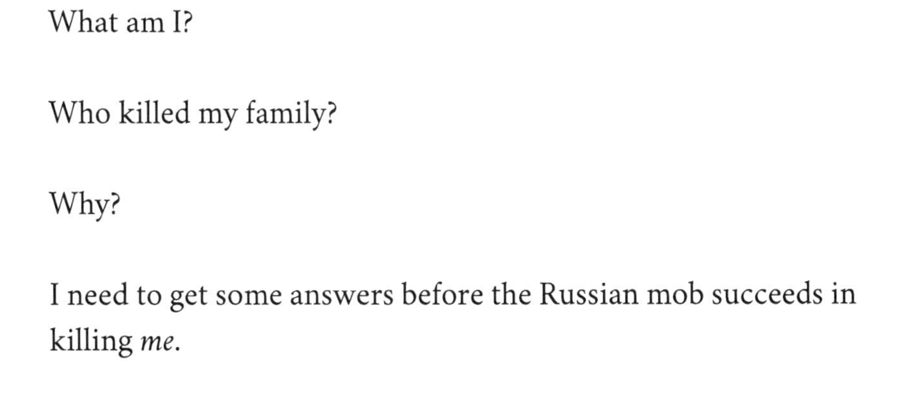

What am I?

Who killed my family?

Why?

I need to get some answers before the Russian mob succeeds in killing *me*.

That is, if my own friends don't kill me first.

1

My phone makes the most annoying noises. Why did I put it next to the bed again?

I grudgingly struggle to wake up. The bothersome noises continue, so I grab the phone.

"Hello?" My voice is gravel-textured in my own ears. How long have I been asleep?

"Darren, it's Caleb. I'm waiting downstairs. Come on out."

The adrenaline rush hits me, and I phase into the Quiet. I'm lying on the left side of the bed near my other, frozen self. There's a pitiful, ultra-concerned look on his face. *My* face.

I reach for my wristwatch on the nightstand. It's 6:13 a.m.

The events of the prior days flash through my mind with startling clarity. The trip to Atlantic City, when I met Mira for the first time. Having my hacker friend Bert look her up. Meeting her and her brother Eugene in their Brooklyn apartment and learning that I'm a Reader. Mira getting kidnapped by the Russian mob, and our going to the Reader community for help. Caleb and Julia helping us. It all comes back to me, followed by the worst part.

I *Pushed* someone.

It's an action that no Reader should be able to do. Something that only Pushers, the people Readers hate, can do.

I took away someone's free will.

And now Caleb is here, at the crack of dawn.

Shit. My heartbeat jumps. Did Mira already rat me out? Maybe to the entire Reader community? And if she did, what does that mean for me? What do Readers do with Pushers? I remember Mira threatening to kill every Pusher she met. What happens if *I'm* one of those Pushers? If the other Readers found out I Pushed that guy to throw himself between Mira and that bullet, what would they do? Nothing good, I'm sure of it. But why would she reveal what I did? The only reason she's alive is because I made that guy take a bullet for her, and she has to know that.

Or could Caleb be here for some other reason? I do owe him a trip into someone's head, as weird as that sounds. Could he be here to collect? That would be preferable to the alternative of him knowing that I'm a Pusher.

If I'm even a Pusher, that is. Yesterday, I seemed to have proven that I'm a Reader. Proven it twice, to two different people. They were quite convinced of my Readerness. Does that mean Readers have no real understanding of what Pushers can or can't do, or does it mean something else entirely . . . perhaps that I'm neither a Reader nor a Pusher? Is there a third possibility? For all I know, there are other groups out there we haven't even heard of.

Or perhaps I'm both. A hybrid. Is it possible that one of my parents was a Reader, and the other was a Pusher? If so, I would be a product of blood mixing—something that Eugene seemed to think was a huge taboo. And he and Mira are half-bloods, so he's probably more open-minded about this issue than pure Readers. Does this mean that my very existence is against some stupid rules? That could explain why my biological parents were convinced someone wanted them dead.

It could explain why they were murdered.

I could sit here in the Quiet thinking for hours, but all the thinking in the world won't make Caleb leave. I need to figure out what he's doing here.

I get out of bed and walk naked toward the door. In the Quiet, no one can see me, so I don't worry about it.

I go down to the first floor wearing only my slippers and exit through the front door. There are actually a surprising number of people—motorists, pedestrians, even street people—frozen in that moment in time. They must be insane to be awake so early.

It takes me only moments to locate Caleb's car. It's parked precisely where he dropped me off yesterday. He seems to be a creature of habit.

He's holding his phone. It's kind of funny knowing I'm on the other end of that call. I examine the inside of the car carefully, looking for any clues as to why he might be here. I find nothing except two coffees in the cup holders. Is one for me? How thoughtful. I do find a gun in the glove compartment, but it doesn't really worry me. Caleb's the kind of guy who probably has guns hidden all over the place, just in case.

I don't go anywhere near Caleb himself—a touch could pull him into my Mind Dimension, as he calls the Quiet, and he'd know I was snooping. Not to mention the wisecracks he'd make about my being naked.

Disappointed that I couldn't get any extra information, I head back to my apartment. I touch my frozen self on the hand that's clutching the phone, and phase out of the Quiet.

"What's this about, Caleb? I just woke up." My voice still sounds hoarse, so I cough a few times, covering the phone speaker with my left hand.

"Come out, and we'll talk," he replies.

I'm not in the mood for a long debate. Knowing Caleb's capabilities, if he was here to do me harm, I probably would've woken up with his gun in my mouth.

"I'll be down in twenty minutes," I tell him.

"Make it ten," he says and hangs up.

Some people have no manners.

I quickly get up, brush my teeth, and get dressed. Then I whip up a green smoothie—my answer to breakfast on the run. Three frozen bananas, a big handful of cashews, a cup of spinach, and a cup of kale go into the blender. A few noisy seconds later, I'm on my way out with a giant cup in my hand. I often do this smoothie thing to save time on those few occasions when I actually go to the office.

Speaking of work, doesn't Caleb understand that normal people have jobs they need to be at on a Wednesday morning? I don't, but that's beside the point. I'm even more annoyed now. Then again, it's early, and this thing could potentially be over before the workday begins.

"You better have an important reason to get me out of bed this early." I open the door to Caleb's car.

"Good morning to you too, Darren." Ignoring my scowl, he starts the car as soon as I get in and pulls out. "Look, kid, I didn't want to wake up so fucking early, either, but Jacob took the red-eye, and he demanded to see you before your workday, so you're not inconvenienced too much. So here I am."

Jacob, the leader of the Reader community, wants to see me? Shit. Maybe Mira did tell everybody about my Pushing, and it got all the way to the top. Then again, Caleb doesn't seem overly hostile, so maybe I'm wrong.

As Caleb navigates a handful of streets, my nervousness over the possible reasons for Jacob's request is quickly superseded by the fear induced by Caleb's driving. I didn't blame him for driving like a maniac when we had to save Mira, but there's no reason to do so now.

"I don't need to be back for work, so please don't kill us," I say. Caleb ignores that statement, so I ask, "What does Jacob want?"

"What he wants is between you and him." Caleb honks at a guy who stopped at a red light, like that's a mistake or something. "I'm trying to make up for the time you took getting ready. We have an extra errand before I take you to Jacob." The light changes, and we surge ahead.

"What extra errand?" As I sip my drink, I realize he didn't make fun of it. Most people at least ask about it. In my experience, in mainstream America, pea-green morning drinks are looked on with either suspicion or ridicule.

"We're going to have some fun," he says in an apparent attempt to cheer me up. "A guy in Brooklyn is our first target."

"Our target?" I'm confused. "What are you talking about?"

"Our deal," he says, scowling at me. I really wish he'd keep his eyes on the road. "I thought of someone."

Our deal. Crap. I'd hoped he'd forget I promised to help him Read deeper into some fighter's memories than he can do on his own—something other Readers refuse to do for him. I was hoping to learn more about *why* they refuse, even though it's too late—I already agreed to do it in exchange for him helping save Mira.

"What can you tell me about this thing we're about to do?" I ask. All of a sudden, his driving isn't my biggest concern.

"Truth be told, not that much," he says contemplatively, looking at the road ahead. "When I did it before, it was with someone who's only a little more powerful than myself. The woman I did it with could only spend a day in the Mind Dimension. The length of time people can collectively spend in the Mind Dimension determines how strongly the minds Join, I believe."

"You believe?" Great. Any confidence I had in Caleb's understanding of this thing goes up in smoke. I wonder if he knows any more than I do.

"It's hard to describe, Darren. All I can say is, let's just agree to stay out of each other's heads."

That's when it hits me: he'll have access to my head. He'll have access to my thoughts in a way I still don't quite understand. If it's anything like Reading, he could theoretically find out what happened yesterday. He could find out I Pushed someone, if he doesn't know already. I have a feeling I'd be in deep trouble if that happened. More than anything, I want to ask him how he feels about Pushers, but that could just get him thinking about it, which could increase the odds of him snooping in my mind.

"The more I hear, the more I don't really want to do this, Caleb."

"Yeah, I'm a little hesitant myself," he says, and I begin to have hope. Then my hope is dashed as he adds, "But it's not like

I get a chance like this every day. Who knows if I'll ever get another one like it. As for you—a deal's a deal."

"What do you mean, you might never get another chance like this? I'll totally do it some other day; you just caught me off-guard. I wasn't expecting you today. I'm not ready, psychologically. I'd like to give it a little thought before I just dive in." It sounds reasonable to me, but Caleb isn't sold.

"Oh, I'm not worried about collecting the debt you owe me." I can't tell if he's joking or threatening. "The chance I'm talking about has more to do with our target."

"Oh, and who's that? And why is it such a rare treat?" Curiosity starts to win out over dread, by a very slim margin.

"His name is Haim. I only found out he was in town when I pinged my contacts about capable people I could actually learn something from. He could leave at any time, given the nature of his work. That's why I want to get to him now."

I absorb this information as we get off the highway in what I think is one of the Heights parts of Brooklyn, an area known for Manhattan skyline views and old brownstone buildings.

Coincidently, we double-park next to one such home, a three-story brick townhouse. It's quaint if you like older architecture, which I don't. I can just imagine how musty it is inside.

The street, though, looks much cleaner than Mira's part of town. It's almost Manhattan-like. I can see why some of my coworkers choose to live here.

"Take us in," Caleb requests without turning off the ignition.

I comply and phase into the Quiet. The jitters from the ride make it easy; fear always helps me with the process. Instantly, the sounds of the engine disappear, and I find myself in the back seat.

I bring Caleb into the Quiet with me, and we make our way to the house in silence.

When we reach the locked door, Caleb breaks it with a few powerful kicks. His legs must be incredibly strong. Then he walks in like he owns the place, and I follow.

Surprisingly, it's nice inside—really nice. There's something exotic about the décor that I can't quite place.

On the first floor, there's a kitchen where we find a man and a woman sitting at a table, eating breakfast. Both are olive-skinned and dark-haired. The guy is fairly well built—which is expected, since Caleb said he's supposed to be some kind of a fighter.

"Him," Caleb says, pointing at the guy.

"How is this supposed to work?" I ask.

"You go about it just like you're going to Read him. Then, once I'm confident you're inside his head, I'll try to Read him at the same time. That's the best way to explain it. You'll feel a strange sensation—your instinct will be to reject whatever is happening. You'll have to fight that impulse. Instead, you'll need to allow me to share your Reading. If you don't, both of us will just end up Reading him separately, like the other isn't there."

"And then? What will it be like if this works?"

"That part is hard to describe. It's easier to just try it. Psychedelic is the best way I can explain it." He smirks—not a pretty sight.

Psychedelic is good, I guess. Some people pay to have that kind of experience. I was never one of them, but still.

"Okay, got it. And we stay out of each other's individual memories," I say, trying to sound nonchalant.

"Yeah, as much as we can, but it's a crapshoot. You'll see what I mean in a second. Good luck."

"Wait, how far into his memories should I go?" I ask, trying to postpone the inevitable.

"Don't go too deep. Your time will be split at least three ways when we do this. I promised not to squeeze your Depth dry, and I want to keep my word. Just try to go for the first violent memory you can. That kind of thing shouldn't be hard to locate when it comes to Haim." This last bit seems to amuse Caleb.

"Okay, fine. Let's do it," I say, placing my hand on Haim's wrist. I start getting into the Coherence state—the prerequisite for Reading. It comes to me almost instantly, despite the extra stress.

And then I'm inside Haim's mind.

2

"Haim, it's been so good having you around," Orit says to us in English. We take a sip of the tea she's prepared for us, trying not to burn our tongue, and reflect on how hanging out with our sister has been a highlight of the year.

"Now it's your turn," we say. "You have to visit me and Grandma in Israel."

Orit hesitates before she nods. Despite her agreement, we know she's not likely to come. We're not actually that upset about it; we're usually in too much danger to have little Orit around. But then again, we think she really ought to visit Israel at some point. Maybe she could find a husband there. Or finally learn a few words in Hebrew.

I, Darren, disassociate from Haim's immediate memory. I'm amazed yet again at the lack of language barriers when it comes to Reading. Haim's native tongue appears to be Hebrew, yet I understand his thoughts, just like I did with the Russians the other day. It seems to prove that thought is language-independent, unless something else explains this phenomenon.

I also reflect on how someone else's feelings become my own during Reading—for example, the olive-skinned woman at this table seemed very plain to me a moment ago, but inside Haim's head, everything is different. Her dark eyes and hair are just like our mother's—and the similarity is further highlighted by her caring nature . . .

I'm distracted from my rumination when I feel something new.

This *something* is hard to explain. Have you ever had a head rush from getting up too quickly or drinking too much? Multiply that lightheadedness a thousandfold, and you might get a glimpse of what this feels like.

All my instincts tell me I need to clear my head of this feeling. To get stability. To ground myself, which means I need to do the opposite—at least if I follow Caleb's instructions.

So I try to remain loopy. It's difficult, but my reward, if you can call it that, is a strengthening of this weird feeling. It now feels less like lightheadedness and more like free falling from a plane—a feeling I got to know recently from Reading my friend Amy's skydiving experience.

And then something completely different begins.

A feeling of unimaginable intensity overcomes me, a combination of overwhelming awe and wonder. There's a strange bliss to it, followed by a feeling of becoming something more than my own self—becoming a new being. It's both frightening and beautiful.

The sensation comes in waves of moments when I feel deep understanding of everything in the world, even the universe—or maybe even the multiverse—as though, all of a sudden, my intelligence has multiplied. That brief sensation of omniscience dissipates the next moment, and what I feel can best be described as cherishing something sacred, like standing in reverence next to a monument for fallen soldiers.

In the midst of all this, the knowledge dawns on me: I'm not alone. I'm part of something more elemental than myself. And then, I understand.

I'm not simply Darren, not anymore. I'm Caleb. And I'm Darren. Both at once. But not in the way Reading allowed me to be other people. This is a much deeper connection. During Reading, I merely see the world through someone else's eyes. This Joint Reading experience is much more than that. I see the world through Caleb's eyes, but he also sees the world though *my* eyes. It almost blows my mind when I realize I can even see through his eyes how the world looks through mine, when filtered by his perception and biases.

I can tell he's trying not to get deep into my mind, and I try to reciprocate by focusing on not getting into his. As this is happening, the positive feelings I was experiencing thus far begin to turn dark. I sense something frightening in Caleb's mind. And the whole universe seems to be shouting one idea in our joint mind: *"We are staying out of each other's heads. We are staying out of each other's heads . . ."*

But before either one of us can actually follow this reasonable mantra, a barrage of memories is triggered, all at once.

On some level, I'm not sure how, I know that Caleb is seeing my most embarrassing and vivid memories. I don't know why it's happening; it could be because they shine so brightly in my mind, or it could be because he's curious about some of this stuff. Whatever the answer, he's reliving the time my moms talked to me about masturbating. If it were possible to turn red right now, I'd look like a tomato at the thought of sharing that particular memory. He's also reliving other things, like the time I first phased into the Quiet after my bike accident. The first time I had sex. The day I saw Mira in the Quiet and realized I wasn't alone.

On some level, I'm reliving all these memories at the same time. All at once, as though in a dream.

And then I realize something else is happening. With dread, I see a mental tsunami coming at me.

It's Caleb's memories.

3

Caleb, the device was found.

We read the text and are overwhelmed with relief.

"We?" a sarcastic voice in my head says. "It's me, kid, Caleb. This is my memory."

"'We' is how I experience it, Caleb," I snap back, hoping he can hear me. "You think I want to be here?"

"So get the fuck out."

"I would if I could."

"Try," Caleb thinks at me, but it's too late. I'm immersed back in Caleb's memory, which continues to unfold like a Reading session.

The text doesn't change our mission, we realize.

We're approaching the car, trying to get as close to it as possible before Splitting. It's a fine balance, this business of attacking someone who can also enter the Mind Dimension. It's a difficult art that we're still developing.

Typically, it's hard to catch someone unawares if he or she

can Split. From childhood, those of us with the ability to enter the Mind Dimension learn to immediately scan the environment around us when we Split. Or at least the paranoid among us do.

The solution is very bold; few would have the balls to try it. The answer is to attack someone inside the Mind Dimension itself.

I, Darren, disassociate for a moment and think at Caleb, "Why attack someone in the Quiet? Nothing you do there has any effect in the real world."

"What did I tell you about getting out of my head?" He sounds angry, if it's possible to sound angry while thinking. "At the very least, stop the fucking commentary. For your information, when one of us dies in the Mind Dimension, it has an effect—a lasting effect. Trust me."

"But still, why not do your attack in the real world?" I ask.

"Look, kid, I'm not here to teach you anything. We're here for me, remember? But if it shuts you up, let me explain. One benefit of attacking someone in the Mind Dimension is that there's no possibility the person will see me until I pull him or her in. It's the ultimate stealth, and the reason for the development of this technique. Another huge advantage is that, in the Mind Dimension, a Pusher can't use random bystanders to aid himself—something that fucker would definitely try. But before going in and attacking people in the Mind Dimension, keep in mind that this technique has drawbacks. In a regular fight, I can leverage the Mind Dimension. It's a huge edge. I can Split and see where my frozen opponent is about to strike me. If the opponent isn't a Reader or a Pusher, I can Read him too, which gives me valuable information about my opponent's actions in the immediate future. Unfortunately, in this case, the opponent is a Pusher. All I can rely on is fighting prowess. This suits me just fine, since I'm confident in my abilities in that department. Still, I always strategize based on the assumption that my opponent is as good as, or better than, me—as unlikely as that is in practice."

"Wow, dude, that's way more than I ever wanted to know about the subject—and extremely arrogant, to boot," I think at him.

"You asked, asshole."

With no more commentary coming from Caleb, I get sucked back into his memory.

A car alarm blares in the distance. We decide that the location we're in now should work for our purposes: far enough that the Pusher couldn't have seen us coming, but not so far away that we can't fight when the moment arrives.

We Split, and the car alarm, along with other ambient noise, disappears.

Now that we're in battle mode, our need to kill the man in the car—the Pusher—is overwhelming. It overtakes our whole being. We rarely get a chance like this. A righteous, completely justified kill. No way will we face an attack of conscience over this. No, there won't be any lost sleep, or even an ounce of remorse this time. If anyone ever deserved to die, it's our current target.

This Pusher has been trying to damage the Readers' gated community for weeks now. He's responsible for the bomb that our men are disarming at this very moment.

So many Readers could have died. On our watch. This possibility is so unthinkable, we still can't fully wrap our head around it. And it was all avoided by mere chance, by a lucky discovery. We saw the telltale signs inside the mind of that electrician. We don't dwell on what would've happened if this had gone undiscovered. The only consolation is that we would've died along with the victims, given where the explosion was set to take place. We wouldn't have had to live with the shame of being Head of Security and allowing such a thing to occur.

Of course, the chicken-shit Pusher did none of the work himself. No. He mentally compelled the staff at the community instead.

Rage wells within us again when we focus on how these nice, regular people got their minds fucked with, simply because they happened to be contractors, plumbers, and gardeners working at the Reader community. We seethe at the injustice of it, at how they would've been blown up along with the Readers, collateral damage in the Pusher's eyes. We would never resort to such a maneuver. The idea of collateral damage is among the things that made us eventually leave Special Ops.

Our rage grows exponentially as we remember what Julia told us she gleaned while Reading Stacy, the bartender—what this slime did to her. The metaphorical rape of Stacy's mind, making her try to hurt the people she worked for, wasn't enough for him. The fucker took it a sick step further and made it literal. He decided to mix his unholy business with the abominable perversion of pleasure, making her do such twisted things . . .

We take a deep breath, trying to suppress our rage, which is beginning to overflow. Rage is not helpful in combat. At least not in the style of fighting we have cultivated. We need to be assessing, analyzing, and then acting. We know that historically, berserkers always died, albeit gloriously, on the battlefield. That's not our way. In fact, we practice something that can be said to be the opposite of blind fury. We call our style *Mindful Combat*. It requires a degree of tranquility. We take some more deep breaths. We mean for one person to die today, and he is in that car. We need to live on so we can hunt down and kill anyone else who's part of this crime, this conspiracy.

We're watching the man in the front window of his car. We're wary. We recognize people like ourselves, former military, and this guy's body language screams Special Ops. The way he parked away from any good sniping spot, the alert way he's sitting. All these clues point to elite training. But this guy is not from the Special Activities Division, our own background. We're pretty sure of that. He might've trained with the Recapture Tactics Team—though this asshole probably Pushed to get his way in, at least at the psych-profiling stage.

Taking a final deep breath, we shoot out the passenger window and punch the frozen Pusher in the face, knowing that the physical contact will bring him into our Mind Dimension. Killing him here is the goal. Doing it slowly, if possible, would be a bonus.

We prepare to shoot as soon as he materializes—but he doesn't. We're taken aback for a second. He should've materialized in the backseat, we think momentarily before a sharp pain in our right shoulder grabs our full attention.

Strangely, the Pusher seems to have materialized outside the car. We don't recall anyone ever becoming corporeal in the Mind Dimension this way. There's no time to wonder how it happened, or where he got the knife that's now lodged in our shoulder. With this injury, our whole world becomes focused on one thing only: survival.

The burn in our shoulder is excruciating, and just holding the gun in our right hand feels like torture. Doing our best to ignore the pain, we turn around and try to fire at the attacker. He anticipates the move, and with a twist, manages to get free. If not for our injury, there would be no way he'd get away with this, but as it is, a moment later our weapon clinks as it falls to the ground. His other hand reaches into his coat pocket.

It's time for a desperate maneuver.

We head-butt him—a move so dangerous that we normally discourage our people from using it.

The blow brings stars to our eyes, and a sense of disorientation, but it seems that the risk was worth it. The Pusher clutches his now-hopefully-broken nose. This is our moment.

Using our good left hand, we punch him in the nose—which he's clutching with his hands—and with the injured arm, we reach into his coat pocket.

We grab his gun, lift our right hand, and let it come down. Using the injured hand this way, with the gun as a makeshift club, hurts us less than a punch would have. The heavy gun handle lands on the same weak spot on the Pusher's nose.

He doesn't pull his hands away. The damage to his nose must be severe.

He tries to go for a low kick, hoping to hit our legs. We move out of the way of the attack, take the gun into our left hand, and take it off safety.

We shoot his left upper arm first. He makes a strange gargling sound.

We shoot his upper right arm next. This time, he screams.

We savor the fact that his pain must be excruciating.

A shot to each leg follows, and he falls to the ground, trying to get into some semblance of a defensive position.

Now the Mindful Combat part is over, and we can let the rage back in.

Still, we don't let the rage make us go too quickly. We kick and take a breath. Then kick again and again.

We're moving in a fog. Time seems to slow.

When our legs ache and we're satisfied with the amount of bone-crunching noises, we finally get tired of this game. After all, unless the Pusher dies of these injuries, he'll be good as new when he gets out. But that's not going to happen. We aim the gun at our opponent's head.

It's time to get to the point. It's time to begin killing this Pusher . . .

I, DARREN, HAVE TO REMIND MYSELF THAT THIS WHOLE experience was just Caleb's horrific memory. I feel sick. But at the same time, I also feel surprisingly at ease with the memory. It's a very strange, contradictory combo.

"No shit," Caleb's voice intrudes. "We're part of the same mind for now, and my half of it is fine with it. How your half, the weak half feels, is irrelevant. You don't like it? Then get the fuck out."

I try, but I can't control it. Unbidden, another memory of Caleb's overtakes me.

WE HEAR A LOUD NOISE AND WAKE UP. THE ALARM CLOCK NEXT to our bed is showing three a.m., meaning it's only been an hour since we went to bed. That's a single hour of sleep after hundreds of miles of running in the span of four days.

We're being dragged somewhere. The weariness dulls the panic a bit, but we know something bad is coming. And that's when the first punch lands. Then the second. Someone pushes us, and we slip on someone's blood and fall to the ground. After all that, they decide to beat the shit out of us?

We try to ignore the pain, making a valiant effort not to Split into the Mind Dimension. Such a reprieve would be cheating, and we want to feel like we earned our place here.

"Don't you want to quit?" a voice keeps saying, and we hear someone agree. That person's beating stops, but of course, he's out of the program. To us, there is no such option. We would give anything to stay in—lose anything, endure anything. We never quit. Ever.

Instead, we slowly begin to get up. A kick lands to our kidney, another to the small of our back, but rather than keeping us down, they have the reverse effect: they spur us into action. It feels like the world is pushing us down. We fight for every inch, every microsecond of progress we make, and we find ourselves standing on two feet once again.

The blows raining down on us from all around stop abruptly.

A large man steps forward.

"This one isn't just surviving—the bastard wants to fight. Look at his posture," he says, surprise mixed with approval in his voice.

We don't have the strength to answer. Instead, we strike at him with our right arm, instantly blocking his countermove.

The man's eyebrows go up. He didn't expect this much resistance.

Once in fight mode, muscle memory takes over, and we start the deadly dance of our personal fighting style. Even through our exhaustion, we feel a twinge of pride as a low snap kick penetrates the man's defenses. His right knee buckles at the impact; he falters, if only for an instant.

We become a flurry of fists, head, knees, and elbows.

The guy is already bleeding when someone yells, "Stop!"

We don't. More people enter the fight. The style we've developed can usually deal with multiple opponents, but not people of this caliber, and not when nearly dead from exhaustion. We contemplate the idea of Splitting to cope, but decide against it.

Fatalistically, we block the deadly barrage of their attacks, but eventually an opponent lands a perfectly executed round kick to the left side of our head, and the world goes dark.

I, DARREN, GET MY BEARINGS BACK.

"What the fuck was that?" I try to scream. Of course, I don't have a body, so the scream just goes into the ether that is our joint mind.

"Just some training," Caleb's thought comes to me in response. "You seriously need to focus. You're on the right track, seeking out the violence, but you're still in the wrong person's head: mine. Get back to Haim. Remember what we came here to do."

I try to remember. It feels like years ago when we came to Brooklyn Heights to Read this Israeli guy. And as I recall this, I realize that I'm still there with Haim and Caleb, still conversing with Haim's/Caleb's/my sister Orit. The shock of becoming a double—no, triple—mind is still with me, but at least I can think on my own again.

"Hurry," Caleb hastens me. "We're about to fall into each other's memories again."

I don't want *that,* so I make a herculean effort to properly get back into Haim's head. I try the trick of feeling light. I picture myself as vapor in a fog, as weightless as a dandelion floret floating in a light morning breeze, and it seems to work.

As I get that now-familiar feeling of going deep into someone's mind, I try to zero in on and recall just a fraction of what I saw in Caleb's mind.

It seems to do the trick . . .

4

THE ATTACKER IN FRONT OF US LEAVES HIS MIDSECTION EXPOSED for a moment; it's the last thing he'll do in this fight, we think as we unleash the burst.

"You did it, kid," Caleb's thought intrudes. "Finally, we're both in Haim's head."

"I got as much. You don't exactly think in Hebrew, do you?"

"Right. Now shut the fuck up and let me see this."

The 'burst' is what we mentally call this quick succession of punches to our opponent's solar plexus. We walk into our opponent as we strike, making the force of our punches that much more potent. We count twenty hits before he tries to block and stage a simultaneous counterattack.

Fleetingly impressed with his economy of movement, we grab his arm and use his own momentum to throw him off balance. He hits the ground, hard. Before he tries to pull us down with him, we kick his jaw—and feel the crunch of bone as the outer edge of our bare foot connects with his mandible. He stops moving.

He'll probably be fine. A couple of rib fractures and a broken jaw are a small price to pay for the opportunity to fight against us. Anyone who tried this outside our training module wouldn't learn a thing. They would die instead.

The training module is our response to the immense pressure from our friends at the Shayetet to teach our unique fighting style to their people. They know we've left Krav Maga, the martial art style of Israel, far behind. What we've developed transcends Krav Maga, transcends every fighting style we've ever encountered.

Fighting in these modules is a compromise. No death strikes, no aggressive groin assaults; no one dies in the training module. Such a compromise defeats much of the original intent, of course. This style was designed with a single purpose in mind: killing your opponent. Now much of our energy is wasted trying not to use the style as it was designed. Not killing our opponent feels unnatural, counter to everything we've spent our life working toward. A hollow imitation of what we envisioned. Much to our dismay, no one else seems to care about these nuances. They clamor for a school where civilians will learn this for their own amusement, refusing to understand that it's impossible to tame this training. This is not a sport for civilians; this is life or death. Anything less dishonors the work we have done, the lives taken in the evolution of our unique fighting style.

"Ha-mitnadev haba," we say in Hebrew, which, I, Darren, understand to mean 'next volunteer.'

We recognize the man who comes in: Moni Levine. He's a renowned Krav Maga teacher. They probably want him to learn from us in the hope that he can teach it afterwards. We hope that it works out somehow. We would welcome any opportunity to be left out of this futile teaching business.

I, Darren, disassociate as I have done during other Readings. This time is different, of course, since I still feel Caleb here. I feel his excitement. He clearly appreciates Haim's fighting style more than I do.

"Don't distract," Caleb's thought comes, and I let Haim's memory absorb me again.

"Azor, esh li maspik," Moni says after five minutes of brutal attacks. Not surprisingly, that means 'stop, I have had enough.'

We graciously tell him he did well and that he's welcome to return.

The next opponent enters. Then another. It must be ten or more in a row. None of them are a challenge. This is another part of the training that we hate. We fight almost robotically, letting our thoughts drift to the upcoming quick trip to the United States. We're concerned that this training module will make us develop deadly habits, like thinking idle thoughts during a fight . . .

I, Darren, disconnect again, only to have Caleb mentally convince me to find another recent memory of the same kind. So I do. It's nearly identical to the previous fight, but Caleb wants to experience it. And then another. And another.

We do this over and over, reliving at least a week—if not two or three—of non-stop fighting. It all starts to blur.

"I can't take this anymore," I think at Caleb eventually. The fatigue that I feel is not physical, but mental. Somehow that makes it more potent, inescapable. The human psyche isn't equipped to do what we're doing right now. I feel like I haven't slept in years, haven't rested in millennia. I'm forgetting the

time when I wasn't Haim. I can't recall a moment when I was *not* doing this accursed fighting.

"Fine," I get a response back. I feel a sudden, enormous sense of loss. It's as though the whole universe imploded.

After a few confusing moments, I understand. Caleb got out. I'm here by myself—no longer part of the joint-mind being.

Not willing to spend a millisecond longer than I have to in Haim's head, I instantly get out as well.

I'M BACK IN HAIM AND ORIT'S KITCHEN IN THE QUIET. I LOOK IN shock at Haim, who's still frozen—with that wax-statue smile directed at his also-frozen sister. He doesn't look nearly as dangerous as I now know he is. In that, he's unlike Caleb, who always looks kind of dangerous with his badass manner and that gleam in his eye. And now that I've gotten a glimpse inside Caleb's fucked-up mind, I know that he's even more dangerous than he looks.

I try not to think too deeply about what I just experienced. It's too late, though; the violent images run through my mind, and I'm overwhelmed. It's not Haim's memories of the never-ending fight that do this to me. It's Caleb's. Those things he did to the Pusher are disturbingly fresh, replaying in my head over and over. I sit down at the breakfast table, in the empty chair next to Haim's sister, and try to take a few calming breaths. If I wasn't in the Quiet now, I think I would be sick.

"Are you okay, kid?" Caleb asks quietly.

"No," I answer honestly. "I'm far from okay."

"For what it's worth, I am never doing *that* again," he says, to my huge relief. "Your mind is too twisted."

"What? *Mine* is too twisted?" I say in outrage, weariness momentarily forgotten. The gall of this guy. I'm not the one who tortures and murders people. I'm not the one who took some kind of weird masochistic pleasure in brutal training. I didn't ask someone to Read a killer, so I could become an even better killer myself.

"You're one odd puppy." He smirks. "But it's not just that. I really hated that feeling in the beginning, when our minds Joined."

"I thought you'd done this before."

He looks serious for a change. "This was different from the other time I did this. Too strange. Way too deep. We didn't experience each other's memories to the same degree when I did it before. This time, it felt almost . . ." He looks away, like he's embarrassed to say the words out loud. "I don't know, like a religious experience. Sorry, kid. The whole thing was just way too deep for me."

Hmm, religious. That's an interesting way to look at it. I wouldn't have called it that, but now that he mentions it, I can see how the word makes sense. Not that I've ever experienced any kind of deep religious experiences myself, growing up under the care of two secular moms. I'd use the words *transcendental* or *trippy* to describe what happened.

"I'm in complete agreement," I say. "I never want to do it again, either." *Especially with a mind as screwed up as yours,* I think, but don't say it.

"And we won't speak of what we saw in there. That's just between us." He looks at me intently.

"Of course. That's understood," I say, a little too eagerly perhaps. I don't know the full catalogue of the things he saw from my past, but I have no doubt he got more than his share of embarrassing tidbits. Thankfully, he seems to have missed the memory I most wanted to hide—what happened yesterday. Otherwise, I might be suffering a fate similar to the Pusher in his memory. The thought fills me with dread.

"You must be capable of even more Mind Dimension Depth than I suspected," Caleb observes. "That Depth determines how far the minds intertwine during this experience. That must be why it was so intense."

I digest this information. If what he says is true, then this experience will be more potent with almost anyone else—Caleb's Depth is allegedly pretty shallow. I'll have to be careful if I ever try it again. Not that I'm planning on it.

"Are you okay to walk back?" he says, interrupting my thoughts.

"Yeah, I guess. I certainly don't see the point of sitting here," I say. "Did you at least learn Haim's fighting style? I'd hate to think we went through all that for nothing."

"Oh, in that sense, this was a huge success. It exceeded all my expectations. He's truly brilliant. Someday, I'm going to visit him in the real world, somehow get him to fight me, like he did with the people in his memory. That's only after I come up with some counters to his best moves, of course," Caleb says, chuckling.

"How does that work?" I wonder out loud. "Learning from Reading? Did I learn anything?"

"It'll help *me* more than you. A practical knowledge base plays an important role. In my case, I'm familiar with Krav Maga, Aikido, Keysi, kickboxing, and many other styles that were clearly influences on Haim's style. Thanks to that earlier knowledge, I'll be able to appropriate a lot of what we both experienced on a direct, conscious level. But for you, I have no clue. You should've learned something, but I don't know how much. And whether you can use whatever stuck in your mind in practice is a big gamble."

And before he even finishes speaking, he's standing next to me, aiming a punch at my face.

What I do next amazes me when I think of it later. I jump out of the chair and throw it at Caleb. Then, without conscious thought, my elbow stops his right hand mid-punch. My elbow hurts like hell, but the alternative would've been my face. What's even more amazing is that my left hand tries to hit him in mid-chest. I remember doing this as Haim. It's Haim's signature move, I think—this punch in the solar plexus.

Caleb takes the hit in the chest, seemingly only raising an eyebrow in response. This should've hurt, I think fleetingly. But then again, some people's abdominal musculature can reduce the impact of that hit. That little tidbit of knowledge comes to me from nowhere. I can't dwell on it too much because he throws a punch, which I manage to block, and then I see another flash of movement. Before I understand what's happening, a horrific pain explodes in my groin.

The world becomes pain. I can't breathe.

I fall to the floor, clutching my balls.

"Sorry about that," Caleb says. "You reacted so well, I thought I'd push you a little. I didn't think you'd manage to not block such an obvious, slow kick. A move that's a cornerstone of Haim's style. You had to have done it yourself, at least a thousand times back in his head."

He's smirking as he says that—the bastard.

If I had a gun in my hand, I would shoot him in his smug face. The pain is unlike any I've ever experienced. The kick might've been 'slow,' but it doesn't matter—it's such a sensitive area. I try to regain control of my breathing. "You. Literally. Busted. My. Balls," I manage to say with difficulty.

"You'll be as good as new when we get back to our bodies," he says, sounding utterly unapologetic.

"Fuck you." Even to my own ears, I sound like the sore loser in a schoolyard brawl.

"Here, lean on me as we walk out," he says, offering me his hand. I make him wait a couple of minutes, standing there in a strange hand-extended pose. When the pain subsides a little, I take the proffered hand.

Barely able to walk, I make my way out of Haim's sister's house. As soon as I'm standing next to my frozen self, I grab my elbow to phase out.

5

THE WORLD COMES BACK TO LIFE, THE PAIN INSTANTLY GONE. The sudden lack of agony feels like pleasure for a moment. It overtakes me as we start our mad drive deeper into Brooklyn.

Immersed in that bizarre lack-of-agony bliss, I'm thankful yet again for this particular property of phasing out: the fact that leaving the Quiet undoes any physical damage you receive while inside. However, I now know there's something irreparable that *can* happen to you in the Quiet.

Dying.

While I'm not yet sure how it works, I know Caleb was trying to kill that Pusher in the Quiet. His thoughts were clear on the matter—the Pusher was going to be erased from existence. Caleb had one-hundred-percent conviction of that.

I guess on some level I knew that death in the Quiet was a possibility, which is why I never tried to off myself there. A little cutting, sure, but I always avoided anything potentially fatal. I always had a feeling, an intuition, that if I died in the Quiet, it might spill over into reality.

"Am I getting the silent treatment the rest of the way?" Caleb says, pulling me from my morbid contemplation.

I realize that we've been driving in silence for a while. Caleb probably assumes I'm pissed about that below-the-belt hit of his. And I am, but it's a tiny part of my concerns at the moment.

"I'm just thinking about what happened. Why we saw the specific memories we did," I say, only half-lying.

"Someone told me once that you tend to find the memory your conscious—or sometimes subconscious—mind is dwelling on," he explains. He shrugs, like he's not sure whether that makes sense or not. "Seemed like a good enough explanation to me."

It makes sense. Caleb asked me to seek out violent fighting memories, and I saw his training. I had been wondering what Readers do to Pushers, and I got *that* memory. Now I just need to make sure my Pusher connection stays hidden. Caleb clearly didn't access that memory of mine, and I want to keep it that way. I'm more certain than ever that I don't want Readers to know anything about my secret.

"So that's why I saw all that violence in your head," I say. It's a calculated statement. I'm trying to cover up, since I just realized I could've given myself away by accessing that Pusher-related memory of his. If I can convince him that a Pusher being in the memory was just a coincidence and that violence was the real reason that moment in time popped up, he hopefully will never draw any other conclusion.

Caleb sighs at my statement. "That's not the only reason. When you get into my head, violence is what you'll find, no matter what your other interests are. There's not much else in there. You won't find two loving mommies, or puppies and rainbows."

Though he's trying to be sarcastic, I can't help but feel a twinge of pity. He sounds almost wistful. Is this cold-blooded killer wishing he had happier memories?

"Darren," he says as I ponder this. His tone is different now, harder to pin down. I'm not sure I like it. "There's something else we need to talk about."

My stomach twists. Does he know about my Pushing abilities after all?

"If Jacob asks you about Julia—which I don't think he will—say you don't know anything," he says, and I expel a relieved breath. I now understand the tone. It's worry, which sounds unnatural for Caleb. That's two unexpected emotions in a row. Did our being in each other's heads do something to him?

"Sure," I say, trying to sound like it's no big deal. "No problem. But why?"

"Since she's recovering, I don't see any need to worry her parents. Plus, she wouldn't want her father to know she helped Mira and got shot," he says curtly.

I get it now. It's not just Julia who doesn't want that. Caleb allowed his boss's daughter to get shot. I get the sense his ass is grass if Jacob finds out the truth.

"Your secret's safe with me," I say, possibly overacting a bit.

He doesn't respond, and silence falls again as we continue riding.

As we leave all the other cars behind in the mad rush to the Reader community, I think some more about what just happened. In theory, I should have some seriously impressive fighting skills for the first time in my life. And I don't mean simply being able to kick ass in a bar brawl either—what Haim did went way beyond kicking some dumb jock's butt. It's an exciting thought. If, by some misfortune, I get into a fight, I'll be able to hold my own. In theory, at least.

Recognizing the view outside, I realize we're passing by the canal—that small body of water on what Eugene called Sheepshead. We're on Emmons Avenue, the street where those mobsters were shooting at Eugene and me just yesterday. We're almost at the community, and I wonder again what Jacob wants.

When we leave the car in the parking lot, we're met by a dude I recall seeing the other day. The one who doesn't seem to like Eugene. Caleb's rude twin—and being ruder than Caleb is a challenge. I really dislike the look he gives me—kind of like a wolf eyeing a stray lamb.

"Sam, take Darren to meet Jacob and bring him back here when they're done," Caleb says.

Sam turns toward the lavish building without a word, walking briskly toward it. I follow him. The silence hangs over us the whole way.

Who knew Caleb would turn out to be the friendly one?

"Sam, you may go now," Jacob says dismissively after Sam leads me into the man's posh office.

"Darren, it's nice to meet you face to face," Jacob says as soon as Sam is gone. He shakes my hand firmly, giving me a reassuring smile.

"Nice to meet you too, Jacob." I try to return his friendliness and hope he doesn't notice how nervous I am.

He looks different in this face-to-face encounter than on

Skype the other day. I guess Eugene brought out the worst in him. Today Jacob seems like a nice guy.

"I wanted to properly introduce myself." He sits down, gesturing for me to take the chair across from his desk. "We don't get new Readers every day."

"I see. There seemed to be an element of urgency for this specific visit." I try not to sound hostile as I take my seat. I also wonder if I should phase into the Quiet and take a look around the office. Given that he's aware of the Quiet, would Jacob leave anything informative lying around? Not likely, I determine, and decide against it.

"No true urgency, I assure you. More like satisfaction of my curiosity, and a proper response to a truly rare case. Your situation is very special. You said you didn't know you were a Reader until yesterday."

"I said it because it's true," I respond, a little too defensively. Modifying my tone, I continue, "I was adopted, you see."

"You have to forgive me if I sounded incredulous—I certainly didn't mean to imply deceit on your part. It's just such an unusual occurrence. Particularly the fact that you discovered on your own that you can Split. Did I get that part right?"

"Yes. It first happened to me as a child," I say. I tell him about the bike accident, about thinking I was about to die and the whole world freezing around me.

He asks more about my childhood, and I tell him a few stories. It's the friendliest interrogation technique I've ever encountered. The guy seems genuinely curious about me. And I have a weakness. Like most people, I like talking about myself. As I realize this, I proceed more carefully. I don't want to blurt out anything that can reveal my Pusher experience.

"The main thing I wanted to talk to you about today is

discretion," Jacob says after I accept his offer of coffee, and he personally makes me a cup.

"Discretion?" I say, blowing on my coffee.

"We Readers have kept our existence a secret from other people since antiquity," he says, his voice becoming preachy and monotone. I get the feeling he's given this spiel many times before. "We have always firmly believed that if the public found out, they would do something terrible to us."

I recall both Mira and Eugene alluding to the Reader community having a non-disclosure stance when it comes to Reader powers. Remembering how Jacob reacted to Eugene on Skype, I decide not to go with 'I've heard this from Eugene before.' Instead, I say, "That's pretty dark."

"Yes," Jacob agrees. "But we can Read people's minds, as you now know, and that ability enables us to accurately assess human nature. Trust me when I say they would not take to us kindly at all. I wish it weren't so, but it's the truth."

"So what do you think would happen if our existence became common knowledge?" I ask, putting my suddenly chilled hands around the warm cup.

"We could become secret slaves to some government agency —and that would be the best case scenario." His jaw tightens. "The more likely possibility would be complete genocide."

Genocide? Wow, he doesn't pull his punches. "Does the prospect have to be so bleak?" I inquire, forcing myself to sip my coffee. I can't resist my tendency to play the devil's advocate. I haven't given this topic much thought after my friends mentioned it, but what Jacob says actually sounds plausible—which is why some pain-in-the-ass part of me questions it. My habit of questioning virtually everything drove my moms and my uncle nuts when I was growing up. "What about progress?" I say. "Surely in modern times, people wouldn't do something like that. It's not like we're that much different from anyone else."

"We're a different species." His tone sharpens.

"Well, strictly speaking, we're not." Even though I risk further eroding the positive tenor of our discussion, I can't help myself. "The ones you call half-bloods are proof of that."

And just like that, the conversation takes a bad turn. Jacob's face goes red. "You're not here to split hairs about semantics." He slaps his palm on the desk. "That so-called progress will just make our annihilation faster than we ever thought possible."

I stare at him, shocked into silence by his outburst. "I didn't mean to upset you," I say in a soothing tone after a moment.

He takes a deep breath and lets it out in an audible sigh. "I'm sorry. This is a sensitive issue for me."

"I understand," I say cautiously. I wonder if he's so touchy because Eugene, a half-blood, used to date his daughter. "You have to realize that I have a deep affinity for normal people—" I use my fingers to make air quotes around the word *normal*, "—since until recently, I assumed I was one. I didn't know Readers existed."

"Right, and that is probably a good reason for you to trust me. My people have had centuries to develop the best strategy for dealing with our situation—and it is *not* to let anyone know of our existence. That's why I thought it important to talk to you. You are new to this, and being young, you're by nature more idealistic, more naïve, than others. As a child, you didn't get the usual Reader upbringing. You didn't learn the horror stories of our turbulent past. Trust me, the danger to our people is real."

I realize now that I might've devil's-advocated my way into

trouble. What if he thinks I can't keep their secret and decides to silence me for the good of the species?

"You make a good case, Jacob," I say solemnly. I pretend to think about it for a few seconds, hoping I'm not going overboard. "Upon reflection, I think you might be right about all this."

Pacified, he smiles. "Mostly everyone comes to that conclusion."

"I should tell you, though," I say carefully, "as a child, I might've inadvertently broken the rules that I intend to follow from now on. I tried telling people about being able to go into what you call the Mind Dimension. I don't think my attempts did Readers any harm, though. Everyone just thought I was nuts." I figure he can find this out anyway if he wants to—my moms' and my shrink's heads would be open books to any Reader—and by volunteering this information, I might be able to forestall any potential snooping. Not to mention, demonstrate my rule-abiding intentions.

As I'd hoped, Jacob shrugs, not looking overly concerned. "What's done is done. Like you said, it was dismissed; that's what matters most. It's not a crime when you don't know the rules. What's important is that you're discreet from now on. If you can mitigate some of your earlier slips, all the better. What's truly forbidden are demonstrations of Reader abilities with the intent to reveal our nature."

"Oh, I've never done that," I say. "If we're talking about Reading, I just didn't have a chance to show off that particular skill. Of course, I've abused going into the Quiet before. In either case, though, I never told—and wouldn't dream of telling—people about how any of this works, so I definitely have no plans to 'reveal our nature.'"

I do wonder if Readers approve of using powers the way I've been using them, for my personal financial gain. I'm not going to ask Jacob about it, though. If he said 'stop doing that,' I'd be out of a job. If it's forbidden, I'll stop when he explicitly asks me to. Better to ask forgiveness than permission, right?

"Good. That's what I thought," Jacob says, smiling again. "You seem like an intelligent young man."

"Thank you, Jacob. You don't need to worry. I work in a field in which confidentiality is important. Besides, I'm a very private person. And don't worry about the people I mentioned earlier, either—the ones who didn't believe me. I'll muddy the waters for them like you asked if it seems needed, but I highly doubt it will even be necessary," I say, meaning nearly every word.

"That's wonderful. Thank you for understanding."

A weight is lifted off my shoulders. I got worried for a second that my moms might be in trouble. Truth be told, they didn't for a moment believe my stories. If mitigation *is* needed, the place to start would be with my therapist. I've told her quite openly about the Quiet. Not that she believed me any more than my moms did. She thinks it's just a delusion. Still, I should probably show her that I doubt that delusion, now that, ironically, I know it's real.

This thought actually answers a question I've been pondering for a while—whether I should keep my standing appointment with my shrink tomorrow. Lately, I've been paying for my hour so I don't lose my weekly spot, but not actually going to therapy. But today, I've been feeling the urge to actually go. I can now conveniently tell myself that all I want from my shrink is to lie to her about no longer having visions of the world being stopped.

Yep, just going to go 'to mitigate,' and not to talk about anything that's bothering me—like the disturbing things I saw in Caleb's mind, for example. Or my guilt about Pushing that guy to kill himself. Or that I'm more adopted than I realized. Or even that I've met a girl—something my shrink has been nagging me about for ages, almost like a third mom. All that babbling about my feelings would imply that I'm sensitive or something—which I'm definitely not. Nope, this visit will be about this discretion business. But, because I'm there anyway, I might as well talk about some of these other issues with my shrink—the ones that aren't prohibited by the Reader code, at least. After all, that's what I pay her for.

"Now that we have the discretion issue squared away, there is another minor thing I wanted to ask you," Jacob says, distracting me from my musings about the upcoming therapy. "Does the name *Mark Robinson* mean anything to you?"

"No," I say, confused. "Should it?"

"No. Never mind. It doesn't matter." He gets up. "Sam will take you back now. I'm happy we're on the same page when it comes to keeping the Readers' existence secret."

He shakes my hand and walks me to Sam, who's waiting behind the door. Sam leads me back to Caleb, as silently as before.

6

"WHERE TO?" CALEB ASKS ME WHEN WE TURN ONTO EMMONS Avenue again.

"Can you please take me to Mira and Eugene's apartment?" I give him the address from my phone.

As we fly through the streets, something suddenly hits me. I *do* know the name Mark. That was the name of my biological father. Could that be the Mark Jacob meant?

If so, could Jacob have known my father?

When Jacob first saw me on Skype, he said I looked familiar. Did he say that because he saw my resemblance to this Mark person? Or is Mark Robinson someone else entirely? After all, Mark is a pretty common name.

I realize I need to ask my moms about my biological father's last name.

"Here we are," Caleb says. He brakes suddenly, just about throwing me through the windshield. We're near the park across the street from Mira's building. "Do you want me to wait for you?"

"No, thanks. I'll just rent a car after this. But there is something I want to ask you," I say, unbuckling my seatbelt.

"What's that?" he asks. "You had a chance to chat on the way over, you know."

I ignore his annoyed tone. "What happens to people who display their Reader powers to the world? Jacob warned me to be discreet, but I forgot to ask him about the consequences. What if I slip up?"

"It's good that you didn't ask him that." Caleb furrows his brows. "But to answer your question, all I can say is nothing good would happen. This isn't a game, kid. It's deadly serious."

"Can you be more specific?" I'm irritated at being called a kid yet again.

"If Jacob told me someone had done that, and if there was proof, I'd probably put a bullet in that person. Is that specific enough?" Caleb says, giving me a level look. "It would never happen, though. No Reader has ever been that stupid, and I doubt you are either."

"But surely someone said something at some point," I persist. "Or else there wouldn't be these rules, right? Plus, there are ideas in regular people's minds that seem like they might've originated with us. Where else would the concept of psychics come from? Just think of the term *mind reading*. And now that I think about it, maybe that's also where the reincarnation myths originated, or even astral projection and remote viewing—"

"Don't forget Bigfoot," he says, looking pointedly at his car door. "Look, I'm no historian. Maybe back in the day, people blabbed, but they don't now. And I'm sure those that did back then were burned at the stake, tortured, or had something equally unpleasant done to them by the ancient Readers. Our ancestors were pretty hardcore in that regard. Back then, for example, you'd get killed for fucking someone other than your assigned mate. And they wouldn't kill just you—they'd kill the person you slept with. I think the reason no one ever does what you describe is that we all know this brutal history. Strictly speaking, no official has ever said, 'We don't do that to traitors anymore.' So I'm telling you the truth: I've never heard of any modern-day lapses. We've looked into a few psychics who talked about reading minds, but it always turned out to be some lowlife con artist trying to scam people out of money, not Readers doing something they shouldn't."

His eyes flash darkly when he mentions the psychics. I wonder what he did to them. I don't want to ask. I've had enough Caleb-related violence for one day.

"Okay, thanks. That explains it, I guess. Now, just one more thing I wanted to ask you," I say tentatively, unsure how to go about this.

He lifts his eyebrows in a silent question.

"Can I have a gun?" I say it quickly, deciding to just blurt it out. As I say the words, I can't help staring at his glove compartment.

"You mean *that* gun?" he says, following my gaze.

"Any gun will do." I'm happy he doesn't seem too pissed to learn I've been snooping. "That gun's a revolver. They have simple mechanisms that should function in the Quiet—I mean, the Mind Dimension."

"Most guns work in the Mind Dimension," he says. "Fine. Take it—quickly, before I change my mind."

I grab the gun and exit the car. I tuck the weapon into the waistband at the back of my pants, feeling very gangster all of a sudden.

"Take the coffee too," he says, handing me the cup. "It was for you. Good luck in there."

Before I get a chance to reply, he reaches over and shuts the passenger door, almost in my face. Then the car takes off, leaving a faint smell of burning rubber in its wake.

As he leaves, I remember another related question. What happens to the people to whom the hypothetically traitorous Reader tells the secret of our existence? I guess Caleb wouldn't know, since he's never dealt with anything like that. Or so he says. I can't imagine it would be anything good. All the more reason to dissuade the shrink of my earlier revelations. I don't want her to get hurt—she's done right by me, even though I think she's full of shit most of the time.

I walk over and sit down on a bench in the park to think things over while sipping the lukewarm coffee.

It's 7:28 a.m. Mira and Eugene are probably still sleeping, like most normal people. If I do what I'm planning, Mira might be upset for more reasons than just my Pushing yesterday. But then again, I doubt I can make things worse—and I have a feeling that the element of surprise will be to my advantage.

Convinced, I sit up and, using the above-average anxiety I'm feeling at the moment, phase into the Quiet. As the sounds of the street go away, I walk toward the building.

The gun helps when it comes to opening the downstairs door. It also works like a charm on the lock of the door to their apartment. My ears still ringing from the gunshot only I could hear, I gingerly enter the apartment, thinking that it's a good thing the damage will automatically be repaired when I phase back to normal.

I begin to question the sanity of my plan again as soon as I walk into what has to be Mira's bedroom.

Mira is asleep on a gray futon. Her room is much less messy than the apartment overall. So it seems like the mess I noticed the other day is more Eugene's fault.

I'm cognizant of a lacy bra and thong lying on the chair next to the bed. I didn't think this part of the idea through. I'm in luck, though. She's clearly not sleeping naked—the shoulder that's visible above the blanket is clothed in a pajama top.

As I stand there, I wonder what will happen when I pull her into the Quiet with me while she's sleeping. I was never able to fall asleep in the Quiet, which seems to imply that Mira will wake up as soon as she enters. I'm about to find out for sure.

I reach out, pull away a few stray strands of Mira's soft dark hair, and gently touch her temple. Then I take a calming breath, realizing the chips are about to fall where they may.

She appears in the Quiet as a second Mira on the same bed, but closer to the edge on my side. This Mira has her eyes open and stares at the ceiling for a moment. Then she turns and looks at her still-sleeping double.

"Please don't panic," I whisper softly.

Hearing me, Mira jackknifes to a sitting position on the bed. Swinging her feet down to the floor, she looks at me, obviously confused.

Dressed in polka-dot pajamas, without all the makeup and the femme-fatale clothing, she looks a lot more approachable than the last time I saw her. Like the proverbial girl next door. A little vulnerable, even. These illusions last for only a moment before I get the most seething look she's ever given me.

"What. The. Fuck," she says somewhat incoherently, and for the first time, I hear a slight Russian accent in her speech.

"I'm sorry to burst in on you like this," I say quickly. "But I really needed to talk to you. Will you please hear me out?"

She jumps up—eyeing her purse, which happens to be behind me.

My heart sinks as I realize she's looking for the gun I recall her carrying in that purse.

Before I can complete the thought about the gun, she's right next to me, throwing a punch. Without consciously planning it, I catch her small fist in my hand a millisecond before it connects with my face. Then I hold it for a few moments, looking into her eyes. She seems shocked at my quick reaction. As soon as she gets her wits back and starts struggling, I let go of her hand.

She tries to kick me in the shins next, and I step back, again without conscious thought.

She almost loses her balance when her leg doesn't connect with its intended target. Her frustration turns into anger, every expression clear on her face, and she runs for the door. I briefly regret my newfound fighting reflexes. Maybe if she'd hit me, it would've been cathartic for her. Maybe afterwards she would've been willing to listen. And I can't imagine her punches would've hurt me that much—given her slim frame and all. And I'm not being sexist here, by the way. Not exactly. If my tiny friend Bert had punched me, seeing as he can't weigh much more than Mira, I doubt I would've felt anything either.

I follow her and realize she's heading into what must be Eugene's bedroom. She must be thinking about pulling him into the Quiet with us. Or getting his gun. Or both.

I wait, letting her do what she wants. I feel fairly safe, figuring that if she didn't kill me yesterday, she's even less likely to do so today after a good night's sleep. Hopefully.

Eugene walks out, wearing only wrinkled tighty-whiteys and looking confused. I don't get a chance to smirk at his appearance because Mira—holding that gun of his—immediately follows him.

The most worrisome part of this is that her hand is steady. I didn't expect that at all. She looks much calmer than yesterday—much more ready to shoot me. How could I have misjudged the situation so horribly?

I hear the gun safety click off.

Is it possible to have a heart attack in the Quiet? If so, I might be flirting with that possibility, given how fast my heart is beating.

She's carefully aiming at my head.

I expect to see at least *some* doubt on her face, but she looks completely calm. Merciless. Her forearm tenses as though she's about to pull the trigger.

I put my hand in front of my face, like that could actually protect me.

"Mira, stop." Eugene puts himself between me and the barrel. "Think about what you're about to do. He can spend *months* in the Mind Dimension."

Either seeing her brother in the way or hearing his words causes her to hesitate.

I'm speechless. She really *was* about to kill me, and Eugene obviously thought so as well. As I take a calming breath, I try not to focus on this fact. The knowledge of what she was about to do stings badly. More than I would've imagined. Thinking about it now, I realize everything I'd convinced myself of was just wishful thinking. I was so sure she wouldn't hurt me. Now, as the hard reality hits, learning that she *would* kill me feels like a deep betrayal—even though it shouldn't.

And speaking of betrayal, Eugene's reasoning for why she shouldn't pull the trigger hurts nearly as much. It sounded like he only wants to spare me because of my power. Forget friendship. 'Don't kill him so we can use his abilities in the Quiet' is what he seems to have meant.

"It doesn't matter how long he can do it," Mira says. "What good is that to us?" Her voice sounds more uncertain, however, and her hand seems less steady.

"You know it can be huge," Eugene says. "We just struck at our enemies. They're bound to retaliate."

"How do you know he's not with them? And if he offered to help us, how could we trust him?" Mira lowers the gun, as though just realizing it's pointed at her brother's chest.

"Snap out of it, Mirochka. You always said that you judge people by their actions rather than their words." Eugene gives his sister an even look. "He saved me, and afterwards he saved you—risking his life in the process. Why don't you judge Darren by his actions?"

What I can see of her face from behind his back looks thoughtful. Eugene's reasoning is spot on. I couldn't have put it better myself. Now it's clear that she's trying to make up her mind. I wish it weren't such a tough decision.

"But he is one of *them*," she says finally. I see her wrestling with the temptation to raise the gun again, but she doesn't. "For all we know, he could've been trying to weasel his way into our confidence for some reason."

"It's unlikely, Mira, and you know it. He wouldn't have revealed his Pusher nature to save you, if that were the case," Eugene says.

"Maybe that was a slip," she says, sounding less and less certain.

"That doesn't make sense," Eugene says. "He did it intentionally; you saw him. Assuming the worst case—that he did have some agenda before yesterday—he *still* decided to save you. That would count for something if it were true. But I don't think things were ever that complicated. I think it's much more likely that he truly didn't know what he was . . . what he *is*."

"Yes, exactly," I finally jump in. "I didn't."

"Shut up," Mira says angrily. "You would say that regardless."

"Well," Eugene says thoughtfully, "maybe there's a way we can figure out if he's telling the truth."

"Oh?" Mira voices my own thought.

"Yeah. I've been pondering this very question last night, and I may have thought of a way." Eugene sounds progressively more excited.

"What way?" Mira asks, and the fact that there's hope in her voice gives *me* hope.

"A test," her brother says.

Mira's shoulders sag in dismay. "You tested him yesterday. You were confident he's a Reader after that."

"And he is," Eugene says defensively. "My test wasn't wrong."

"Fine, maybe Pushers can Read as well as fuck with people's minds," Mira says stubbornly.

"They can't Read," Eugene objects. "Father was certain of that. I remember him telling me about it, and I've gone over his notes. Plus, you saw Julia make the same assumptions as me, in front of a bunch of other members of that Reader community. If anyone knew Pushers could Read, they would've corrected Julia, but they didn't. No, Mira. He *is* a Reader. That usually would mean that he's not a Pusher. Only in this case, for some reason he is. Any way you slice it, he's a strange case—in terms of his growing up with no knowledge of Reading or Pushing, and now everything that he can do."

"Fine, so he's a strange case," Mira concedes. "It doesn't mean he's telling the truth about anything."

"Which is why there's another test I want him to take. It won't tell us everything, but it will tell us if he's being honest with us. See, using my equipment, I can set up a pretty good polygraph test." Eugene is beginning to sound almost giddy at the mention of equipment.

"A lie detector test?" Mira frowns.

"Exactly." Eugene beams at her. "Like what regular people use, only better, using my research and equipment. Ever since I learned that a Reader can't Read others of our kind, I've been trying to figure out how we can keep each other honest. This is the best idea I've had so far. I can re-purpose some of the neurofeedback and other biofeedback devices that—"

"But can't people beat those things?" Mira asks, interrupting him. I'm starting to feel like I'm not even in the room. "Will it be a hundred-percent accurate?"

"Nothing is that accurate. And I suppose he *could* beat it, but it's unlikely. People can learn to beat the standard tests, but even then they need to do all this research into the methods used, and then train themselves to modify their natural responses. None of which Darren's had time to do—especially since he doesn't even know the methods I'll be using. This is the first he's even heard about being tested, so he's had no time to prepare."

"Okay, Darren—if that's even your name." Mira stands up on tiptoe to look at me over Eugene's shoulder. "If you agree to submit to my brother's test, I'll listen to what you came here to say. And I might not shoot you afterwards."

"Sure," I say readily. "I'll take the test; I have nothing to hide."

That's pretty much the truth. With only one small caveat I don't mention: Eugene is wrong on many points when it comes to this whole plan. First, I actually do know a quite a bit about these kinds of tests. I'm one of those people who did the research into how to beat them. The theory of it isn't actually specific to the test being given, since they all relate to biorhythms. Regardless of what Eugene changed about his test, I'm sure it still works on the same principles. Principles that can be taken advantage of—if I choose to do so.

"Okay, great," Eugene says. "I'll get ready. You leave the Mind Dimension and come back here to our apartment." He walks into his bedroom—I assume to reach his frozen body and phase out. And hopefully put on some pants.

Mira lingers for a moment and gives me a hard-to-define look. "You better pass," she says, and without giving me a chance to respond, goes into her own bedroom.

7

In a strange stupor, I make my way back to my body on the bench and phase out.

The world comes alive, and I consider making a run for it rather than going back. If Eugene messes up his science, I could be in real trouble. Plus, from what I know of lie detection, it's not even an exact science. It's actually part scam, often meant to scare guilty people into confessing things they're trying to hide. That's the biggest secret I learned while researching this.

A polygraph test is certainly not something I'd trust with my life.

I *would* make a run for it, but I want Mira to stop looking at me the way she has been, like I'm some kind of a monster. Like I had something to do with her parents getting killed. Also, there is that practical matter—the reason I came here in the first place. This second element is what decides it for me.

I cross the road again, only in the real world this time.

Eugene buzzes me in and opens the door. He's now dressed

in jeans and a T-shirt, and he informs me that the equipment is set up.

I try to make myself as comfortable as I can while he hooks me up to his laptop. I must look even more ridiculous than during the Reader test he gave me the other day. I have electrodes attached all over my head, presumably to measure my brain waves. I have a heartbeat monitor on my finger and a device that looks like a rubber band around my chest. I assume the latter is for detecting increased respiration. Another gadget seems to measure skin conductance—the measure of how sweaty you get. Finally, there are a few cables with purposes I don't understand. These make me nervous. I hope they're not meant to administer electric shock or something; that's what comes to my mind when I look at them.

Through all the setup, Eugene seems as excited as a kid at a birthday party.

After making what seems like a thousand adjustments, he finally seems satisfied. "I'm done," he yells, looking at the door.

Mira enters the room—carrying a gun, of course. She's swapped her PJs for skinny jeans and a low-cut tank top, a casual outfit for her. I can't believe I have the bandwidth to think *hot* about someone who wants to shoot me, but that's exactly what comes to mind when I look at Mira.

As she stares at me, her serious expression alters, and I see tiny crinkles form in the corners of her eyes. Great. She's amused at how ridiculous I look. I probably would be too, if I were in her shoes. I don't mind being mocked in this case; I'd sooner she laugh than point that gun at me. Maybe I should get myself a jester's hat so she doesn't feel the constant urge to shoot me.

She puts the gun down and sits crossed-legged on the floor,

settling herself on top of a bunch of papers, cables, and other random stuff Eugene has lying around. I make sure *not* to look down her low-cut tank top—despite the fact that it would be possible. From what I've read, arousal can be misinterpreted as a sign of lying with these tests.

"Okay, Darren, what's two plus two?" Eugene asks.

Don't ask me why I bothered to learn how to beat the polygraph exam. Let's just say if my investing activities ever led to my having to take one, I wanted to be ready. Anyway, I know what this inane question is about. Eugene is establishing a baseline. His readings of my answers to the obviously true statements will later be compared to readings after I answer more important questions. So, if I wanted to cheat, I could make myself nervous as I answer this question. That wouldn't be difficult for someone like me, who's spent most of his life making himself nervous in order to phase into the Quiet.

But I decide against trying to cheat, also known as *using countermeasures*. First, I don't really have anything to hide, so why bother? Second, as unlikely as it sounds, Eugene could be right. The fact that he's using his own version of the test might mean there's some physical reaction he's monitoring that I might not have under control—some new principle I haven't read about. If that's the case, he may think I'm messing with the test. And messing with these tests is as good an indicator as any that you're hiding something. In our case, that's the last thing I want Mira to think. The whole point of this is to gain her trust.

"Please answer quickly," Eugene says, bringing me out of my thoughts. His expression is darkening, and I realize I already started my test on the wrong foot.

"I'm sorry," I say. "I'm a little nervous. I really want you guys to believe me."

"Fine. Take a deep breath," he says, looking at the monitor.

I do as he says, taking a couple of relaxing breaths.

"Good. Now, just answer what I ask you, when I ask you," Eugene says. "What's two plus six?"

"Eight," I answer quickly, letting him get a clean baseline.

"And what's your name?" Eugene keeps his eyes on his laptop.

"Darren," I say simply.

"Did you know that either I or Mira existed before you met her in Atlantic City the other day?"

"No."

"Did you save Mira yesterday?"

"Yes."

"Are you a Reader?"

"I'm not sure. I hope so."

"Are you a Pusher?"

"I'm not sure. I hope not."

"Did you know you might be a Pusher before yesterday?"

"No."

"Are you running a con game with us as targets?"

"No."

"Do you have a crush on my sister?"

"What?" I say, caught completely off-guard with this one. Then, realizing I'm messing up, I reluctantly admit, "Maybe. Well, yes. Not a crush, but—"

"Thank you," Eugene says with a smirk, his eyes leaving the screen for the first time during this barrage of questions. Then he turns toward his sister. "He's telling the truth."

I glance at Mira and catch a strange look on her face. Was she just blushing? That seems unlikely. I must be imagining things due to my embarrassment over being put on the spot like that. But I know why Eugene did it. He wanted to ask something that I would react to, so he can be sure his device detects lies when they happen. That last question was perfect for that. He's even more clever than I thought. *Asshole*.

"Okay, that's great. He's not lying." Mira turns away from me to look at her brother. "That still doesn't tell us what the fuck he is."

"You know he's not someone who means you any harm," Eugene says, his voice unexpectedly stern. "Shouldn't that be enough?"

This is the first time I hear that kind of tone in his voice. Mira looks taken aback too, so it must be a rare occurrence.

I decide to jump in. "Mira, I want to know what I am even more than you do. Eugene is right—I don't mean you any harm. The opposite, actually."

"Oh, shut up," she says dismissively. "The opposite. Right. You are so selfless. Please. I know your type. All you care about is yourself."

I look at Eugene for help. Eugene doesn't meet my eyes. I'm on my own.

Her lip curls. "You know I'm right. Quick, while you still have to tell the truth, why don't you tell us why you came? Was it to help us? Or was it to save your own skin?"

"Well," I say uncomfortably, "I guess under the circumstances I won't deny it. I came to ask you not to tell other Readers about what you saw me do."

"Exactly," she says, her voice dripping with disdain.

"You don't know what I know. You don't know how brutally Readers kill Pushers," I say, losing my patience. "It's not being selfish if I don't want to be murdered by Caleb or someone like him."

"And how would you know anything about Readers killing Pushers?" She gives me a suspicious look, making me realize I just goofed.

"I saw it in Caleb's mind, okay? He made me do that Joint Reading thing with him earlier today, and I saw through his eyes how he killed one of them." I realize I'm going back on my word to Caleb about not sharing what we saw in each other's minds, but I can't help it. I'm desperate to prove my case to Mira.

She doesn't have a comeback. She just looks at Eugene in shock.

"That was the truth," he says. "Now can we stop this foolishness? Darren is clearly not against us, so I'm going to unhook him. Meanwhile, Darren, I want to hear every little detail about the Joining."

As he gets me out of the cables, I tell them about my Joining with Caleb, omitting things that Caleb and I would consider too personal. I also swear both Mira and Eugene to secrecy, and hope that Caleb never finds out I divulged even the few details I shared.

"Unbelievable," Eugene says when I finish. "I would give my left pinkie to try that. I only did it one time, with Julia, but it was nothing like what you describe. Dad was right. This experience changes based on how powerful the participants are . . ."

As he speaks, Mira begins to glower at him. "No way," she interrupts. "I see where you're going with this, and the answer is *no*. I'll shoot him before I let you Join minds with him."

"What? Why?" Eugene says, clearly disappointed.

"Because even if he didn't know he was a Pusher before, he

knows it now. Once he's inside your mind, he'll have you in his power." She turns to glare at me.

"Is that true?" Eugene asks me. He doesn't look scared; if anything, he looks excited. I guess the scientist in him is relishing all this.

"I have no idea," I say honestly. "I didn't realize that was a possibility until Mira suggested it just now. It was so confusing in there, I'm not sure if I would've been able to figure out how to do that, even if I wanted to try. Our minds were as one. I could've just as easily Pushed myself to do something while trying to influence him. And, of course, I wouldn't want to try it, especially with Caleb or you, Eugene. Him, because if it failed, he would kill me or worse. And you, because . . . well, I just wouldn't."

"There, you see, Mira? He wouldn't Push me," Eugene says. "And if I Join with him, that would beat any lie detector test when it comes to learning the truth."

"Do you even hear yourself?" She gives him an exasperated look. "Of course he says he wouldn't Push you. And besides, why are you trying to use truth-seeking as an excuse? Didn't your test just prove that he's telling the truth?"

Eugene says, "Well, yes—"

I'm beginning to get tired of their bickering. "I'm sorry to interrupt, Eugene," I say, "but this isn't necessary. I don't want to do any Joint Reading with you. The one time with Caleb was enough, trust me."

Mira gives me a grateful look. I guess I'm her ally in this. Eugene is doing a terrible job hiding his deep disappointment. I can't believe he still wants to do this, given what Mira just told him. If I thought someone could Push me under some circumstances, I'd avoid the said circumstances at all costs.

"It wouldn't be the same if you did it with *me*," he says pleadingly. "It wouldn't be like what you experienced with Caleb. This thing varies depending on participants' Depth and intellect. The higher those things are, the deeper the Joining. Also, the mind of the subject might make a difference. And possibly—"

"You're not helping your case with that," I say. "It was deep enough for me. I wouldn't want to make it deeper."

"Think about it," Eugene insists. "I think if we did it, you wouldn't regret it. You had a bad experience, so you're obviously going to be wary. I probably would be too, if I glimpsed something as frightening as Caleb's mind."

"Hey, that's not fair. Caleb saved me," Mira reminds him. "No need to get all high and mighty."

"So Caleb is a good guy, but me, who also saved you, you're ready to shoot," I say bitterly. "Did Eugene tell you why I did this crazy thing with Caleb to begin with? That it was actually payment to your precious Caleb for saving you?"

"Is that true?" she asks Eugene, giving me an odd look.

"Yes. I didn't get a chance to tell you." Eugene looks uncomfortable.

"I see," she says slowly. "Okay, Darren. Maybe I won't shoot you anytime soon. And I'm not a rat, so your secret is safe with me. Even if we don't really even know what that secret is. Are you happy now?"

"Yes. Thank you," I say, relieved. I'm okay with her attitude for now. It beats being shot or revealed as a potential Pusher.

"Great. Now that it's settled, can we get some breakfast?" Eugene gives us a big smile. "I'm starving."

Mira rolls her eyes. "How are you not much, much fatter?" she asks rhetorically before saying, "Sure. Let's go get something. I have some more questions for Darren, and we might as well kill two birds with one stone."

"I'm in," I say, though I'm not sure I want to answer any questions Mira is thinking of asking me. The green smoothie I had earlier was more of a snack, so a real breakfast sounds like a wonderful idea.

It takes them a few moments to put on shoes. One elevator ride and a flight of stairs later, we're walking through the lobby.

We approach the door. I feel chivalrous for some reason, so I hold open the glass door that leads outside the building. I'm doing it for Mira, of course, but Eugene benefits too.

"Thank you," Mira says, exiting after Eugene. "Where are we going to eat?"

"The diner?" Eugene suggests hopefully.

As I follow them, I have a sense of déjà vu. She's about to bring up the food poisoning story again. They'll fight. Then she'll get her way and choose the breakfast place she wants. I guess it's a thing with siblings; they have the same fights over and over, with the same results. Must be kind of nice.

Suddenly, there is a loud noise—a strange sound that scrapes at the inside of my ears.

I'm caught off-guard. Instinctively, I phase into the Quiet.

The argument between Mira and Eugene stops, their faces frozen. The sound also stops.

I turn around.

It's the glass door. It's shattering in a strange pattern. From a spot in the middle, the glass is flying out in small fragments. Farther out, the glass is falling in larger chunks.

Something struck that glass at high speed and with high force.

I feel cold as I rush into the building, fearing what I'll find there. It takes me less than a minute to discover the culprit.

It's a bullet.

A bullet is lying on the floor in the hallway.

I run outside and cross the street, frantically looking around. I see nothing, so I go through the park, straining my eyes as I scan the area. Finally, I spot something in the distance. I run toward it. As I get closer, I hope against all hope that it's just a large fly.

When I'm standing next to it, though, I know my hope is futile. The thing frozen in mid-air is what I feared it would be.

It's another bullet—flying at one of us.

8

I SWIVEL MY HEAD FROM SIDE TO SIDE, FRANTICALLY TRYING TO figure out where the shooter might be.

My brain almost subconsciously provides the solution for me as my legs take me where I need to go.

I run through the little park, almost tripping over frozen parents watching their frozen kids on the silent playground.

The shooter is sitting in a large van, holding a long rifle pointed in our direction.

The anger that I now feel is difficult to describe. I've never felt this enraged before.

This fucker just shot at me and my friends—and he's shooting at us through a park where little kids are playing.

Before this moment, I thought I would never consider Pushing anyone again. The reality of what I inadvertently did to that guy yesterday still horrifies me.

But now I feel ready to Push again—intentionally this time. It's the only option.

I approach the guy and grab him by the neck with all my strength. For a second, I forget why I'm here. I just relish choking him.

Then I give myself a mental shake. I don't know if Pushing works with corpses, so it's best if I don't continue with this. I loosen my grip and try to start the session.

I find it extremely difficult to get into the right state of mind while overcome with so many turbulent emotions. I must, however, so I concentrate.

I do synchronized breathing for a few moments, and begin to feel the necessary state of Coherence coming on. Suddenly, I'm in the shooter's vile head . . .

We're shooting at the target the second time and mentally cursing the boss in Russian. Why the fuck did he give this order on such a short notice?

The first miss is his fault. He didn't give us a chance to get our favorite rifle. The one with the scope that has been perfectly calibrated. Instead, we got this piece of shit.

We're not used to working like this. To not being a hundred-percent sure we're going to hit the target. It's unprofessional. The only silver lining is that, due to the urgency, we came here alone, so no one witnessed that embarrassing miss. Our marksman's reputation is unblemished.

I, Darren, disassociate from the Reading. This is yet another Russian mobster. He has been ordered to kill, and it's clear that he won't stop until that grim task is complete. But he doesn't know anything useful to me.

I begin my unsavory task. I try to repeat Pushing—the thing I did the other day.

I'm still unsure how I did what I did, so I rely on instinct and intuition.

I picture this fucker packing his rifle, closing the van door, and getting behind the wheel. I try to imagine hearing the van door close and feeling the ignition keys under my fingers. There is a huge urgency to get out of here. To be away. I visualize the switching of gears and the frantic clutching of the wheel, knuckles white, followed by the flooring of the gas pedal. I put my fear of that bullet into my vessel—his mind. I become fear. I channel it. There is only one escape from this fear, and that is to leave instantly and to go fast. As fast as humanly possible. No stopping, no slowing down, just a mad rush to safely, safety that's many miles away from here . . .

I do this thing for what feels like a half hour, battling a growing feeling of mental exhaustion mingled with disgust. When I finally can't take it for another second, I exit the guy's mind.

I RUN BACK THROUGH THE PARK, SHUDDERING WHEN I PASS BY THE bullet again.

I want to grab it, throw it on the ground, and stomp on it, but I resist the urge. It would be futile—nothing I can do to the bullet in the Quiet will change the fact that it will resume its potentially deadly path when I phase out.

Random thoughts enter my head. Should I have done the Pushing? Am I becoming the monster the Reader community is afraid of? The monster *I'm* afraid of?

Yes, I should've done it, I try to convince myself. It was necessary. If I didn't do something, the bullet that's still in the air would've been followed by more, until the shooter's job was done. Until he killed his target—one of us. Pushing was the only way I could think of to stop him. I didn't have a choice.

Besides, it's not like I'm going to cause his death, like the other time. Not that it was, strictly speaking, my fault yesterday—the second guard had been the one to actually pull the trigger. In this case, I think I merely caused the shooter to drive away. Admittedly, he will go fast, which has risks associated with it, but I didn't commit him to a definite fatal outcome.

I stop worrying about my actions when I find myself next to our frozen bodies again.

I look us over.

My frozen self's face looks scared, but knowing what I know now, the expression on his/my face is not scared enough.

Eugene just looks confused, not scared yet.

Mira is the only one of us who looks like she has it together. She looks focused and alert, ready to pounce into action, and her head is beginning to turn toward me.

No matter how much I stare at the three of us, I can't seem to make myself feel more confident in the idea I hatched up.

The plan is ridiculously simple. I will fall, and by doing so, I will try to get Mira to fall as well. She'll fall into Eugene. We should all go down like a stack of dominos—in theory, at least. And quickly, which is vital.

My hope is that the bullet will miss all of us if I do it right. This sort of tackling maneuver works for the Secret Service in the movies, so I figure it should work in real life. It *has* to work.

Not letting my brain come up with counterarguments for this plan, I focus on just going for it.

I reach out and touch my face. At the same time, before I'm even in my body, I put every ounce of my energy into willing my leg muscles to begin the movement that will cause me to spring in the right direction.

My whole world becomes the command I'm sending to my brain—the command for my leg muscles to act so I can fall.

My body seems to move before I even become aware that I've phased out of the Quiet. I feel my arms spread around Mira before they actually do so.

I only fully realize I'm out of the Quiet when I hear Mira's surprised yelp at the impact of my body falling on her.

I know I'm out because the street noises have returned. And then I feel the most unpleasant scraping sensation in my head. It's like a dental drill, but multiplied a hundredfold. It's quickly followed by intense pain. It's as though I just got hit on the head with a baseball bat—a baseball bat made of hot iron.

Everything is happening as though in slow motion. I feel like I'm going to phase back into the Quiet, but I manage to fight off the sensation.

In the next instant, I'm on top of Mira, who's on top of Eugene.

That part of my plan has worked.

They're both cursing, which means they're alive. Then I feel an explosion of pain in my head as I roll off the pile of bodies we formed.

I'm unable to get up. My head is pulsing with pain. It burns. It stings. It's horrible.

I bring my hand to the epicenter of the torment, and I feel warm liquid there.

In a moment of lucidity, I realize I've been shot. In the head.

"Darren, what the fuck—" Mira begins, but stops mid-sentence. "Oh, Darren, I am so sorry. Why are you bleeding? Did you hit your head when you fell? What happened?"

I feel her hands on my shoulder. She's turning me over.

"Eugene, please call 911," I try to say. "I think I've been shot."

"Zhenya, zvoni 911, bistrey!" she yells in Eugene's direction, and I don't know if she spoke in Russian, or if I'm losing my ability to comprehend English.

"Darren, look at me," she says to me gently. "You're going to be okay. I'm going to try to stop the bleeding."

I was right; that liquid I felt means I'm bleeding. This thought comes to me as though from a distance.

I hear the sound of ripping cloth, and in the next moment, I feel the pain intensify. She must've pressed the makeshift bandage to the wound. Some part of me realizes this must be an attempt to stop the bleeding.

I begin to reach for my head again, but she puts her hand on mine, preventing me from doing so. Her hand feels good, reassuring, so I just leave it there.

"Take deep breaths," Mira's voice says softly. "Yes, like that, slow and steady, this should help with the shock. How much does it hurt?"

I try to tell her it isn't so bad, but the words come out all jumbled.

"It doesn't matter, Darren, just talk to me," she says in a desperate, hushed tone. "Open your eyes, now."

I obey her command and open my eyes. At the same time, I lift my hand, the one that touched my head earlier, and take a look. My hand is covered in blood, and I can feel it streaming down my neck.

The world begins to spin, and then everything goes black.

9

I WAKE UP.

How much did I drink last night?

My head hurts like hell.

I try to remember what happened. I'm not in my own bed, but lying down in some kind of bed in a moving vehicle. Ambulance?

I try to open my eyes, but the light strikes a hammer-blow of pain, so I close them again.

"Darren, I'm here," says a familiar soothing voice.

It's Mira's voice—and the reason I'm here comes back to me.

I was shot.

In the head.

That would explain this excruciating pain. I try to open my eyes, squinting cautiously.

"He's conscious," I hear Eugene say.

"That's good news," says an unfamiliar male voice.

"You're not a doctor to be saying what constitutes good or

bad news." Mira's tone is sharp. "I want a doctor to see him right away."

"We're on the way to the hospital," the unfamiliar voice says defensively. He must be a paramedic, and the moving object I find myself in must be an ambulance, I realize.

"My head really hurts," I decide to complain. Talking makes the pain intensify, though, and the feeling I now have is like being carsick, only ten times worse.

"You got shot," Mira says gently. "Is there anyone I should call for you? Friends or family?"

There is care and concern in her voice. She sounds like she's actually worried about me and wants to help. She doesn't sound like the girl who was just about to shoot me herself not so long ago. The headache intensifies further when I try to think about this, so I stop. The idea of calling someone makes some sense, though.

"In my phone. Sara and Lucy are my family. Bert is my friend," I say, trying to reach for my pocket. Moving sends waves of nausea through my body. Am I dying? I wonder if that would end the pain.

"I got it," she says, putting one of her hands on mine and reaching into my pocket with her other hand.

Usually, I would have dirty thoughts in a situation like this—having Mira dig through my jeans this way—but I guess getting shot takes its toll. I feel like I might actually puke if the ambulance keeps on shaking the way it does, and I want Mira as far away from me as possible if that happens.

I take a few deep breaths and decide that maybe I woke up too soon. I think I need to rest for a few more minutes.

"What hospital are we going to?" Mira asks the paramedic as my thoughts grow progressively cloudier.

"Coney Island," I hear him respond as though in a dream, and then my mind goes blank again.

I WAKE UP AGAIN. THIS TIME I KNOW THAT I'M NOT IN MY OWN bed. I remember being shot. I also remember feeling sick in the ambulance, and I'm relieved that I'm feeling somewhat better. I even recall talking to someone. The reason for my feeling better is on the tip of my tongue, but it escapes me.

"When is the doctor going to see him again?" It's Mira's voice. "All he did was give him something for the pain."

Ah, that explains it. I recall telling someone I was in terrible pain. Or did I say something else? It's still a bit blurry, and the weightless feeling running through my body is not conducive to recall.

There's a trick I learned at the dentist's office. When a dentist asks me if I feel something during a procedure, I say that I do until I can't feel my face from all the Novocain. I must've automatically used this same technique when I spoke to the doctor in my woozy state, and he must've believed me and given me something pretty strong for the pain.

"The doctor will see him again after he gets the X-ray," says a different female voice. A nurse, I'm guessing.

"Okay, then when is he going for that X-ray?" Mira's voice rises. "Why is this taking so long?"

"Please calm down, miss. We're doing the best we can," says the nurse in a rehearsed monotone. "We have a lot of patients today and are very understaffed."

They have a back and forth, but I ignore it. Instead, I try to examine this feeling I'm experiencing from whatever is making me feel better. It's like a warm flow through my whole body. Like I'm hovering and floating in a warm bath at the same time.

Whatever they gave me for the pain must be really beginning to kick in.

"That bullet was meant for me," Eugene says after the person Mira was bugging about my care is gone.

"Yes. I hate to say it, but I told you so." Mira sounds angry. "When will you develop a sense of self-preservation?"

"You're right, of course," Eugene says morosely. "We should've slept at a hotel. I didn't think they would come after me again. Not this soon. I didn't even think the ones involved in your kidnapping bothered to share our address with anyone else—"

"Oh, spare me all the bullshit." Mira's tone is scathing. "I heard it yesterday, and now Darren is hurt because I listened to you. You just wanted to be near your precious equipment, as usual. That's all you think about."

With the nice feelings spreading though my body, I have a hard time following the conversation. But one thing I do get from it: Mira seems to care about me. At least she's upset that Eugene's lack of regard for her earlier concerns resulted in my injury. As I think this, the feelings of warmth in my body intensify. What drug did they give me? Maybe I should get a prescription.

"I really am sorry, Mirochka." Eugene sounds genuinely remorseful. "In the future, I will do what you say when it comes to paranoia."

She gets pissy about the word *paranoia,* and they argue some more, with occasional lapses into Russian. I feel myself slowly floating down from whatever cloud the pain medication had taken me to. Their sibling squabble is totally ruining my buzz.

"I can't believe Darren took the bullet for me," Eugene says at some point, and the comment catches my attention.

Truthfully, I can't believe it either. Well, strictly speaking, that was not my intent. I'd hoped to save everyone. But still. His remark makes me feel good, though some of that might still be the drug.

"He did," Mira responds thoughtfully.

They sit in silence for a bit, and I feel the buzz coming back, intensified. As it gets a hold on my body again, I feel decidedly drowsy and don't fight it. My consciousness flees, and I find myself going for a nice nap.

10

"ARE YOU BERT?" I HEAR MIRA'S VOICE AGAIN AS I WAKE UP.

"Yes," Bert responds. "Thank you for calling me, Mira. Nice to meet you. How did Darren get hurt?"

I open my eyes.

"He—"

"Wait, I think he just opened his eyes," Bert cuts off Mira's explanation.

"Darren," she says, looking at me worriedly. "How are you feeling?"

I examine myself.

I'm hooked up to a monitor and have an IV in my arm, but the effects of the drug they gave me must've worn off. My head is throbbing again. But it doesn't seem to be as bad as before, which could be remnants of the medication, or a result of healing. I'm not sure which it is. The whole thing still feels a lot like a hangover, but at least the nausea has lessened, and having my eyes open doesn't make me feel like I have icepicks piercing my temples.

"Okay." I try to sound brave, but my voice comes out hoarse and pathetic-sounding. "Better."

"Here." Mira hands me a cup of water from the little table near my bed, and I drink it carefully.

"Where is Eugene?" I ask, looking around in confusion.

"He went to visit Julia," Mira says, and I detect a note of disapproval in her voice. Is she mad he left before seeing me recover, or does she just disapprove of him visiting Julia?

"How is she?" I ask.

"You're worried about Julia, now? She's doing better than *you*, I can assure you." Mira smiles. "She didn't get shot in the head."

"Oh, right," I say. "How am *I* doing?"

"I don't know," she says in frustration. "They took you to get X-rays of your head. Don't you remember?"

"No, I was kind of out of it," I say.

"Yeah, it must be the stuff they gave you for the pain. You looked quite loopy, drooling and mumbling something. In any case, that was a long time ago, and I haven't seen a doctor with the X-ray results, or even a nurse."

"Hmm," I say worriedly. "That sucks."

"Tell me about it." Mira frowns. "I'm thinking of getting you some food, and if they don't give you some attention by the time I'm done, I'm going to go around and try to talk some sense into these people."

The way she mentions talking to them sounds rather sinister. I wouldn't want her to piss off my doctor at this stage. But I really wish the X-ray results would arrive, so I could find out what's going on with me. Head trauma is nothing to sneeze at, especially for people who like to use their heads as much as I do. Also, I realize that Mira is planning to give this hospital's staff a hard time on my behalf, which is a strange idea.

"Bert, will you keep him company while I grab him something to eat?" Mira says, interrupting my train of thought.

"Of course," he says, getting that bashful look he always wears around girls.

"Do you want anything?" she asks him.

"No, thank you." He blushes.

"And you, Darren?" she says. "We never made it to that breakfast."

I consider the idea. Though my nausea has subsided a bit, I don't yet feel like eating. Or getting up. Or doing much besides talking. The IV they have in my arm feels a little itchy, and I wonder what will happen when I need to go to the bathroom. I'd better ask a medical professional when I get hold of one. On the plus side, I'm not wearing one of those goofy hospital gowns. Probably because they needed access only to my head. It still doesn't prevent me from looking ridiculous, of course. I can feel that my head is bandaged up like a mummy's, probably making me look like it's Halloween.

"No, I think I'll pass on the breakfast for now," I tell her. "I bet they're about to bring me some Jell-O, the hospital food of choice."

"I am going to get you one of those and a pudding of some kind," she says decisively. "If you haven't been told about the X-rays yet, what makes you think you can rely on these people for food?"

"Okay, Mira, thank you. I'll try the pudding if they have it," I say, looking at her in confusion. This caring side of Mira is odd and will take some getting used to. "Maybe something like apple sauce if they don't?"

"Okay, don't worry, I'll get you something," she says and turns to go.

As Mira is walking away, I notice Bert looking her up and down. For some reason, I'm annoyed at him for doing that. Then I mentally smack myself. Am I being jealous and protective of *Mira*?

"Dude," Bert says as soon as Mira is out of earshot. "Is that *the* Mira I looked up for you? Wow, I have to say, she is *so* your type. Why didn't you tell me you found her? And how did you get shot? And who's Eugene? And Julia? What the hell is going on?"

I sigh and concoct a story for Bert. I can't tell him anything about Readers or Pushers, so the story focuses on other things instead. I tell him that I stopped by Mira's house and that her brother and I ended up being friendly. It's almost what happened. Then I tell Bert how I learned about Mira and Eugene's parents being murdered by some unsavory Russian characters. I explain the murder by saying that their father had problems with someone back in the motherland—which could be true. I also say that Mira's quest for revenge backfired, and she got kidnapped as a result—which is false, but a much simpler explanation than the truth.

"You participated in a rescue? Is that how you got shot?" Bert says incredulously. "Are you crazy?"

"Actually, no," I say. "I was unscathed during that rescue. That was yesterday. This shot, obviously, happened today. I think it's safe to assume these thugs were from the same group as yesterday's kidnappers, though. They tried to kill her or her brother this time around, but missed and got me instead. I could actually use your help with this, Bert. There's someone I want to ask you to look up using your skills. Someone who might be giving orders in that organization."

"Yes, sure. I mean, they shot you, so it's the least I can do," Bert says. "Just never mention my name to those sorts of people."

I assure him that I'm not going to mention his name in the unlikely event that the gangsters and I have a friendly face-to-face chat. I then give him the name, Arkady, and the phone number I got the other day. I guess there is a silver lining to getting shot. I was out of favors with Bert when it comes to what he rightfully considers shady hacker activities, but he's not thinking about favors right now.

Seeing how willing he is to help, I decide to milk the situation a bit further.

"There are two more people I was hoping you could try to learn something about. These two are not Russian," I say.

"Who are they then?" he says to my dismay. I really hoped I could play the 'getting shot' card once more, and Bert would do this for me without further questions, but it sounds like I might have to go into this strange topic with him.

"They might be my parents," I say, and watch Bert's eyes go wide with surprise. "My biological parents."

I give him the story of how, *coincidentally,* I also found out that Sara is not my biological mother. I explain that it's a woman named Margret, whom I know very little about, and that my dad now also has a name—Mark. I also tell Bert that I plan to get my biological parents' last names from my moms when they arrive at the hospital.

"All right," he agrees when I'm done. "Text me their names as soon as you know. Also that mobster's number and name. In for a penny, in for a pound. But you've got to do something for me when you get better."

"I can promise to try," I say carefully. "What do you need?"

As I watch Bert's face, I begin cursing myself mentally for being greedy. When it was just the Russian guy I asked him to look into, he didn't need favors back. Whatever it is he's about to ask me, he's looking for the best way to say it—which, knowing Bert, means it will be something big.

"Can you ask Mira if she has friends she can introduce me to?" he finally says, his face turning red.

I blow out a relieved breath. I thought he was going to ask me to give him a kidney or something.

"I doubt she does, but I'll find out for you," I say, smiling. "If not, I will, in general, be on the lookout."

"Thanks," he says, shifting his weight uncomfortably.

I'm actually happy with this development. Bert finally found a workable approach to meeting women—asking me for help. It might work. I've always thought that Bert's biggest problem with women had been a lack of trying.

"I brought something for you," he says, reaching into his man-purse-looking shoulder bag in an obvious effort to change the subject.

He takes out a blue Gameboy 3DS and then a golden one.

This is our little guilty pleasure. When I'm in the office for the whole day, and when things are boring—which is often—we sneak away to a meeting room, sit with our backs toward the glass walls of the room, and play video games. To our coworkers, it might look like we're busy studying reports or reviewing financial statements.

This love of video games is what initially established our

friendship back at Harvard. Well, that and the fact that we were both teens surrounded by adults.

Taking my hands from under the blanket that covers me, I use the incline function of my hospital bed. A few seconds later, I'm in a sitting position with a Gameboy in my hands. The IV in my hand feels a little funny, but manageable.

We load the devices and start playing a goofy fighting game Bert brought for this occasion.

"You're only slightly better than this game's AI," Bert says halfway into the first round. This is his version of trash talk.

I let it slide this time. There are so many things I can say. For example, I can point out that the character he chose to fight me with, Pikachu the Pokémon, is a yellow, goofy little creature that looks suspiciously like Bert himself. Or I could point out that he *should* be better at this game, given how much time he spends with games in general. However, that would be like saying he has no life, which is close to the truth for Bert. I wouldn't be so mean-spirited as to point that out, plus I don't want to piss him off until he gets me the information I need.

So, instead of saying anything, I try to go for a thrust with the sword of my own favorite character. I play as Link, the silent hero from my favorite game series of all time, the Legend of Zelda. The hit lands, and Bert goes quiet, clearly trying to concentrate on his comeback.

Soon I'm dodging thunderbolts as I catch Bert with my signature spin attack. The 3D of the screen begins to make the nausea come back, but I try to ignore it, determined to win.

"By the way, did I tell you that Jerry Buchmacker is dead?" Bert says, blatantly trying to divert my attention. Bert knows how much I hate to lose. I once threw a controller at his head back in college.

"What happened?" I say, knowing full well this is Bert's conspiracy-theory time. Even though we're playing, I have to indulge him to stay in his good graces. "And remind me who Jerry Buchmacker is, again."

"He was working on new artificial intelligence applications. Think self-driving cars, but in medicine."

"Oh yeah, I remember you talking about this guy when you consulted me about the company where he was the CTO. I told you it would be a good investment for Pierce's portfolio," I say, and start a new game, playing as the same character.

"Right, that one, and now he's dead. Another *suicide.*" Bert tries to make air quotes on the last word with the Gameboy in his hands. "I learned of what happened when Mr. Pierce asked me to find out if Jerry's death means we should liquidate the portfolio."

"Okay then, why is the guy *really* dead?" I say, mimicking his air quotes. I know full well where this is heading. I think I've heard this specific conspiracy theory before, and it's not as crazy as some other stuff Bert comes up with.

"It's the secret Neo-Luddite group again," he whispers, looking around as though they have ears in this hospital.

As I learned some time ago, a Luddite, as defined by Bert, is someone who's against any kind of progress. The Neo variety seem to be specifically against modern technological progress. From what I've gathered from my friend's admittedly biased description of them, they are a bunch of crazy people who would have humanity go back to living in caves if they could. The Unabomber was a flavor of one of these people, according to Bert.

This specific conspiracy theory states that there is a secret group that takes out talented scientists in critical fields, such as robotics, genetics, informatics, and nanotechnology. Their motive is to prevent the transformative changes these fields can bring.

I don't believe in this conspiracy, of course, but I do know there are people who fear progress and change. To them I say, "Go into the forest and try living for a day without sanitation, without your iPhone, without a gun to shoot wolves that want to eat you, and without antibiotics for the gangrene you might get from a simple cut. Then come back and tell me you still want to go back to the caveman days."

I certainly wouldn't.

"What makes you think this wasn't suicide?" I ask, even though I know I'm just encouraging Bert's craziness.

"Well, it's their MO," he says, and inside the game, gives me a particularly nasty punch.

"Right, of course," I say sarcastically, blocking the next kick and countering with a sword thrust.

Bert is clearly unhappy with my lack of faith in his theory, and the yellow creature on my screen throws my hero off the game platform as a manifestation of his grumpiness.

We go back and forth like this, with me playing the devil's advocate about the conspiracy and Bert kicking my ass in the game and stating more reasons for why the guy couldn't have committed suicide. A lot of it sounds rather persuasive, actually. There was no mention of depression in any of the files Bert got his hands on. There were long-term plans for vacations and conferences. Finally, and a clincher for Bert, the guy had a gorgeous girlfriend and had just proposed to her.

"What are you guys doing?" I hear Mira's incredulous voice from my left. It comes just as I'm about to deliver my theory of how the guy possibly killed himself as a weird manifestation of cold feet. Marriage can be a scary thing—at least as far as I'm concerned.

"Playing," I say defensively to Mira. I feel like I was just caught doing something obscene.

"Did the doctor say it was okay for you to play that stuff?" she says, frowning.

"I have no idea; the doctor hasn't come yet," I say. "But I doubt video game playing can be bad for you."

"That thing's 3D screen gives me, a person without head damage, a headache," she counters.

I can see what Bert is thinking without needing to do a Read. *Hot and into video games?*

I am impressed myself.

"So you have actually played before?" I ask.

"Of course." She narrows her eyes. "Why is that such a surprise?"

"No reason," I say swiftly.

"I'll tell you what. Before I go find the doctor, I'll play whichever one of you wins," she announces, crossing her arms. Our eyes nearly fall out of our sockets as the move pushes up her cleavage.

I can tell that Bert's and my thoughts converge on the same idea.

I have to win.

11

I PERFORM A COMBO ATTACK, WHICH CONSISTS OF MY BEST strategies. Bombs, boomerangs, sword thrusts—all go in desperation at the little Japanese creature on the screen in front of me.

The need to win is very strong, and I wonder if it's some primal part of my brain wanting me to be the victor in front of a female.

Whatever the reason, I throw all I have into this next attack.

It's futile, though. It seems like the prospect of playing with a real girl is a stronger motivator for Bert than for me. Plus, he's already better at this than I am.

He blocks my onslaught, and then, in mere moments, manages to wipe the game floor with my poor character.

He ignores the sour expression on my face as I hand him the Gameboy.

Mira and Bert begin the game, and Bert is practically beaming with excitement.

I try not to sulk while I eat the pudding and Jell-O Mira brought me.

"Is Eugene coming back?" I ask when I'm done with the food.

"Yes, he should actually be here soon," Mira says absentmindedly, not taking her eyes off the game screen. "I had him rent a car, in case they have my car's plates. I want us to give you a ride once you're discharged."

Their game is lasting an unbelievably long time—causing me to think in dismay that she might actually be better at it than I am. I probably would've lost to Bert already. Unless my sneaky friend is toying with her, trying to make this game last longer.

I look around for a doctor or at least a nurse. There are none in sight. My bed is one of a dozen such beds standing in a circle around the large room. It all looks very dreary and makes me want to check out of here as soon as physically possible. I hope the bullet hasn't done any serious damage to my head.

Most of the folks in here seem to be in a sadder situation than I am. There is a man all bandaged up like a mummy in the neighboring bed. Further down, there is an older person with an IV and a breathing machine. After a few seconds, I stop looking. In a hospital, you can easily see something you'll later regret. But then something catches my attention in the distance.

It's Sara, my more panicky mom.

"Guys, I need a favor," I say. "One of my moms is approaching, and I kind of want to have a private conversation when she gets here. Why don't you go look for that doctor together? Or just walk around?"

Bert chuckles. He knows my real concern. He knows Sara's

tendency to say embarrassing stuff. I can picture a whole diatribe about her 'baby' in the hospital, or something even worse, like a nervous fit.

With a curse, Mira slams closed the Gameboy, signifying her defeat, and glances in the direction Sara is coming from.

"Hello, Mrs. Goldberg," Bert says, getting ready to leave.

"Hi Bert," my mom says. "And you must be Mira?"

"Hi, Mrs. Goldberg," Mira says uncomfortably.

"Please call me Sara," she says. "You too, Bert, how many times do I need to ask you?"

"Sorry, Sara," Bert says sheepishly.

"Nice to meet you, Sara." Mira attempts to smile at my mom. "Bert and I were just about to go look for a doctor, to see when Darren is getting his X-ray results."

"Thank you." Sara gives Mira an approving look. "That's very thoughtful. Let me know if they give you any attitude."

Great. I picture a scenario where Mira is arguing with my doctor, and then, after sufficiently pissing him off, she unleashes my mom on the poor guy. If disgruntled restaurant workers spit in your food, can you imagine what an upset doctor might do to you?

"If they give us any attitude, I will crush their servers," Bert says.

"Albert, you will do no such thing," my mom says sternly. "People could die."

"I'm sure Bert was kidding," I say, giving my friend a warning glare. He probably wasn't.

"I will keep him in line, no worries, Sara," Mira says with a smile.

"Good, thank you," Sara says, apparently satisfied.

As my friends give me the Gameboys and walk away, I

realize with amazement how calmly my mom has been behaving. Was it Mira's attitude that calmed her so?

"Sweetie, what happened? You were shot. Does it hurt?" The barrage of questions begins as soon as Mira and Bert are out of the room, and I curse myself for the jinx. My amazement was clearly premature.

I go into a new variation of the story. In this one, Mira is a new friend who happens to live in a bad neighborhood. The shot was just a fluke, the result of being in the wrong place at the wrong time.

"I like Mira. She's smart and very pretty," my mom says when she stops her verbal version of hyperventilating. "And she clearly cares about you. But you should have her visit you in the city instead of the other way around. It'll be safer that way."

I now understand why the freak-out is not as bad as I expected. I think the fact that my mom found me with a girl—something she's been nagging me about for ages—trumps my getting shot in her twisted version of reality.

"Sure, Mom. It actually just so happens that Mira and her brother will be moving anyway," I say.

"Good." She pats my knee. "Let me know if you need suggestions for safe neighborhoods."

"Okay, Mom. Where's Lucy?" I say, trying to change the subject.

"Your mother will be here soon. She just texted me. Kyle dropped her off at the hospital entrance and is parking. She'll be here in a moment."

I'm actually a tiny bit worried about Lucy coming here. I hope she doesn't play detective with me. She sometimes can't help it.

I keep those concerns to myself, though, and say instead,

"Okay. In the meantime, there's something I want to ask you . . ." I pause, thinking about it, and then I decide to just blurt it out. "What were the last names of my biological parents?"

Sara looks taken aback for a moment, but recovers quickly. "They were the Robinsons, and your biological mother's maiden name was Taylor," she answers readily.

The Robinsons. So Jacob was indeed asking about my father, Mark Robinson. Does that mean my father was a Reader? Maybe even part of that specific community? I make a mental note to try to learn more about this. Maybe I can find a reason to chat with Jacob again, or ask his daughter Julia about it when she recovers. Perhaps I can even talk to Caleb, as scary as that option sounds. Also, Mark worked with my mom Lucy and Uncle Kyle. I can try to pump them for information—though, of course, they don't know anything about Readers and Pushers.

I see Sara wave her hand at someone, and it takes me out of my thoughts.

Following her gaze, I see Lucy approaching.

"How are you, kiddo?" Lucy says when she gets to my bed. "What happened?"

I tell her the same story that I told Sara and how I don't yet know the details but that my friends are trying to get a doctor, or someone, to pay attention to us. As I talk, I can't tell if she's buying it. Lucy is like that; you don't know what's on her mind when she doesn't want you to. Must be a detective thing. However, as I learned over the years, the mere fact that she's hiding her expression signifies trouble.

"You guys catch up, and I'm going to go try to find Mira and Bert," Sara says and walks off without giving me a chance to respond. Did she pick up on Lucy's lack of expression also? The idea of her joining the doctor search is the very definition of overkill. If someone is not back here in a few minutes, I will be extremely surprised. Images of lionesses killing gazelles and bringing the bloody carcasses to their fluffy cubs spring to mind for some reason.

"Okay, now tell me what really happened," Lucy says as soon as Sara gets out of earshot.

My mom the detective. She's the reason I can usually lie so well. As a kid, I had to take my lying game to stellar levels in order to fool Lucy. I'm usually very smooth at it, but that's when I'm not worried about head wounds and don't have secret societies I have to keep quiet about.

"I didn't want to worry Sara," I say. "So I simplified things a bit, that's all."

"I gathered as much." A slight smile appears on Lucy's face. "Spill it."

"The short version is that some Russian mobsters want my friends dead. Before you ask, I truly have little idea as to why. Suffice it to say, these same people might've murdered their family first."

"What are your friends' names?" Lucy says calmly. She's acting as though I tell her about attempted assassinations all the time.

I give her Mira and Eugene's last name and everything I can recall about their parents.

"I'll look into it," she says, writing something in a small notebook.

She can actually find out quite a bit. She still knows people in the organized crime division, including my uncle Kyle, who's probably on his way up here as we speak. But it's doubtful she'll be able to help much. The Pusher who's behind all this, according to my new friends, would be beyond a regular detective's capabilities.

"Just information, Mom. Please don't go after anyone," I say and finally get a full smile out of her.

"You sound like your mother," she says. "You don't need to worry. I'm in the white collar division for a reason."

"Someone reported a gunshot wound?" an unfamiliar male voice says, and Lucy and I look up to see a stocky policeman approaching. Great. The staff at this hospital can't be bothered to get me my X-ray results, but they managed to file a report about my wound.

"It's all right, Officer," Lucy says, pulling out her badge and showing it to him. "I'm already on it."

The policeman immediately turns around and departs, muttering something under his breath about incompetent Coney Island nurses, and I suppress a chuckle. There are certainly benefits to having a detective for a mom.

"There you are." My uncle Kyle enters the room at that moment. "How's the injured soldier?"

Uncle Kyle is not my biological uncle, obviously. He's not even my adoptive uncle. He's Lucy's coworker. However, he's played the role of my uncle since I was little, and I'm used to thinking of him as such.

"Hi Kyle," I say, sitting up so I can shake his hand. It's our thing. We don't hug—we shake hands.

"Kyle, I'm glad you're here. I want to check on this doctor situation," Lucy says. "Please stay with him."

"Of course," Kyle says. "Give them hell."

And Lucy joins the doctor hunt, which I would find comical if it weren't for the fact that Mira is involved in it, too. Having Lucy there is literally bringing out the big guns—though I doubt she'll draw her weapon on the medical staff. At least not unless they really piss her off.

"I heard there is a girl involved in this shooting," Kyle says, winking at me. If there's one thing I always liked about Kyle, it's his lack of smotheringness. He doesn't ask me how I got shot. He probably isn't all that worried about me. And there is something refreshing about that.

This attitude of his has served me well over the years. There are tons of fun, albeit unsafe, things a boy wants to do but needs adult backing to actually do. For example, Kyle is the reason I know how to hold a gun. It's the result of a secret trip we took to a shooting range. To this day, my moms still think we went to the New York Aquarium and would probably still retroactively give Kyle a beating for taking me to a shooting range instead.

"Yes, there is a girl. If you stick around, you might meet her." For some reason, I'm hoping that he does. Since when do I care what Kyle thinks?

"I'll try," he says, smiling.

"I have something here that you might be interested in," I say, reaching for the Gameboys.

When I was little, Kyle was my go-to video game partner. For all his faults, I'm thankful for the hours he spent playing Mortal Kombat with me. Ripping his head off, literally—well, the head of his character at least, via the Fatality move in that game—is one of my favorite childhood memories.

"I haven't seen these before," he says. "Is there a way to make it less blurry?"

Kyle and his lack of technology know-how. I'm forced to teach him how to turn off the game's built-in glasses-free 3D effect. That's what he calls blurriness. It's a sacrilege to not see this game in 3D, but I'm not about to get into a verbal fight with him. A virtual game fight will have to suffice. Once the 3D is off, he chooses his character—Donkey Kong, who happens to be a tie-wearing giant gorilla. I myself go for the cartoony variation of Link, my usual princess-saving character.

As he did when I was a kid, Kyle plays cheap. He chooses a move that works and repeats it over and over. In this case, it creates the rather funny effect of a dancing gorilla.

As I'm about to execute a cunning plan of attack, Kyle's phone rings.

"I have to take that," he says, pausing the game.

He picks up the phone. As soon as whoever is on the other line starts talking, Kyle's expression turns somber, and he walks away from my bed. Must be detective business.

I make myself busy by exiting the fighting game and checking to see if I can get onto Wi-Fi in this place. That would let me buy more games if I'm bored, which I'm bound to be when everyone leaves. Assuming I need to stay here, which I hope I don't.

"I have to go," Kyle says when he comes back. He looks upset. "Something urgent has come up."

"Aren't you Lucy's ride?" I ask.

"Yes, but she'll have to cab it. This can't wait."

"See you later. Thanks for stopping by," I say, trying to hide my disappointment.

As he leaves, I realize that boredom might come sooner than I anticipated. Wi-Fi is a no-go, though at this point, given my experience with this hospital, I'm not surprised.

Luckily for me, the fighting game has a mode where you can fight the computer, so I start playing.

I'M IN THE MIDDLE OF A PARTICULARLY NASTY FIGHT WHEN I realize my bed is moving.

I look back and see a woman in a white coat pushing it.

"Where am I going?" I ask. "And who are you?"

"The doctor wants to have a private conversation with you," says the woman in a monotone while continuing to push the bed. "I'm your nurse."

I try to process this information. Why would a doctor need to take me to a private room to talk? How bad is the news he wants to give me? Or did my family and friends cause such a ruckus that there is going to be a 'tell Darren off' session?

We don't end up going far. There is a little office room to the side of the large hall. The nurse closes the door and starts preparing some kind of medication.

"What are you doing?" I say, trying to sound calm. I'm afraid of needles, and the stuff she's prepping looks to be a shot.

"Just something for the pain," she says.

"I don't need anything," I say. "I'd rather have the pain I have now than the pinprick of a needle."

She approaches me, smiles, and takes the cable that goes from my IV to my hand. She unplugs it and connects it to the syringe she's holding.

"See, no shot," she says.

"I still don't want the shot until you tell me what's in it—"

Her pressing the syringe cuts me off.

My heart rate picks up.

Did she just give me a shot after I explicitly told her not to? Why would she do that?

Suddenly, a wave of warmth begins to spread though my body, causing some of my worries to dissipate.

No, something is not right. I force myself to think through the happy, comfortable feelings spreading through me. It's beginning to be difficult to care, but with a herculean effort, I make myself worry again.

Maybe she wants to steal your organs, I tell myself, trying to come up with the scariest scenario.

Time seems to slow down for a moment, and then the noises of the hospital disappear.

I find myself lying in bed next to my other self, and I'm overcome with momentary relief.

I made it. I phased into the Quiet.

My head is now completely clear of whatever she gave me, and I'm determined to figure out what the fuck just happened.

12

I GET UP AND LOOK AT MYSELF. MY FROZEN SELF'S PUPILS ARE tiny, like pinpricks. This must be the effect of whatever drug she gave me, as her own pupils are the normal black circle one would expect in a well-lit room.

Fleetingly, I note the bandage around my head; it looks as ridiculous as I thought, but that's not what I care about right this moment. I'd be willing to walk around Times Square bandaged up like a mummy, if that would help me get out of this predicament.

I notice that not only do I feel free from the drug she gave me, but the pain from my wound is also nonexistent, as is always the case in the Quiet.

I walk over to the woman and look through her pockets.

She has a real-looking hospital ID, which is a good sign. She's an RN named Betty March. That's encouraging to some degree—she knows about drugs and how to deliver them. But surely they aren't allowed to force something into someone's veins under these circumstances.

Time to do a little Reading, I decide, and touch her temple.

"YOUR BOYFRIEND WILL BE SEEN SOON. PLEASE GO BACK AND wait," we say to the girl who's been pestering the staff.

I, Darren, realize that this is a memory in which *we* just spoke with Mira. She's without Bert or my mother, which means this memory happened a while back. Whatever I'm looking for in Betty's memories—and I'm not yet sure what that is—happens later. I decide to experience every moment from here to the present to make sure I understand why she did what she did.

As the memories go by, I develop a healthy respect for the nursing profession. It's tough. Finally, I get to what I think I need. She's in the ladies room at the time.

We're sitting on the toilet, and time stops. There are now more of us in Betty's head.

The feeling I have is the same as the one I had in the head of that Russian gangster, the one controlled by the mystery Pusher. I feel the presence of another mind—a spooky apparition that has no gender or identity. It's just a feeling that there's someone else here.

Like before, the Pusher starts giving instructions. This time, though, as I follow the instructions Betty is getting, I feel a chill overtake my disembodied mind.

'Walk up to Darren Wang Goldberg,' is accompanied by mental images of where my bed is located and what I look like, plus a desire to help a person in need.

'Take the patient to a private room,' is accompanied by mental images and instruction that the doctor wants to have a conversation with the patient. A conversation that is likely going to upset the rest of the people in the room.

'Administer 10mg of morphine by injection,' is accompanied by images of a patient suffering, doctor's orders, and a warning about a patient who's confused and who might resist the shot.

'Forget the injection,' is the next instruction, and it is accompanied by a feeling of blankness. Of emptiness. A Zen-like state of not thinking about anything at all and being at peace.

'Take the pillow, place it on the patient's face, and hold it there.' This macabre instruction is accompanied by a whole mental story. In this story, the person Betty is to smother has been begging her to do this for years. He's suffering terrible pain that even drugs can't make better. Incongruently, feelings of hatred for the patient are also introduced. The Pusher's instructions seem to say that this is the person who beat Betty and put her in the hospital, the monster who killed Betty's little boy.

Although somewhat in shock, I manage to think of how interesting it is to witness the way Pushing is supposed to work. I mean, when I tried it, I did it intuitively, using only a very basic example of this Pusher's work. This is much more subtle. Much more sick. If Betty does what she's instructed to do—and I have no doubt that she will—it will be proof that Pushers truly can make a person do anything they want. The justifications given don't even need to make complete sense. Just some hook into the person's mind is all that seems to be required. Just provide any rationale, and the victim does what you mentally force them to do.

Morbidly fascinated, I let the memory unfold. With precision, Betty carries out each instruction the Pusher has given her. As Betty performs each task, she seems to genuinely believe the instructions and the back stories the Pusher provided. When I asked her where she was taking me, she was convinced that I was going to speak to the doctor. She wasn't being deceitful at all. What I find particularly frightening is that each step of the way, she seems to have only a vague idea of what happened previously. It's a lot like a dream in which things seem to make sense, but don't upon awakening.

It's likely that by the time she starts killing my drugged, unconscious self with a pillow, she won't even recall the morphine shot she gave me.

The full implications of my position begin to dawn on me as I exit Betty's mind.

I'M BACK IN THE QUIET WITH THE KNOWLEDGE THAT THE PUSHER is trying to kill me—that maybe he has already killed me.

If that dose of morphine was too much, I might die of an overdose before the nurse even gets to me with the pillow. And if the injection doesn't kill me, the suffocation certainly will. I don't doubt that the Pusher knows what he's doing, nor do I doubt that Betty is going to do as he instructed her.

Why is he trying to kill me? Is it because of my helping Eugene and Mira yesterday? That doesn't fully make sense to me. If anyone did something outstanding to save Mira, it was Caleb. Or did the Pusher think I was the brains of the operation? That's flattering, I guess, but completely wrong in this case.

I can't think about this too long, though. Not when I'm uncertain whether I can still save myself.

A dozen possibilities run through my mind. Can I Push the nurse myself and override what my nemesis just did? But what if she kills me anyway? Or changes tactics? Or does it even faster? I don't dare trust my life to something like that. Not unless I first put something more surefire into play.

Exiting the room, I look around.

Jackpot.

Just outside the room is a mountain of a man. An angry mountain named Frank, according to his name tag.

I touch his arm and focus.

THIS FUCKING HOSPITAL IS LIKE A ZOO, WE THINK ANGRILY. No one has paid any attention to Lidia for hours. We have to find someone in charge and try to talk some sense into them.

I disassociate from Frank's thoughts. His plight is familiar. This place is definitely a dump. From what I gleaned in his mind, his wife needs attention much more than I do.

I feel a twinge of guilt over what I'm about to do. Frank might end up in trouble. Plus, I will be messing with his mind—and he's done nothing wrong.

But self-preservation wins over other scruples, and I try to replicate what I did earlier today.

'There is a woman in the other room who needs help. She's having a seizure and needs someone strong to hold her down until the doctors arrive. Otherwise, she might hurt herself or others. Perhaps helping her will get someone to want to do us a favor, and Lidia will get help faster. It's simple: just walk in, give the woman in there a huge bear hug, and don't let go. If she starts struggling too much, fall on the ground with her in your arms. Lie there until the doctors arrive to save her.'

I work different variations of the same scenario in Frank's mind. Compared to what I saw in nurse Betty's mind, a lot of my instructions are probably redundant. But now is not the time to try to perfect my Pushing technique. I need to cover all the bases.

Hopeful that the whole 'smothering me with a pillow' bit might now be avoided, I leave Frank's mind.

NEXT, I GO SEARCHING FOR A DOCTOR.

If I overdose from the shot the nurse gave me, a doctor might be able to save me. They do it to TV junkies all the time. Maybe I need an adrenaline shot to the heart, like in *Pulp Fiction*.

In general, I read that it's rather difficult to die in a hospital if you have doctors around. That's why people sign those 'do not resuscitate' papers. They don't want to be saved under certain conditions.

But first you have to *find* a doctor. I run around the floor in the Quiet, trying to stay within a short distance of the room where my unconscious self is.

I don't find a doctor, but there is a young woman whose ID states that she's a resident. I touch her earlobe and focus.

TWENTY-TWO HOURS ON THE JOB. WE DRINK THE ESPRESSO-spiked latte, but it's now as effective as chamomile tea when it comes to holding on to some semblance of sanity.

I, Darren, disassociate from Jane's thoughts. I'm wary of entrusting her with the mission I have in mind, given how tired she is. That she's here in this condition and expected to treat patients borders on criminal negligence. I don't have much choice, though. She's the only person I can use in close proximity to the room where my physical body is.

First, I need to pillage her memories for a solution, to zero in on a memory of a specific topic. I did something like that once before, when I was searching for memories of my biological parents in Sara's mind.

I decide to try the same method, only being more intentional about it. The topic is morphine overdose. I try to feel light, as if I'm trying to get deeper into someone's memories. At the same time, I try to think of ODing patients.

"Jane, you will want to see this procedure," Dr. Mickler says as we're half-running after him.

"What's wrong with him?" we ask, looking at the thin, pale-looking guy on the table.

"Heroin," Dr. Mickler says.

I let the rescue scene unfold. There was no shot to the heart as in the movie. Instead, they used a drug called Narcan, which has a Naloxone Hydro-something as an active ingredient. It's very promising, as it saved the guy from that heroin overdose, and his vitals were very bad.

I scan more of Jane's memories, trying to find information about this drug. I learn that it will work for morphine just as well as it works for heroin.

I begin Pushing.

'Get Narcan. Go to a room.' I provide a mental picture of the path to the room.

'Don't get sidetracked when you see the nurse having an episode there. She's being held by the police. The key priority is to help the patient the nurse accidentally hurt. She gave him 10mg of morphine.'

I play out different ways the whole thing could unfold. When I feel like there's no other path for Jane but to save me, I reluctantly exit her mind.

I FEEL MARGINALLY BETTER NOW THAT I'VE DONE SOMETHING TO fix the situation. I decide to get back to my body, phase out, resist falling asleep, wait a few moments, and then phase into the Quiet to see if my unwilling helpers are beginning their assigned work.

I walk back into the room, touch my frozen self's hand, and hear the noises of the hospital return.

13

I FEEL GREAT. I'M NOT EVEN ALL THAT CONCERNED THAT BETTY IS about to try to kill me. The only thought I have is that it's no wonder people ruin their lives taking this morphine stuff. It's pretty awesome.

Somewhere I hear a door open. I'm only mildly interested.

I see Betty with a pillow in her hands. This reminds me that I'm supposed to remember something, but I'm distracted by this strange itch that I'm feeling on my arm. When I scratch the itch, it feels amazing.

Then Betty lowers the pillow on my face.

My respiration rate is slower than usual from the morphine; a memory surfaces, and through my opiate haze, I realize this pillow will make it even harder for me to breathe.

Phase into the Quiet, that's what I'm supposed to do. But it requires me to be scared, which is hard at the moment, even with the knowledge that I'm being suffocated.

Suddenly, the pillow is gone from my face.

I hear a thud, which is supposed to mean something to me.

I make my best attempt to phase into the Quiet, but I feel like I'm floating instead.

My lids feel heavy. Very heavy.

I close my eyes, hoping this will help me concentrate.

Maybe if I snooze just for a moment . . .

I'M WIDE AWAKE AND COMPLETELY SOBER.

Every hint of pleasantness from the morphine is but a distant memory.

I'm feeling sick.

Something is in my arm, something that's hurting me, so I rip at it. There is a moment of pain and then relief.

I open my eyes and see that I'm holding the IV.

In front of me is Jane, the resident I Pushed, who looks surprised to be there.

She's holding the other end of the IV cable I just took out of my arm; attached to it is a syringe. I assume the drug, Narcan, is in it, which means my Pushing worked.

On the floor is Frank, the guy whom I used to tackle Betty, the nurse who just tried to kill me. She's cursing and trying to escape Frank, but he doesn't let go.

I'm overcome with a powerful wave of nausea and get sick onto the bed.

After all the pudding and my morning smoothie are gone from my system, I feel a tiny bit better. Well enough to unhook myself from the monitor, get up off the bed, and get away from the mess.

"You might want to help them," I tell Jane and quickly exit

the room, heading back to where my bed was standing previously.

The whole gang—Mira, my moms, and Bert—are standing there. Their chat is interrupted by Sara, the first of them to see me. She begins waving.

I inhale deeply, smile, and wave back at them as I approach.

"Hello," I say, trying my best to ignore another wave of nausea. My intent is to make it seem like I'm feeling much better, or in other words, to lie.

"What are you doing up?" Sara says instead of a greeting. I guess, unlike me, she doesn't feel like it's been days since we saw each other.

"I needed to use the bathroom," I lie. "I'm feeling much better, having walked a bit."

"That's good. Movement is life," Sara says. She likes to dish out such pearls of wisdom from time to time. I'd normally tease her about it, but I'm in no mood right now.

"Where is your bed?" Mira says, her eyes narrowing.

She's sharp, this one. I should've probably talked to her in the Quiet first. She's not the one I'm trying to fool right now.

"I think they're changing the sheets," I say, having no idea of the plausibility of this statement.

"Well, you'll be happy to know that we spoke to the doctor," Sara says. "The bullet just grazed your head. The X-ray shows no fragments of the bullet and no skull fractures. Those couple of stitches are all the damage done. You hurt yourself worse that time you fell off the monkey bars."

"Or that time you fell off the shopping cart in Key Food," Lucy adds.

"Great," I say, interrupting the torrent of embarrassing incidents. "That means I can check out when I want, right?"

"The doctor promised he really would come by to see you after lunch. He said that if you want to check out at that point, he'll let you," Lucy says. "I'd make sure you're feeling one hundred percent before doing that."

Bert clears his throat. "Well, dude, I was just waiting to say good-bye. I have to go. Work, you know."

"Sure, thanks for stopping by." I pat him on the shoulder.

"We actually have to go also," Sara says, looking at Lucy. "Now that we know you're going to be okay. But you should eat something. According to your friend—" she nods her head toward Mira, "—all you've had is pudding and some Jell-O."

I can't believe my luck. I was just about to invent a way to get rid of them, but they're doing it for me.

"Sure, Mom, I'm actually going to head into the cafeteria right after you leave," I say. "Mira, do you want to go with me?"

"Of course," Mira says. "But there's a better option. My brother is almost here, so we can take you to a restaurant, get you some real food. Afterwards, we can have you back for that conversation with the doctor."

"Great," I say. "That works even better."

In reality, food is the last thing I want right now. I'm still feeling sick. What I do want is to be far away from this hellhole.

"Okay then," Sara says, giving me a hug. "Albert, let's walk out together. Let Mira and Darren decide where they're going to eat."

I think I catch her winking at Bert as she says that.

"Oh, Lucy, Kyle had to leave, so you don't have a ride," I say, remembering Kyle's quick departure.

"Right. He texted me. That's why I'm leaving now. I'm sharing a cab with your mother." She smiles and kisses my cheek.

"It was great to meet you, Lucy . . . Sara . . . Bert . . ." Mira gives each of my moms a hug, and Bert a kiss on the cheek. Must be a Russian thing.

"So where do you want to go to eat?" Mira says when they get out of earshot.

"I'm not actually hungry. I want us to get out of here quickly, though," I say, and start walking toward the exit.

"What's wrong?" Mira says, catching up with me.

"I'm feeling pretty sick—I just didn't want to worry my moms," I say. "I need fresh air."

"If you're sick, you should stay at the hospital," she counters, but I keep increasing my pace.

"There's something more going on," she says when I avoid the elevator. "You're taking the stairs on purpose. You don't want to run into your family and friend on the way out."

"You're right. Can I please explain when we get out of here? Otherwise, we might get delayed by hospital security or something worse," I say. "I got into a bit of trouble. I want to tell both you and Eugene about what happened. He would want to know."

"Okay," she says. "Let me check on him."

We walk the rest of the stairs in silence, Mira messing with her phone.

"Okay, he's parked near the south-side exit," she says. "It's this way."

I follow her.

"You know you're very lucky," she says out of nowhere.

"I am? Why?" Spotting Eugene's car, I head for it.

"Your family," she says. "It must be nice to have people who care about you so much."

"I guess," I say, shrugging. "Though it can sometimes be a nuisance."

"People never appreciate what they have." There's a bitter note in her voice, and I wince internally as I remember that her parents are dead. Shit. I didn't mean to be so insensitive. I rack my brain for something to say as we approach Eugene's car, a Camry, and get in.

"How are you?" Eugene says, giving me a concerned look.

"I'm fine. Just a scratch. Please start driving—I want to get out of here. There's something I need to tell you guys."

In the moments that follow, I describe the attempt on my life. When I get to the part about the Pusher, Mira orders Eugene to stop the car. He complies, pulling over to the side of the road as I continue with my tale.

I don't sugarcoat my Pushing, even though I know that I might be losing whatever pity-induced goodwill I might've had with Mira. I hope she appreciates my honesty, though. I hope she sees I had no real choice in the matter.

"That's pretty insane," Eugene says when I'm done. His eyes are wide with shock.

Mira doesn't say anything. Instead, she looks like she's concentrating.

"Darren's right about the Pusher," she says after a moment. "The fucker who killed our parents was there, at the hospital."

14

"WHAT? HOW DO YOU KNOW THAT?" EUGENE GIVES HER A startled look.

"I Split to the Mind Dimension just now, of course," Mira replies. "Then I walked back to the hospital and Read the people there. I had to see if I could learn something more than Darren discovered about our enemy."

"And," Eugene prompts impatiently.

"And I didn't find any sign of the bastard. Only that tell-tale presence Darren described in the woman's mind." She looks upset as she says this.

"But how do you know it's the same Pusher?" Eugene asks.

"I just feel it. I can't explain it," she says curtly, and I know exactly what she means. There was almost a tone of voice to the Pushing instructions I glimpsed in the nurse's mind—the same tone that I heard in the Russian mobster's head the other day.

"What did the people I Pushed think about the whole

ordeal?" I ask worriedly. "Are they going to call the police? Do you think I'll be wanted for questioning?"

"No. The resident and the visitor have amnesia, as does the nurse," Mira says, her expression now hard to read.

"Amnesia is a known side effect of Pushing," Eugene explains. "If you get someone to do something small, something they can justify to themselves, they can internalize the story the Pusher gives them or invent their own reasoning, creating an illusion of free will. But when it's something big, something they can't fathom doing by free will, the brain chooses to forget the incident altogether. It's a type of defense mechanism, I guess. They either don't remember what happened, or have only a vague recollection. My father thought it was akin to alcohol-induced amnesia."

I sort of understand. The alcohol amnesia thing happened to me once. I woke up next to Jen, this woman that I couldn't picture myself being interested in, beer goggles or not. Yet apparently we'd hooked up, and she told me a story that sounded like it happened to someone else.

"Right, so you're off the hook," Mira says to me. "I don't think anyone is going to be questioning you for that."

"Okay, good," I say, starting to feel cautiously optimistic. "Let's keep on driving. Start the car."

"What if he's still there?" Mira says, frowning. "Maybe we should go back."

"No, that's a terrible idea," Eugene says firmly.

"I agree," I say. "Being nearly killed twice in one day is plenty for me."

"You guys are such wimps," Mira says scornfully.

"I am not," Eugene objects. "We're blocks away from Brighton Beach, where the Russian mafia hangs out all the time

—and the Pusher has used them in the past. He can Split, walk over, find a lackey, and make him come kill us. In fact, the hospital is so close that the Pusher can just call them on the phone. For all we know, they're already at the hospital by now. I'm all for vengeance, but if we get killed, we won't get any."

"Exactly," I say. "I'm too sick from the drugs and the head wound. I need to rest before I take another bullet for the greater good."

"Fine." Mira blows out an annoyed breath. "You're probably right. So what now?"

"I'm going to stay at a hotel," I say. "They now know my name, which means they might know where I live. I'm not taking any chances. In your case, it's even simpler. They do know where you live, so I suggest you follow my example."

"That's a good idea," Eugene says. "They are really after us, so it pays to be cautious. Needless to say, give a different name when you book your room."

"Right. And no going to the apartment to get shit, Eugene," Mira says, and I hear her also mumble something along the lines of 'a couple of pussies.'

"Wait, I just realized I forgot some stuff at the hospital," I say, patting my pockets.

"Are you looking for this?" Eugene says, getting a gun from the glove compartment.

"I was actually thinking of the Gameboys I left in that room, but that's also mine," I say. "Where'd you get it?"

"Mira got it out of your pants before the paramedics got to you," he says. "I've been holding on to it."

"Okay, thanks," I say, trying not to focus on the image of Mira getting something from my pants.

We don't talk much more on the way to the city, other than

my asking Eugene to stop near a juice bar. A beet-carrot jumbo cup of juice is all I want today. I don't think I can keep anything more substantial down.

As I drink the juice, we make plans, which are very simple. Keep our heads low for a couple of days, and then regroup. Mira suggests we don't use credit cards for the time being, and we all stop by a bank to get cash.

I suggest a hotel that I know is halfway decent, but they refuse, preferring to stay in Brooklyn. I decide to go to that hotel anyway, having had enough of Brooklyn, and we agree to split up.

After that, I doze from the sugar high of my juice, only to be awakened later by the sudden stop of the car.

"This is you," Eugene says.

Looking out, I see the Tribeca Grand Hotel—my destination.

"Thank you," I say. "Thanks for the ride. And thank you, Mira, for looking out for me at the hospital. I really appreciate it."

She leans over her seat and gives me a peck on the lips.

I get out, my brain too overwhelmed with near-death experiences to puzzle out the meaning of Mira's little kiss.

Operating on autopilot, I get inside the hotel. It's nice, but its grandioseness is presently lost on me. I buy some Tylenol and water at the hotel kiosk, take four pills, and hope my liver doesn't fail. Then I request the biggest room they have available.

As they're setting everything up, I text Bert the names of my biological parents and the phone number of Arkady.

On the way to my room, I get some ice for my head. Then I

get in, plop on the bed, order some Pay-Per-View, and mindlessly watch TV.

The Tylenol and the ice make the throbbing in my head subside a bit, and the exhaustion really hits me. It's still early, but I don't care. I'm going to go to sleep early yet again. If I keep this up, I might become one of those early-bird people.

As I get in bed, I set the alarm for eleven a.m. I know I'm being overly cautious, given the current time, but I do it anyway. My shrink appointment is during my lunch hour, and this time around, I'm determined to make it.

15

I BECOME AWARE OF SOME ANNOYING NOISE. IT'S MY PHONE alarm. *Why did I set it?* I wonder lazily, opening an eyelid.

Then I remember. I wanted to make it to my appointment. All of a sudden, the whole thing seems like a drag, and I try to go back to sleep. I rarely, if ever, keep my appointments with my shrink, so why rock the boat? It's not like I need to express my feelings and get in touch with my emotions. What possessed me to even think about going?

But as some of the ideas why I *should* see her begin buzzing in my head, sleep eludes me. After a few minutes of just lying there, I grudgingly get up.

I order room service and check my phone. I have five missed calls from Sara and one from Lucy, so I call both of them back.

Yes, I'm doing better. No, it doesn't hurt anymore—at least not much. Yes, Mira is a nice girl.

Done with my moms, I see an email from Bert.

I'm using an app Bert personally put on my phone. Allegedly, the email sent through this app is seriously encrypted, to the point where even the NSA might not be reading Bert's correspondence. He's paranoid like that. If you ask me, hiding so much might actually make the NSA more curious about you, but there is no way I can convince Bert of this. In any case, as I read, I see that this specific email is among those that I do need to stay private:

Dude,

The guy whose phone number you got is named Arkady Bogomolov. He's extremely dangerous. Not worth fucking with, trust me, even for someone as hot as Mira.

As for your parents, I'm surprised. I'm not finding much. Lucy has a case file on the murder, but don't tell her I know this. Glancing through it, I have to say, it seems very shady how they died. No clues as to who did it. Lucy clocked an unbelievable number of hours on that case without any luck, though you probably already know this. Anyway, I can get that case file for you if you swear to never talk to her about it. There was this OB-GYN, Dr. Greenspan, that your mom was going to, but his digital records don't go that far. I tried my phone con on them, but, get this, the physical records were stolen recently. Weird coincidence. I will keep digging, but don't expect too much. Sorry.

Bert.

I write my response:

Can you find out more about this Arkady character? Particularly, I want to know where he can be found in the near future. I just want to look at him from a distance, so don't get your panties in a bunch.

Yeah, and get me those files if you can. I don't want to ask

Lucy for them. I won't tell her about the files, obviously, since I realize that you're much too pretty to go to jail.

When room service brings in my breakfast, I order a cab. The breakfast order turns out to be too small. I wolf everything down and still feel a bit hungry. I guess not eating much and throwing up the prior day is good for the appetite. I wouldn't be surprised if I lost a few pounds. There's no time to get more food, though, so I guess I'll have to make do. The shrink always has doughnuts at her office.

As I get dressed, I realize the biggest problem with staying in a hotel. All I have is my prior day's clothes, which have been through a lot. Thankfully, they're dark, so no blood or dirt shows. I will have to go shopping, but that can wait until after the appointment.

Leaving my room, I grab a cab and make my way to Midtown.

"DARREN," THE SHRINK SAYS WHEN I SIT DOWN ON HER COMFY office chair. "I'm glad to finally see you here."

"It's good to see you too, Liz," I say, smiling. "Sorry it's been so long. Things have been hectic."

Her perfectly plucked eyebrows rise in surprise, and I can't blame her. I don't normally apologize for missing sessions—nor do I normally call her *Liz*. She asked me to call her that a while ago. Just Liz. Not Dr. Jackson or Miss Jackson. Not just Doctor. Not Ma'am or Madam. Not Mrs. Jackson or Mrs. or even Elizabeth. But, of course, I very rarely obliged in the past, so I can see how she might find it surprising that I didn't do the usual—which is to invent a new way to address her that she most likely would prefer I not use. Like Mrs. J, for instance.

She now knows things are different today. More serious.

"It's fine, Darren. I knew you would come visit me when you were ready for it—when you felt like you needed it. And as usual, this is a safe place, so please don't hesitate to share whatever is on your mind—whatever brought you here again."

"Thank you," I say. "I don't actually know where to begin."

"You're hurt," she observes, looking at the bandage on my head. "That might be a good place to start."

"Yeah, I got shot, actually. Came face to face with my mortality and all that. It was bad, but it's not exactly what I wanted to talk about today. At least not at first," I say as I shift in the chair. "If you don't mind."

This gets me another barely detectable expression of surprise. Her face is hard to read. I suspect she's had something done that interferes with showing emotion. Botox or something like that. Or she just developed that unreadable expression as part of her job. It's hard to say for sure.

"Of course, Darren. We can talk about whatever you want." She crosses her long, black-stocking-clad legs. "Start where you want to start."

I look her over while thinking of what to say next. She looks like the epitome of a MILF mixed with a bit of sexy librarian. The latter is due to the stylish spectacles she's wearing. She's slender, but with noticeable muscle definition on her exposed arms, particularly around her shoulders. She must be hitting the gym regularly, and it shows. Her long hair looks like it belongs to a woman in her twenties or teens. She always dresses in outfits that border on hot, but still pass for professional. I have no idea how old she is; it's not a gentlemanly thing to ask. All I know is that she already looked this way—awesome and middle-aged—when we first met almost a decade ago. She hasn't visibly aged since then.

As you'd expect, I used to have inappropriate thoughts about her in my early teens, but it was just a phase. Nowadays, I sometimes suspect that the tables might've turned, and it's not just because of the cougar-like vibes she gives off. It goes deeper. There are little things. Like, for example, when I talk, she seems to genuinely care about what I have to say. True, it could be just her doing her job. In fact, a good therapist *should* behave that way. But I find it hard to believe that the amount of attention and the heartfelt advice she gives me is merely her doing her professional duty. Her attention to me changed as I got older—or maybe I just started noticing it at that point. Then again, it could, of course, be wishful thinking and conceit on my part; it's beyond flattering to think a woman of this caliber wants me.

Oh, and besides the way she listens to me, there's also the fact that I think she's available. At least I've never heard her mention any family, and her desk lacks any pictures of children or a husband. Then again, these sessions are to talk about me, not her, so it's possible I just don't know about her personal life.

"Have you stopped time recently?" she asks, pulling me out of my jumbled thoughts. "You haven't talked about that for a long time, something I consider to be a good sign."

"Surprising you should mention that," I say, considering my next words carefully. She just opened the door to the issue of covering up my blabbing about the Quiet. "I think I made a huge breakthrough when it comes to that. Sorry it hasn't come up before in our sessions, but yeah, I don't believe that stuff anymore."

"Interesting," she says, but the expression on her face is anything but curiosity. She looks almost upset. Or, more specifically, she looks disappointed and perhaps a tiny bit worried. It's hard to tell with the Botox or whatever. "What brought this on so suddenly?" she asks, gazing at me.

"Not suddenly. It's been a while now. I guess I grew out of it. Isn't that the way of these things? Don't your other patients go into remission? Get cured? Shouldn't you pat yourself on the back?"

I find her reaction odd. She's acting like she doesn't believe me. Or doesn't want to believe me. Is it because she's afraid I'll stop visiting? After all, that was the reason for my getting into therapy when I was growing up—my so-called delusions. But doesn't she realize that that's not why I've been seeing her since I moved out of my moms' house? Then again, how would she know that? I don't even know why I'm still visiting her, or why I have this standing appointment that I so seldom keep, but pay for. My shrink tax, as I always jokingly think of it.

She gives me a penetrating stare. "I think something else is going on with you. Something like denial, perhaps? Maybe you met a young woman and want to seem sane for her? Whatever it is, I'm very curious to learn more about it. Some people think mental illness is like an infection: take the right antibiotic, and you can be cured. The truth is that there's no such thing as mental illness to begin with. Just different people with quirks and traits, some of them maladaptive. When it comes to these problematic features of the psyche, we usually have to treat them on an ongoing basis. There are few silver bullets in my profession. Catharsis is a myth of fiction. But then again, yours was always a special case. My biggest question is: if you're cured, what are you doing here?"

"That's unusually insightful," I say, impressed. "Almost creepy. I *have* met a woman that I'm interested in, but that's not why I say I'm cured. As to your last question, I'm not even sure why I'm here. I guess I have some new issues on my mind, and I feel most comfortable discussing them with you for some reason."

As I say it, I realize it's the truth. The irony of this doesn't escape me. I'm someone who has always been a huge skeptic about psychology as a treatment for anything. In fact, I always doubted it on a deeper level, going as far as to call it pseudo-science, though never to Liz's face. Of course, the fact that I came for therapy today doesn't prove the earlier me wrong. I just think I'm here more to talk to someone who's known me for a long time and who's acted like she cares about me. Here I can talk about things that I don't think my friends and family are equipped to help me with.

"I'm flattered that you feel like you can discuss things with me. Maybe a big change has occurred within you after all. And I'm very excited to hear about your relationship," she says, sounding sincere. If my meeting a girl makes her jealous on any level, she's extremely good at acting happy for me instead. So good that I concede that perhaps I was wrong about that whole business of her wanting to sleep with me. Then again, wanting to sleep with someone is not mutually exclusive with wishing him a happy love life. There are lots of Victoria's Secret models I wish I could sleep with, but if I learned that they had a great guy in their life, I would wish them luck. I think I would, anyway.

"Yes, the girl thing is interesting, but that's not exactly what I wanted to talk about either," I say. "At least not at first. It's this other thing. I did something to a man to save her when she was in big trouble. Mind you, I was morally justified, but the thing that happened to the man as a result was very bad, and now I'm feeling guilty."

Therapy has this effect on me. I say things there that magically put me in touch with my true feelings as soon as I say them, even if I didn't fully register those feelings until that moment. The skeptic in me would, of course, say that this doesn't justify the institution of psychotherapy. He would point out that I could've probably used a pet parrot instead of Liz to bounce words off of in this capacity. Regardless, it feels good to talk to her like that.

"Okay. If that's what you want to talk about." I notice she stops writing in her notebook and is looking at me with an unusual intensity. I rarely express feelings this way, and something about what I said must've resonated with her.

"I don't know if it is," I say. "There are other things that happened. I witnessed something terrible, and my life was in danger a few times. It's all difficult to deal with, especially when I can't discuss it with my family."

"I see." She gives me an encouraging look. "I can tell you have a lot going on. Just start at the beginning and tell me whatever you feel comfortable talking about. Start with this man you mentioned. What exactly did you do to him?"

"I sort of *persuaded* him to do something that ended up causing him great harm," I say. This is the closest approximation of the truth I'm able to come up with at this time. Even this, once I say it, I regret. It's risky. What if the Readers decide to Read my family and/or therapist for some reason? They might understand what sort of persuasion I'm talking about.

"You *guided* someone to hurt himself?" Liz says in a strange tone. She sounds almost excited. It's not the reaction I would've expected at all. "This is very important, Darren. Can you tell me as much as you can about this event?"

Something is off. My heart starts pounding in my chest, and I phase into the Quiet to give myself a moment to think. Liz's reaction is really odd. Now that she's frozen in that moment, I see her eyes gleaming with very non-shrink-like excitement. I've never seen her react this way, and I've told her some crazy shit over the years.

Is this some weird thing for her? Does she get off on stories of patients doing something shady? That doesn't make sense at all. Doesn't seem like her. However, there is something I can do to figure this out. I haven't done Reading for a while, and now is as good a time as any.

In fact, there is some poetic justice in getting inside the head of your therapist. It could be a lot of fun feeding her insights about herself that I glean from her mind. But most importantly, I can find out what's behind this strange reaction—as well as maybe settle the whole 'does she want me' debate once and for all.

I approach Liz and look for a place to touch her. Though I have phased into the Quiet in her presence many times before, I've never used the opportunity to do anything inappropriate, like touching her very temping cleavage area—and yes, I was tempted. I've never tried to analyze why I exercised this restraint. It just didn't feel right to do something like that. Not with a person whom I told about myself doing exactly this to girls at school back in the day—actions she told me not to worry about because they were just mild delusions, a slightly exaggerated version of a normal pubescent boy's fantasy.

I end up going for a light touch on her neck with the tips of my index and middle fingers. It's the sort of gesture I have seen doctors make when trying to get someone's pulse.

As my fingers touch her skin, I instantly pull my hand away, my heart rate picking up.

A second version of Liz is standing in the room, watching me pull my hand away from her frozen double. As the avalanche of confused thoughts hits me, some part of me is happy her neck was the part of her body I opted for. Otherwise, this would be not just the biggest surprise of my life, but also incredibly awkward.

"Thank you," Liz says, smiling. "I was about to do this to you myself. I now have very little doubt that you are sane . . . and probably one of us."

16

I'M SO STUNNED THAT I FIND MYSELF IN THAT RARE SITUATION where I have nothing to say. I just look at her—the woman I thought I'd known all this time.

As it turns out, I didn't know her at all.

As moments pass, I begin to digest the severity of this deception. I recall all the conversations where I described the Quiet, and she acted like a shrink listening to a delusional patient. All the therapy meant to get me to stop imagining something that she clearly had always known was real. In a way, the anger I begin to feel is akin to the way I felt when I thought Sara had been a Reader but never told me—and sent me to a shrink, to boot. This is the shrink I eventually ended up with, and Liz's deception is worse than Sara's would've been had my mom turned out to be a Reader. Liz actually pretended to be fixing a problem she knew full well I didn't have.

"I know you must be confused and upset," she says,

obviously reading my expression. "Before you make a final judgment, please allow me to explain."

I try to get my emotions under control. It's difficult. I have had a Reader in my life, all this time, and she allowed me to think I was crazy. When I feel like I won't shout obscenities at her, I say, "Why did you wait for years to reveal to me I wasn't the only one?"

She flinches for a second. I guess she's not used to my voice being so icy.

"I had many reasons for this deception, and my choices were pretty limited," she says, looking at me. "In the beginning, there was a chance that you might've been a rare, truly delusional case. This has happened before. Also, you were young enough when we met that you could've been making things up for attention. When you showed off your power to me, by knowing things in my books, I knew that you were sane and that you could do what you said. But you still could've been a Leacher—which would've been a big problem. You still might be, though I doubt it. I just didn't know what to do, so I waited. When you just told me about the way you protected your new friend, I was about to take things to the next level—"

"A Leacher? What are you talking about?" I stare at her, my head spinning.

"Before I say any more, I have to test you to be sure. I know you essentially admitted that you Guided someone, but I still have to do this."

"I did what?" I give her a confused look.

"You have to do the test first. I will not speak another word until after the test. Follow me," she says and walks out of the room.

I follow. What choice do I have? At least this time I'm not at gunpoint during the testing.

"Her," she says, pointing at the waiting room receptionist. "Make her walk into my office and say, 'Sorry, we're out of doughnuts.'"

Have you ever had a car accident? You know that feeling just before the accident, when you slam on the brakes with all your might? A situation where all you want to do is hit the pause button on the world? This is what I feel like right now.

I had been convinced that she was a fellow Reader, which would by itself have been odd. But now I begin to understand the enormity of this situation.

"What do you mean?" I say, wanting to hear it.

"Oh, come on, Darren. You're smarter than this. I think you know what to do," she says, smiling. "And you know what I'm talking about, even if you're not familiar with the terminology."

"Since it's a test, I want to be sure," I say. "What exactly do you want me to do with her?"

"Okay then. Do what you did to that man you mentioned. The one you Guided to do something that caused him harm in order to defend your new girlfriend. You had your hands on him after you 'stopped time,' didn't you? You willed him to do something, and then you saw that he actually did it? That's what you feel guilty about, isn't it? Just do that again—only this time no one will be hurt, and Camilla will just walk into the office and say that silly phrase. That's all. Then I can be sure that you're one of us." Liz's voice takes on the same gentle tone as when she gives me all sorts of mundane advice.

Except this time she's talking about Pushing, not how to best deal with stress. This can only mean that I'm right about my suspicions.

Liz is a Pusher, so the *us* she just mentioned is other Pushers. Liz wants me to prove I'm one of *them* by Pushing her receptionist.

My head feeling like it's about to explode, I walk up to the receptionist.

She's frozen in an unnatural position while starting a phone call. I gingerly place my finger on her right hand, the same hand that's pressing the number dial.

"OKAY, MR. DAVENPORT, I WILL RESCHEDULE YOUR APPOINTMENT for two p.m., Monday of next week. Thanks for letting us know," we say and hang up.

I, Darren, separate my thoughts from Camilla's. I'm here for a reason, and I need to do what I came here to do.

I visualize getting up, opening the door, and saying 'I'm sorry, we're out of doughnuts.'

Just to be sure the whole thing makes sense in Camilla's head, I add a story around it:

'The patient Darren requested a doughnut. He explained how hungry he is and how difficult it is to go on with the session without the treat. However, he's diabetic and allowing him to take the doughnut from the box that's sitting on the desk would be a bad idea. So let's walk in and say, 'Sorry, we're out of doughnuts.' The box can be hidden when he gets out. And it's okay to interrupt the session for this reason. In fact, it's critical to get this out of the patient's mind, so he can focus on the rest of the session.'

Hopeful that my Push will work, I exit Camilla's head.

17

"OKAY," I SAY. "LET'S GET OUT."

Without waiting for Liz's response, I walk back into the office and touch my forehead.

The ambient noises of the office come back. Liz is sitting in front of me, her arms crossed in anticipation.

There is a hesitant knock on the door.

Liz doesn't respond. I don't either.

Slowly, the door opens and Camilla walks in, looking extremely uncertain. I find it fascinating to watch this. On some level, this woman knows that interrupting the doctor with her patient is wrong, despite the rationalization I placed into her mind. However, she's clearly unable to fight the compulsion.

"Sorry, we're out of doughnuts," she says, looking at me. Then she reddens and runs back out of the office.

"That's very good," Liz says, putting her hands on the

handles of her chair. She was clearly tense the last few moments.

"Will I get some answers now?" I ask, figuring that's what I should say. "Am I one of you?"

I have a dilemma. I know more than I probably should. I decide not to show it. If she's a Pusher who assumes that I'm a Pusher too, then she would likely react negatively if she knew I was a Reader as well. She clearly isn't the Pusher who tried to kill me—whoever that is must know what I look like. Of course, it makes sense that the first Pusher I would meet face to face would not necessarily be the one who wants me dead. There are probably as many of them as Readers—not that I know how many Readers there actually are in the world. Still, I need to be careful: Liz could know that Pusher.

"Yes, you are one of us," she says. "We call ourselves Guides, for obvious reasons."

Guides. That's much nicer-sounding than Pushers. "Because we can force people to do what we want?"

"Force is a crude word for it, but yes—though I don't like to think of it that way. We don't force as much as provide guidance for people to wish to do what we intend. It's not all that different from making a thoroughly persuasive argument."

Yeah, right, I think, but don't say it. What argument could I have given someone to take a bullet for Mira? But then I realize that one could say that the Secret Service agents have been persuaded to do exactly that for the President.

"What are some of the other things you mentioned?" I resume my questioning. "What are Leachers? Why are they so dangerous? Why did you think I could be one?"

"Let's talk more privately," she says and looks like she's concentrating for a moment. The next instant, I'm standing in the middle of our chairs, looking at her touching my frozen self on the cheek. Was her touch a bit too gentle, almost sensual, or is that my imagination?

The room is silent again, which makes me realize that Pushers can also phase into the Quiet and pull others with them. Not a huge surprise, but I can't take anything for granted.

"Okay," she says after winding up her watch. I wonder if she's concerned about spending too much of her Depth, or whatever Pushers call it. "Leachers are a group of people who can also 'stop time,' which we call *Splitting*. Only instead of Guiding people, they do something disturbing and unnatural. They Leach people's minds of information—which is the ultimate violation of privacy. Make no mistake, this is not the harmless telepathy you might've seen in movies, where a mind reader gleans some surface thoughts. No, Leachers go much deeper. They can ferret out every secret, uncover every desire and forbidden fantasy. No memory is hidden, no interaction is sacred for them—they can access it all." Her nose wrinkles with barely concealed disgust as she adds, "And yes, they're very dangerous."

Given how void of emotion her face usually is, her disgust is that much more striking.

So, as I was beginning to suspect, Leachers are Readers. Leachers are considered an abomination by the Guides, just as Guides—Pushers—are considered a crime against nature by Readers. This isn't that surprising. Two groups who hate each other will always vilify one another.

Until now I had the Reader outlook, and I assumed Pushers were diabolically evil. After all, one of them killed Mira's parents, while another one, in Caleb's memories, wanted to blow up the Reader community. A Pusher also tried to kill me at the hospital. Or have me killed. That Pusher/Guide was likely the same one who killed Mira's parents. So in my short experience with them, Pushers don't have a good track record. But *I* can do what they do, and I'm certainly not a lost cause. Liz being one of them confuses things further. She's a good person. At least I thought so before I learned that the Liz I knew is not the real Liz.

I also realize something else. Clearly, Pushers/Guides can't Read/Leach the way I can—she's condemning the Reading ability, in fact. Nor did she expect a Reader to be able to pass that test with the secretary. All this adds up to something I already suspected: I *am* something different.

I decide I'm going to call Pushers *Guides* in my mind going forward, since it's a nicer term, with the exception of the fucker who's trying to kill me. He'll remain the Pusher.

"Why are Leachers so dangerous?" I ask, realizing that I've been quiet for too long.

"That's harder to explain without going into some history. I have to warn you, no real records of the time I'm going to tell you about exist. A lot of this is verbal tradition combined with hearsay and conjecture," she says and proceeds to tell me a story, a bit of which I already heard from Eugene. She doesn't talk about how phasing into the Quiet works or go into Eugene's Quantum Mechanics theory. Instead, she tells me something that sounds like an origin myth.

As she explains it, Guides and Leachers started off from the same selectively bred branch of humanity. It all started, as these things sometimes do, with a crazy cult. There were people who began a strange eugenics program. It focused on breeding people who had one thing in common: they described the world slowing down when they were under extreme stress and having out-of-body experiences in near-death situations. This breeding, over many generations of arranged couples, led to a branch of humans that could bring about, at will, something like a near-death experience for variable lengths of time—only back then, they thought it was the spirit leaving the body. After this point, the breeding focused on extending that length of time in the spirit world—what I term the Quiet.

Almost a century later, two new aspects manifested among the people who, at that point, could spend some minutes in the spirit world. Some could Read, or Leach, as Liz put it, and some learned to Guide, or Push, as Readers would see it. The cult split into two groups. At first, they just lived apart, but soon, each group started to view the other as heretical. There was a leader on both sides, and Liz's version painted the Leacher leader as particularly evil and responsible for starting the war between the groups that would go on for ages.

Later in history, one Leacher was advising Alexander the Great, according to some accounts—or, according to others, Alexander himself was a Leacher. In any case, in the process of conquering the city of Thebes, he destroyed almost the entire Guide community of that time, along with six thousand regular people. And this was just the first of the genocides that Leachers tried to commit against Guides, according to Liz.

"Do you now see why I had to make sure you weren't a Leacher—as unlikely as that possibility was?" she says when she's done.

"No, not fully," I reply honestly. "I mean, what happened in history sounds really abhorrent, but are modern-day Leachers so bad? Plenty of countries and ethnic groups have dark histories in the past, but now they're mostly civilized. Just look at Europe. Why do you think Leachers still want to wipe us out?"

"Because they tried to wipe us out as recently as World War II," she says harshly. Then, moderating her tone, she adds, "Granted, that is now also history. Personally, I just don't trust them. They view everything as wrongs done to *them*, and they'll never forgive and forget. With their skewed perspective, they'll always want to get revenge. Of course, there are many among us who feel stronger about this issue than I do—and many who are more liberal and think bygones should be bygones. You'll probably meet both kinds, though most of my friends hold liberal views. This is Manhattan, after all." She smiles at that last tidbit.

"Okay," I say, though the idea of meeting more Guides seems of questionable safety. "So why did you think it unlikely that I was one of them? If one can Split, isn't there a fifty-fifty chance that the person is a Leacher?"

"Actually, the chance is more than fifty-fifty in Leachers' favor. There are more of them than of us—which is why I had to be extra careful. As to why I suspected you were one of us, well . . . you *look* like a Guide. Many of us have the look I'm talking about. It's a certain facial bone structure, a prominent nose—the look of a born leader, if you will. Of course, these things alone are not very reliable. A much bigger clue for me was the fact that you were adopted."

"Oh? How would that be a clue?"

"Leachers have strict taboos about breeding outside their little clique. They shun anyone born as a half-blood, as they call them. We're much more open about it. It was even encouraged to some degree in the past, when our numbers were particularly small."

"Really?" From what Eugene told me, a Reader's power is directly related to how long one can spend in the Quiet, and having children with non-Readers seems to reduce the latter ability. I wonder if it's the same for Guides, but I can't ask that without showing that I know too much.

Liz nods. "Yes, after one of the worst genocides, we were down to just a dozen or so individuals. If we hadn't become more open-minded, we would've had serious inbreeding problems. Even now, our genetic diversity is fairly low. Of course, back in the day, our stance on having kids outside the Guide community was the same as that of Leachers. And to this day, there are some people—we call them the Traditionalists—who want us to have assigned mates. Fortunately, they're a tiny minority and are usually ignored. The only downside, and the thing that scares the Traditionalists, is that children born of such mixed lineage usually have diminished Reach. So, theoretically, if we keep diluting our gene pool, we might lose the very thing that makes us different."

"What's Reach?" I ask, guessing that she gave me a segue into learning about the power variation that Readers value so much.

"It has to do with how long you can freeze time, which impacts how deeply and for how long you can Guide someone," she says, confirming my suspicions.

"Interesting. So how long can you freeze time and how does that affect your control over people?" I say, wondering if Guides have the same taboo when it comes to talking about this stuff.

"It's not a topic for polite conversation," she says, confirming my suspicion. "But if you agree to keep it confidential, I would be willing to share. You have, after all, shared your life with me all these years."

"Sure, I won't tell anybody," I say. "And your telling me this only begins to scratch the surface when it comes to making up for all this 'therapy.'"

"Fair enough," she says with a wry smile. "I can spend almost an hour in the Mind Dimension, which is what we call this place where we are right now. When I use my power to aid in therapy, I'm able to get my patients to change their undesirable behavior for as long as a week—but my Reach is much less than that. I'm just good at getting people on the right track with my suggestions, so they continue doing what I meant them to for a while. This works out nicely, since my patients usually see me once a week."

"You use Guiding for therapy?" I don't know why that surprises me, but it does.

"Of course, the ability can be—and has been—used to help people. I'm one of the few psychologists who can truly modify a patient's behavior. That's why people value my services so much, and why my fees are so high. Other doctors can only boast of being able to do this. My Guiding ability is invaluable when it comes to treating conditions like OCD and other disorders."

"But in my case, you couldn't use it because you thought there was a chance you could pull me into the Mind Dimension?"

"Right. Had I been sure that you were just a delusional patient, I would've helped you, after you were old enough."

"Old enough?"

"We don't Guide young children. It's one of the ancient taboos that we still follow in modern times. And it's a good thing. From what I know about developmental psychology,

Guiding a child might leave adverse, long-term effects," she says.

"What about adults? Are there side effects to Guiding?" I wonder.

"It depends on the situation. The way I Guide my patients is completely harmless and improves their quality of life."

I think about all this. The taboo makes sense. I can see a number of creepy reasons someone might have a rule not to touch children, even in the Quiet. And especially in order to mind control them. The therapy she does is interesting, though. I picture using Guiding to stop someone from obsessive hand washing. It wouldn't be hard. The person would just think his OCD is going away rather than that he's being mind-controlled by his therapist. And would it be so wrong to do this? Probably not.

"You know," I say, looking at her, "I would've thought a Leacher's power would be more helpful to a therapist."

"Perhaps it would be, but I wouldn't know," Liz says with a shrug. "To me, some of the usefulness of talk therapy is in the talking itself. A Leacher wouldn't need to talk to the patients as much."

"I have to admit, you're making me feel better about this power. Upon first hearing about it, I thought it sounded a little creepy," I say, watching her face to see if she takes offense.

She doesn't. In fact, the corners of her mouth turn up in a smile. "Yes, I could see how it might seem that way. That's certainly how Leachers justify their hatred of us. Our ability seems unnatural if you don't think about it deeply. That's mostly due to the misconception we have about free will. Specifically, that it exists."

"Do Guides think free will is an illusion, then?" As soon as I ask the question, I realize I made a mistake. This is a philosophical discussion—and those, in my opinion, have as little place in polite conversation as money, politics, sex, and religion.

"I'm not sure if that's a group-wide view," Liz says. "I, personally, don't believe in free will. I've read studies that have convinced me of this. People concoct reasons, after the fact, for behavior that's outside of their control. A classic example of that is how a person's brain signals an arm to move before a person is conscious of deciding to move it."

"That doesn't fully make sense to me," I say. "I like to think that we can choose what happens to us. Otherwise, if it's all outside our control, people can get fatalistic."

She laughs, ending our debate. "You know, you'll feel right at home when I introduce you to my friends," she says, still smiling. "I can tell you're going to get along with some of them."

She wants to introduce me to her friends? That could be a problem.

"Actually, Liz, I'm not sure how eager I am to meet any Guides besides you," I say slowly. Pausing, I look at her, and then decide to just say it. "You see, I think a Guide is trying to kill me."

18

"What?" Liz's whole demeanor changes. "What are you talking about?"

I give her a carefully edited version of what happened to me at the hospital. I describe the attempt on my life, and lie that my mom—the detective—spoke to the nurse who tried to kill me. I say that the nurse reported blanking out during the whole ordeal, and that my mom, who is a seasoned investigator, seemed to believe her. This is as close as I dare get to the truth —which is that my friend, one of the 'evil Leachers,' read the nurse's mind and found out that the woman has amnesia.

"That is very strange," Liz says when I'm done. "It's true that if the nurse had been Guided to do something so out of character, she would've forgotten the event completely. But how do you know that she's not a Leacher agent just trying to make it look like one of us was after you? Or that it wasn't a strange coincidence?"

"Even if she was a Leacher, she wouldn't be able to lie to my mom any better than a regular person, I would imagine," I tell Liz. "And coincidence sounds like too much of a stretch to me. I mean, how often do people just forget something that they did, unless they're under the influence, or on drugs?"

"That does seem suspicious," she concedes. "But in any event, even if you're right, meeting the Guide community would be your best course of action. Trying to kill one of our own is not tolerated. If some Guide did try to harm you, he or she would face serious consequences."

"Oh? What exactly would happen to him?" I ask, intrigued.

"I'm not sure. We don't have much Guide-on-Guide crime. Back in the day, someone like that would've been sterilized or even killed. Now, I'm not sure. I know that we wouldn't let this person be taken into the regular judicial system. Not given what we can do. Most likely, this person would either face the Elders or receive vigilante-style justice from our community."

The Elders? I vaguely register the term, but I'm too interested in the topic at hand to ask her to explain. "So you're certain I would be safe?" I say instead.

She nods. "Even if someone wanted to kill you, I can't think of a safer place than where I want to take you," she says. "Not everyone will be there, only the more open-minded folks, who also happen to be my friends. And I'll introduce you to Thomas. He was in the Secret Service, so if anyone can protect you, it would be him."

Secret Service? It's funny that I thought about that agency just a few minutes earlier. "Unless this Thomas is the person trying to kill me," I say, half-jokingly. "Then I'll have brought myself to him on a silver platter."

"That's impossible," Liz says. "He was a patient of mine, like you, so I know what he's capable of. He wouldn't have any motive to try to kill you, in any case. If anything, he would find you a kindred soul. You were both adopted—" she says, then suddenly stops. "I'm sorry. I shouldn't have said that. Doctor-patient privilege and all that."

I think about this for a moment. It's not so much her certainty of my safety, but sheer curiosity on my end that helps me make the decision. If I accept Liz's invitation, I can meet more Guides. More people who can do what I do. I can learn things that I wouldn't be able to learn otherwise.

"Okay, I'll meet your friends," I say. "How do we arrange it?"

Liz smiles. "There's a party tonight, and now you're invited. Every one of them is going to be there." Then, glancing down at her watch, she says, "We best get back to our bodies. We've talked for quite a while, and I don't want to deplete my time."

Without giving me a chance to respond, she approaches her body and touches her frozen face, bringing us out of the Quiet.

I find myself back in that chair, looking at Liz and unsure what to say.

"Would you like to use up the rest of your hour? And do you plan to continue with your therapy?" she says, her therapist mask back on.

"I think I want to go now," I say after a moment of consideration. "As to the long-term therapy, can I get back to you on that?"

"Of course," she says. "It's entirely up to you. I have your contact information, and I'll get in touch with you about the party later today."

I leave Liz's office, chuckling slightly at the sight of the doughnut box in the trashcan. I bet Camilla threw out some perfectly good food to stay consistent with her earlier lie.

My head itches from the bandages, and I shudder at the

thought of meeting new people while looking like this. On impulse, I make a decision to visit Doctor Searle across the hall from Liz's office.

"You have to make an appointment," the lazy-looking receptionist says, barely looking up from her computer. "We're booked through this month."

The conversation with Liz has altered some of my perceptions. I don't feel as much hesitation about Guiding people to do what I want. Somehow, it's better than Pushing them. It's semantics, I know, but it seems to work for me. Without any guilt, I phase into the Quiet and make the receptionist realize that the doctor will indeed see me now.

The good doctor needs a similar treatment. Without it, he failed to see why he, a dermatologist, should be dealing with gunshot wounds. After he's properly Guided, however, he gladly takes my bandages off, thus expanding his specialty. I even learn that my stitches will dissolve and disappear with time—so if all goes well, there will be no need to see another doctor. I'm healing quite nicely, all things considered. I just have to be careful when getting my next haircut.

The mirror in the doctor's bathroom improves my mood another notch. There's a small patch of shaved hair around the stitches, but nothing too obvious. If I brush my hair more to the side, you can barely see anything.

With that taken care of, I'm off to Saks Fifth Avenue.

If I'm going to a party, I need to get some clean clothes.

19

Wearing my new getup, I return to the hotel. The leather jacket I bought for the occasion is a touch warm, but I should make a good impression on the Guides I meet.

My phone rings, and I see that it's Mira's number.

"Hi," I say, picking it up.

"Hi Darren." She sounds uncertain. "How are you feeling?"

"Much better today," I say, trying to sound both cheerful and sick at the same time. "Thank you for checking."

"That's good," she says, now sounding more sure of herself. "I'm happy to hear that."

Mira is checking on my wellbeing? It's both amazing and difficult to believe.

"So what are you up to?" she asks.

Suddenly, it hits me. She wants to see me. She's just being coy about it. But I already have plans, and I know that I can't bring her with me. Not to this party, not with her attitude toward Pushers.

"I think I'm going to try to take it easy tonight." I feel like an ass for lying, but I see no other choice. "I'll drink some chamomile tea and turn in early."

"Add honey and lemon to your tea," she suggests. "That's how my grandma cured almost any ill. Well, that and fatty chicken broth, but I don't recommend that one."

"Yep, I'll do the honey and lemon, thank you. I'd like to see you, though, as soon as I'm better—which should be after a good night's sleep. Would you like to have lunch with me tomorrow?"

"Yes, I think I would," she says softly and somewhat out of breath. Her voice sounds almost sensual. "Let's get in touch in the morning. Okay?"

"Okay, I'll call you. Thanks, Mira," I say, trying to sound more confident than I feel. "Say hello to Eugene for me. Bye."

"Bye," she says and hangs up.

Well, that was interesting. All of a sudden, I'm less excited about the party. If I hadn't agreed to go, I could've met up with Mira tonight. I bet catching her in this weird, pity-inspired 'let's not kill Darren today' mood would've been fruitful. By tomorrow, she might remember how she really feels about me.

The excitement about the party slowly comes back to me during my room-service meal as I speculate on the different ways the whole thing might go. I am all ready and psyched again by the time I get a text from Liz.

Where are you now?

I text her my hotel address. I guess I trust Liz with my life at this point. Then again, if something goes awry, I can always switch hotels.

The limo will pick you up in ten minutes.

Now I'm impressed. My therapist definitely knows how to get attention. A limo to a party is seriously stylish.

I'm downstairs when I see the limo pull up. It's a black, high-end limo, not one of those new Hummer-types. It comes fully equipped, right down to a guy in a chauffeur hat who calls me *Sir* and opens the door for me.

On the way, the driver doesn't talk much, and I return the favor. I only have time to drink half of my glass of champagne before we arrive somewhere in the Meatpacking district. I don't recognize the place, but Liz is standing outside. She looks stunning. Her usual office attire is already sexy, but it pales compared to what she's wearing now. I have to make a concentrated effort to keep my eyes above her neck.

"I'm glad you came," she says. "Let me show you inside the place."

We go past the long line and the huge bouncers as though we're invisible. I have no idea if Liz just used her persuasive power, or if Guides own this club and Liz comes here so often that the bouncers recognize her. We also don't pay anything, even though places like this usually try to get you to pay a cover or buy bottle service to get in.

We go down half a flight of stairs and make our way into the most fancy club I've ever been in. I am not a fan of clubbing, but as a guy who has to carry on conversations with girls in their early twenties, I have to at least know the names of the more trendy clubs. However, this one I'm not familiar with—which is pretty suspicious. Can the Guides somehow *Guide* NYC denizens to keep their club a secret?

We walk onto a giant dance floor, and I follow Liz as she navigates through the crowd and toward a different set of stairs. As we make our way, I see some Hollywood stars on the dance floor, plus an heiress who's been in all the tabloids and at least one Victoria's Secret model. Actually, the model might be from Playboy—it's hard to tell them apart. The heiress might've also been in Playboy, come to think of it. As to why I know what's in Playboy—well, I subscribe. For the articles, of course.

Once we reach the stairs, we go down a floor and find ourselves in another large hall. Only here, things are much quieter. It's a cocktail party, and it's full of people dressed in suits and nice dresses. They walk around leisurely, holding champagne glasses, seemingly oblivious to the anarchy happening just above. I see the Mayor of New York City chatting with the Governor, and at least a dozen CEOs from Fortune 500 companies. What is this place?

Not our destination, it seems, as Liz leads me through this room. On the way, I see more prominent government and business leaders whose faces I recognize.

We walk down another flight of stairs. How deep does this place go? I didn't think New York building codes allowed so many things to be happening in the basement areas. Then again, given the people I just saw, whoever runs this place knows people who can bend the rules if needed.

The activity on this next floor is downright creepy. It's a masked ball. A bunch of people dressed in cocktail dresses and suits are wearing an assortment of medieval-looking masks. I half-expect to see an orgy or some kind of pagan ritual. Did these people see *Eyes Wide Shut* one too many times? To my disappointment, this isn't our destination either. Liz just waltzes right past the masked people.

This is when I realize something. Nobody seems to notice us. They act as though we're not here. Has someone Guided them to behave in this strange manner? That's the assumption I have to make.

This new floor features a room that's noticeably smaller than the others. A bunch of people I don't recognize are gathered in the center of the room, listening to someone sing. More people are sitting around on comfortable chairs and sofas located on the edges of the room. The place looks like a cross between a lounge and a country club.

To my surprise, I recognize the man singing in the middle of the room. He's a famous blind opera singer, whose name escapes me at the moment. He has dark bushy hair with some white strands around his face and a white beard. I notice he looks a little fatter than I remember him being.

"We're here," Liz whispers in my ear. "Let's wait for the end of the concert."

The opera singer is a genius. I am not a connoisseur, but I find the concert extremely moving. Possibly my mental state at the moment—alert anxiety—is a good fit for this sort of music.

When the singing is over and my hands are hurting from enthusiastic clapping, I look around the room. And this is when I get my first shock. There is a man looking intently at me—a man I recognize.

It's my boss, William Pierce—or Bill, as I call him in my head and behind his back.

He waves at me. When the clapping subsides, I make my way toward him. As I walk, I see him look down at his phone and then look up at me with a smile.

"I don't know what to say," I exclaim when I reach him. On instinct, I extend my hand for a handshake. It's not something I do in the office on a day-to-day basis; in fact, I can only recall shaking his hand twice—one time before and one time after my interview with him—but it just feels right for some reason. It's like we meet for the first time again.

He shakes my hand with a bemused expression. "Darren, what a pleasant surprise. It's an interesting coincidence that you're here now, given that I just received the most interesting email from you about the stock I asked you to research. The write-up is outstanding, as usual, and it's particularly impressive given that you managed to send the email while listening to the opera with me. Great multitasking. Particularly admirable given that Bert informed me recently that you'd been shot. Most diligent, even for you."

I am so busted.

"Okay, Bill, I fess up. I might've scheduled that email to go out at an opportune moment," I say, figuring the fact that my boss and I are both Guides changes our professional relationship anyway. And that does seem to be the case—he doesn't so much as blink at my familiar use of his first name.

"I figured that much. In fact, I've been onto this little practice of yours for a while. But so you know, I actually appreciate it—the people you copy on those emails believe that you really are working your ass off, and it sets a good example for them. Along with mitigating the impression they have of you as a slacker. Although I guess that's not the most important thing to talk about right now, given the circumstances."

"Yeah, I guess not," I say. "Did you suspect about me?"

"No. If I'd thought you were one of us, I would've brought you into our community a long time ago. Truth be told, I always thought you were one of the other guys. You're so good at knowing things that I thought you were Leaching the information from the CEOs and other execs I asked you to talk to. Seems like I was wrong. Seems like you've come up with some ingenious ways to use the Mind Dimension."

"You thought I was a Leacher, and you still employed me?" I say, surprised. "I thought they were public enemy number one in Guide society."

"I'm not sure what Liz told you, but we're not so dogmatic in this group."

"Right. She said that you guys are quite open-minded. But there's a difference between being open-minded and hiring your enemy," I say, genuinely puzzled.

"Having Leachers investigate companies seems natural to me. They can cut through the bullshit and just read people's minds. Direct and effective. Seems like good business to me," he says, his eyes crinkling with mirth. "If I could ask someone for that skill in the job application, I would."

From the corner of my eye, I see a girl approaching us. She seems to have overheard the last thing Bill said, and instead of being shocked, she's nodding approvingly. This whole thing is a huge contrast to Mira's hatred for Pushers.

"So you're the new guy?" says the girl, handing me her tiny hand for a handshake. She's extremely short and petite. I'd guess she's under five feet, even with high heels.

Bill graciously introduces us. "Hillary, it turns out that I have known Darren for a number of years. He was right under my nose, so to speak."

"It figures," Hillary says, furrowing the eyebrows on her small face. "You've had one of us working at your hedge fund, and you didn't even notice. People are just cogs in that financial machine of yours, aren't they?"

Bill sighs. "Please, Hillary, can we have one conversation without your Occupy-Wall-Street rhetoric?"

"It's very nice to meet you, Hillary," I say in an effort to change the subject. "What do you do?"

"I'm an anthropologist. I'm also involved with a couple of charities," she says, turning her attention from Bill to look up at me. Her big blue eyes twinkle, and with the yellow cocktail dress she's wearing, she looks a bit like a doll.

"Right, and she has nothing to do with the spread of veganism in New York," Bill says. "Or with the bans on ape research."

Am I hearing what I'm hearing? Is Bill being playful? I never thought I would witness such a thing.

"I make a difference for the better," Hillary retorts. "I'm sorry that what I do is something someone like you wouldn't be able to understand. Certainly, protecting the animals isn't profitable. That's your favorite word, isn't it? *Profit.* Or is it *bottom line?*"

"Bottom line is two words," Bill corrects her, grinning at the annoyed expression on her face.

He's clearly pushing her buttons, and she's falling for it. It's a very odd exchange. If I didn't know that Bill is happily married, I'd think he was flirting with Hillary. Flirting in a juvenile, pulling-the-girl's-ponytail style. Something I learned early on they do *not* appreciate. And speaking of his wife, is she one of us? I wonder, but I don't feel comfortable asking at the moment.

Bill's phone rings. He looks at it, then at us, and says, "I'm sorry—I have to take this." And with that, he walks to a corner of the room to get some privacy.

"So you guys don't get along?" I ask Hillary as soon as Bill leaves.

"I wouldn't go as far as to say that." Hillary shrugs. "William is just William, bourgeoisie personified."

Politeness would dictate for me to say something affirmative about Bill's inadequateness, but I don't want to. In a lot of ways, I admire the guy. He's on a very short list of people I've always looked up to and respected. In fact, seeing Bill at this party dispels all of my remaining doubts about the Guides. If he's a Guide, that fact, more than any of Liz's reassurances, tells me that they're not all members of some evil cult. They're just a group like any other, with good and bad types in the usual distribution—with the Pusher hunting me being on the scumbag end of the spectrum. Returning my attention to Hillary, I say, "Since I work for him in that hedge fund, what you say about him could easily be applied to me."

"Somehow, I doubt it. You don't look like the type. Besides, you didn't know your nature. Now that you do, you might change your profession to something more meaningful." She gives me a hopeful smile.

I think she means this as a compliment, so I don't argue with her. I also wonder what I would do if money weren't a variable at all. I went to work for Bill because I wanted to work the least and make the most money doing it, not out of some burning passion for stock picking. Would I become a detective like my mom, perhaps? I think I'd consider that, especially if the job weren't so dangerous.

"So, anyway, Darren, tell me about yourself," Hillary says, bringing me out of my musings. Her earlier smile transfers to the corners of her eyes, and the last remnants of annoyance disappear from her face.

I tell her a little bit about my life. I assume she'd be

interested in my being adopted and discovering phasing into the Quiet on my own, so I focus on those things.

As I tell the story, Hillary's little face continues to be highly animated. Though petite girls aren't my type—at least if Bert is to be believed—I think they have a unique cuteness about them. If I had a girlfriend like this, I'd mentally call her Nano, like that iPod Nano I had as a kid. Back then, as now, everything was becoming more and more portable, and a pocket-sized girlfriend like this is just the next logical step.

Size aside, something about Hillary looks familiar to me. I can't put my finger on it, though. I wonder how old she is. Twenty-four? Twenty-five? It wouldn't be gentlemanly to ask. She could easily be older than she looks; it's one of the benefits of being that size. As I focus on her features, I become certain that this is the first time we've met, and yet there's something nagging at my brain.

"So what was that thing Bill alluded to? The vegan thing?" I ask when I feel like I've shared enough of my life, and it's only courteous to learn a bit about her.

She grins. "Oh, he's blaming me for the rise of vegetarianism and veganism in New York. He thinks that just because I'm a vegan, I go around nudging people to follow in my footsteps."

"Wow. I'm still not used to thinking this way. Can you actually do that? Guide a meat-eater to go vegan?" I ask, impressed by the very idea of it.

"I can, and maybe I have strategically done that with the biggest trendsetters upon occasion," she admits. "But my humble efforts are not the sole reason why things are moving in that direction in New York—and other places, for that matter. People are just becoming more aware of the impact of their diet on the environment, of animal suffering associated with it all, and, of course, the one that matters to them most: their health. With the spread of books such as *The China Study*—"

"Hillary, we're trying to make a good impression here, and your propaganda will not help in that goal. I have to borrow Darren, if you don't mind," Liz says, startling me by appearing right next to me seemingly out of nowhere.

Hillary opens her mouth, looking like she's about to object. Before she can say anything, however, Liz grabs me by the elbow and drags me to the other side of the room.

20

"I didn't need to be saved. I was actually quite enjoying Hillary's company," I say to Liz as we walk away.

"Oh, good," Liz says with relief. "That girl can be insufferable. Still, I want you to meet Thomas right now. Then you'll be able to go back and finish your conversation."

We approach a sharply dressed guy who's about my height. He's a bit broader in the shoulders than I am, which is something I don't see often. He's also muscular. Not steroid-big like Caleb, but he clearly works out regularly, like I try to do.

"Thomas, I want you to meet Darren," Liz says, giving the guy a thorough kiss on the lips. The kiss part is really odd. Didn't she say earlier he was a patient of hers, like me? I catch myself before I get more bothered by it. It's not like I'm jealous. Okay, fine, maybe a tiny bit jealous. Thinking that a woman like Liz was interested in me had been a pleasant fantasy—and helpful for my self-esteem.

"It's great to meet you, Darren." Thomas shakes my hand

with one of those excessively firm handshakes that I'm used to getting from men in finance.

As we shake hands, I realize that he seems to be part Asian. What makes this stand out is the fact that everyone else in this room is white. And now that I think about it, all the Readers I've met were also white. I guess it makes sense when you consider both of the groups' histories. After all, they—or *we*—began from a cult that did that whole selective breeding thing somewhere in Europe, according to what I've learned from Liz. Thomas's origins must be a bit different. It proves what Liz told me: that this group of Guides will welcome you regardless of your lineage, so long as you are somehow a Guide. I wonder if this means they would be okay with whatever I am. I'm not going to risk them finding out, of course, but their attitude does give me hope.

"Good to meet you too, Thomas," I say, realizing I'm staring at the guy.

He doesn't seem bothered by my staring at all. He's just standing there, looking at me, seemingly comfortable with the silence.

"So Liz told me that somebody's trying to kill you," he says casually after a moment. "She said that this person is one of us, a Guide."

"Yes, unfortunately, that's the case," I say, almost defensively. The way he emphasized the word *Guide* made it sound like he was skeptical.

"Can you tell me exactly what you told her?" he asks calmly. "Liz didn't give me many details because of the doctor-patient confidentiality."

"I'll leave you two to get acquainted," Liz startles me by saying, and walks away. I was so lost in my thoughts that I'd almost forgotten she was still there. I note Thomas following the sway of her hips with a very non-doctor-patient look and file it away as curious, but unimportant for the moment.

When he turns his attention back to me, I repeat the story I told Liz.

As I go through it, Thomas asks me a bunch of pointed questions. He's obviously familiar with the investigative process, perhaps from his Secret Service job. Had I not grown up telling lies to my mom Lucy, the detective, I might've been in trouble. As it is, I'm not sure if he completely believes me. My mom probably wouldn't have. Unlike her, though, he doesn't know my 'tells.' I hope.

"I find it hard to believe one of us would do such a thing," he says when I'm done explaining about the attempted killing. "But in any case, you did the right thing, getting a hotel room. I would also suggest ditching your phone and getting another one, and maybe getting out of town for a bit while I look into this."

"That's a good idea about the phone, Thomas," I say. "I should've thought of that. As far as getting out of town, my family is here, and so is my work. Where would I go?"

He shrugs. "Take a vacation. Visit friends or relatives you haven't seen in a while. Though, if you want to be completely safe, you should probably stay clear of your immediate family for the time being."

"I don't think I like that plan," I say, frowning. "I don't want to stay in hiding forever."

"Well, if you had more information—"

"I might be able to obtain it," I say, starting to feel hopeful. "I can't commit to anything, but if I did find out more, do you think you'd be able to help me deal with this person?" I know it's a lot to ask, but I could really use someone like Thomas on my side.

"Sure." He hands me a business card. "Here's my number. If you learn who this mystery Guide is, let me know immediately."

"I will, thanks," I say, and put his details into my phone. By habit, I call his number, so that he has mine. When the call connects, he looks at his phone and grunts approvingly.

"You know," he says, looking back at me. "If this whole thing is true and you figure out who this Guide is, he or she will try even harder to get rid of you."

"I don't think this person could be trying any harder," I say, meaning it to be a joke, but Thomas responds with a stony expression.

"The attempt on your life was very subtle," he says. "Our ability, if misused, can be much more harmful. If someone tried to kill you without subtlety, every member of that hospital staff would've tried to go for your throat. It wouldn't have been pretty."

I picture that with a shudder. He's probably right. The Pusher was being subtle because he knew there were Readers around, and he was trying to keep his or her identity a secret. Had secrecy not been part of it, things might've gotten truly ugly. Then again, I can do what the Pusher can—and I'm reasonably certain the Pusher doesn't know it.

"Do you think there is a chance this Guide might be in this room?" I ask, because I have to at least pose the question. I don't think it's Thomas, since Liz appears to trust him, but the other people in this room are still unknown to me—Bill excluded, of course.

"No, I doubt it," Thomas says. "I know everyone here, and I

don't think any of them are capable of something like that. Not to mention, they would have no reason to be after you."

"Can you think of anyone who *would* have a reason to be after me?"

I expect Thomas to say no, but he looks thoughtful instead.

"Are both of your parents Guides?" he asks.

"I don't know. I'm still learning about them, but probably not both of them." This is as close as I dare get to the truth of my origins. "Why?"

"Well," he says slowly, "when I joined this group, I was warned about the Traditionalists. I was told they might go after me—which hasn't happened. So if you're not a pure Guide, they could be behind this. Though in your case, I'm not sure how they would know about your heritage."

"The Traditionalists?" I ask, confused. "Liz mentioned them before, but she didn't give me much detail. Why would they want to come after you?"

"They're extremists who have some archaic attitudes about purity of blood, and they're against marrying outside the Guide community, among other things," he says with distaste. "In a way, they're like those inbred Leachers. So you can see how I could be their target. You can tell I'm not 'pure' by just looking at my face."

"I see." I have a growing conviction that I'm not going to be a fan of these Traditionalists, even if they're not the ones trying to kill me.

"I wish I could tell you more about them and why they might target you, but I know very little. Like you, I didn't grow up with this stuff," Thomas says, and I remember Liz mentioning that he was also adopted. Despite his stoic demeanor, he must see us as kindred souls, given that our stories are so similar.

I want to hear about his background, but first, I need to find out more about these Traditionalists. "Is there anyone I could talk to about them?" I ask, and Thomas nods.

"You can try talking to Hillary," he says. "She knows more about this than most of us."

"All right, I will, thanks." I wonder why the tiny girl knows about this, but that's a topic I'll broach with her.

Thomas looks at me, falling back into his silent pattern, so I ask, "What did you mean when you said you didn't grow up with this stuff?" Since I'm not sure whether Liz meant to reveal his adopted status to me, I figure it's best to pretend complete ignorance. I don't want to get her in trouble.

He hesitates for a moment, but then he says, "Like you, I was adopted. My parents didn't tell me this until I was six years old." As he says this, I catch a glimmer of some emotion behind his expressionless mask.

"That's amazing," I say. "This is something we share. Well, almost. I guess the difference is that I always thought I had one biological parent, Sara. I assume you learned that both your parents were adoptive?"

"Yes," he says. "They told me a woman gave me to them. A woman they'd never met before or after the adoption. Someone whose identity I was never able to discover."

There seems to be a deep sadness to that part of the story. He clearly yearns to know more about his origins. I can relate, but I don't want to share my version of this story. Not if I have to reveal the names of my parents. So instead I say, "What about your abilities? Did you, like me, discover what you can do on your own?"

"Yes. It was during a car accident that I discovered that I was able to stop time—what everyone here calls Splitting into the Mind Dimension."

"For me, it was a bike accident," I say, smiling. "And I called it the Quiet."

Thomas returns my smile. "Did you also Guide someone on your own?" he asks. "I called it Hypnotizing."

"No. The first time I was able to do that deliberately was today, when Liz decided to test me to see if I'm a Guide," I say. "You discovered it on your own?"

"Yeah, it happened during a fight. I got into a lot of those as a kid," he says, his eyes getting a faraway, nostalgic look. "I stopped time to practice punching the bully I was fighting. As I was practice-hitting him in that mode, I also really willed him to trip. He was much bigger, and getting him on the ground was my only chance to walk away without some serious damage. Afterwards, he did trip. I, being a kid, wondered if that was because I'd willed it so hard. So the next time I got into a fight, I tried to repeat that trick. I did it during other fights until one day, I realized that I could do more than just make people fall over."

"Oh, I am so jealous," I say earnestly. "The fun I could've had if I'd discovered this as a kid."

"It only sounds fun in theory," he says seriously. "I thought I was completely insane."

"Ah, I was about to ask how it happened that you know Liz also."

"Well, before I was able to Guide people, I tried telling my parents about time stopping—"

"I did that too," I interrupt, excited.

"Right. So the result was probably the same too. They took me to see a psychiatrist," he says.

"Yep," I say, nodding my head.

"Did Liz tell you how in cases like ours, all roads lead to her?" he asks, glancing in her direction.

"No, she didn't. Are you saying I was led to Liz on purpose?"

Thomas smiles again. "This is how it works," he says. "She made herself known as an expert on the exact sort of 'delusional symptoms' someone like us might report. She wrote a few articles on the step-outside-the-world delusion, giving this phenomenon a psychobabble explanation, something about it being a way for some intelligent and slightly-too-introspective kids to cope with the world going too fast around them. So after a few doctors didn't know what to do with me, they referred me to her, the expert. The same thing happened to you, I bet."

"That's exactly what happened, yes."

"I think that happens to pretty much anyone in our situation in NYC—not that our situation is common, of course. Once I met Liz, and once I shared my Guiding experiences with her, she brought me into this world," he says, waving his hand in a gesture meant to encompass the whole room.

"Okay, I'm even more jealous now. Just to think, had I not avoided getting into fights, I would've discovered Guiding and joined this community much earlier in my life," I say.

"You don't want to have had my childhood." Thomas's face darkens. "Trust me, you wouldn't have wanted to join the Guides at that price."

"I'm sorry. I didn't mean to trivialize. I'm just saying it must've been cool to know what you are and that you weren't crazy. Besides, I bet eventually the bullies had to leave you alone."

"They did," he says curtly. I have a feeling some bullies of Thomas's past got a lot more than they bargained for. Good for him. Hell, if people stop trying to kill me for a few days, I'm tempted to make the time to find John, my own childhood nemesis. Now that I can Guide, he might get the urge to literally go fuck himself.

"It was nice to know I wasn't insane," Thomas says in a lighter tone when I remain silent. "I guess you had it tough in your own way. But hey, all's well that ends well, right?"

"Exactly," I say, happy that the topic is getting less sinister. I'm about to say more, but I notice Liz making her way back to us.

"Can you guys continue this later?" she says, sipping a pink drink. "I still need to introduce Darren to everyone, and since I have to leave early today, I'd like to get that task out of the way."

"Of course. I have to leave anyway," Thomas says.

"Okay, I'll give you a call, and maybe we can do coffee in a few days," I say.

"Sounds like a plan," he agrees with a smile.

"Okay, now that you have a man date, let's go," Liz says teasingly. Seeing my shrink joking and clearly buzzed is weird, to say the least.

As we walk away, she takes me by the arm and leads me around, introducing me to the people in the room.

I'm terrible with names, so I hope there isn't a quiz later, because I would fail it. I do notice a pattern, though. We all have some facial features in common, in the way Liz alluded to earlier. And whatever it is, I haven't noticed it with Readers. All these people seem rather interesting in their own ways, and I hope that with time, I'll get to know all of them.

What I also notice is that no one seems to be displaying any animosity toward me. So either my nemesis is an excellent actor, or the Pusher from the hospital isn't here.

The whole thing is beyond tiring. Maybe it's all that going-to-bed-early stuff from the last two days messing up my circadian rhythm, or maybe I'm still not fully recovered from my injury. Whatever it is, I'm beginning to get a serious craving for my bed back at the hotel.

Hillary is the last stop on this intro-tour. "See, I promised I'd give him back to you," Liz says to Hillary, smiling. "He's all yours to brainwash. Now, if you'll excuse me, I have some business to take care of."

"I heard you might know about something I find kind of interesting," I say to Hillary when Liz is gone.

"Sure, what is it?" she asks, grinning at me.

"I was hoping you could tell me about the Traditionalists," I say.

Her grin disappears without a trace. "You're new, Darren, so you don't know that this is a sensitive subject for me. But it is, and I'm sorry, but I don't want to talk about it," she says, her voice unusually harsh.

"Oh, I'm sorry. I didn't know that. Let's talk about something else." I feel like an oaf. Her face is so expressive that upsetting her just feels wrong. Like being mean to a little girl. It must be her petiteness messing with my brain.

"Do you want to get out of here?" she says consolingly. "I'm starving, and they never have anything edible."

I don't point out the large buffet filled to the brim with choice finger foods and consider this for a moment. I'm tired, but something about Hillary makes me want to get to know her better. I'm not sure what it is. It's almost as though there's some kind of connection between us.

"I'm game, but I have an errand to run on the way. Do you mind if I stop by the Apple store for a minute? They're open late, and I urgently need to get a new phone."

"No problem." She grins at me. "Let's go."

21

As we get out of the cab, I finish texting everyone my new phone number.

The place we end up is one that Hillary describes as a raw vegan restaurant. She swears it will be the best meal I've had in years, but as I look at the menu, I'm rather skeptical. As expected, they have many salads, but I'm surprised to find that they have other options as well.

"I guess I'll order coconut water for now," I say to the dreadlocked waiter who smells suspiciously like weed.

"That's an excellent choice, full of electrolytes. It's very good for you," Hillary says, smiling. "I'll have the same."

"I'll also get the spiral zucchini pasta with cashew-nut Alfredo sauce," I say hesitantly. This is the most promising-sounding dish on the menu, but that's not saying much.

"You should leave room for dessert. They're amazing here," Hillary says, ordering her own choice: a kale salad with honey-glazed pecans, plus guacamole with 'live chips'—whatever that is.

"So what did you think about our little community?" she says when the waiter leaves.

"They seem like good people," I answer honestly. "I can't wait to get to know everyone better."

"They are good people. I wish the rest of the Guides were more like them," she says, almost wistfully.

I figure she must be talking about the Traditionalists, but I don't press her, given her earlier reaction. Instead I say, "Yeah, I know what you're saying. Some Guide is trying to kill me."

"Kill you?" She looks stunned. "Why? How do they even know you exist?"

I share as much as I can for the umpteenth time today, telling her the same story I told Liz and Thomas. "So you see, someone is trying to kill me, but I have no idea how they know that I exist."

"Is that why you were asking about the Traditionalists?"

"Yeah, Thomas said it sounded like something they might do, and he said that you were the best person to ask about it," I say carefully.

"Then I guess you had a good reason to ask before. But I don't understand why they would want to hurt you. I mean, with Thomas, I can see it, but you . . ." She narrows her eyes, studying me intently.

"I don't know why he made that guess," I say, not wanting to raise the question of my heritage. "Maybe he was wrong."

"Maybe," she says. "I guess I can tell you what I know, in case it helps."

"That would be great."

She squares her shoulders. "Okay, to get a sense for the

Traditionalists, try this thought experiment. Take the close-mindedness of any sort of extreme fundamentalist, add eugenics, dogma, fear of the unknown, and mix in an overwhelming, blind, and bigoted hatred of the Leachers."

"Okay. I'm picturing this and not liking the results."

"Well, that's just step one. Step two: now imagine growing up with people like that as parents," she says somberly.

I blink. "Oh, is that why—?"

"Yeah, that's why I was touchy earlier. But don't worry about it. You didn't know."

"Still, I'm sorry I upset you."

"It's okay. My folks are probably not even the worst of what's out there. Yes, they're obsessed with fear of exposure to regular people. And, yes, they're afraid of new technology or—more correctly—of progress of any kind. Oh, and if they had their way, life today would be like the good old days of yesteryear that I suspect never existed in the first place. All of those things are true, but even with all those things in mind, I don't think my parents would go as far as trying to Guide someone to kill anyone."

She stops talking and looks thoughtful. Is she wondering if she just told the truth? If her parents might be capable of murder in the name of their beliefs? I guess this topic is off the table for the time being.

Food and drinks arrive just in time to fill the silent moment we're having. She starts wolfing down her chips with the guacamole and offers me some.

"This is surprisingly good," I say, trying the chips. Apparently, they were made in a dehydrator, which slowly dried them without officially cooking them. That doesn't sound very 'raw' to me, but they taste a lot like corn chips, so I'm not going to complain. My own dish of the pseudo-spaghetti made from zucchini is also pretty good, though it has as much in common with the real thing as a hot dog with a real canine. I taste the drink too, like it, and tell Hillary, "This coconut water is different from the stuff I've gotten before."

"Of course, you probably got the one from the can," she says, and starts eating her salad. Her hands are so small that the fork looks big in them.

I wonder how Hillary and her friends would react to knowing the truth about me, so to test the waters, I ask, "The way you talked about the Traditionalists hating Leachers before, you made it sound like the rest of your community likes them."

"Compared to the Traditionalists, we're practically in love with them, sure," she says, spearing another bite of salad with her fork.

"Hmm, but I thought, at least from talking to Liz, that Leachers are to be avoided," I say, pushing the inquiry further. I hope she doesn't find the topic suspicious. I really want to find out how much danger I'd be in if my fellow Guides learned about my Reading abilities.

"I don't know about Liz, but I, personally, don't hate the Leachers. Not even a little bit," she says, giving me a guileless look. "In fact, I'm curious about them."

"Oh. And is that a common view?"

"No. Mine is probably a rare attitude. The rest of the group would consider me weird, even though they're pretty liberal. Even outside the Traditionalists, most Guides dislike Leachers with a passion."

"Is it because of the genocides?" I ask, remembering Liz's history lesson.

"Yeah, that's part of it. Bad history does that to groups. But there's more to it. It's widely believed that Leachers still, to this day, actively hate us—so disliking them back seems like a natural response," she says.

"But *you* don't," I clarify.

"Well, I wouldn't go as far as seeking them out. I agree that it's wise to avoid Leachers. Not because I believe they're evil, but because I think some of them may have the same 'us versus them' mentality that a lot of Guides do, even outside the Traditionalist clique."

"So we're supposed to dislike them because they hate us, and avoid them for the same reason. If they apply the same logic, isn't that a Catch-22?"

"You're a man after my own heart," Hillary says with a smile. "That's actually a pet peeve of mine, and I think you verbalized it perfectly. The entire human race has this tendency—the inclination to cling to their own group. This obsession with sub-dividing ourselves is responsible for practically every evil in the world. Everyone fails to see that the hatred between our people is just another example in a series of these meaningless feuds. They all start with people who are extremely alike, and then a tiny difference creeps in, and people separate along that difference, after which insanity ensues. Sooner or later, you get that 'we hate you because you hate us' deadlock, or worse."

"Wow, you really have given it some thought," I say, impressed.

"How could I not? It's so obvious. Take anything arbitrary, like skin color, income, politics, religion, nationality, or in this case, types of powers. You name it, and at some point, people find a way to separate over that arbitrary trait—and some become willing to kill over it. Once that thinking sets in, the groups start thinking of one another as less than human, which further justifies all manner of atrocities. The whole cycle is so pointless that I sometimes want to give up." She sighs. "But I don't. Instead, to quote a wise man, 'I try to be the change I'd like to see in the world.'"

"I wonder what Gandhi would've said about all this," I say, sipping my drink. "And, for what it's worth, I'm not racist, sexist, or any other *ist* myself. In fact, since I didn't grow up with these stories about Leachers, I don't plan on hating them either. Like you, I'm curious about them, so I don't think you're weird at all."

"Thank you," she says, rewarding me with a wide, white-toothed grin. "You know, even though we just met, I feel like I know you already. Like I can trust you. But I don't know why. Is that strange?"

"No. I know what you mean," I say, and I do. It actually *is* strange. I'm drawn to this girl, but not in the way I'm usually drawn to pretty girls. It's more that I just like her.

She grins at me. "Good. I'm glad we're on the same page. And about your troubles . . . If you need help dealing with whoever's after you, I'd be glad to be of assistance."

I suppress a smile as I imagine her swinging her tiny fists in a fight. "Thank you, Hillary. I really appreciate the sentiment."

"But you don't think I can be of help," she guesses astutely. "Why? Because of my height?"

"No," I lie. "Because you seem so peaceful. I would've pegged you for a pacifist." I learned long ago that if a woman asks you a question pertaining to her size, you have to say whatever she wants to hear, and quickly. A special case of this rule is the dreaded 'does this make me look fat' question. The answer to that is always NO.

"You're right," Hillary says. "I'm not a violent person, but my Reach is probably the longest in our group." She flushes a bit as she says this last part, and I remember Liz telling me that this subject—the measure of a Guide's power—is considered impolite among them. I guess Hillary just told me the equivalent of her bra size or something along those lines.

"Your Reach?" I ask, looking at her. Liz explained the concept a bit, but I want to understand it better.

Hillary nods, her cheeks still pink. "Yes. Your Reach determines how much, how deeply, and for how long you can Guide a person. Mine is so great because all of my ancestors, including my parents and grandparents, adhered to the barbaric custom of breeding for this quality. In fact, had I been a good girl and mated with whomever I was told, my children might've grown up to become the Elders."

"Okay, brain overload," I say. "How can you Guide someone 'deeper'? And what are the Elders?"

"The quick version about Reach is this: let's say you Guide someone, and then let's presume I come along and I want to Guide them away from your course of action. Reach differences will determine my success."

"So even if I program someone, if you're more powerful than I am, you can reprogram them?"

"We never use such a derogatory term, but you got the gist of it, yes," she says. "And the Elders are those Guides who can spend lifetimes in the Mind Dimension. I don't know much about them. The rumors say that they live in the Mind Dimension together, each one taking a driver's seat pulling others into a weird community that, for all intents and purposes, exists outside time."

I stare at her, fascinated. "That's incredible."

"Yes, it is—although it freaks me out a bit. I find it difficult to imagine even talking to one of the Elders. Just think about it. In the time it takes you to blink, they can Split into the Mind Dimension, join their friends, and live a lifetime of experiences together. It boggles my mind, and I like my mind's equilibrium."

She's right. It's difficult to comprehend what she's describing. In a nutshell, it's life extension—and I find it beyond cool. I'd like to try living in the Quiet for a long time with a bunch of friends, or hopefully even with a girlfriend.

"So, anyway, back to Reach," Hillary says, pulling me out of my excited imaginings. "Mine is quite formidable, which means that if that Guide tries to use civilians to kill you, I could override his or her directive, provided I got involved in time."

"That would be amazing," I say, impressed. "I really appreciate it, Hillary. Here, let me get your phone number." I hand her my new phone. One of the 'Geniuses' at the Apple store transferred all my contacts, and it's as though I've had this phone for ages.

She inputs her number and hands it back to me. "I put my name there, but you can write in a nickname, like you seem to do with everyone else."

I take the phone back, vaguely embarrassed that she saw the nickname stuff. It's this thing I do. I come up with ridiculous nicknames for everyone, and then have fun with voice dial. Her nickname is going to be Tinker Bell. Imagining saying the words 'call Tinker Bell's cell phone' in a crowded bus is my kind of fun.

I look at the screen and see the words *Hillary Taylor* written there, along with the phone number. I decide that the nickname can be added later. For now, I dial her number, so that she has my contact info as well. It's when the phone is dialing that it hits me.

Taylor.

Sara told me that my mom's maiden name was Margret *Taylor*.

No.

It can't be.

Can it?

It *is* a small community. How many namesakes can there be?

"Are you an only child, Hillary?" I ask, not fully thinking of the consequences of this line of questioning.

She looks stunned by my question. "Yes. No. Sort of. I had an older sister a long time ago, but she's dead. Why do you ask? And why do you look so shocked?"

Her sister.

Older . . . likely much older, given that Hillary looks to be only in her mid-twenties.

An older sister who's dead.

It has to be.

I can't believe it—but the resemblance is there.

With hindsight, that's what's been fascinating me about her face. We have the exact same shade of blue eyes. The same chin, similar cheekbones, and her nose is a miniature, feminine version of mine. Aside from the big height difference, we look like we could be related—and now I know why.

Because we are.

"I think you're my aunt, Hillary," I blurt out, unable to suppress my excitement.

22

The look on Hillary's face would be comical if it weren't for the fact that I'm feeling exactly like she looks.

"I found out today that my biological mother's name was Margret, and her last name was Taylor, like yours," I explain, my heart pounding with excitement.

She looks me over, and I see the dawning recognition on her face. She must've noted the resemblance also.

"But—" she starts, then swallows, staring at me. "This is such a shock. You have to forgive me."

"Yeah, I'm still kind of digesting it also."

"Margie had a child?"

"She must have," I say. "If I'm right, that is."

"But that can't be. Margie died more than twenty years ago. This has to be some kind of a mistake."

I just sit there and let her ruminate on it.

"You do look like her," she says after a pause. "And you look like our father . . . who's your grandfather, I guess. But how is this possible?"

"I'm not sure," I say, coming to a decision. "Before I tell you any more, you have to promise me that what I'm about to say will stay between us. Just us. Can you do that?"

I know it's dangerous telling someone the whole truth, but all my instincts say that I can trust Hillary. She was not anti-Leacher even before she knew we were blood relatives. So she could've been okay with my ability to Read even before this. I was thinking of telling her eventually, when I got to know her better. This just expedites the whole thing. I could've enumerated the pros and cons for trusting her all night long, but it all comes down to a simple matter of being able to judge people—and I judge her trustworthy.

"This is very strange, but I know I'll die of curiosity if you don't tell me whatever it is you know. So yes, I swear on my sister's grave that I will keep your secret," she says in a hurried whisper. "Tell me everything."

I tell her the whole story. I begin in Atlantic City, when I met Mira for the first time. I explain about how I learned to Read and then Guide, and how I discovered the truth about Liz. As I speak, Hillary listens with rapt attention, seemingly holding her breath in fascination.

"It all fits," she says when I'm done, and I see a growing sadness in her eyes. "You couldn't have known this, but your story fits exactly with what I know about my older sister."

"Is there anything you can tell me about my mother?" I ask. "I mean, your sister? I only recently learned of her existence."

Hillary nods. "I was little at the time, only about five or six," she begins, "but I know she was a rebellious teen."

I almost smile, listening. It must run in the family. I was

definitely rebellious myself, and my moms would probably say I still am to some degree.

"She was not as bad as I later grew up to be," Hillary continues, "at least according to my parents. Still, they said she was pretty bad. She was also very powerful, and from what you just told me, she might've had more Reach than me."

"How do you figure that?" I ask, surprised.

"Don't you see it? Your adoptive moms, how they said they couldn't talk about your origins for years? How the subject almost became taboo?"

"Yeah . . ."

"That sounds like they were Guided not to talk about it by Margie," she says.

"But that's *years*." Now that I understand the concept of Reach better, I realize how extraordinary my birth mother's power must've been—and begin to feel better about Lucy and Sara keeping this important secret from me.

"Yes, amazing, I know. This Reach is exactly why my parents put extra pressure on her to marry and, more importantly, to *breed* with a person of their choosing—or rather that of the Elders' choosing." Hillary's jaw flexes, and her expression darkens with anger. "Margie not only refused that, but she ran off with a non-Guide lover. That he was actually a Leacher isn't something I knew, and I doubt our parents did either."

"So what happened after?" I say, my chest tightening.

"They disowned her," Hillary says through gritted teeth. "They tried to tell me I had no sister."

"That's horrible." I feel anger rising within me, too. What kind of parents would do that?

"Yes, it is," Hillary says furiously. "But I knew, of course, that

I had a sister, and that she was my favorite person in the whole world. I've never forgiven my parents for that. Never."

Her blue eyes fill with moisture, and I have no idea what to do. I want to comfort her, but I don't know how. So I just put my hand on hers on the table and give it a reassuring squeeze.

"I'm sorry," she says, blinking rapidly to contain her tears. "As you can see, this is still very painful for me. But I shouldn't cry. This is a happy moment. Meeting you. Her son. My nephew."

"And to think, we almost ended up flirting with each other," I say in an effort to amuse her.

"Almost? Darren, darling, I've been flirting with you all evening," she says, a hint of a smile appearing on her features. "But I quickly saw that you weren't interested in me in that way, so I settled for making an awesome new friend."

The idea that my newfound aunt had been interested in me would've been funny, in a Jerry Springer sort of way, if it weren't for the fact that I had also been drawn to her. But she's right—the attraction hadn't been of the kind I feel for Mira. Still, I'm glad we found out the real situation before the night was over.

"So do I call you Aunty?" I ask, making another attempt to cheer her up.

It seems to work. She smiles, her infectious grin back in full force. I recognize this smile. On several occasions, I saw it on my own frozen face when I was in the Quiet. Would Liz say that our initial attraction, if that's what it was, was some kind of narcissism? Or would she bring up some Freudian crap to explain it? I'm not sure, nor do I know why I so often wonder what Liz would say.

"No way," Hillary says in response to my question. "No Aunty, please."

"Aunt Hillary, then?" I say, trying to sound innocent.

She rolls her eyes. "Please. I'm twenty-seven—way too young to be an aunt to someone your age."

"Fine, Hillary it is," I concede. We share a smile, and then I say, "So I have a grandmother and a grandfather? But they would hate me?"

"I'm afraid they likely would," she says. "If you're right about having a Leacher—or *Reader*—father. I should get used to saying this more PC term, I guess. I'm sorry, Darren, but as soon as I was old enough, I left Florida behind—mainly to get away from your grandparents."

"I see," I say, but I'm not overly upset. A few minutes ago, I didn't have an aunt, and now I do. That my biological grandparents are assholes is something I can deal with. Maybe the ones on my father's side are better? Unlike Hillary, I have two sets of much less fucked-up grandparents from my adoptive moms.

"How much do you know about what happened to my mother?" I ask, wondering if Hillary can shed some light on my parents' murder.

"Not much," she replies. "I tried to find out what happened with Margret in New York. What I learned was all public information. She got married and was murdered with her husband shortly thereafter for some unknown reason." Hillary looks thoughtful for a moment. "You know, I just realized that if your father had really been a Reader, that could've been why they were killed."

I nod. "Right. I'm beginning to suspect the same thing."

"If so, it had to have been the Traditionalists," she says, and I see angry color blooming on her face. "Not the ones connected to my parents, but probably some other group. As crazy as my parents are, they wouldn't kill their own daughter. At least I hope not."

"That's a redeeming quality for sure," I say drily.

We sit there silently. She's deep in thought.

"It has to be the Traditionalists," she says again, as though she just had an epiphany. "Your existence goes against everything those fuckers stand for."

"You mean the whole mixing of the blood taboo?" I say, surprised by how detached I feel about the whole thing. It's as though we're talking about someone else, not me.

"Yes. In fact, I can hardly believe you even happened. That a child that's both us and them could even exist," she says wonderingly.

"Why not?" Readers seemed to believe such a thing possible, though highly undesirable.

"We have something like an urban myth that says that nature wouldn't allow such an abomination to even exist," she says, making a point to do air quotes around the word *abomination* and looking at me apologetically. "Mainly, this comes from these legends of Leachers raping Guide women. According to these myths, there have never been any children in such cases."

I raise my eyebrows. "You guys think the two groups are sexually incompatible?"

"Yes, but I take those stories with a big grain of salt. I believe that a lot of Leachers happen to be exactly like our Traditionalists in their attitude—the ancient Leachers, especially. This means they wouldn't have had sex with their enemy, under any circumstances, even to rape them."

"Yeah, given what I heard from my Reader friend Eugene, you might be right. He couldn't believe a Reader would ever donate to a sperm bank out of risk of this 'horrible' occurrence," I say, surprised by the bitterness in my voice. It sucks to think you're forbidden to exist.

"Exactly. Those ancient Leachers would've killed the prisoner women instead. I'm sure of it," she says. "All this just makes your existence that much more revolutionary."

"What's so revolutionary about it?"

"Oh, come on. Just think about it. What's the best way to mend centuries-old feuds?"

"I know the answer you're looking for is to intermarry, but I'm not sure it's that simple—"

"It is," she says confidently. "This was the reason why kings of warring nations sometimes married into each other's families. It's also why Americans—products of the melting pot —have forgotten many, if not all, of the prejudices of their European ancestors, who hated each other's guts."

My skepticism must be showing on my face because she continues, "I've thought about this a lot, Darren. There are examples all over the place—I'm an anthropologist, after all. If you have two groups who hate each other, you need to break the group identity that results in the whole 'us versus them' setup we talked about earlier. And what better way to break such identity than having children around that are representatives of both groups? Especially when they are as charming as you." She winks at me playfully.

"As flattered as I am to be the future and all that, allow me to play the devil's advocate for a moment and take your idea to its logical extreme. It wouldn't be just Readers and Guides who would need to intermarry. You're saying the human race should do so also?"

"Right," she says.

"But don't you think something would be lost if everyone assimilated into one giant human race? All those cute little cultural diversity things would go away, for example. Like ethnic foods, different languages, even ethnic music or mythologies." I'm not necessarily convinced that she's wrong, but I want to hear her counterpoints.

"I'm not sure you're right about that." She downs her glass of coconut water in a big gulp. "Certain things would stay. Take holidays such as Easter that stem from ancient pagan holidays. They're still around—colored eggs and the bunny and all. But even if we did lose some of this cultural heritage, it would be worth it if it meant world peace."

"But why stop at someone like me?" I ask. "That logic can be used to say that both Guides and Readers should intermarry with regular people."

"That's right," she says.

"But that would essentially wipe out our abilities. You'd get the same genocide sort of situation that Readers were trying to perpetrate on Guides—only in this case, it will be voluntary."

"That's not true. We'd have less divisiveness. And who said our abilities would go away? They might spread. In any case, once Guides and Readers accept you for what you are, I believe it will open a new dialogue between the groups."

"Or I would get killed to maintain the status quo." I'm no longer arguing for the sake of argument, but with a growing sense of peril.

"I won't let that happen," my aunt says seriously, and despite her size, she seems astonishingly formidable all of a sudden.

23

AFTER HILLARY AND I SPEND HALF THE NIGHT TALKING, I WAKE up late—but thankfully, not too late for lunch. I text Mira to confirm our plans, and she gives me the address where I'm to pick her up.

This time, when I go to a car rental agency, I get a much nicer car. I also wholeheartedly agree to buy the insurance, in case I end up in another high-speed chase with Russian mobsters.

After a frantic drive to make sure I'm not late, I park my shiny black Lexus near the lobby of Mira and Eugene's hotel.

Once I notify Mira of my arrival, I finally take a moment to check the emails on my phone. And there it is, the email from Bert I have been waiting for:

Dude,

I was able to find a good location where you can look at Arkady Bogomolov. It was an ingenious hack, if I do say so myself. I'll tell you all about it when I see you next. If I see you, that is, because this guy is bad news, and you best stay away from him. Your best course of action is to delete this email right now and go hang out with Mira.

Oh well, you have always been stubborn, so I guess you're still reading. The guy will be at a Russian banya called Mermaid. It's in Brooklyn, and the address is 3703 Mermaid Avenue. Hence the name, I take it. In their system, he's listed as getting a massage at 4:00 pm today. From a guy named Lyova—yuck.

Your mom's murder case files are attached.

You owe me.

Bert.

I quickly write a response:

Thanks, I owe you big.

Bert really outdid himself this time. I should take the time and figure out a way to help his girl troubles, as he requested. If the subject comes up, I will ask Mira if she has any girlfriends. I suspect she might not. There is something of a loner vibe about her. Also, the person for Bert would need to be pretty short, unless the girl wasn't into traditional gender binary.

Aware that I have little time, I quickly research the place Bert wrote about. As I learned from reading that gangster's mind the other day, *banya* is a kind of spa. I now confirm and expand on that memory online. Apparently, it's not the kind of place where girls get their manicures and pedicures. Instead, Russians go there to sit in extremely hot saunas and—I kid you not—to get spanked by brooms made out of birch tree branches. Yeah. It's essentially a public bathhouse with some weird S&M spin. Sign me up. Not.

This specific place is located not far from Coney Island Park, according to the map in the phone.

I guess I should tell Mira about this development. Maybe after we eat something, though—I'm starving. And, while I'm at it, I need to talk to her about meeting the Pusher community. This one is trickier. But then again, she'll be away from her gun, so it might be the perfect opportunity. Yes, she might freak—likely *will* freak—and I might ruin the date, if this is a date, but holding out on her might lead to an even bigger disaster.

And then I see her.

She walks out of the hotel lobby wearing tight Capri pants, sandals, and a strappy tank top. Her hair is done in a simple tight ponytail. This look is pretty casual, compared to her usual high heels, war-paint makeup, and skimpy cocktail dresses. I'm not sure what this dressing-down act means, but I think it's a good sign. After all, she usually dresses to kill when she's out looking for revenge.

I get out of the car and wave. She smiles and approaches. With a strange impulse of chivalry, I walk over and open the car door for her. She kisses me on my cheek—a surprise. Either based on my reaction to the smooch or because of my opening the door for her, I get rewarded with an even bigger smile and a thank-you.

"Where to?" I say when I get in.

"I'm in the mood for Russian food. Have you ever had any?"

"I had some blinis with caviar at the Russian Samovar place in the city, but that's kind of it," I say.

"That's an appetizer and isn't the kind of thing people eat every day. Not unless they're some kind of oil oligarchs," she explains. "But it's a decent example."

"Okay, that settles it. Can you direct me to a good place?" I say.

"Yeah. Take two lefts over there. We're going to this place called Winter Garden," she says, and I start driving.

A couple of turns later, I'm getting a bad feeling. "What part of Brooklyn is this place located in? It *is* in Brooklyn, right?"

"Yes. It's located where most good Russian food can be found. Brighton Beach," she says. "Have you ever been there?"

"No. But, Mira, isn't that the place where all the Russian Mafia hang out?" I try to sound nonchalant.

"A lot of people hang out there," she says dismissively.

"Right, but we're on their shoot-to-kill list," I say. "Other people are not."

"You're such a worrier." There is a hint of laughter in her voice. "Brighton Beach is a big place, and it's the middle of the day on a Saturday, with tons of people around. But if you're scared, we can get sushi."

"No, let's go to this Winter Garden place," I say, trying to sound confident. I don't point out that the last time we got shot at by those people, it was in the morning, or the fact that the bullets went right through a very public playground. I figure the odds are on our side, but even if not, I don't want to reinforce the idea that I am a 'worrier.'

"Great, turn onto Coney Island Avenue at that light. Yes, there." As I turn, she says, grinning, "I have been meaning to ask you, do you always drive this slowly?"

"What's the point of going fast when I see the light changing to red?" I say, realizing that she's beginning to talk and act like the Mira I'm more familiar with. It's oddly comforting and even fun in a way.

"You could've totally made that green," she says. "Next time, you should let me drive."

I picture her driving like Caleb, only worse, and make a solemn vow never to let her drive, unless it's an emergency. I also don't dignify her jibe with a response.

Her grin widens. "How is your head?" she asks when I stubbornly remain silent.

"Much better, thanks." With everything going on, I'd nearly forgotten about the wound. "Just a little itchy."

"That means it's healing."

"Cool. I hope that's the case. How was your day yesterday? How's your brother doing? Did he visit Julia again? How is she recovering?"

For the rest of the way to the restaurant, she tells me how boring it is at the hotel. How Eugene is impossible to be around when he doesn't have his 'science stuff' with him. He wants to run ideas by her, share epiphanies, and carry on conversations. Mira's only reprieve was his visits with Julia, who was let out of the hospital today. Now, Julia is apparently staying in the same hotel as Mira and Eugene until she's completely recovered—she doesn't want her family to know about her adventures.

"So Eugene is off your back, it seems," I say as we pull into a public parking lot. "He'll probably be busy with Julia from now on."

"Yeah, I guess," she says and makes a face before climbing out of the car.

"What's the problem?" I ask as I feed the parking meter.

"I'm not a fan of that relationship of his," she says as she walks toward a pathway that leads to a large wooden boardwalk. "Last time, Julia's father interfered with their relationship, and Zhenya was really hurt."

"Is Zhenya Eugene's nickname?"

"Yes, that's what I call him sometimes."

"What about you, do you have a nickname? I can suggest a few, like Mi—"

"No," she says. "Please don't. My name is already short."

She walks a few seconds in silence, and I wonder if I touched on a sensitive topic. Maybe her parents called her by a nickname, and this made her think of them?

"We're here," she says, bringing me out of my thoughts.

We're standing next to a place that has a sign that reads "Winter Garden." If no one tries to kill us during our meal, I'll have to admit that Mira made an excellent choice when picking this place. The tables are situated on a wooden boardwalk, with the beach and the ocean beyond it. The weather is beautiful, and the ocean breeze brings sounds of the surf and smells that I associate with vacation.

When we take our seats, I look at the menu.

"It's all in Russian," I complain.

"Think of it as a compliment," she says. "They must think you're Russian, though I personally have no idea why."

"That's okay. I don't want to be mistaken for a Russian. I don't have too high of an opinion of them after the last few days. Present company excluded, of course." I smile at her.

"Of course," she says sarcastically.

"In any case, I guess I'll have to behave like a tourist and ask for the English menu," I say, not looking forward to it.

"Or you can take a chance and let me order for you." She winks at me mischievously.

Did I mention how hot Mira looks when she's being intentionally mischievous?

"First you pick the place," I say, folding my left pinky finger.

"Now you want to order for me?" I fold the ring finger. "Who's taking whom out?"

"Don't forget that I also wanted to drive." She chuckles and holds out her middle finger as though she wants to fold it in the same fashion. Except it looks more like she's flipping me off, and I suspect she's doing that on purpose.

My witty retort never comes because our waiter arrives and begins speaking in rapid-fire Russian.

Mira looks at me, and I nod, resigned.

Mira and the waiter have a long, incomprehensible discussion in Russian while I get distracted by a smell coming from somewhere. It's a nauseating aroma, and it takes me a few moments to realize that it's some idiot smoking a cigar.

The last time I saw people smoke in restaurants was in 2003. Did this guy not get the memo about the smoking ban? I guess he thinks the fact that we're outside is a loophole of some kind. If you ask me, it's an unthinkable breach of etiquette, and I'm tempted to tell the guy off.

I look the offender over. Okay, so perhaps I won't give him the stern lecture he deserves. He doesn't look like he'd get it. What he does look like is a mountain. Only mountains are peaceful and serene things, and this motherfucker looks extremely mean.

I contemplate forgetting about it, but I can't leave it alone. The smoke is going to ruin my meal. Deciding to take a different course of action, I phase into the Quiet.

The restaurant patrons freeze in place, and the ambient noises of people and the ocean surf disappear.

I savor the silence. It makes me realize that I haven't done this in a while. Not once today, in fact.

I approach the guy with the cigar.

Frozen in place, he looks a lot less intimidating. I reach out and grab his ear, like they used to do back in the day to spoiled children—or so Kyle told me.

Physical connection in place, I want to establish a mental one. The lack of recent practice shows. I need to consciously relax to go into his mind, but once I focus on my breathing, I'm in.

We're puffing on the Cuban cigar and wondering when Sveta will get here.

I quickly disassociate, not willing to smoke that monstrosity even in someone else's head. If it were possible to cough mentally, that's what I'd be doing right now.

I make a snap decision on how to proceed and instantly feel good about myself. I'm about to do this guy a great service—and help everyone around him.

I prepare to do the Guiding, which is a better term than Pushing for what I'm about to do.

'Smoking is bad.

If you keep it up, it will give you cancer.

Feel a strong desire to put out this cigar. Feel disgusted, appalled, and sick to your stomach.

Doesn't the cigar look like a turd?

Do you want to put shit in your mouth?

You will never smoke cigars, or cigarettes, ever again. You have the willpower to quit—for the rest of your life.'

To add to those indoctrinations, I try to channel my memory of the negative emotions I felt during anti-smoking ads. Some of those ads are so disgusting that I can't believe anyone can see them and go on smoking.

I'm convinced the guy will not be smoking for a long while.

For how long is an interesting question. According to Hillary, my biological mother made my adoptive parents avoid the topic of my origins for years. I suspect my Reach might be just as impressive. If I understand it correctly, Guiding Reach works a lot like Reading Depth. Both are based on another variable: the amount of time you can spend in the Quiet. I don't know the limits to my time in the Quiet, but I do know my Depth amazed Julia and others, and they didn't know the full Depth I was capable of. It would be reasonable to assume my Reach is equally long.

All that considered, I might've permanently cured the cigar smoker of his deadly addiction.

As I prepare to get out of his mind, I wonder how regular Guides do their Guiding. It must be very different for them. They don't get the experience of being inside the person's head the way I do. That's a Reader thing. For them, it must be more like blind touching and wishing. I'll have to ask Hillary more about it, maybe get some tips on how to Guide more effectively.

Realizing that I'm still inside the now-non-smoker's head, I focus and instantly get out.

My good deed done for the day, I walk over and Read the waiter, since I'm in the Quiet anyway. He thinks Mira is as hot as I do, but I can hardly blame him for that. The good news is that nothing Mira ordered for us thus far sounds life-threatening.

Satisfied, I phase out.

"Ee dva compota," I hear Mira say to the waiter with finality.

As the man leaves, I see my new non-smoker friend begin to cough with a funny look on his face. Then, staring at his cigar as though it's a cobra, he violently sticks the object of his distress into his water glass.

Success. I mentally pat myself on the back, but don't say anything to Mira. The last thing I want is to remind her of my Pushing abilities.

"Thank you for ordering," I tell Mira instead.

"See if you like the food, then thank me." She smiles. "Besides, you're paying, so I should thank you."

"Oh, good, you'll at least let me pay. That makes me feel like I *am* taking you out after all," I say, winking.

"Sure. I have to look out for your masculine pride and all that. You almost ran out of fingers counting your grievances," she says. "And of course, this has nothing to do with my being broke."

I consider this for a moment. "Don't you have all those gambling winnings?"

"Yeah, but I don't keep much of it."

"Where does it all go? Shoes?" I joke.

"Well, in fact, shoes do cost a pretty penny, but no. The bulk of our money ends up feeding my brother's research," she says, pursing her lips with displeasure.

"Oh, I didn't realize you support his research this much." In fact, I'd gotten the impression she disapproved of it. "What exactly does he study? I mean, I know it has something to do with how our powers work."

"I support his research mainly out of spite. Because I know it would piss off the fuckers who killed Mom and Dad." She glowers darkly. "And because I love my weirdo brother. As to what his research is all about, I wish I could tell you, but I don't really get it. When he starts talking about it, it's as though a part of my brain shuts off."

I chuckle at that, remembering how she always goes out of her way not to hear Eugene talk about his work.

A waiter comes back with drinks and says something to Mira in Russian.

"Try it," Mira says. "I think you'll like it."

I taste the liquid in my glass. It seems to be some kind of sweet fruit punch. "Yum."

"Yeah," she says knowingly. "That's Russian compote, made out of dried fruit. My grandmother used to make it all the time."

"It's a great start," I say.

"Good, the appetizers are coming too."

Sure enough, the waiter comes back with a tray.

"That's julienne, escargot, and you already tried blinis before," she says, pointing at the tray. "Give it a try."

I oblige, piling samples onto my plate.

"You know," I say when I'm done chewing. "This tastes a lot like French food."

"I'm not surprised," she says. "Czarist Russia's nobility had French chefs, and French cuisine is now part of Russian culture. Still, these dishes should be a little different."

The escargot, snails in butter and garlic, are outstanding. The julienne thing is a mushroom and cheese dish that reminds me of mushroom pizza, without the dough—meaning you can't go wrong with it. Blinis are very similar to the crepes I had before, only these come with red rather than black caviar.

"So far, it's awesome," I tell her, trying my best not to burn my tongue on the hot cheese of the julienne dish—which, so far, is my favorite.

"I'm glad." She sounds so proud that you'd think she cooked the food herself.

"I was wondering about something," I say as I blow on my food. "What are you planning to do after you get your revenge and all that?"

She gives me a vaguely surprised look, as though she's never been asked this before. "I plan to get my GED, since I never finished high school. After that, I'm going to enroll at Kingsborough College."

"Kingsborough? I've heard of it, but know very little about the place. Is it good? What do you want to study there?"

"Kingsborough is a community college. We locals call it 'The Harvard on the Bay.' It's probably not up to your high standards, but I can get my RN license after I get my Associate's degree and afterwards get a job."

"You want to be a nurse?" I ask, surprised. I wonder if she said the Harvard bit because she knows I graduated from there. Maybe she Googled me? I find the idea that she cared enough to do a search quite pleasant.

"I would make a good nurse," she says. "I'm not squeamish, and I don't faint at the sight of my own blood like some people." She gives me a pointed look.

"I didn't faint," I protest. "I lost consciousness because I was shot. That's completely different. I saw a ton of blood the other day, remember? No fainting."

"Methinks the gentleman doth protest too much . . ." She gives me a teasing smile. "I'm pretty sure you saw your own bloodied hand and fainted yesterday. But in any case, I think I would make a great nurse. My plan is to work in a neonatal unit, if I can. To deal with newborn babies." Her face softens as she says that last bit.

"Really?" I can't picture her working with babies. Being a kickass professional spy, maybe. But a nurse working with babies? It just boggles my mind.

She nods. "Yes, I like helping people. And I want to work in a place like that, a place where people learn the happiest news of their lives."

So she likes to help people. That's news to me. But something about that worries me a little. Could that urge of hers explain why she was so nice to me when I was hurt? Was she only acting like that because that's how she would've treated any person in pain?

"I imagine it's not all unicorns and rainbows at the neonatal unit. Don't babies get sick?" I ask, picturing all the crying, and worried parents breathing down your neck. I don't know about other guys my age, but for me, crying babies are on par with scorpions and snakes.

"Of course. But I can Read them and figure out what hurts." She smiles again. "And then the doctors will be able to help them."

"You can Read a baby?" I don't know why that hadn't occurred to me before. If that's the case, then working with babies does sound like a uniquely helpful way to use Reading. Similar to what Liz does with her Guiding of OCD patients, but perhaps even cooler.

"Sure. You can Read many creatures," Mira says. "I used to Read my cat, Murzik, when he was alive."

"You could Read your cat?" Now I'm flabbergasted. "How was that? Do they have thoughts, like us?"

"Not thoughts, at least not my old lazy cat. But I was

immersed in his experiences, which had something like thoughts in them, only fleeting. In that way, babies are similar. They feel more than think, and when you Read them, you can learn if something hurts or why they're unhappy."

"Wow. I'll have to try Reading some creature. And, I must say, yours sounds like an excellent plan. I hope you get your revenge soon, because this sounds much better than what you've been doing." As I say that last part, I realize I might've inadvertently criticized her.

"You don't say." Her voice drips with sarcasm. "Helping people is better than underground gambling with monsters?"

"Never mind," I say, sorry I blabbed too much. "Yes, obviously you'll be happier once you put that plan into motion. Besides, I assume your gambling days are over?"

"You assume?" she says, finishing her last crepe. "It's an interesting assumption. But I think we've spent enough time talking about me. Quid pro quo, Darren. What do *you* plan to do after you get out of this mess?"

"I'm going to take a vacation," I say without hesitation. "Go someplace warm, or maybe travel someplace interesting, like Europe. After that, I don't know. I already have a job at a hedge fund, but it's not the kind you described. It's not my passion or anything like that. It's just a means to make money."

"The horror," she says in mock shock. "Money is the root of all evil, don't you know?"

"Hey, I'm not complaining. It's just that you actually want to help people, and you've thought about a job that would make you happy. I haven't thought about that yet. I was thinking about being a detective the other day, but the paperwork and danger might be a drag. Not to mention the very thought of going back to school—"

"You can be a private detective," she suggests, interrupting. "You can do as much paperwork as you feel like doing—since it would be your own business. And, you can take only jobs that have the amount of danger you're comfortable with. Wives wondering about their philandering husbands, that sort of thing." There's only a little bit of mockery in her voice as she says the word *danger*.

I stare at her, struck by the idea. "You know, that could actually work. I could even use Reading to help me solve cases. I could be like one of those psychic detectives on TV. Only I'm afraid that taking on boring cases would defeat the original purpose of my enjoying the work."

She's about to respond, but the waiter comes again, with a bigger tray this time. He takes what's left of the appetizers, and we get our plates with the main course.

"That's called *chalahach*," she says.

"Really? It sure looks like lamb chop to me." I glance down at my plate. "A lamb chop with mashed potato and green beans. How very not exotic."

"Not exotic? This is a traditional dish from freaking Uzbekistan, or some other former Soviet republic. It's as exotic as it gets. And the way they make it here is amazing." She cuts off a piece and puts it in her mouth, closing her eyes in bliss as she begins to chew.

I try it and have to concur. "It's been sautéed in a different way than your usual lamb chop," I say.

"Exactly. Also make sure to use the sauce." She points at the red ketchup-like stuff in a saucer on my plate.

I follow her suggestion and admit, "It's even better with the sauce."

"Told you," she says, wolfing down her chop. "The sauce is Uzbek also. Or Tajik. I'm not sure."

For the remainder of the meal, we talk about why Russian food is so full of other cultures' cuisines, and I challenge her to come up with some original Russian dish. I also unsuccessfully try to think of a way to bring up my knowledge of Arkady's location without ruining our lunch.

"No dessert?" I say when the waiter brings us the check.

"I wanted to leave room for you to try something else," she replies as I pay the waiter with cash.

"Something else?" I say curiously, rising to my feet.

She gets up as well. "I wanted to get you a *pirozhok,* this meat-filled dough. It's definitely, positively a Russian food. They sell them all over the boardwalk."

"Great, more food, and the street variety to boot. I can't wait," I say, teasing.

Without saying a word, she goes into the indoor portion of our restaurant and comes back a minute later with a strange-looking pastry.

"This one is not street food. I assure you, it's safe," she says. "Try it."

The pastry tastes baked, not fried, and seems to be filled with something like apple preserves.

"I like it," I say. "But wasn't this supposed to have meat in it?"

"You wanted dessert, so I got you the apple variety. A pirozhok can have all kinds of fillings," she says and rattles off a weird list that includes eggs, cabbage, cherries, and—my favorite—mashed potatoes. Yes, Russians apparently eat starch filled with starch.

"Thank you, Mira," I say when I finish my pirozhok. "That was awesome."

"Don't mention it. Now let's walk it off by going toward Coney Island," she says. "I'm in the mood for a stroll."

"Okay. But now that we're done with our meal, there's something I wanted to talk to you about." I pause, and then at her expectant look, I say carefully, "I think you might get your revenge sooner than you thought."

24

"YOU SHOULD'VE TOLD ME EARLIER," SHE SAYS AFTER I FINISH telling her the story about how I got Arkady's name out of the mobster's head and how my friend Bert found out about his whereabouts.

"I'm sorry. I didn't really get a chance before. Not with all the guns you kept pointing at me, and then getting shot and everything else."

"Fine," she says curtly. "We have to go to the banya. Now."

"But what about our walk? Besides, his massage is at four p.m., and it's two-thirty now," I say, already regretting that I told her.

"Listen, Darren, I'm sorry, but the walk will have to happen another day," she says. "Thank you for the lunch and for telling me this now, but I can't relax and enjoy myself, knowing about a lead like this. Plus, the guy is already there, I assure you. I know how a banya works."

We walk back to the car. I learn on the way that going to the banya is usually a full-day event and that our target is likely to want to get a couple of *parki*—the spankings with the birch brooms—before getting his massage.

I start driving, and she continues telling me what she knows of the Russian bathhouse culture. I'm beginning to feel that Russia is the one place I won't need to visit anytime soon. I suspect I have already learned and seen everything a tourist would have by just going on this one date— if this *is* a date —with Mira.

"Stop here," she says when, according to the GPS, we're a few blocks from the place.

I look around. The neighborhood looks a bit rundown and sketchy.

"We're going into the Mind Dimension," she says, clearly seeing the hesitation on my face. "So we're not really going to leave the car. Please Split and pull me in."

I do as she asks and phase in.

Immediately, I'm in the backseat looking at the back of my own head and that of Mira. I tap an exposed part of her shoulder, and in a moment, a livelier version of her is sitting next to me.

"Let's go," she says, and we make our way to the banya on foot.

We go inside, and I gape at the scene in front of me.

Picture Russian Mafia. Now picture them sitting with regular middle-aged Russian men and a small handful of women—all of them in their swimwear—at what looks like a mix between a cafeteria and a shower stall. Picture all that, and you'll begin to get an idea of what the inside of this Mermaid place looks like.

"Okay, which one is he?" Mira starts walking around. "They all look like a bunch of regulars."

"I say we Read people one by one until we find him or verify he isn't here yet. We can also look for the masseur," I say. "His name is Lyova."

"All right. You take the steam rooms, and I will do this area. The masseur is likely to arrive close to the appointment."

"You sound like you've been here before," I say, heading toward what must be the steam rooms.

"Of course," she says over her shoulder. "It's the best banya in Brooklyn."

I walk over and open the wooden door that leads to the steam room. The people here are even less covered than their counterparts in the lunchroom. They're also wearing pointy woolen hats that are supposed to protect their heads from overheating. If I hadn't read about this previously, I'd burst out laughing at the ridiculous sight. Completing the bizarre picture are two people lying on wooden shelves and getting the birch-branch spanking treatment.

I've never seen steam frozen in place before. It's weird. When my body touches it, it condenses into tiny drops of water on my skin. The room is not hot here in the Quiet, but I can tell that in the real world, this place is scorching. Everybody in here is covered with droplets of sweat.

I start Reading people, one after another. Two guys are programmers, another is an electrical engineer, and the majority are retired old men. No gangsters, no Arkady, no luck.

I leave this room and head over to a room that has a sign stating that it's a Turkish Spa. The glass entrance door is fogged up from thick steam. I'm going to come out wet if I go in there.

"Darren, over here!" I hear Mira call out from the table area, and I'm more than happy not to enter the room I was about to go into.

As I walk toward her, I see them. These guys stand out for a number of reasons. First, they are buffer and meaner-looking than the rest of the patrons. But the main reason I know we found what we're looking for is that I see the guy who tried to shoot me yesterday. He must've managed to handle the car safely, even after I Guided him to leave fast and to keep on driving. I guess I shouldn't be surprised, since I didn't command him to do anything truly suicidal.

He's sitting there, a shot of vodka held halfway to his mouth. Vodka in a steam room? Really? Someone has a strong cardiovascular system, or a death wish.

"That's the fucker who tried to shoot me," I tell Mira, pointing at the guy.

"Right, and that's the man we came here to Read." She gestures toward a particularly large specimen, who has tattoos of stars on his shoulders and a large silver cross hanging around his neck. His face is frozen in a scowl—probably his usual expression.

I approach and gingerly touch one of his meaty biceps. The muscle is so big, it looks like a strange tumor.

I focus momentarily, and I am in.

WE'RE JUMPING INTO THE COLD WATER OF THE SPECIAL POOL BY the steam room. There are ice cubes floating in it, we notice with satisfaction. Instead of the shock of cold water, our body just feels tingly, and the dip is extremely refreshing. The resulting pins-and-needles sensation on our skin, combined with the buzz from the vodka, almost makes us forget the unfortunate fact that we'll have to leave banya in a half hour and miss our massage, all because of that fucking phone call.

I, Darren, disassociate.

Something is odd about this mind. Something I've never come across before, but I can't quite put my finger on it.

I focus on the memories Arkady has about the phone call. I get vague images of it being from someone important, but someone outside the Russian organization.

Sounds a lot like our mystery Pusher, I decide.

Determined to investigate this, I almost instinctively feel lighter and rewind Arkady's memories to that point.

"On the Brooklyn Bridge?" we ask, confused. "Why the fuck would we meet there?"

"Because, I don't trust you, Mr. Bogomolov."

"That's a fucking joke, right? You don't trust me? Out of the two of us, I have far more reasons not to trust you, Mr. Esau, much more than the other way around," we say. "I'm still not convinced you're not setting some kind of a trap for me and my people."

"Well, you're just proving my point for me then. That's even more reason to meet in a public place, with lots of people around," says Esau. His voice sounds unnaturally deep. We're fairly sure he's using a voice scrambler.

"How will I find you?" we ask. "What do you look like?"

"I'll find you, so don't worry," says Esau.

"Oh, I'm not worried," we say. "But if you don't bring my money and the list, you should be worried. Very worried."

Images of the torture we would inflict on Esau in that scenario flash in front of our eyes.

"You will get the cash and the list," says Esau. Is that fear coming through the voice scrambler? "You're actually going to get two lists. One will contain more business for you."

Esau had ordered kills on and off from us for some time, but this is the first time he decided to put together a whole fucking list of people.

"We don't do bulk discounts," we say sarcastically. "This isn't fucking Costco."

"I wasn't asking for a discount. The list is merely a way to make sure I keep these pleasant conversations with you to a minimum. Your usual rate applies."

"Good," we say with satisfaction. "And if we're going to play this distrust game, then you better bring a downpayment for each name on this new list of yours."

"Of course, half the usual for each target," Esau says. "But, just as a heads up, since we're going to be bringing so much money with us, the memory card that contains the lists is encrypted. We're going to give it to you today, but will only provide the key to decrypt it once we're safely away from our meeting."

We're both impressed and annoyed. This last precaution might well have saved the man's life. Maybe. Depends on how well protected he'll be. The passcode can be gotten out of him if enough skill is applied in questioning. We haven't had anyone not talk before.

As if reading our mind, Esau says, "Furthermore, you should know that if something were to happen to me, I've made arrangements. The people on the list that you want, the ones in witness protection, will get a warning, and you wouldn't want that."

"Sounds like we have an understanding," we say, wondering if Esau is bluffing about these arrangements. Even if he is, we can't take the chance. Esau will survive today's meeting—which is fine with us. This way, we get more money down the line and can off him later. "I'll see you later today."

"Four-thirty, sharp," Esau says and hangs up.

We wonder if this could be a trap from the FBI or some other agency. Then we dismiss the thought. Those people wouldn't order hits. They go as far as using drugs and things like that, but assassinations are a line they wouldn't cross. Particularly the petty kinds of kills that this Esau guy had ordered—like the American kid Slava managed to screw up killing yesterday.

The American kid? I, Darren, take a mental step back, struck by the wording. Eugene is Russian, and at almost thirty years of age, he's not exactly a kid. If Arkady was thinking about him, wouldn't he call him a Russian guy or something along those lines? Unless . . .

Unless the shooting this morning wasn't directed at Eugene, like we all thought.

Suddenly, it all becomes clear. Of course. It was the Pusher. He tried to kill me, not once but twice—first via the shooter and then again in the hospital.

I'm the un-killed American kid in question.

Shit. Whoever this Pusher is, he's serious about eliminating me. Is it possible he had something to do with my parents' deaths? Or Mira's parents' deaths? Had he used this exact puppet—Arkady—to do it? I need to dig deeper into Arkady's head to find out.

I focus on going back a long time . . .

We spit out a tooth, but don't slow down. Instead, we execute our plan of attack on the Captain. A punch to the liver, another to his Adam's apple. The Captain has been teaching us

Systema for the last couple of weeks. Learning the unit's secret martial art was one of the main reasons we joined this training. Well, that and curiosity. We wondered if this, of all things, will take away the boredom.

I, Darren, realize I'm too deep inside Arkady's past, so I try to go for more recent events.

The Chechen woman is shot in the neck. She falls, bleeding, convulsing, and trying to scream. We feel nothing, though we know that most people would feel pity at the sight. We vaguely understand the concept. We wonder if it's pity that compels us to think about how the woman was beautiful, and it's a shame we didn't get a chance to fuck her. No, that's more regret than pity. Pity is an emotion that still eludes us.

I'm still in too deep. Also, I finally understand what the strange thing about this mind is. The guy is a real-life, certifiable psychopath. He doesn't feel the usual range and intensity of emotions that other people do.

I decide I have to be careful about poking around in his head. His experiences make Caleb's disturbing memories seem like summer camp. The atrocities Arkady committed in Chechnya are there, in the back of our shared-for-the-moment mind, and I don't want to experience something like that. No amount of therapy with Liz would undo it.

So I mentally tiptoe around, trying to look at experiences that shed any light on the murders of the past. I'm drawing a blank, though, whenever I try to focus on anything having to do with my parents' murder. He must not have been involved in that.

I do come across many signs of the Pusher, though. And the explanation of why Arkady thinks he met Esau recently. The Pusher regularly makes Arkady forget things—like missions from this Esau. In fact, he often makes Arkady forget Esau's existence completely. To me, that means only one thing.

Esau and the Pusher are the same person.

I want to scream in excitement.

Unfortunately, it seems like the Pusher took obsessive precautions to never be seen by Arkady. Even when he Pushed Arkady, he probably walked over to him in the Quiet, rather than being physically in the room. This Esau identity must be the Pusher's way to control his pet Mafia goon by more conventional means—via the phone.

I look further into Arkady's memories.

We finish setting up the explosive device and get back into the car. As we sit there, we wonder why this Tsiolkovskiy guy needs to be eliminated in such a fancy manner. Bullet to the head would've been much cheaper and less risky. Every assassin knows that explosives can hurt the man who works with them. We've heard of this happening on many occasions. It's understandable for someone high-profile, but doing it to kill some Russian scientist? It doesn't make sense. But the client said he would pay double, claiming that Tsiolkovskiy might see it coming otherwise, so explosives it is.

I feel cold all over at my discovery. I can't even imagine what Mira will do when I tell her.

With a shudder, I get out of Arkady's head.

"Fuck," I say unimaginatively when I'm out and catch Mira's gaze.

"I take it you heard the phone conversation," Mira says. "We've got to hurry." She turns and starts to briskly walk away.

"Mira, wait." Catching up, I place my hand on her shoulder.

"What?" She gives me an annoyed look. "Didn't you Read the same information I did?"

"Yes, a Brooklyn Bridge meeting," I confirm. "But I learned something else, too. Something you might not have, given your Depth . . . "

Her face turns pale. "Tell me."

I take a deep breath. "He remembers planting a bomb under a car for a Russian scientist with the last name of Tsiolkovskiy. That had to have been your dad—"

Her reaction is so violent and sudden that I don't have time to say anything else. Grabbing a chair, she starts whacking Arkady's frozen body with it, over and over.

Then she puts the chair on the floor and sits down on it, propping her elbows on her knees and covering her eyes with her palms.

"Mira," I say softly, approaching her. "If you want, I can try to make him drown himself in that cold pool over there."

I don't know if I can actually do what I just said, both from a practical standpoint and from an ethical one. But trying it will certainly make more sense than beating up a man in the Quiet—an action that will have no impact in the real world.

"No, don't." Lowering her hands, she looks up, her eyes glittering brightly. "He's the key to the fucker who's pulling the strings."

I exhale, relieved she didn't take me up on my hasty offer. I might've balked at doing something *that* cold-blooded.

"So you want to go to the meeting at the Brooklyn Bridge?" I ask as she gets up from the chair.

"Yes. Once he brings us to the Pusher, I'll kill them both."

Her voice is cold and sharp. "If we kill him now, the Pusher might get spooked."

"Okay, but—"

"Let's get back to the car. Let's not get into any particulars just yet," she says, striding toward the door.

I reluctantly follow her. As much as I want to catch this Pusher, I'm really not looking forward to confronting Arkady and his colleagues.

"Sorry about earlier," she says over her shoulder. "I just needed to vent."

"Of course, no worries," I say, and then we walk in silence for a few moments.

When we reach the car, I touch my neck through the open Lexus door, and the world comes back to life.

25

"Please let me drive," Mira says as soon we're out of the Quiet.

Given her mental state, I decide to comply. Arguing with an angry Mira doesn't seem like a good idea to me. The girl definitely has a short fuse. Besides, I have some phone calls to make, given where we're heading.

As soon as she's behind the wheel, she floors the gas pedal, causing the Lexus to make a tire-screeching sound.

I take out my phone, happy to focus on something other than the streets of Brooklyn that are flashing by the car window much too fast.

"I'm calling Caleb," I tell Mira as I locate his number in my phone.

"That's a good idea," she says approvingly. "I was going to ask Julia to do this at the hotel, but this is even better. You two have a nice rapport."

"If Caleb and I have a nice rapport, I shudder to think how

he treats people he dislikes," I say and dial the number on my screen.

The phone rings for a while. I wait.

Then it connects, but no one says anything on the other line.

"Hello?" I say carefully.

"Who? Oh, Darren." I hear Caleb's surprised tone. "Miss me already?"

"I can use your help, Caleb," I say, ignoring the jibe. "*We* can use your help."

"Oh, cutting right to the chase? I like it." Caleb sounds a bit less sarcastic. "What do you—the plural you—need?"

"Some of your unique help tonight," I say. "There's this—"

"Darren, let me stop you right there," Caleb interrupts. "I'm not in town. In fact, I'm out of state."

"Shit," I say.

"What's going on, Darren? Is it something serious?"

"Yes, it is, but I don't want to go into it right now," I say. "Not over the phone. I've got to think of something else."

"Are you in trouble? I can put you in touch with Sam or one of my other people."

"Sam the Asshole? You're kidding, right?"

"Sam's in charge in my absence, so he's the logical choice."

"No, thanks. I think we'll manage."

"Suit yourself—there's nothing I can do that Sam can't. The man is a machine. If I weren't the one with charisma, he'd be in charge," Caleb says, and I can't tell if he's joking or not.

"I appreciate that," I say. "And I may call you back about it, but I really think I'd rather work with someone I know."

Mira parks the car in the hotel parking lot, so I tell Caleb I have to get off the phone.

"Sure," he responds. "Let me know if you change your mind about Sam or if there's anything else you need."

"Well," I say as Mira exits the car, "I do have one quick question . . ."

"What is it, kid?"

"Do you know a guy named Mark Robinson?"

There is a moment of silence. Then: "Why do you ask? Where did you hear that name?"

"Jacob mentioned him," I say noncommittally.

"Hmm, that's odd. He's ancient history. One of our people who was murdered. A nasty affair. Do you know why Jacob mentioned him to you?"

"No," I say. Then, cognizant that Mira is about to come back and drag me out, I add quickly, "Thanks, Caleb. I'll call back later if we end up needing Sam."

"Okay." He hangs up, probably still wondering about my weird question. I guess he has no idea Mark had a son.

I phase into the Quiet and take a moment to digest what I just learned.

My father was a Reader. There is no doubt about that now. And my mother was a Guide. What I suspected ever since discovering my Guiding abilities has now been confirmed. And the theory of my parents being killed for their forbidden union is beginning to sound more plausible.

I phase back out and join Mira outside.

"So, judging by what I overheard, Caleb isn't available?" Mira says as she briskly walks toward her room. She's texting as she goes, and I assume she's communicating with Eugene.

"Yeah. Caleb offered the help of that Sam guy, but I wasn't sure about that idea."

"You did the right thing. Sam and I, we don't have good history," she says through clenched teeth.

"Oh?" I ask, hoping that this is not an ex-boyfriend or something along those lines.

"He beat up my brother," she says angrily. "It was on Jacob's orders, most likely, but still, there's no way we're going to deal with him."

"Shit. Sounds like we wouldn't want him involved, for sure. I've met the guy twice now, and I know he's a jackass. I just didn't realize to what extent."

We make our way to Mira's room and find Eugene waiting by the door. She lets us in, and we all grab seats around the room. Loveseat for Mira, an office chair for me, and Eugene sits on the bed.

"I think I should talk to Julia," Eugene says once we bring him up to speed on the whole situation. "If not Sam, she might know someone else who can help us."

"If you tell Julia about this, she'll most likely want to come," Mira says. "And I suspect you wouldn't want that."

"She wouldn't; she just got out of the hospital," Eugene says, but there is uncertainty in his voice.

"Even assuming that she would do the prudent thing and not join us, there is another problem with getting her involved," Mira says. "It might end up pulling her father, Jacob, into this, and I don't want to do that."

"Why?" I ask curiously.

"Because of his fear of exposure," Mira says. "This meeting is happening in a very public place—meaning that there's a chance that the confrontation with the Pusher could involve a lot of civilians."

"It's not like Jacob is this great humanitarian," Eugene

chimes in. "It's just that, as you learned the other day, he's obsessed with keeping Reader existence hidden. He's a Purist."

"Exactly," Mira confirms. "The last thing we want is him stopping us from acting."

"But the three of us stand no chance," Eugene says, his shoulders sagging. "So we might want to risk talking to Julia.

"The two of us," Mira corrects. "There is no reason for Darren to join this. It's not his fight. And not Julia's either—so no Julia."

"I'm going to help you," I surprise myself by saying. "You forget that this Pusher tried to have me killed."

He also might've killed my parents, but I don't mention this. That might be a topic for later.

"Okay, but that's still just the three of us," Eugene says, looking at me gratefully.

The look Mira gives me is harder to read. She seems to be reevaluating me again. I'm reevaluating myself too. Mira just gave me a way out, and instead of taking it, I'm volunteering to join them. And dealing with the Pusher who tried to kill me is only a fraction of my motivation. The bigger part is staring expectantly at me with those beautiful blue eyes.

"There might not just be the three of us," I say, growing uncomfortable with Mira's intent stare. "But before I get into that, I need to ask you: what's a Purist? You said Jacob was one. What does that mean?"

"Purists are Readers who try to stick to archaic traditions, such as assigned mating," Eugene says bitterly. "Their biggest fears are things like exposure to the outside world and dilution of the Reader blood."

"The only good thing about them is that they want to exterminate Pushers," Mira says.

That one hurts. And doesn't bode well for what I'm building up the courage to tell them. It especially hurts because I no longer think of myself as *that* kind of Pusher. The Pusher she hates would hate her also if he's a Traditionalist. It's ironic how much these Purists sound like the Traditionalists Thomas and Hillary described. I almost regret we can't get Jacob involved. It would be a sort of poetic justice to let the two orthodoxies fight it out. They sound like they deserve each other.

"Mira," Eugene says uncomfortably, "you don't mean that. Darren is a perfect example of why thinking that way is wrong."

"It's okay, Eugene," I say graciously. "I kind of understand Mira's hatred for Pushers. I mean, I hate the guy who tried to kill me in the hospital. But it's also a fact that not all Pushers are the same. In fact, I think only a tiny minority are like that fucker."

"I didn't mean you, Darren." Mira drops her gaze, as if embarrassed. "You're something else entirely."

"And if I were as much a Pusher as you are a Reader, would you try to kill me again?" I say, deciding to put my cards on the table.

"You know that I wouldn't." She looks at me again. "In any case, you said you don't even know who or what you are."

The good news is that she isn't taking out a gun. Yet.

"Right, I didn't," I say carefully. "But I learned more about myself yesterday—and even more just a few minutes ago. Most importantly, I learned that not all Pushers—or Guides, as they call themselves—are the evil monsters you think they are. In fact, most of them are regular people, just like me and you."

In the dead silence that follows, I tell Mira and Eugene an abbreviated version of what happened yesterday. About my shrink, about my aunt, about Thomas.

"So these Pusher Traditionalists are like our Purists?" Eugene says, staring at me.

"Yeah, and they sound just as fun too," I say.

"So it must've been one of *them* who killed Dad because of his research," Eugene whispers.

"I'm not sure you should blame whole groups of people, be it Pushers or Traditionalists among them," I say cautiously. "It might be just one crazy Pusher who took it upon himself to hire the Russian mobster we Read . . ."

"So you yourself are really a Pusher?" Mira says, clearly having a hard time digesting my story.

"I prefer Guide, but yeah, at least halfway, on my mother's side, I am. I still don't know much about my father, except I just confirmed that he was a Reader."

"But that's forbidden," Eugene says, his eyes widening.

"You're not one to judge," I say defensively. "Don't your people think half-bloods are forbidden, too?"

"It's different," he says uncertainly.

"Is it? Why couldn't you date Julia?" I say.

Eugene doesn't respond, and Mira seems to be trying to drill holes in me with her gaze.

"You lied when you said you were not feeling well when we spoke yesterday?" she finally says. To my surprise, that seems to upset her more than my being a Reader-Pusher hybrid. "You were actually going to a *party*?"

"I'm sorry I lied to you about that," I say to her honestly. "I just didn't think you'd like it if I told you the truth. 'Sorry, Mira—can't hang out, going to a Pusher party.'"

Eugene lets out a nervous chuckle and gets a furious look from his sister.

"And how do we know you're not lying right now, or haven't

been lying to us all this time?" Mira says, turning to glare at me. "You lie so well when it suits you. How do we know this isn't some kind of a Pusher trick?"

"A trick to do what, exactly?" I'm getting tired of constantly being accused. "Hand you the Pusher who killed your parents?"

"He's right, Mira," Eugene says soothingly. "I don't see what possible nefarious Pusher purpose could be served by all this."

"Fine. Let's say I believe you." Mira's expression doesn't soften. "What does it change? What do I care if some Pushers think they're good and call themselves Guides? It doesn't change the fact that one of them should die today. It doesn't change our lack of plans. And no matter what you say about the few people you've met, the fact remains that they, like you, can fuck with people's minds—and that's wrong."

"It does change things because I have a plan in mind," I retort. "And Reading can also be said to be fucking with people's minds. I think a lot of people would rather be made to do something than have their deepest secrets stolen."

"Just like a Pusher to twist the truth," Mira says angrily. "Mind fucking is obviously—"

"Mira, please stop," Eugene interrupts forcefully. He's using that rare 'big brother knows best' tone of voice. "Let Darren tell us how we can deal with the situation at hand. We can exchange xenophobic drivel later."

"Fine," she says, folding her arms across her chest. "Do enlighten us, Darren."

"Okay," I say. "Thomas, the *Guide* from the Secret Service I mentioned earlier, offered to help me. Originally, it was in the context of what to do if I learned the identity of the person who tried to kill me at the hospital. Still, I'm sure he might be helpful in this situation, too."

"And you think you can trust him?" Eugene asks doubtfully. "You only met him yesterday."

"And he's a Pusher," Mira mutters under her breath.

"I think I can trust him, yes. If I didn't trust him, it would certainly be for reasons other than his being a *Guide*," I say, emphasizing the politically correct term. "The person I *really* trust is my aunt, but I don't want to involve her in this situation."

Mira gets a look of concentration on her face for a moment. "Fine. I just talked to Eugene, and he convinced me to give this insane idea a shot."

"You talked—" I begin, but then I understand. She phased into the Quiet and pulled her brother in for a private conversation again.

"I'm sorry about that, Darren," Eugene confirms my suspicion. "We had to think about such an unusual proposition. I vouched for you because I now see you as a friend. I hope I don't regret it."

"So you didn't want to trust me," I say, looking at Mira. Figures.

"If she didn't, she wouldn't," Eugene says. "Mira doesn't—"

"Shut up, Zhenya," Mira says, giving him an icy stare. "Don't you understand the concept of a *private* conversation?"

"Let me check to make sure Thomas even wants to help us," I say. "Otherwise, this is all pointless."

Since no one objects, I take out my phone and call Thomas.

"Thomas, this is Darren," I say as soon as he picks up. "You said to call you if I needed help with the Guide who's trying to kill me."

"I did. What's going on?" Thomas sounds instantly alert. "Did you learn his identity already?"

"Not exactly," I say, trying to get my thoughts organized. "But I do know where he'll be later today, and I want to confront him. I'm with some friends of mine, but it's only the three of us."

"Okay, hold your horses," Thomas says. "Start from the beginning."

"What I didn't tell you yesterday was that I had a clue I was investigating. A clue related to the connection this Guide seems to have to some Russian criminals. My friend and I found out that he'll meet the people he controls on the Brooklyn Bridge today," I say.

"I see." Thomas sounds calm, as though people call him up with this sort of convoluted story all the time. "Your friends, who are they?"

"Well, that part's complicated," I say, cursing myself for not telling him about my Reader connection the other day. "They're what you would call Leachers."

"What?" His tone sharpens. "How do you know Leachers? What are you doing in their company? Are you okay?"

"It's three-twenty already," Mira says from the couch. "We have to start preparing."

"Look, Thomas," I say, realizing that she's right. "This thing is happening at four-thirty, so we're quickly running out of time. I am okay. My friends can be trusted. I have a very good explanation for everything, but we really have to get moving. Can we meet in person and talk in the Mind Dimension? This way, no time will pass on the outside."

He's silent for a very long moment. "Listen, Darren . . . We just met, and this is a lot to take in and not a lot of time for me to make decisions."

"I know, and I would be cautious too if I were you." I'm

cognizant of the fact that if I actually were him, I would've told me to go fuck myself. "There's something else you should know, something that might help you trust me. I learned at the party that Hillary is my aunt. You can ask her about that. She knows the whole story."

Another silence.

"You know," he says finally, "I actually think I see it. There's a distinct familial resemblance. I just didn't realize it until you told me. That's incredible."

"Yeah, I know," I say. "Does that help? We're running out of time here, Thomas."

"Assuming I agree to help, then yes. It takes care of a big problem I was going to raise before you brought up the Leachers."

"What problem?"

"You said there'll be a bunch of Russian gangsters and at least one Guide. To make matters worse, this thing is happening on a public bridge. Do you understand what that adds up to?"

"No, I am not sure that I do," I say, confused. "Trouble?"

"You can say that again. It means that this Guide will have a lot of people he can potentially turn against us. We might not survive this encounter, and even if we do, there might be severe civilian casualties."

"Shit," I say, looking at Mira and Eugene in despair. I hadn't thought that part through.

"There is a solution, though," Thomas says. "I need to make a call. Where are we meeting?"

"Let's meet at the South Street Seaport. Behind the mall. The part that faces the bridge," I suggest. "It seems fitting, given the view and its proximity to the meeting."

"Okay. I'll bring some supplies," Thomas says. "Can you be there in an hour? That would leave us enough time to get to the bridge even if we have to walk."

"Yes," I say, looking at Mira and mentally cringing at the thought of the drive ahead. "We can probably get there even sooner."

"Okay. See you there," Thomas says and hangs up the phone.

I meet Mira and Eugene's expectant gazes. "I think he'll help," I say, trying to sound more confident than I feel.

"Well, we need to get to the bridge regardless," Mira says matter-of-factly. "So meeting this guy is not going to sidetrack us too much. So long as it's not some Pusher trap."

"If it is, it would have nothing to do with me," I say.

"I know," Mira says. "It's not you that I don't trust."

I almost say 'since when,' but I hold my tongue. "Mira, I'm a good judge of character. It's a part of what I do for a living," I say, deciding that bending the truth might help ease her anxiety. "I think Thomas is going to help. I really do."

"We don't have a lot of choices, Mira," Eugene adds. "We can't take them all on with just the three of us. At least this guy works in the Secret Service."

"I said meeting this guy is not going to sidetrack us," Mira says, getting up and walking to a night stand. "So stop selling me the car I already bought."

She takes a gun from inside the night dresser. "Zhenya, do you have yours?" she says as she stuffs it into the back of her pants.

"Yes, in my room." Her brother also gets up.

"Okay, go get it, and meet us downstairs," she says to Eugene in a commanding tone.

It looks like she's bossed him around before, because he rushes out of the room without hesitation or backtalk.

"What about you, Darren?" she says, her voice getting a bit softer.

"I have a gun in the glove compartment of the rental," I say. "But I hope I don't need to use it."

"We have to be ready for anything," Mira says and walks out of the room.

26

"You're going to kill us, Mira." Eugene is plastered against the passenger door as we run the second red light. We exited the Battery Tunnel just moments ago, but we've already flown though five blocks. "Seriously, we're not *that* pressed for time."

"We never should've taken that fucking tunnel," she says, swerving suddenly. I think she just scared a cab driver—and those guys have seen everything. I've always thought they were the ones driving like maniacs, but they've got nothing on Mira. Hell, even Caleb isn't as bad. But she's still eighteen, and thinks she's indestructible. I, by the way, never had that delusion. I'm only too aware of how destructible I am.

"There was traffic leading up to the bridges," Eugene mumbles, still defending the suggestion he made earlier to take the tunnel.

The constant bickering Eugene and Mira engage in makes Mira's horrible driving an even worse experience. They argue about how fast she should drive, which cars not to cut off, and the best route. Until now, I thought my moms were the worst people to be in a car with, but apparently I was wrong. Is this how all siblings behave, or am I just lucky to be in a car with a particularly bad example?

The rest of the trip lasts about three deep breaths, and then Mira swerves into a parking garage, tires screeching. I estimate that she enters it at about thirty miles per hour, but I could be lowballing it.

When I open the car door, there is a definite smell of burned tires.

As she hands the valet the keys, the expression on the guy's face is priceless. I give him a hundred-dollar bill to get him out of his stupor and instruct him to wait at least twenty minutes before parking the car. We might return right away if we decide to drive to the Brooklyn Bridge after our talk with Thomas.

We run from the garage to the meeting spot. Despite the tenseness of the situation, I notice the beautiful view. It's soothing to see the old ships anchored here at the Seaport, and it makes me wonder about the days when this was an active port. Near-death experiences seem to do that for me—they bring out my sentimental side.

It's a nice Saturday afternoon, and we're soon confronted with a crowd of people. They're mainly tourists, but there are some locals here as well. Mira makes way for us through the crowd, rudely elbowing everyone aside.

We're near the corner of the meeting spot, near the benches looking out onto the water, when the world goes silent. The crowds around us freeze, as do Mira and Eugene.

"Hello, nephew," says a familiar, high-pitched voice. "You should really return my calls."

Hillary is standing next to my frozen self, with her hand on the frozen self's cheek. Thomas is standing next to her.

"You called me?" I say, surprised to see her there.

"Yeah, like twenty times."

"Sorry I missed it. I was too busy keeping my lunch in my stomach. Mira's driving is insane." I'm finally getting rid of the strange shock that accompanies forced phasing. It's always spooky being in the Quiet in a crowded and noisy place like this. My brain expects people to start walking and talking, but they don't. Being pulled into this state without warning makes the disorientation worse.

"Which one is Mira?" Hillary examines a couple of pretty girls.

"Who's Mira?" Thomas peers at the crowd. "Is that one of the Leachers you mentioned?"

"I didn't fill him in yet," Hillary says. "You might want to tell him the full story."

Before I tackle the mystery of Hillary's presence, I do as she suggests and tell Thomas everything. I have to give Thomas his due. He doesn't freak out about having to deal with Readers, unlike my Russian friends' reaction to working with Guides. He also takes in stride the fact that I'm a weird hybrid of both groups. I suppose his upbringing—not being part of the Guide community from birth—can explain it. Still, bigotry is all too easy to adopt, so the fact that he seems to have an open mind on the matter only reinforces my positive impression of him.

"So which one is she?" Hillary says. "I'm going to die of curiosity."

"There," I say, pointing at Mira. "The one who's slicing through the crowd like an impolite knife through butter."

"Very pretty." Hillary smiles her approval. "But then I assumed she would be."

"Yeah." I shrug. "Can I bring her in? That guy with glasses is Eugene, her brother."

"Hold on," Thomas says. "Let's talk privately first."

"Okay," I say, "now that I've explained myself, why don't the two of you tell me why Hillary is here?"

"If you took my calls, you'd know my reason for being here." She gives me a determined look. "I'm joining this mission."

"What? No, you're not." I turn to Thomas. "Tell her it's not happening."

"You need me," Hillary insists, and Thomas nods.

She gives me a smug look. "See? And you're not in a position to tell me what to do."

"Of course not," I say quickly, not wanting to offend her. "That was not my intent. I just don't want you getting hurt, that's all."

"That would be sweet if it weren't insulting. Why am I more likely to get hurt than your girlfriend, for example?"

"I don't want her to be here, either. It's just that I can't stop Mira from going. She's a bit tougher than you . . ." I'm completely failing at finding a graceful exit out of my verbal mess.

"Uh oh, Darren. Are you saying Hillary isn't as tough because of her size? You're new to the community; otherwise, you'd know she doesn't like her size criticized." Thomas's tone is serious, but the corners of his eyes are crinkling with amusement.

"My size has nothing to do with anything," Hillary says, elbowing Thomas in the hip. "In this situation, I'm the one person you all need."

Thomas nods again. "Right. Remember that problem I told you about?" he says. "How the Guide can use everyone on that bridge against us?"

I look at Hillary, remembering what she told me about her Reach. "You think you can override anyone he controls?"

"The person we're going after could be a *she,* but yes," Hillary says. "I have the best chance of anyone I know."

"It's true," Thomas confirms. "You have to trust me, Darren. Hillary has a very good reason to be here. I wouldn't have brought her otherwise."

"And I wouldn't have come if he didn't drop your name, Darren," she says. "I'm still a bit hesitant, but I think my presence can actually help avoid any unnecessary violence."

"Now that we have established who should be here, it might be a good moment to point out who probably shouldn't," Thomas says, pointedly glancing at Mira and Eugene.

"We can't *not* take them. It's Mira's revenge," I say, my eyes lingering on Mira's face. "She's been doing nothing but dreaming about getting this person."

"You're just building the case against taking her. She sounds like she could be a liability," Thomas says. "She's likely to do something reckless and get herself or us in danger."

"I don't think we have much choice," I say. "She'll be there, no matter what we do. If we want to avoid violence, we better take her with us."

"Also, we might actually use them for my plan," Hillary says. "It's very crowded there, and they can help Darren with the Reading."

"Fine," Thomas says cautiously. "But I don't like it."

"Duly noted," Hillary says, winking at me. "We'll put that into the report, Mr. Secret Service."

"Pull them in," Thomas says, and I do.

In a moment, Eugene is staring at me, his jaw slack and his eyes wide. In contrast, Mira seems calm, and she's studying the new people inquisitively.

I make quick work of introductions.

"Hillary has a plan," I say. "Do you mind telling us what it is, Aunty?"

"I thought I told you not to call me that," she begins saying, and then cuts herself off. "Never mind. You're just like your mother in this. If I let it bother me, you'll just do it more often." She chuckles before turning to face Eugene and Mira. "I do have a plan," she says. "Why don't we walk over to those benches before I explain it? It might take a few minutes."

"Sure," Mira says, and makes us a path again, violently shoving frozen people aside. I guess this is her way of expressing her feelings about having to work with Pushers.

"She's feisty," Hillary whispers as we walk through a tunnel made of bodies left in Mira's wake.

"Tell me about it," I whisper back, making my voice as low as possible.

"Gorgeous ambience," Hillary says when we get to our destination. She's right; this place is famous for its awesome view of the Brooklyn Bridge.

"We didn't come here for sightseeing," Mira says testily. "Let's hear your plan, Pusher."

"First and foremost, young lady, you will not use that derogatory term on me." Hillary gives her a stern look. "I prefer *Guide,* if you must talk about my abilities at all."

"She didn't—" Eugene begins.

"I can speak for myself," Mira interrupts. "I'm sorry. I'll call you whatever you want if you'll just please hurry up."

"Sure," Hillary says. "Here's what I have in mind . . ."

And in the silence that follows, she walks us through her idea.

"That sounds as good as anything I could've thought of," says Thomas.

"Coming from you, I'll take that as a huge compliment." Hillary beams at him.

"I'm game," Mira says. "This should work."

"Me too," Eugene says.

"I guess I'm okay with it also," I say. "Sounds fairly safe."

"Exactly," Hillary says. "My main objective is that no one gets hurt."

I notice Mira's eyes gleam dangerously every time Hillary says something along those lines, but I keep quiet. There isn't much to be said.

We all walk with Hillary to where her body is. She's the one whose version of the Quiet we're all in.

"How are we going to get there?" I ask as Hillary is about to take us out of the Quiet.

"It's walkable," says Thomas. "But I'd rather drive there. If the plan goes south, we might need a ride nearby."

Everyone agrees, and Thomas convinces all of us that his car should be the one we take.

As soon as we get out of the Quiet, we walk to his car—a black minivan half a block away.

"How did you *not* get your car towed, parking there?" Eugene asks, impressed. "Or at least not get a ticket?"

"I have special plates," Thomas says, opening the side door. "I can park wherever I want."

Inside the car, behind the second seat, is a whole arsenal of weapons. No wonder Thomas wanted to take this car.

"I'm not touching a gun," Hillary says as soon as she sees Thomas's stockpile. "Don't even try to convince me."

"You're staying in the car anyway, so you should be okay." Thomas smirks. "Besides, I bet that if you needed a gun, you'd forget all about your pacifist principles. Just like if you were starving, you'd eat bacon. How about you guys? Can I interest you in a weapon, just in case?"

"I have my own," I say, tapping the back of my pants where I have the gun Caleb gave me.

"Same here." Mira mirrors my tap.

"Me too," Eugene echoes.

"Okay," Thomas says. "Then it's just me." He straps on a holster and puts a gun in it. He also puts a huge hunting knife in a scabbard on his belt.

"There's really no need for this," Hillary objects. "My plan doesn't require any guns."

"It's just for contingency," he says. "Now, everyone, please get in. We have to go."

"I call shotgun," I say and get into the front seat.

Mira, Eugene, and Hillary climb in the back.

"Buckle up," Thomas says and starts the car.

It takes us two or three minutes to get to the spot where the traffic is turning onto the Brooklyn Bridge.

"Here," Thomas says. "Darren, since you insisted, Split, now."

I find that the pre-plan jitters aid me in phasing.

That's part one of the plan.

I now need to pull everyone into the Quiet with me.

Originally, Hillary wanted to do this herself, saying she's the most logical choice as one with the most Reach. I insisted that it be me. I explained to her that I have previously spent hours in the Quiet, so the relatively short amount of time the plan requires should be a snap for me.

I'm not sure why I did it. Probably to show off in front of Mira. But there was a practical side to it, too. Hillary needs to worry about bigger, more important aspects of the plan.

I phase and end up outside the car. That's interesting. Usually, I would show up in the back seat. Because the seat is taken by my friends, however, it seems that my body chose to show up outside. I wonder how this works. The Pusher in Caleb's memory was able to control this process. Maybe I can figure out a way to do the same? Then I remind myself that maybe it's bad luck to want to be like that Pusher at a time like this. After all, Caleb killed him.

The cars around us are standing still. No honking or sounds of any kind. The silence seems foreboding all of a sudden.

Okay, I need to snap out of this funk. The plan is simple and easy. No danger.

To bring the rest of the crew into the Quiet with me, I touch them, one by one, through the car window.

"We walk from here," Thomas says when he shows up.

We cross in front of the frozen cars and walk away from the road. Right over on the other side is the pedestrian portion of the Brooklyn Bridge.

As expected on a nice Saturday afternoon, the place is extremely congested, but the plan allowed for this eventuality.

"As we agreed, I'll go ahead," says Thomas. "My job is to recognize the Guide. Otherwise, you risk pulling him into the Mind Dimension with us, and that wouldn't be smart."

"I'm still not sure about this part. It's actually one of the weaker points of the plan," Eugene says.

"How so?" Hillary says, looking up at him.

"How do you know that you'll recognize him?" Eugene says to Thomas.

"Well," Thomas says, "from what all of you have told me, it seems a near certainty that this Guide lives in New York. I mean, there's no way someone from out of town would be able to Guide so many people here and over such a length of time. And if he's indeed local, I will know him."

"I guess it could work," Eugene concedes, "if you have a good memory."

"There aren't that many of us," Hillary says. "Even I could do it, and I'm a bit of a recluse. Thomas is new, so he's recently been explicitly introduced to everyone by his girlfriend, who's our official social butterfly."

"Who's the girlfriend?" I ask, although I already suspect the answer.

"Liz, of course." Hillary smiles. "You didn't figure that out?"

"No, not really. The fact that he's her patient kind of threw me off," I say, hoping I don't piss off Thomas. Now that I think about it, I realize that the lack of significant-other pictures in Liz's office is explained by the semi-forbidden nature of her relationship with Thomas. Obviously, she wouldn't want to acknowledge him as her boyfriend in the work setting.

"Focus, people," Thomas interrupts. "I need your heads in the game. You can gossip later, when we're done with this."

"Yes, sir. Sorry, sir." Hillary salutes him.

Mira watches the whole exchange with a strange expression on her face. I wonder if her world just became more complicated. Before meeting these two, she'd thought all Pushers were evil, so everything was simple and clearcut. But now she's met her so-called enemies, and they—especially my aunt—probably don't fit Mira's evil-villain stereotype.

Thomas leaves, ignoring Hillary's mockery. As he moves a few feet away, he becomes difficult to see in the crowd. This place is much too packed to suit me.

"We have a lot of work to do," I say, looking over the crowd.

"Then let's start working instead of talking," Mira says and approaches a buff-looking guy to the right of us.

"She just skipped those four people," Hillary says, pointing at two elderly couples nearest us.

"Right, they're the Russian Mafia, for sure," I say, unable to resist a snarky tone. "I know you said we need to identify the mobsters in the crowd, particularly if any are trying to be stealthy, but I'm pretty sure they're all going to be much younger than these four."

This is the part of Hillary's plan that found good use for Mira and Eugene. They're supposed to help identify the gangsters in this crowd by Reading. I have my doubts about this being necessary, as I suspect mobsters won't be trying for stealth. I bet we'll find them hanging out together someplace. Still, since finding a use for Mira and Eugene meant they got to come along, I kept my mouth shut.

In any case, if any Russian gangsters are found in this way, Hillary will supply them with some special instructions. Then my aunt, Thomas, and I will instruct everyone else to leave the bridge as fast as humanly possible, but in an orderly fashion. This way, we'll clear the place of any innocent bystanders.

"It's ageism," Hillary says stubbornly, interrupting my thought process. "You're implying that people of a certain age are not capable of something that someone younger can do. And where do you draw the age line? Fifty? Sixty?"

"Hillary, we might end up spending a day in the Mind Dimension if we check every single one of these people," I say, trying to placate her. "Let's say, due to this profiling, you tell a mobster or two to evacuate the bridge by mistake. It won't be the end of the world."

"Fine," she says and approaches the elderly couples.

Because Hillary can do her thing by a simple touch, Mira, Eugene, and I leave all the unlikely candidates for her.

I get to my job, which combines Guiding uninvolved people to evacuate with the work Mira and Eugene are doing—since, like them, I can Read.

I approach the first candidate, a muscular guy, with a scar on his cheek. He, in theory, could be one of Arkady's men.

I touch his forearm and concentrate.

WE WORRY ABOUT THE WHITE LIES WE PUT IN OUR DATING profile. Particularly those lies by omission.

Will she want to date a war vet? And if so, what about a vet who might actually have PTSD? Or do we have panic attacks? Would the difference even matter to her?

I disassociate with the conclusion that this one is not a mobster.

That established, I begin part two.

'The date is going to happen in Battery Park instead of here. It's a much longer walk and probably much less crowded. Text the date and change the venue. Walk off the bridge in an orderly fashion. Focus on not trampling anyone. When you begin to have the next PTSD episode or a panic attack, you'll feel relaxed, the anxiety will leave your body, and you'll begin to forget what caused this problem in the first place.'

Convinced the guy will leave the bridge and potentially have less of a PTSD problem, I exit his head.

One down, hundreds more to go. I take out a magic marker that I got from a pack Thomas had in his glove compartment, and put a big X on this guy's head. This way, Hillary will know he's been processed already. Eugene is putting a circle on his targets' heads to signify that they're clean and should be Guided to evacuate. Mira is using lipstick to draw her circles. In case it isn't obvious, the forehead marking was my idea.

I look around and see a guy with a shaved head. He looks more like an athlete, but it's feasible that he could be a mobster. He becomes my next target.

I quickly learn that the athlete is actually a plumber with a bodybuilding hobby. More importantly, though, he's not a criminal of any kind.

I am out of his head and ready to draw my X when I get approached by Thomas.

"I checked about a quarter of the bridge and didn't see anyone I recognize," he says. "How are things going back here?"

"Just look at the foreheads. These two big guys are clean," I say.

"Those four over there also," Eugene says, overhearing our conversation.

"That guy too," Mira adds from a few feet away. "And that woman."

Why she even checked a woman, I have no idea, but I don't say anything lest Hillary accuse me of sexism this time.

"I just took care of those elderly people and two children," Hillary says. "Even if we skip the unlikely targets, as Darren suggested, this will take a really long while. I didn't anticipate this many people being here."

"It's not like we're getting older or missing any appointments, with the time stopped and all," Eugene says.

"True, but this can be very tedious," I say. "We might need to get more selective in our choices. Rather than just younger, buffer men, why don't we focus on ones that have a criminal look to them also?"

"That's even worse profiling," Hillary says unhappily. "And it can lead to a lot more mobsters walking away. I'm not comfortable with that."

"I have an idea that can at least take care of the second problem," Thomas says. "We can add a compulsion for anyone remotely suspicious to give up their gun to the next police officer they see."

"That's clever," Hillary says, looking relieved. "People without guns simply won't comply. They won't have the context for the induction. So only the guilty will be impacted."

"Of course, some mobsters might not have a gun," I say. "And some innocent people might have a permit to carry a concealed weapon."

"What kind of criminals would they be without guns? But if they are, I say it's their lucky day—they get away free," Eugene says. "And the people who lawfully carry a concealed gun will end up showing their permit to the cops, get a breathalyzer test for doing something so wacky, and get let go. No harm, no foul."

"I agree," Mira says. "If we miss a few, it's not going to be that big of a deal."

"We still need a good number of mobsters to deal with the Guide. He might not be here alone," Thomas reminds us.

The plan is to have a bunch of Russian mobsters prohibit the Guide from leaving the bridge. Because Hillary is going to command them, in theory at least, the Guide we're targeting won't be able to override her because of her longer Reach. That's why she's so critical for this plan—and why I'm supposed to give any real mobster I find to her.

"I wouldn't worry about that," Mira says. "Most likely, the men we saw at that table in the banya are all here in one large group, and there will be plenty for that part of the plan."

"Okay, then that settles it," says Thomas. "I'll also take part in the evacuation now that we have a better way of doing it."

"Just mark up the people as you finish with them, like these guys have been doing, so we don't duplicate our efforts," Hillary says.

"Does anyone have anything to write with?" Thomas says.

"Here, use my eye shadow pencil," Mira says, handing him the strange writing instrument.

She uses way too much makeup, I decide. Especially since I know for a fact she looks amazing without it. I saw her first thing in the morning the other day, and she was drop-dead gorgeous. Unless she sleeps with makeup on. Can that be done?

"Put an X on the foreheads of everyone you Guided to evacuate," I remind Thomas as he takes Mira's pencil.

He walks off, saying nothing about the indignity of this marking. He had a problem with this part when we were talking about Hillary's plan. Indeed, he had an even bigger problem with my original idea for this—taking people's pants off, or just pushing them to the ground, like logs. This current system is actually a compromise.

I choose two new potentials. Both end up being civilians, and both get instructions to get off the bridge and give their concealed guns to the next police officer they see. Both get marked.

I fleetingly wonder how many non-mobster people who happen to have illegally concealed guns will end up getting into trouble today because of us. Oh well, that's their problem for carrying a gun without a permit.

I'm approaching my next target when I feel a delicate hand on my shoulder. "Darren, I wanted to speak to you," Mira says quietly when I turn to face her.

"What's up?" I ask, matching her volume.

"When we find the Pusher, the one responsible for my parents' death, I'm not going to follow the plan," she says, standing up on tiptoes to speak almost directly into my ear.

"Mira, please, this is a good plan. Don't do anything rash," I say, my heart beating faster—and not just because of her soft lips brushing sensually against my ear.

"I'm not an idiot," she whispers. "I'm going to wait until he's trapped first. But once he's trapped, instead of handing him over to the rest of the Pushers like Hillary wants, I'm going to kill him."

"I don't think that's a good idea," I say, confused as to why she's even telling me this. I'd wondered why Mira took that portion of the plan so calmly, given her desire for vengeance. Now I know. She never intended to go along with it. She wanted to double cross Hillary and Thomas.

"I'll need your help," she says. "I'll need you to lock the car after I run out, and slow them down in any way possible."

"No, Mira, I don't think I can do that," I say. "But how about this? As soon as we get back to reality, I'll Split and pull you in.

Then we can talk about this. Okay? Promise you won't act until we talk?"

"Fine, we'll talk," she whispers. "But with or without your help, Arkady and the Pusher are not leaving this bridge alive."

And before I get a chance to respond, she walks away.

Thomas was right; we should've come without her. It's too late now, though. Maybe I can do something to stop her, like locking the car *before* she runs out. I can also phase out and warn Thomas and Hillary. But Mira trusted me, and I'm having a hard time picturing myself betraying her trust like that. Plus, there's a tiny part of me that agrees with her. My aunt is much too peaceful. Arkady's men repeatedly tried to kill me and my friends, and it was the Pusher who was pulling their strings. If those two die, I won't cry over them at all.

I walk further, avoiding a few people Thomas had marked, and head toward a small clearing in the crowd. Thanks to the clearing, I see Thomas in the distance.

And that's when I register the sight in front of me.

It's as Mira suspected.

All the Russian goons from the banya are standing in the middle of the Brooklyn Bridge. Only they're dressed now and very likely armed.

There's a clearing around them, probably because people were instinctively giving this group a wide berth. I don't blame the prudent pedestrians. I would've avoided these Russians myself.

Approaching them, I put circles on each forehead with an X underneath. A sort of skull and bones mark I came up with to signify the mobsters. None of them were otherwise marked, which means that Thomas isn't insane in his profiling. He rightfully realized these aren't innocent bystanders.

Now we need Hillary.

"Hillary," I yell, looking back. "Best come take a look at this. I think we're pretty much done with one part of the plan."

I see a tiny hand wave above the crowd for a moment. Did my aunt have to jump to make that happen? Or did Eugene lift her?

I decide to follow Thomas and tell him the news, because it doesn't seem like he heard me yell for Hillary.

As I head in his direction, I see Thomas.

He's touching someone.

Someone I recognize.

"Thomas, no! Stop!" I yell, hoping it's not too late.

But it is.

In a moment, we're going to have a new presence in the Quiet—someone who shouldn't be here at all.

27

I RUDELY PUSH ASIDE THE PEOPLE IN MY WAY, TRYING TO GET closer. As if getting closer is going to change anything.

Thomas's hand is resting on Jacob's shoulder, his fingers almost brushing against the man's neck.

Yes, Jacob—the leader of the Reader community. The man who gave me that 'no disclosure of powers' lecture the other day and mentioned the name of my father.

The last person I expected to see on this bridge.

I look closer and get another surprise. Next to Jacob is Sam, the guy Caleb mentioned as potentially helping us. A man Caleb called a machine. That Jacob is with Sam makes sense. Sam is security, like Caleb. But the fact they're *here* makes no sense at all.

The world seems to slow, even in the Quiet—or maybe it's just my thoughts that speed up.

Did Caleb call in Sam despite my being against it? No, that

wouldn't explain anything. I never told Caleb any details about this meeting. It has to be something else.

Did Eugene talk to Julia after all, and did she tell everything to her father? Eugene never left my sight, but maybe he did it in the Quiet? Would Eugene be so stupid? I can't imagine that he would be. There must be another explanation.

Then I wonder if the Readers might be after the same Pusher as us, for their own reasons, and they're here trying to get him too. This is a more plausible guess, but the coincidence of it would be too great. And why only Jacob and Sam? Why wouldn't they bring Caleb's whole team, plus the man himself?

And then I notice a briefcase in Jacob's hand.

A briefcase. The man on the phone was supposed to bring money for Arkady, and a briefcase seems like a good way to transport bundles of cash.

Can it be?

Is it possible that instead of a powerful Pusher, it had been Jacob—a Reader—on the phone?

That would explain why the mysterious puppet-master used the phone in the first place. True, it's easier to call people than walk over and touch them in the Quiet, but phone calls are easier to trace, and the mastermind in all this always seemed to be extra paranoid. And why waste money on a convoluted hit list if you can just make Arkady kill whomever you want for free?

If Jacob is the man on the phone, everything changes.

Thomas is within an inch of touching Jacob. I take out my gun, confused thoughts still buzzing in my head.

Could it have been Jacob who ordered me to be shot? Maybe he saw my resemblance to my father? He did mention on Skype that I looked familiar. If he knew whom my father married, it's not a big leap to assume that I'm a hybrid. And what could be worse than a hybrid to a Purist like Jacob? Not much, I imagine. Is it possible that Jacob had Caleb bring me to him in order to observe my reaction to the name *Mark Robinson*? With hindsight, it does make sense. There was no reason for Jacob to personally warn me against revealing my powers; Caleb or any other Reader could've done that.

As I think these thoughts, the fear that overtakes me is so intense, I half-expect to phase into the Quiet—except I'm already there. So I don't phase; I just feel odd as the feeling intensifies. Phasing must provide me some relief in tense moments like these because I've never felt so much like jumping out of my skin before.

And then I see a second, not-frozen Jacob show up behind Thomas. This Jacob looks around him in confusion for only a moment. When he sees Thomas touching his frozen body, he seems to realize what happened. I can tell what he's thinking: someone pulled him into the Quiet.

Someone he doesn't recognize.

If Jacob's here for the reason I suspect, then he'll be scared now. He'll be feeling cornered.

For my part, the feeling is one of stunned immobility. I watch, in a trance-like state, as Jacob jumps back. He throws the briefcase he's been holding to the side, and begins to reach with the freed hand into the back of his pants.

When the briefcase hits the ground, it breaks open. Bundles of hundred-dollar bills spill onto the pavement.

There's no longer any doubt.

Jacob *is* the man on the phone—the paymaster for whom we laid this trap.

And that means Thomas is in danger, I realize instantly. We all are.

Metal flashes as Jacob removes his hand from the back of his pants. He's holding a gun now.

Why hasn't Thomas turned around already? I think in mute terror. Couldn't he hear the sound of the briefcase landing and splitting open? Or is he so focused on the Guiding that he's oblivious to his surroundings?

I raise my own gun and fire, aiming upwards.

It would've been better to shoot at Jacob perhaps, but I don't trust my marksmanship skills. Not with him so close to Thomas. Besides, I'd rather wound Jacob than kill him. That, unlike death, is reversible upon phasing out and would allow us to ask Jacob several pertinent questions.

The noise of my gun is deafening. It's like a roar of thunder, made stronger by the fact that my ears had adjusted to the almost absolute silence of the Quiet.

Thomas instantly turns around—which, of course, was my intent. There's no way he could've missed *that* terrible noise.

Everything that follows happens with astonishing speed.

Thomas turns and sees the man he just tried to Guide standing behind him, holding a gun. I would've expected Thomas to be confused, but instead, his reaction is lightning-fast.

With one swift motion, Thomas kicks the gun out of Jacob's hand. I wonder if my gunshot disoriented Jacob, causing him to become an easy target for that kick. Some Caleb-and-Haim-forged part of my mind also registers an extra detail about Thomas's maneuver.

It was a kickboxing move.

Almost immediately, Thomas punches the now-disarmed Jacob in the face.

That's a traditional boxing uppercut, the same fight-attuned part of my brain informs me.

Jacob staggers backwards. His movements seem to slow. That hit must've really taken his brain for a spin.

Thomas closes the distance between them in one powerful lunge and executes another punch. Boxing again, but this time mixed with something I can't even place.

Jacob staggers back again and falls. He looks drunk, like boxers do when they get that final knockout punch. Only he doesn't stay down. Instead, he begins crawling on the ground a little to the left of Thomas.

I see Thomas watching him. It's hard for me to tell if the expression on Thomas's face is disgust or pity, but what's clear is that he's not hurting Jacob for the moment. Maybe, like me, he wants him alive for questioning. Otherwise, it would be an easy thing for him to end the fight with just a single shot, or even a few well-placed kicks.

But then I understand what Jacob is trying to do.

"Kick him!" I try to scream at Thomas, but my voice is hoarse. Seeing that Thomas doesn't hear me, or doesn't understand what I'm saying, I raise my gun and point it at Jacob. At the last moment, I hesitate. I still don't trust my aim, and they're way too close to each other. So instead of shooting, I clear my throat, preparing to let out the loudest scream of my life. At the same time, Jacob speeds up his crawl, and his hand is by Sam's pant leg.

Jacob is about to pull Sam into the Quiet.

"Fucking shoot him, Thomas!" I scream, this time loudly. "Now!"

Thomas looks at me instead. I point at Jacob with an exaggerated gesture and slice the edge of my palm across my throat in the universal 'kill him' signal. Nodding, Thomas turns toward Jacob and raises his gun.

Only it's too late. Jacob rolls up Sam's jeans and grabs the big man's ankle.

"Watch out!" I yell at Thomas again. I also ready my own gun, determined to risk taking that shot if I have to. If Caleb is to be believed, Sam's a much more dangerous opponent than Jacob. He's on par with Caleb himself—and I've seen what Caleb can do. It's ironic that the man we almost asked for help is the very one we need help from.

I try to focus. I can't miss the moment Sam materializes in the Quiet. When he does, I'm taking my chances with my aim. There's no other choice.

Meanwhile, Thomas, after a brief hesitation, shoots Jacob in the chest. I'm startled by the noise, and also shocked by this turn, even though I was the one who suggested it. I hope that Thomas knows what Jacob just did, that he pulled in reinforcements. Is that why Thomas made that shot? Did he make a decision to keep his enemy's numbers controllable?

I'm still looking around for Sam, and so is Thomas.

And then another gunshot threatens to damage my eardrums. I look around and see, in absolute horror, that Thomas is clutching his chest. There is a circle of red spreading there.

No. This can't be happening. That's the only thought in my mind as Thomas makes a whimpering sound and slowly falls to his knees.

"No!" I hear a high-pitched voice echoing my thought from

a foot away from me. It must be Hillary and the others, catching up with us. I have no time to check, however.

Now that Thomas is on his knees, I see where Sam materialized in the Quiet. He was directly behind Thomas from my vantage point. That's why I heard the shot, but didn't see the shooter.

The shooter who's now looking in my general direction and carefully aiming his gun.

I fire. The good news is that I at least don't shoot Thomas. He's still clutching his chest, but the fact that he's still upright, albeit on his knees, fills me with a sliver of hope. Maybe Sam's bullet went through his body without damaging any vital organs? Maybe it's just a flesh wound?

The bad news is that I clearly missed Sam, because he's standing unharmed.

Standing unharmed and firing his own gun—which is pointed at me.

Sam's gunshot is the scariest sound I have ever heard in my life. It seems to vibrate and fill my very being with dread. But as the feeling that my ears might bleed fades, I realize that I'm intact.

And then I see why.

Sam wasn't aiming at me. He was aiming at Thomas. I'm numb with disbelief as I watch Thomas falling to the ground, a pool of blood forming around his head.

The enormity of this loss is worsened by the knowledge that Thomas was the only one of us who would've stood a chance against Sam. And now Thomas is dead.

And we're fucked.

As I stand there, dazed, I see a gun appear from behind me. I recognize the slender long-fingered hands holding the weapon.

It's Mira's hands.

As I register this fact, she pulls the trigger.

At the same time, Sam does some military maneuver, where he rolls on the floor. I've seen this in movies, but never in the real life. Mira's shot must've missed him because I see Sam roll up to Thomas's dead body and turn it sideways, using our dead friend's body as a makeshift shield.

Sick with dread, I aim and take another shot. At the same time, two more shots get fired. It must be Eugene and Mira shooting at the same time, I realize vaguely.

"Darren, run!" Hillary yells, and I hear her acting on her suggestion.

"We should follow her." It's Eugene, sounding frantic.

I hear the sound of his departing feet, and then Mira yells, "We should cover them!" and fires another shot at Sam.

I glance back to see Mira backing away. I follow her example, shooting in the general direction of Sam as I begin to back away myself.

Sam peeks from his hiding place and fires another shot. I brace for the pain, but instead I hear an agonized shriek behind me.

From where Eugene and Hillary are.

Forgetting about creating the cover fire, I rush toward my friends. Mira does the same.

We see Eugene standing over Hillary, who's on the ground.

"She's alive," Eugene says quickly. "It's her leg. She's been shot in the knee."

He must be babbling in shock because it's obvious my aunt is alive. She's wailing like a banshee and clutching her leg.

In shock myself, I realize that I've kept my eyes off Sam for too long. I turn around—and see Sam standing much closer to us. Having abandoned his makeshift human shield, he's now in a half-kneeling position, using his knee to stabilize his gun while aiming at us.

Both Mira and I raise our guns in unison and fire. Sam's own shot echoes ours.

I brace for pain, but it doesn't come. Instead, I hear a thumping sound nearby. I again feel like I'm about to phase into the Quiet, only this time the feeling of frustration at it not happening is even more intense. Filled with terror, I look back. The pavement behind me is covered with blood.

And then I see its source.

It's Eugene. He's on the ground, convulsing, blood and brain matter seeping out from what's left of his head.

I feel sick, but I can't vomit. My brain feels woolen, my thoughts slow with stunned disbelief. Surely this is just a nightmare that I'll wake up screaming from. Eugene can't be dead. He can't be. It's only now that I realize how much I liked him. How I had begun to think of him as a friend. He can't be gone.

But I don't wake up in bed screaming. Instead, I turn and shoot again, over and over, trying to channel my hatred for Sam into every bullet.

The fucker seems unharmed, however. He's impossible to hit, with all the stupid rolling maneuvers that he does. I shoot again, but he rolls forward, doing something that looks almost like a somersault.

When he lands, I squeeze the trigger again, but my gun makes an empty clicking sound.

"Run, Darren!" Mira yells, taking a step forward. "You need to get out. Before he gets you too."

She takes careful aim and shoots. I hear a grunt and see Sam clutching his hand. Mira managed to hit his gun hand. I feel a wave of relief.

Emboldened by her success, Mira shoots again, but this time she misses. Sam does another one of those cursed rolls.

"Run, I said!" Mira screams, but I can't bring myself to move. Does she really expect me to leave her to fight Sam on her own? No fucking way.

And then it hits me. Maybe I do have to do what Mira says. If I get out in time, get back to my frozen self in the car, and phase us all out of the Quiet, I can at least save Hillary. No matter what damage Hillary received here in the Quiet, once she's pulled out of it, she'll be whole again. But what about Mira? If I leave her behind, she might be dead before I can get us all out.

"You run!" I yell at Mira. "I'll follow you."

Not waiting to see if she will follow my command, I frantically glance back at Sam. He's holding a knife now.

I know what I have to do. I have to attack him, to slow him down. As I think about this, I again experience that feeling. Like I'm about to phase into the Quiet. This time, though, it does something.

Time seems to slow down for me.

In this slow motion, I begin running toward him. As I run, I watch Sam's left hand grip the knife by the blade. His arm swings back, and then he lets the deadly projectile fly. In this same slow motion, I see the knife rotating in the air as it flies toward us. I try to brace myself—but then I see that the knife is not flying at me.

It's flying at Mira.

With an explosion of despair, I see the knife make the last deadly rotation as it strikes Mira's chest. It penetrates deeply, almost to the hilt, and I hear a scream of agony escape Mira's mouth.

Some irrational part of me wonders if I can run, phase us out before the knife does its deadly work, but then I remember the distance to the car and abandon that option. It's too far.

Mira's hands clutch the hilt of the knife, and a look of utter dread crosses her face. For the first time, I see her as the young and fragile woman that she is. Our eyes meet as she begins to cough up blood. Slowly, almost gracefully, she falls down. By the time she hits the ground, those deep blue eyes that are still staring into mine lose their focus.

She's dead.

No. I can't accept that—because if I do, I'll fall on the ground in grief. And I can't fall. Not now. Not after everything.

I feel my grief and terror transform into something else. A violent and uncontrollable fury.

I become wrath. I become rage.

A part of me registers Sam approaching, but instead of fear, I feel elation at what I'm about to do. The world becomes focused on a single point. On a single target.

A person. No, not a person—a thing, a piece of meat that I must destroy. A cancer that I must cut out.

A roar, like that of a wounded animal, leaves my throat.

I run at Sam.

He runs at me.

In a mixture of Haim's and Caleb's moves, I land blows to his stomach and face before he registers my intent. I kick his shin next, and Sam blocks it, but he misses the kick that goes for his balls. As my foot makes contact, he gasps and turns pale, but doesn't stop blocking and manages to deflect my jab at his solar plexus.

Recovering from my surprise attack, Sam attempts a punch of his own. I block his punch with my left forearm and slam my right fist into Sam's jaw with all my strength.

Excruciating pain explodes in my forearm and right fist, but it doesn't matter. All I can think about is the satisfying crunch his jaw just made. It's like music to my ears, and I want to hear more of his bones break. I want to hear it even if I need to break what's left of my own fingers in the process.

I feint with my right fist, and when Sam reacts to it, I try to hit his nose with my left elbow.

The pain in my arm is unbearable, but I ignore it, the elation of hearing the bone-crunching sound overriding everything else. His nose is bleeding now, likely broken.

He doesn't pause, though, and my moment of triumph is followed by an eruption of agony in my side. Air leaves my lungs with a whoosh, and I desperately try to regain my balance. Sam's knee connects with my ribs somehow, and I don't get a chance to stabilize myself. Not when Sam kicks my knee next, and I begin falling. As I fall, he manages to kick my flying body several times. I'm only able to block a few of the blows before I fall face down on the ground.

My body feels broken, and the metallic taste of blood is in my mouth. I try to spit it out, but I can't. My body doesn't obey me as kicks continue to rain down on me. I lose count of them, the pain blending together into an avalanche of suffering.

I don't know how I'm still conscious, but I suddenly become cognizant that he stopped. And before I have a chance to wonder why, I feel his hands grab my head, holding it in a viselike grip.

No, I scream in my mind as my head turns to the side with

an impossibly loud crunch. There is an explosion of pain in my neck, followed by an awful numbness.

A numbness that engulfs my entire body.

In the horrifying absence of pain, I realize that I'm looking at Sam from a strange angle. This shouldn't be possible. I shouldn't be able to see him at all, since I'm lying on my stomach. And then I begin to understand.

I understand the numbness and the crunching noise.

I understand why I now feel like I'm choking.

My neck is broken. The spinal cord has snapped, and my head is twisted backwards. This is why the guillotine was considered a merciful death. When your head is separated from the body, there is no pain. You simply die. In seconds.

As my consciousness begins to slip, I stare at the sky, knowing it's the last thing I'll ever see.

28

SOMETHING SMACKS ME IN THE FACE. THE PAIN IS A WELCOME surprise. That I can feel anything at all fills me with a sense of wonder.

I was never a believer in the afterlife, but I was apparently wrong. Something exists after death, or so it seems.

I open my eyes to even more confusion.

Why would there be an airbag in my face in the afterlife?

I'm suddenly fully alert.

Somehow, I'm back in Thomas's car. Next to me, I see Thomas himself. He's behind the wheel. He also has an airbag in his face, but he's moving.

He's alive.

"Ouch," I hear a high-pitched voice from the back.

Hillary's voice.

"You should've fucking let me drive." It's Mira's voice now. Sharp and annoyed, but unmistakably alive. The joy and relief that fills me is indescribable.

"Mira," I almost yell. "You're alive!"

"Why wouldn't she be?" Eugene's voice says from the back. "What the fuck happened after I was shot in the Mind Dimension?"

"Yeah, what happened?" Thomas echoes.

"You're alive too, Eugene! You're *all* alive. I can't believe it!" I'm hoping this isn't some hallucination or a trick of my dying brain. "I saw all three of you die. *I* died."

"Just the three of us?" Thomas asks. "So, Hillary, you didn't?"

"No," she says. "I was injured and bleeding, but when that monster killed Darren, I was still alive."

"Then we still stand a chance," Thomas says.

"Yes. In fact, the plan is almost unchanged," Hillary says. "Who were those men?"

"A leader of the Readers and his guard," I answer on autopilot as I try to process the fact that somehow we are all alive.

"What? How did one of us end up being one of them?" Hillary sounds almost as confused as I feel. "You know what, there's no time for that. I saw the mobsters with the marks Darren left on their heads. I can take control of them and then evacuate the rest of the people."

I manage to push away the airbag and look behind me.

Hillary has a look of concentration on her face.

"Okay, I just tried to take care of it," she says, her features returning to normal after a moment. "I hope it goes smoothly."

"What do you mean?" Mira and I say in unison.

"And how are we even alive?" I add, barely able to contain the turbulent mixture of emotions swirling inside me. "I thought we died—"

"Darren, when you get killed in the Mind Dimension, you don't die in the real world," Hillary says, looking at me. "We all feel like something bad is going to happen if we die in there, and it does—but it's not death. It's more of a major inconvenience."

"What? No, wait," I say, confused. "Yes, you do. You die, I'm sure of it. I—"

"No, you don't, as we obviously didn't," Mira says. "But we did lose something."

"Try to Split, Darren," Eugene says, looking at me. "Then you'll understand."

I do as he says. Phasing into the Quiet right now should be the easiest thing in the world. I've got all this residual fear and adrenaline stored up.

Only it doesn't happen. The frustrated feeling is familiar. It's exactly how I felt in those scary moments in the Quiet. It's like trying to phase and hitting a mental brick wall.

"The three of us are Inert now," Thomas explains as he gets his airbag situation under control. "We can't Split into the Mind Dimension."

It must be the overflow of emotion because the sense of loss I feel is intense. "We lost our powers?" I say in disbelief.

"Yes. For a while," Thomas says. "Not forever."

"So it's not permanent?" The wave of relief is nearly as powerful as my sense of loss a second ago.

"No, it's not. When you die in the Mind Dimension, it's a lot like using up your time, only the Inertness lasts much longer," Eugene explains.

"I've never run out of time in the Quiet before," I say, and I hear the note of unease in my voice. Logically, I know that temporarily losing my powers is in no way comparable to dying, but it still feels frightening. The Quiet has been my security blanket, a safety net I've used since childhood, and I feel its loss keenly.

"I understand, Darren." Hillary gives me a sympathetic look. "Like you, I've never run out of time, so I can't even imagine what that would be like. I'm so sorry it happened to you."

"He'll be fine. It'll come back," Thomas says. He doesn't seem overly concerned about his own loss of powers, but then again, his are more limited than mine or Hillary's.

As he speaks, something occurs to me. "So is this why you were so cavalier when you pointed that gun at me yesterday?" I ask, staring at Mira. That never made sense to me. Not after I saved her life the day before. "You weren't threatening to kill me. You were threatening to strip me of my power?"

"Right," she says. "Honestly, I was just bluffing. I wasn't really going to make you Inert. Not given what I knew about your insane Depth. I'm sorry about that whole incident. I wouldn't have done it if I'd known you were actually scared for your life." She pauses, then adds, "Most likely."

The puzzle pieces begin to fall into place. "So that's why Eugene said that weird shit about not shooting me because I can spend months in the Mind Dimension?"

"Yeah." Eugene nods. "It would've been a sacrilege to take away so much power. I couldn't let her do it. She can be cranky when she wakes up, so I didn't even realize she was bluffing."

I blow out a relieved breath. So it wasn't that Eugene wanted to use me, as I'd originally thought. He had been aware of the true cost of death in the Quiet all along and was simply trying to protect me.

Everything starts to make sense now. When Caleb said

during our Joining that dying in the Quiet has a lasting effect, he didn't mean death; he meant the Pusher would be Inert. This also explains Caleb's slightly odd thought about it being time to 'begin' killing the Pusher. He must've meant that step one was making the man Inert. Without powers, it must be much easier to dispatch one of us outside the Quiet. And this is why Caleb tried to phase into the Quiet from not too far away. Once the Pusher was killed in the Quiet and therefore rendered Inert, Caleb, who still possessed his powers, would've made short work of him.

I'm still not solid on the details, but things are beginning to be clearer.

"How long will it take me to recover?" I ask.

"It varies for everyone," Eugene says.

"Wait," Thomas says, turning toward me. "Hold on a second. Is your 'Depth' the same thing we call Reach? And if so, are you saying that yours is *months*? You never mentioned this, Darren."

I shrug, still thinking about my Inert state, but Hillary smiles proudly. "He is my nephew, after all."

"Is this why you didn't run when I asked you to?" Mira stares at me, her eyes shining. "You thought we were in mortal danger?"

"Well, yeah," I admit, somewhat embarrassed. "I couldn't just leave you there. Sam was right on our heels. I didn't realize you were trying to save my powers."

"I was actually trying to end her suffering," Mira explains, glancing at Hillary.

"Thank you," my aunt says.

There is a moment of silence as everyone seems to relive those terrifying moments.

"So what's with this car crash?" I ask finally. "How does that fit into everything?"

"That's my fault," Thomas says. "The shock of dying and then finding myself behind the wheel again was too much, so I rear-ended that guy."

"I took care of that driver," Hillary says. "He'll think he backed into a fire hydrant."

"You keep saying that you took care of things," Mira says. "But you're not explaining what you did or how you did it. What's happening on that bridge?"

"Oh, that. I Guided the mobsters to hold down your fellow Leachers—I mean, Jacob and Sam. The mobsters are probably moving in on them as we speak," Hillary explains.

"I still can't believe it," Eugene says through gritted teeth. "It's been Jacob all this time." In an uncharacteristic move for Eugene, he punches my seat in frustration. It doesn't hurt, so I don't say anything. I understand exactly how he feels.

"Wait, it just occurred to me. The name Jacob," Hillary says. "Didn't you say that the name of the person on the phone was Esau?"

"Yes," I say. "So?"

"Jacob and Esau were brothers in the Scripture. The guy practically gave you a hint as to who he is," Hillary says.

"So Jacob ordered that explosion," Mira says slowly, and I realize that this fact is only now beginning to dawn on her. "It was a Reader who ruined our lives, not a Pusher."

"Yes, it was Jacob using an alias of Esau," I confirm softly. "He ordered Arkady to use the explosives." Mira's entire world must be turning upside down. Pushers are not her enemies, while Readers, her own people, seem to be.

"I don't understand." Eugene sounds bewildered. "There was

definitely a Pusher involved. He pops up in many of the gangsters' memories."

"There must be more to this," Hillary says. "After the police question everyone involved, we can access their files. Maybe something will turn up."

"What police?" Mira's voice gets soft. Dangerously soft. "What are you talking about?"

"I'm about to call them," Hillary explains. "That's the part of the plan that's now different. Easier, in fact. The gangsters should be able to hold those two Leachers down, and instead of us calling our Guide friends, I'll let the cops handle this. Guides are not equipped to deal with Leachers. They'll kill them, and I can't have that. Don't worry, though. Unlike Guides, Leachers can't get out of jail. Right?" she says, apparently missing the hard gleam in Mira's eyes.

"No fucking way—"

Mira's harsh words get interrupted by the sound of distant gunfire. One shot is followed by several in rapid succession.

Hillary turns pale.

Mira's head whips toward the bridge, and I see her coming to a swift decision. Before I can say anything, she springs into action. She opens the door, presses the door lock button, slams the door shut behind her, and begins running toward the bridge.

"Fuck!" Thomas fumbles with the lock. "I told you she'd be a liability."

I frantically unbuckle my seatbelt to go after her.

"Stop her," Thomas barks at Hillary as he finally unlocks the doors. "You're the only one who can."

"I can't," Hillary objects. "She's got a gun. She could shoot a civilian if I try to use them."

"This is not the time for pacifism." I don't see the expression on my aunt's face, but I hear Thomas curse and then say, "Fine. Improvise something. You there, hand me that rifle—"

I don't hear Eugene's response because I open the door and start running after Mira. Immediately, I'm reminded of the fact that I'm no longer in the Quiet. The cars around us are moving at full speed, and I almost get run over twice before I reach the sidewalk. When I hear screeching brakes, I attempt to phase in, but it's futile. I can't go into the Quiet.

I've been Inert less than five minutes, and I already hate it.

"I was barely able to control that last car, you know," a cab driver says cryptically from his window as I run past him. He's wearing a turban and speaking with a slight Indian accent. I'm pretty sure I've never met him. "You're my blood relative, Darren, and I desperately want you to live. Please be careful."

My attention shifts from the strange cabby to the road I just crossed as I hear loud honking, followed by a thump. Glancing back, I see Eugene on the ground in front of a car. My heart skips a beat, but I don't stop.

I have to get to Mira.

As I get close to the bridge, I see a crowd of people rushing toward me. It must be Hillary's improvised Guided evacuation. Here and there, I notice familiar faces—people I'd Read and Guided myself.

At my approach, the crowd parts, leaving a wide path for me. It's odd, but it serves me, so I don't question it.

"Darren, hurry, she's almost there," says an old lady as I run onto the boardwalk-like portion of the bridge.

"It's me, Hillary, by the way," a little kid says as he runs by me. "Why do you look so shocked?"

Now I get it. The cabby, the old lady, the people giving me

room to run, and now the kid. Hillary is Guiding these people to aid me, and she's giving me messages through them. I'd be very impressed if I weren't in such a panic.

Then I hear tires screech behind me again.

"A car almost hit Thomas. He's okay, though. Still running your way. Eugene is also okay; he just hurt his leg. He might not make it there in time," the buff guy with PTSD says as I pass by him.

Before I get a chance to feel reassured, there is a strange wail. At least a hundred people all around the bridge scream in unison like some hellish chorus, "No, Mira, don't!"

And then the people in front of me fall to the ground. What makes that move extra-spooky is that they do it simultaneously, like they were all stricken with some deadly poison at the exact same moment.

This gives me a clear view of what's about to happen—a view that explains why Hillary made them do that. She wouldn't give so many civilians bruises without good cause.

On the far end of the bridge, I see two large men fighting. Fighting to the death, by the looks of it.

One of them I recognize instantly. It's Arkady, the psychopath from the banya. He must be under Hillary's control. The other one is Sam.

The fury that gripped me earlier returns as I see Sam holding the same knife that he threw at Mira in the Quiet.

And then I register what Mira is doing.

This is what Hillary wanted me so desperately to see.

Mira is aiming her gun at the two fighting men.

In that instant, I also take in the rest of the scene. On the ground next to Sam and Arkady, two of Arkady's men are holding down Jacob. The rest of the mobsters, including the one who tried to shoot me the other day, are lying on the ground bleeding. Those must've been the shots we heard. The gangsters were probably shot trying to get Sam's and Jacob's guns away from them—and it looks like they succeeded.

"Mira, there is no need to kill anyone!" Arkady screams as he continues wrestling with Sam. Hillary must be speaking through his mouth as well.

Sam grunts and yells out in response, "Mira, stop him, and you and your brother will be welcomed with open arms in our community! This man is being controlled by a powerful Pusher. I need your help. Jacob needs your help. Shoot him! Now!"

"It's you I'm going to kill first, not him," Mira hisses, her aim unwavering. "And Jacob—I'm going to make him suffer." And with that, she squeezes the trigger.

At the deafening gunshot blast, Sam rapidly twists his body, and it's Arkady's head that explodes into little pieces instead of his own.

As I watch all this, I continue running.

Mira, unfazed by her miss, shoots at Sam. To my horror, Sam does the rolling thing he did in the Quiet. Only he does it even faster, avoiding Mira's bullet with uncanny precision. He seems to have started moving before Mira even squeezed the trigger. And then I understand: he can phase into the Quiet. He must be using that ability to anticipate Mira's movements.

Mira begins to back away toward me, still shooting in Sam's direction. Sam rolls again and stabs one of the Russians who are holding Jacob. There is a loud scream as his knife connects with the gangster's shoulder.

"Stop it, you insane Leacher! Stop or you'll be killed," the injured man screams, letting go of Jacob to clutch at his shoulder. Ignoring his words, Sam stabs the man again, this time in the heart.

"Okay, fine," the guy rasps out, blood bubbling up on his lips as he falls to the ground. "You leave us no choice."

That's Hillary talking, I remind myself again.

"Darren, move to the right!" yells a chorus of civilians who are lying on the ground around me. My aunt again. "Now!"

Without thinking, I jump to the right and immediately hear a gunshot. Glancing back, I see Thomas standing a dozen yards away with a rifle in his hands. When I turn back to the scene ahead, I see Sam falling, with the top of his head blown into pieces.

"Now, you fucking stay down, Leacher," the other Russian who was holding Jacob says. I can't believe it's Hillary again. She sounds utterly cold. I guess if anyone could drive my pacifist aunt to bloodlust, Sam was the guy.

And then I realize she's not gloating at Sam being shot. She's talking to Jacob. He's managed to free himself from the Russian's hold and is reaching for the knife Sam dropped when he died.

"Mira, you're in Thomas's way," the Russian says. "Move, so he can take the shot."

I raise my own gun, but this time I'm somewhat reluctant to pull the trigger. If this were Sam, I would've shot him without a second thought. But this is Jacob. He knew my father. He can give me answers about my family.

Instead of moving as Hillary commanded, Mira is also raising her gun. She's apparently determined to kill Jacob on her own.

Taking aim, she squeezes the trigger.

Instead of a bang, there is a quiet click. Jacob is still standing there, unharmed.

Her gun is out of bullets.

Jacob blinks. He looks almost surprised to still be alive. Then he looks at the knife in his hand and, grabbing it by the blade, raises it over his shoulder.

I'm gripped by a horrible sense of déjà vu. He's raising the knife for a throw at Mira—just like Sam did in the Quiet.

This can't be happening again.

I won't let it.

Without thinking even a second longer, I shoot. The knife is still in Jacob's hand, so I fire again and again. Mindlessly. Furiously.

I don't stop squeezing the trigger until I'm out of bullets.

As the haze of rage clears from my mind, I see that the knife is no longer in Jacob's hand. It's on the ground, and so is the man himself, his chest covered with blood.

Numb, I stand there and stare at the man I killed, one thought foremost in my mind.

Mira is okay. That's all that matters.

"Let's go, Darren," the people lying around me chant in Hillary-Guided chorus. "It's time to go."

Shaking off my stupor, I begin to head back, only to realize that Mira is not with me. Instead of following me, she's walking to where Jacob's body is lying. Reaching him, she starts going through his pockets. Then she picks up another gun off the ground and shoots Jacob in the head.

I wonder if that means my own shots didn't kill him—and then I wonder why I care either way. He was about to kill Mira. How could I not shoot?

Her grisly task accomplished, Mira picks up the briefcase

Jacob had been holding earlier—the one that flew open in the Quiet but is still intact here—and walks toward me.

"Let's get out of here," she says, her face pale and resolute.

I look at her without comprehension.

"It's over," she says gently. "Now we go." And looping her arm through mine, she starts pulling me away.

As we walk, the enormity of what just occurred dawns on me. Arkady, Sam, Jacob, the other Russian mobsters—they're all dead, and we were nearly killed ourselves. To say that I'm pushing the limits of my ability to cope with seeing Mira nearly die would be a massive understatement.

Lost in thought, I let her steer me toward Thomas, who's standing there waiting for us. Eugene is limping our way as well, looking extremely relieved to see Mira and everyone else intact.

"Good work," Thomas says to me as we approach. "I'm sorry that I couldn't take my own shot. She was in the way."

"Thanks," I mumble, feeling incredibly drained.

"You," Thomas says, looking at Mira and shaking his head. "You're the most reckless woman I've ever met."

She doesn't respond. For the first time since I've known her, she looks subdued. Serene, almost.

Thomas's black van, now with a broken bumper, is waiting by the curb as we head back to the road. Some guy I've never met is sitting behind the wheel.

"I prefer stick shift," Hillary explains from the back seat. "So I had this guy bring the car over."

"Thanks," Thomas says. "He can go now."

"Thank you, Robert," Hillary says to the driver. "Your car is where you left it. You can go."

The guy gets out and starts walking away, a blank look on his face.

"Well, don't just stand there." Hillary motions for us to get in. "It's over. Now let's get out of here."

Her words prompt everyone into action. Thomas gets behind the wheel, and we all get inside.

I look back as we drive away and see people still running away from Brooklyn Bridge.

29

As we drive uptown, I realize that I need to pull myself together. The drained feeling is overwhelming.

"I killed someone again," I finally say, speaking to no one in particular. "I really didn't want to."

"Don't feel bad about that," Mira says. "That fucker killed our parents. And possibly your parents, too. Besides, you just shot him. I'm the one who actually killed him."

So Jacob wasn't dead when Mira got there.

"I don't know if that helps," I say. "I knew him, you know. That makes it different, somehow."

"You should talk to Liz once everything settles down," Thomas recommends. "She can help."

Yes, talk to my therapist. That would be a good start. But I need something else right now. Something more immediate.

I need some information and some time to think things through.

"Can someone please tell me who the hell those men were?"

Thomas inquires. "The people we just killed. What the hell was all that about? They were some of yours, obviously . . . Some Leachers, weren't they?"

"They were *Readers*," I say, emphasizing the proper term. I don't like double standards, and if Hillary and Thomas want to be called Guides rather than Pushers, they should return the favor. "The big bodyguard type you shot was one of their top security personnel, and the older, less-threatening-looking one that I killed—or Mira killed—was Jacob, that community's leader."

"Okay. But we came to get one of us—a rogue Guide," Thomas says patiently. "What happened? How did you guys get it so wrong?"

"Darren, do you want to play the detective?" Mira suggests. "Your guess is going to be as good as mine."

"Well," I say slowly, trying to think through the fog still filling my mind, "it sounds like Jacob killed your family because of your father's research. Because Jacob was a Purist, the research your father was doing might've been unacceptable to him." That's the only thing that makes sense to me, at least.

"What's a Purist, and what is this research?" Thomas asks.

"Purists sound a lot like the Reader version of Traditionalists," I explain, amazed to be the one who has the answers for once.

"And my brother's research is none of Pushers' business," Mira says before her brother can start going into an explanation.

"But what about the Guide we went to see in the first place?" Hillary says, confused. "You're saying there was no such Guide?"

"No," I say. "That's the weird part. Mira found signs of a

Guide when she researched her parents' murder. And she wasn't the only one. I saw signs of a Guide when we were rescuing Mira the other day, and again when that nurse tried to kill me. That means that unequivocally, there's one involved. Maybe he was working with Jacob?"

"Working together?" Hillary says. "I doubt our Traditionalists would even talk to a Reader, let alone work with one."

"Same for our Purists," Eugene says.

"Be that as it may, evidence seems to suggest otherwise," I say. "In Arkady's mind, I saw the Pusher erasing Arkady's memories of Jacob sanctioning some hits. That would only make sense if they were working as a team."

"If they did team up, it would be a hypocrisy of unbelievable proportions," Hillary says. "Traditionalists are the very people who hate Readers the most, and I'm guessing the same applies to their Purist brethren."

"Purists hate you people with an almost religious fervor," Eugene confirms. "Working with a Pusher would be like making a deal with the devil for them."

"Maybe these two joined forces to fight an even bigger devil," I speculate. "A temporary alliance, perhaps? I mean, we saw today how powerful a team of Readers and Guides can be. Maybe they united for some common cause . . . like to kill *me*—the abomination."

"I don't know about that. After all, you didn't exist to them until recently," Eugene says. "Unless their union goes way back to your parents' time—which is possible, I suppose. But getting rid of my father's—and now my—research is a more likely motivation."

"So you mean I'm not done." Mira sounds more weary than

angry. "You think there's another person, a Guide, who had something to do with our parents' death."

"I think I speak for everyone when I say you can call *that* person a Pusher, Mira," I say. "But my intuition tells me that Jacob is the one to blame for your parents' death. After all, he was the one who ordered the hit on them."

"You're more than done, Mirochka," Eugene chimes in. "You killed the people directly responsible for it. It's time to move on. Start to live your life again."

"He's right," I say. "Let Guides deal with that Traditionalist Pusher problem. Let *me* deal with it. Maybe it's as simple as ratting out this Pusher to his fellow Traditionalists. They might not approve of his allegiances. What do you think, Hillary?"

"That could work. Let me think about that," Hillary says pensively.

Mira just sits there quietly, her expression unreadable. I guess she has a lot to mull over. I sure hope she decides that her revenge is officially over. I want that for her. I want her to go to college and become a nurse working with babies, regardless of how uncharacteristic of her that plan seems.

What I don't say is that my own quest for revenge is definitely not over. Jacob and the Pusher knew about me somehow. They knew even before I was born. I'm certain of it. They must be the reason my parents went into hiding—the reason why they gave me to Sara and Lucy to raise.

It can't be a coincidence that right after I saw Jacob, I was shot at by his pet mobsters. Nor is it a coincidence that a half hour after that, the Pusher found me in the hospital and tried to kill me. One must have told the other about me. Jacob must've noticed that I look like my father and told the Pusher about it. It might also explain the OB-GYN records that Bert mentioned disappearing. Maybe this is the first time my parents' murderers realized my parents had a child. My birth mother's medical records could've helped them verify that.

"Darren, we should talk more about this," Thomas says, breaking into my thoughts. "As soon as the dust settles a bit."

"Sure," I say.

"There's one more thing," Mira says, reaching into her pocket. "Something that might help you, Darren. I found this."

She's holding a small black object in her outstretched hand.

"That's the flash drive Jacob brought," I say, understanding why she went through the dead man's pockets before she shot him.

"Yes. Except it's encrypted, remember?" Mira says.

"What's supposed to be on there?" Thomas asks.

"A list of targets the mob was supposed to kill for Jacob, and a list of witnesses that Arkady needed eliminated, I think," I say. "You know, with hindsight, I can see how a Reader could have an easier time getting a list of witnesses like that compared to a Guide."

"Indeed. With hindsight, a lot of things become obvious," Hillary says. "The trick is to see them beforehand."

"Give me the drive, and I'll get some people in the Service to try to crack it," Thomas offers.

"I'll give it to Darren," Mira says. "Whatever he decides to do with it is fine with me."

"I'll send you a copy," I say to Thomas. "But I have a friend who'll likely crack this thing faster than any of your experts."

The problem will be explaining to Bert why I'm having him crack this code. It might be tricky, but I'm sure I'll manage it.

"Okay, so now let's talk about what happened," Thomas says,

looking at Hillary in the mirror. "Are we now fugitives from the law? How bad was it down there on the bridge?"

"Not too bad," my aunt says, sounding tired. "No one will remember any of us being there, for starters."

"That's good," Thomas says approvingly. "What about evidence? Did we leave any DNA on the scene?"

"I just twisted my ankle," Eugene says. "So no blood."

"Everyone else?" Thomas asks.

"I'm fine," I say. "Not a scratch."

"Same here," Mira echoes.

"And obviously, I never left the car in the real world," Hillary says. "Only in the Mind Dimension."

"Good. We might not go to jail after all." Thomas looks relieved. "Now give me your guns. I'll properly dispose of them."

We all place our guns in the back next to the rest of Thomas's artillery stash.

"Okay, I'll keep an eye on the police investigation," Thomas says when we're done. "It might have to wait until I regain my abilities, but if needed, I'll clean things up. Which brings me to the next bit of business. We all need to disappear for a while. Particularly those of us who are Inert."

"Disappear?" Eugene says nervously.

"Yes, get out of town," Thomas clarifies.

That's it, I realize. This is exactly what I need. A vacation. Some rest. Some time without being shot at.

"How do you guys feel about Miami?" I say, my mood lifting a little. "I sure could use some time in the sun, with an umbrella drink in my hand."

"I can't leave for a few days," Hillary says, "and Florida is far from my favorite place, but I might join you there in a bit."

"I'll pass. Liz and I will want to do our own getaway," Thomas says. "But Miami for all of you will work out perfectly. This way, you can tell your friends and family the truth—that you're taking a vacation. Darren, if you need help convincing your boss, Hillary and I can talk to him."

"No, it'll be fine. Bill knows that awesome resources like me can sometimes do strange things like this. He won't mind," I say dismissively. Then, turning toward Mira, I say, "What do you think? Will you join me? It'll be my treat, too."

"Oh, you forget." The tiniest of smiles appears on Mira's otherwise somber face. "I'm not broke anymore. It actually might be me taking you on vacation, not the other way around."

"What are you talking about?" Eugene gives his sister a puzzled look. "We *are* broke."

"This briefcase," she says, pointing at her feet. "It's filled with cash."

"Be careful with that." Thomas frowns, looking at Mira in the mirror. "That money can be traced to you if someone knows what he's doing."

"So we have a challenge, it seems. We'll need to spend all the money in Miami," Mira says. "And spend it as quickly as possible."

"I'm sure we can manage," I say drily. "We'll just have to drink a lot of champagne and get all-day spa treatments."

"The horror," Mira says, her smile widening. "I see a lot of expensive shoes in my future. All that time I'll have to waste shopping. Such a drag."

"If push comes to shove, you two can also go gambling," Eugene adds, getting into the spirit of it. "The money you win will be clean."

"That's a good way to launder money," Thomas says, chuckling. "Using a cash business like that."

"And it's only fitting," Hillary says, looking at me and Mira. "Given how these two met for the first time."

I take out my phone and do a little online searching.

"How's tomorrow for a flight?" I say. "Is that too soon?"

Mira shrugs. "Works for me."

"Sure," Eugene says. "But can we stop by our old apartment?"

"No," Mira and I say in unison.

"We don't know if Arkady ordered someone to watch the place and wait for you," I explain.

"Fine," Eugene says sadly. "Maybe some of that cash can go toward some new lab equipment."

"Maybe," Mira says. "Do they have stores that sell that type of stuff for cash?"

"I don't know." Eugene perks up a bit. "I'll have to look into it."

"I'm booking the tickets now," I say and begin navigating the airline's website.

"Okay, great," Thomas says. "That takes care of that. Now I need to know where to take everyone."

"Well, I see that you've been driving toward my place," Hillary says.

"Yeah, I assumed—"

"Good call," Hillary says, interrupting Thomas. "You assumed correctly. I'm going home."

"I'd like to go back to the hotel. Pick up a few things and talk to—" Eugene starts saying and stops abruptly.

"I'm sorry, Zhenya," Mira says softly. "You can't talk to her."

I look back and see Eugene's face turn pale.

He just connected the dots.

Without Reading, I can tell what Eugene is thinking right now. He was part of an operation that resulted in the death of Jacob—Julia's father. Whatever she is to him, it might be over now. He certainly can't see her any time soon. I have to say, I feel really sorry for him. Hell, I feel sorry for Julia also. She didn't seem to be best pals with her father, but I'm sure she'll be hurt when she learns what happened.

"If I may offer a piece of advice," Thomas says. "The three of you should get a brand-new hotel for the night."

We take his suggestion and use the remainder of the way to Hillary's place to decide on the hotel. We choose a nondescript one near the JFK airport. The logic is that a longer drive today will make our lives easier tomorrow when we fly out in the morning.

"Bye, Darren," Hillary says when the car stops. "Get in touch if you really meant it when you invited me to Miami."

"Of course I meant it," I say. "Join us when you can."

Blowing me an air kiss, Hillary leaves.

Thomas waits until she walks into her high-rise condo building and then starts driving.

The atmosphere in the car is that of complete exhaustion. It seems all of us have been through so much that we need to digest things in silence. I myself am so drained, I can't even think. Instead, I try to make my mind go blank and do the breathing meditation Sara taught me.

A meditation that I now realize she must've learned from my father, her colleague Mark Robinson.

As my breathing slows, I feel my eyes getting heavy, and I close them for a moment.

"Darren, wake up, we're here." Eugene's voice penetrates my drowsiness, and I realize I must've dozed off.

"I don't think we'll hear from each other for a while," Thomas says, clearing his throat as I unbuckle my seatbelt. "But when things settle down, I'd love to hang out with you."

"Sounds like a plan, Thomas," I say, opening the door. "Thanks for all you did for us today. I owe you."

"I, too, want to thank you," Mira says. "I'd be dead if it weren't for you."

Thomas looks as surprised as I feel. Mira sounds genuinely grateful. "You're welcome, Mira," he says, a bit uncomfortably.

We get out of the car, and Thomas pulls away with one last wave.

As we walk, I begin to feel more awake. Approaching the front desk at the hotel, I get three separate rooms for each of us.

We ride the elevator in silence.

"Yours is 505," I tell Eugene when we reach his door. "Yours is 504," I say to Mira. "And I'm in 503, right across the hall."

"Thank you, Darren," Eugene says.

"Sure, Zhenya," I say, winking as I use Mira's nickname for him.

Mira doesn't say anything, but as she takes the key from me, her fingers linger for a second, brushing against mine. Her touch is soft, sensual. Before I can say anything, though, she goes into her own room.

I follow suit, entering my room.

First order of business, I eat all the candy bars and peanuts from the minibar. I hadn't realized how starved I was until this moment.

Next, I take the longest shower of my life. As water streams over me, the tightness in my shoulders begins to fade. It's all going to be fine, I tell myself, feeling revived by the hot water.

As I towel off, I begin to feel a tinge of excitement for the trip to come. I love Miami—and Miami with Mira? That might be something else entirely.

My musings are interrupted by a knock on the door.

"Who is it?" I ask, wrapping the towel around my waist.

"It's me," Mira says behind the door. "I hope I'm not disturbing you."

"No," I say, opening the door and stepping back to let her in. "I was just taking a shower."

She comes into the room. Her hair is wet, and she's wearing a hotel bathrobe. She must've also just showered. Her face is clean and completely free of makeup, reminding me of the time I woke her up in her apartment in the Quiet.

As she looks me up and down, I realize that I'm wearing only the towel. I don't feel self-conscious at her stare, however. With all the time I invested in gym workouts, moments like this feel like payoff.

"I came to say thanks for saving my life," she says, lifting her eyes to meet my gaze. "And, well, for everything."

"Of course." I grin at her. "I hope that means you'll stop pulling a gun on me now."

"Yes, it does." She grins back. "If you're good, that is."

"Oh." I lift my eyebrows. "And what about if I'm bad?"

She steps closer, staring up at me. "If you're bad, then I'll find a way to deal with you," she whispers and stands up on tiptoe to give my earlobe a playful nibble.

I react instantly. This smallest of flirtatious gestures makes the towel around my hips begin to look like a tent.

All my earlier tiredness forgotten, I wrap my arms around Mira's back and lower my head to kiss her. The kiss is hungry, intense. It seems to last and last—all that near-death angst compacted into one moment.

When she pulls away to catch her breath, we're both panting and her hands are clinging to my shoulders.

"I came here to thank you," she murmurs, looking up at me, "and also to give your reward."

Stepping back, she unties the robe and lets it fall down to the floor.

The night that follows is easily the most rewarding of my life.

SNEAK PEEKS

Thank you for reading! If you would consider leaving a review, it would be greatly appreciated.

Darren's story continues in *The Enlightened* (Mind Dimensions: Book 3). Please visit www.dimazales.com to get the book.

If you enjoy sci-fi/dystopian novels like *The Hunger Games, Divergent,* and *The Giver,* you might be interested in my new series, *The Last Humans.*

If you like epic fantasy, I also have a series called *The Sorcery Code.* Additionally, if you don't mind erotic material and are in the mood for sci-fi romance, you can check out *Close Liaisons,* my collaboration with my wife, Anna Zaires. You can visit www.annazaires.com to get your copy.

If you like audiobooks, please visit www.dimazales.com to check out this series and our other books.

And now, please turn the page for a sneak peek at *The Sorcery Code, Close Liaisons,* and some of my other works.

EXCERPT FROM OASIS

My name is Theo, and I'm a resident of Oasis, the last habitable area on Earth. It's meant to be a paradise, a place where we are all content. Vulgarity, violence, insanity, and other ills are but a distant memory, and even death no longer plagues us.

I was once content too, but now I'm different. Now I hear a voice in my head, and she tells me things no imaginary friend should know. Her name is Phoe, and she is my delusion.

Or is she?

Fuck. Vagina. Shit.

I pointedly think these forbidden words, but my neural scan shows nothing out of the ordinary compared to when I think phonetically similar words, such as *shuck, angina,* or *fit.* I don't see any evidence of my brain being corrupted, though maybe it's already so damaged that things can't get any worse. Maybe I need another test subject—another 'impressionable' twenty-three-year-old Youth such as myself.

After all, I might be mentally ill.

"Oh, Theo. Not this again," says an overly friendly, high-pitched female voice. "Besides, the words do have an effect on your brain. For instance, the part of your brain responsible for disgust lights up at the mention of 'shit,' yet doesn't for 'fit.'"

This is Phoe speaking. This time, she's not a voice inside my head; instead, it's as though she's in the thick bushes behind me, except there's no one there.

I'm the only person on this strip of grass.

Nobody else comes here because the Edge is only a couple of feet away. Few residents of Oasis like looking at the dreary line dividing where our habitable world ends and the deserted wasteland of the Goo begins. I don't mind it, though.

Then again, I may be crazy—and Phoe would be the reason for that. You see, I don't think Phoe is real. She is, as far as my best guess goes, my imaginary friend. And her name, by the way, is pronounced 'Fee,' but is spelled 'P-h-o-e.'

Yes, that's how specific my delusion is.

"So you go from one overused topic straight into another." Phoe snorts. "My so-called realness."

"Right," I say. Though we're alone, I still answer without moving my lips. "Because I *am* imagining you."

She snorts again, and I shake my head. Yes, I just shook my head for the benefit of my delusion. I also feel compelled to respond to her.

"For the record," I say, "I'm sure the taboo word 'shit' affects the parts of my brain that deal with disgust just as much as its more acceptable cousins, such as 'fecal matter,' do. The point I was trying to make is that the word doesn't hurt or corrupt my brain. There's nothing special about these words."

"Yeah, yeah." This time, Phoe is inside my head, and she sounds mocking. "Next you'll tell me how back in the day, some of the forbidden words merely referred to things like female dogs, and how there are words in the dead languages that used to be just as taboo, yet they are not currently forbidden because they have lost their power. Then you're likely to complain that, though the brains of both genders are nearly identical, only males are not allowed to say 'vagina,' et cetera."

I realize I was about to counter with those exact thoughts, which means Phoe and I have talked about this quite a bit. This is what happens between close friends: they repeat conversations. Doubly so with imaginary friends, I figure. Though, of course, I'm probably the only person in Oasis who actually has one.

Come to think of it, wouldn't *every* conversation with your imaginary friend be redundant since you're basically talking to yourself?

"This is my cue to remind you that I'm real, Theo." Phoe purposefully states this out loud.

I can't help but notice that her voice came slightly from my right, as if she's just a friend sitting on the grass next to me—a friend who happens to be invisible.

"Just because I'm invisible doesn't mean I'm not real," Phoe responds to my thought. "At least *I'm* convinced that I'm real. I would be the crazy one if I *didn't* think I was real. Besides, a lot of evidence points to that conclusion, and you know it."

"But wouldn't an imaginary friend *have* to insist she's real?" I can't resist saying the words out loud. "Wouldn't this be part of the delusion?"

"Don't talk to me out loud," she reminds me, her tone worried. "Even when you subvocalize, sometimes you imperceptibly move your neck muscles or even your lips. All those things are too risky. You should just think your thoughts at me. Use your inner voice. It's safer that way, especially when we're around other Youths."

"Sure, but for the record, that makes me feel even nuttier," I reply, but I subvocalize my words, trying my best not to move my lips or neck muscles. Then, as an experiment, I think, "Talking to you inside my head just highlights the impossibility of you and thus makes me feel like I'm missing even more screws."

"Well, it shouldn't." Her voice is inside my head now, yet it still sounds high-pitched. "Back in the day, when it was not forbidden to be mentally ill, I imagine it made people around you uncomfortable if you spoke to your imaginary friends out loud." She chuckles, but there's more worry than humor in her voice. "I have no idea what would happen if someone thought you were crazy, but I have a bad feeling about it, so please don't do it, okay?"

"Fine," I think and pull at my left earlobe. "Though it's overkill to do it here. No one's around."

"Yes, but the nanobots I told you about, the ones that permeate everything from your head to the utility fog, *can* be used to monitor this place, at least in theory."

"Right. Unless all this conveniently invisible technology you keep telling me about is as much of a figment of my imagination as you are," I think at her. "In any case, since no one seems to know about this tech, how can they use it to spy on me?"

"Correction: no Youth knows, but the others might," Phoe counters patiently. "There's too much we still don't know about Adults, not to mention the Elderly."

"But if they can access the nanocytes in my mind, wouldn't they have access to my thoughts too?" I think, suppressing a shudder. If this is true, I'm utterly screwed.

"The fact that you haven't faced any consequences for your frequently wayward thoughts is evidence that no one monitors them in general, or at least, they're not bothering with yours specifically," she responds, her words easing my dread. "Therefore, I think monitoring thoughts is either computationally prohibitive or breaks one of the bazillion taboos on the proper use of technology—rules I have a very hard time keeping track of, by the way."

"Well, what if using tech to listen in on me is also taboo?" I retort, though she's beginning to convince me.

"It may be, but I've seen evidence that can best be explained as the Adults spying." Her voice in my head takes on a hushed tone. "Just think of the time you and Liam made plans to skip your Physics Lecture. How did they know about that?"

I think of the epic Quietude session we were sentenced to and how we both swore we hadn't betrayed each other. We reached the same conclusion: our speech is not secure. That's why Liam, Mason, and I now often speak in code.

"There could be other explanations," I think at Phoe. "That conversation happened during Lectures, and someone could've overheard us. But even if they hadn't, just because they monitor us during class doesn't mean they would bother monitoring this forsaken spot."

"Even if they don't monitor *this* place or anywhere outside of the Institute, I still want you to acquire the right habit."

"What if I speak in code?" I suggest. "You know, the one I use with my non-imaginary friends."

"You already speak too slowly for my liking," she thinks at me with clear exasperation. "When you speak in that code, you sound ridiculous and drastically increase the number of syllables you say. Now if you were willing to learn one of the dead languages..."

"Fine. I will 'think' when I have to speak to you," I think. Then I subvocalize, "But I will also subvocalize."

"If you must." She sighs out loud. "Just do it the way you did a second ago, without any voice musculature moving."

Instead of replying, I look at the Edge again, the place where the serene greenery under the Dome meets the repulsive ocean of the desolate Goo—the ever-replicating parasitic technology that converts matter into itself. The Goo is what's left of the world outside the Dome barrier, and if the barrier were to ever come down, the Goo would destroy us in short order. Naturally, this view evokes all sorts of unpleasant feelings, and the fact that I'm voluntarily gazing at it must be yet another sign of my shaky mental state.

"The thing *is* decidedly gross," Phoe reflects, trying to cheer me up, as usual. "It looks like someone tried to make Jell-O out of vomit and human excrement." Then, with a mental snicker, she adds, "Sorry, I should've said 'vomit and shit.'"

"I have no idea what Jell-O is," I subvocalize. "But whatever it is, you're probably spot on regarding the ingredients."

"Jell-O was something the ancients ate in the pre-Food days," Phoe explains. "I'll find something for you to watch or read about it, or if you're lucky, they might serve it at the upcoming Birth Day fair."

"I hope they do. It's hard to learn about food from books or movies," I complain. "I tried."

"In this case, you might," Phoe counters. "Jell-O was more about texture than taste. It had the consistency of jellyfish."

"People actually ate those slimy things back then?" I think in disgust. I can't recall seeing that in any of the movies. Waving toward the Goo, I say, "No wonder the world turned to this."

"They didn't eat it in most parts of the world," Phoe says, her voice taking on a pedantic tone. "And Jell-O was actually made out of partially decomposed proteins extracted from cow and pig hides, hooves, bones, and connective tissue."

"Now you're just trying to gross me out," I think.

"That's rich, coming from you, Mr. Shit." She chuckles. "Anyway, you have to leave this place."

"I do?"

"You have Lectures in half an hour, but more importantly, Mason is looking for you," she says, and her voice gives me the impression she's already gotten up from the grass.

I get up and start walking through the tall shrubbery that hides the Goo from the view of the rest of Oasis Youths.

"By the way"—Phoe's voice comes from the distance; she's simulating walking ahead of me—"once you verify that Mason *is* looking for you, *do* try to explain how an imaginary friend like me could possibly know something like that… something you yourself didn't know."

Oasis is currently available at most retailers. If you'd like to learn more, please visit www.dimazales.com.

EXCERPT FROM THE SORCERY CODE

Once a respected member of the Sorcerer Council and now an outcast, Blaise has spent the last year of his life working on a special magical object. The goal is to allow anyone to do magic, not just the sorcerer elite. The outcome of his quest is unlike anything he could've ever imagined—because, instead of an object, he creates Her.

She is Gala, and she is anything but inanimate. Born in the Spell Realm, she is beautiful and highly intelligent—and nobody knows what she's capable of. She will do anything to experience the world . . . even leave the man she is beginning to fall for.

Augusta, a powerful sorceress and Blaise's former fiancée, sees Blaise's deed as the ultimate hubris and Gala as an abomination that must be destroyed. In her quest to save the human race, Augusta will forge new alliances, becoming tangled in a web of intrigue that stretches further than any of them suspect. She may even have to turn to her new lover Barson, a ruthless warrior who might have an agenda of his own . . .

There was a naked woman on the floor of Blaise's study.

A beautiful naked woman.

Stunned, Blaise stared at the gorgeous creature who just appeared out of thin air. She was looking around with a bewildered expression on her face, apparently as shocked to be there as he was to be seeing her. Her wavy blond hair streamed down her back, partially covering a body that appeared to be perfection itself. Blaise tried not to think about that body and to focus on the situation instead.

A woman. A *She*, not an *It*. Blaise could hardly believe it. Could it be? Could this girl be the object?

She was sitting with her legs folded underneath her, propping herself up with one slim arm. There was something awkward about that pose, as though she didn't know what to do with her own limbs. In general, despite the curves that marked her a fully grown woman, there was a child-like innocence in the way she sat there, completely unselfconscious and totally unaware of her own appeal.

Clearing his throat, Blaise tried to think of what to say. In his wildest dreams, he couldn't have imagined this kind of outcome to the project that had consumed his entire life for the past several months.

Hearing the sound, she turned her head to look at him, and Blaise found himself staring into a pair of unusually clear blue eyes.

She blinked, then cocked her head to the side, studying him with visible curiosity. Blaise wondered what she was seeing. He hadn't seen the light of day in weeks, and he wouldn't be surprised if he looked like a mad sorcerer at this point. There was probably a week's worth of stubble covering his face, and he knew his dark hair was unbrushed and sticking out in every direction. If he'd known he would be facing a beautiful woman today, he would've done a grooming spell in the morning.

"Who am I?" she asked, startling Blaise. Her voice was soft and feminine, as alluring as the rest of her. "What is this place?"

"You don't know?" Blaise was glad he finally managed to string together a semi-coherent sentence. "You don't know who you are or where you are?"

She shook her head. "No."

Blaise swallowed. "I see."

"What am I?" she asked again, staring at him with those incredible eyes.

"Well," Blaise said slowly, "if you're not some cruel prankster or a figment of my imagination, then it's somewhat difficult to explain . . ."

She was watching his mouth as he spoke, and when he stopped, she looked up again, meeting his gaze. "It's strange," she said, "hearing words this way. These are the first real words I've heard."

Blaise felt a chill go down his spine. Getting up from his chair, he began to pace, trying to keep his eyes off her nude body. He had been expecting something to appear. A magical object, a thing. He just hadn't known what form that thing would take. A mirror, perhaps, or a lamp. Maybe even something as unusual as the Life Capture Sphere that sat on his desk like a large round diamond.

But a person? A female person at that?

To be fair, he had been trying to make the object intelligent, to ensure it would have the ability to comprehend human language and convert it into the code. Maybe he shouldn't be so surprised that the intelligence he invoked took on a human shape.

A beautiful, feminine, sensual shape.

Focus, Blaise, focus.

"Why are you walking like that?" She slowly got to her feet, her movements uncertain and strangely clumsy. "Should I be walking too? Is that how people talk to each other?"

Blaise stopped in front of her, doing his best to keep his eyes above her neck. "I'm sorry. I'm not accustomed to naked women in my study."

She ran her hands down her body, as though trying to feel it for the first time. Whatever her intent, Blaise found the gesture extremely erotic.

"Is something wrong with the way I look?" she asked. It was such a typical feminine concern that Blaise had to stifle a smile.

"Quite the opposite," he assured her. "You look unimaginably good." So good, in fact, that he was having trouble concentrating on anything but her delicate curves. She was of medium height, and so perfectly proportioned that she could've been used as a sculptor's template.

"Why do I look this way?" A small frown creased her smooth forehead. "What am I?" That last part seemed to be puzzling her the most.

Blaise took a deep breath, trying to calm his racing pulse. "I think I can try to venture a guess, but before I do, I want to give you some clothing. Please wait here—I'll be right back."

And without waiting for her answer, he hurried out of the room.

The Sorcery Code is currently available at most retailers. If you'd like to learn more, please visit my website at www.dimazales.com.

EXCERPT FROM CLOSE LIAISONS

Author's Note: *Close Liaisons* is the first book in the erotic sci-fi romance trilogy, the Krinar Chronicles. While not as dark as *Twist Me* and *Capture Me*, it does have some elements that readers of dark erotica may enjoy.

A dark and edgy romance that will appeal to fans of erotic and turbulent relationships...

In the near future, the Krinar rule the Earth. An advanced race from another galaxy, they are still a mystery to us—and we are completely at their mercy.

Shy and innocent, Mia Stalis is a college student in New York City who has led a very normal life. Like most people, she's never had any interactions with the invaders—until one fateful day in the park changes everything. Having caught Korum's eye, she must now contend with a powerful, dangerously seductive Krinar who wants to possess her and will stop at nothing to make her his own.

How far would you go to regain your freedom? How much would you sacrifice to help your people? What choice will you make when you begin to fall for your enemy?

Breathe, Mia, breathe. Somewhere in the back of her mind, a small rational voice kept repeating those words. That same oddly objective part of her noted his symmetric face structure, with golden skin stretched tightly over high cheekbones and a firm jaw. Pictures and videos of Ks that she'd seen had hardly done them justice. Standing no more than thirty feet away, the creature was simply stunning.

As she continued staring at him, still frozen in place, he straightened and began walking toward her. Or rather stalking toward her, she thought stupidly, as his every movement reminded her of a jungle cat sinuously approaching a gazelle. All the while, his eyes never left hers. As he approached, she could make out individual yellow flecks in his light golden eyes and the thick long lashes surrounding them.

She watched in horrified disbelief as he sat down on her bench, less than two feet away from her, and smiled, showing white even teeth. No fangs, she noted with some functioning part of her brain. Not even a hint of them. That used to be another myth about them, like their supposed abhorrence of the sun.

"What's your name?" The creature practically purred the question at her. His voice was low and smooth, completely unaccented. His nostrils flared slightly, as though inhaling her scent.

"Um..." Mia swallowed nervously. "M-Mia."

"Mia," he repeated slowly, seemingly savoring her name. "Mia what?"

"Mia Stalis." Oh crap, why did he want to know her name? Why was he here, talking to her? In general, what was he doing in Central Park, so far away from any of the K Centers? *Breathe, Mia, breathe.*

"Relax, Mia Stalis." His smile got wider, exposing a dimple in his left cheek. A dimple? Ks had dimples? "Have you never encountered one of us before?"

"No, I haven't," Mia exhaled sharply, realizing that she was holding her breath. She was proud that her voice didn't sound as shaky as she felt. Should she ask? Did she want to know?

She gathered her courage. "What, um—" Another swallow. "What do you want from me?"

"For now, conversation." He looked like he was about to laugh at her, those gold eyes crinkling slightly at the corners.

Strangely, that pissed her off enough to take the edge off her fear. If there was anything Mia hated, it was being laughed at. With her short, skinny stature and a general lack of social skills that came from an awkward teenage phase involving every girl's nightmare of braces, frizzy hair, and glasses, Mia had more than enough experience being the butt of someone's joke.

She lifted her chin belligerently. "Okay, then, what is *your* name?"

"It's Korum."

"Just Korum?"

"We don't really have last names, not the way you do. My full name is much longer, but you wouldn't be able to pronounce it if I told you."

Okay, that was interesting. She now remembered reading something like that in *The New York Times*. So far, so good. Her legs had nearly stopped shaking, and her breathing was returning to normal. Maybe, just maybe, she would get out of this alive. This conversation business seemed safe enough, although the way he kept staring at her with those unblinking yellowish eyes was unnerving. She decided to keep him talking.

"What are you doing here, Korum?"

"I just told you, making conversation with you, Mia." His voice again held a hint of laughter.

Frustrated, Mia blew out her breath. "I meant, what are you doing here in Central Park? In New York City in general?"

He smiled again, cocking his head slightly to the side. "Maybe I'm hoping to meet a pretty curly-haired girl."

Okay, enough was enough. He was clearly toying with her. Now that she could think a little again, she realized that they were in the middle of Central Park, in full view of about a gazillion spectators. She surreptitiously glanced around to confirm that. Yep, sure enough, although people were obviously steering clear of her bench and its otherworldly occupant, there were a number of brave souls staring their way from farther up the path. A couple were even cautiously filming them with their wristwatch cameras. If the K tried anything with her, it would be on YouTube in the blink of an eye, and he had to know it. Of course, he may or may not care about that.

Still, going on the assumption that since she'd never come across any videos of K assaults on college students in the middle of Central Park, she was relatively safe, Mia cautiously reached for her laptop and lifted it to stuff it back into her backpack.

"Let me help you with that, Mia—"

And before she could blink, she felt him take her heavy laptop from her suddenly boneless fingers, gently brushing against her knuckles in the process. A sensation similar to a mild electric shock shot through Mia at his touch, leaving her nerve endings tingling in its wake.

Reaching for her backpack, he carefully put away the laptop in a smooth, sinuous motion. "There you go, all better now."

Oh God, he had touched her. Maybe her theory about the safety of public locations was bogus. She felt her breathing speeding up again, and her heart rate was probably well into the anaerobic zone at this point.

"I have to go now... Bye!"

How she managed to squeeze out those words without hyperventilating, she would never know. Grabbing the strap of the backpack he'd just put down, she jumped to her feet, noting somewhere in the back of her mind that her earlier paralysis seemed to be gone.

"Bye, Mia. I will see you later." His softly mocking voice carried in the clear spring air as she took off, nearly running in her haste to get away.

If you'd like to find out more, please visit Anna's website at www.annazaires.com. All three books in the Krinar Chronicles trilogy are now available.

ABOUT THE AUTHOR

Dima Zales is a USA Today bestselling science fiction and fantasy author residing in Palm Coast, Florida. Prior to becoming a writer, he worked in the software development industry in New York as both a programmer and an executive. From high-frequency trading software for big banks to mobile apps for popular magazines, Dima has done it all. In 2013, he left the software industry in order to concentrate on his writing career.

Dima holds a Master's degree in Computer Science from NYU and a dual undergraduate degree in Computer Science / Psychology from Brooklyn College. He also has a number of hobbies and interests, the most unusual of which might be professional-level mentalism. He simulates mind reading on stage and close-up, and has done shows for corporations, wealthy individuals, and friends.

He is also into healthy eating and fitness, so he should live long enough to finish all the book projects he starts. In fact, he very much hopes to catch the technological advancements that might let him live forever (biologically or otherwise). Aside from that, he also enjoys learning about current and future technologies that might enhance our lives, including artificial intelligence, biofeedback, brain-to-computer interfaces, and brain-enhancing implants.

In addition to writing The Sorcery Code series and Mind Dimensions series, Dima has collaborated on a number of romance novels with his wife, Anna Zaires. The Krinar Chronicles, an erotic science fiction series, is an international bestseller and has been recognized by the likes of Marie Claire and Woman's Day. If you like erotic romance with a unique plot, please feel free to check it out. Keep in mind, though, Anna Zaires's books are going to be much more explicit.

Anna Zaires is the love of his life and a huge inspiration in every aspect of his writing. She definitely adds her magic touch to anything Dima creates, and the books would not be the same without her. Dima's fans are strongly encouraged to learn more about Anna and her work at www.annazaires.com.

To learn more about Dima and his books, please visit www.dimazales.com.

Printed in Great Britain
by Amazon